BOOKS

FRANKEN-FATALE, 2018

TROUBLE IN UNDEAD DETROIT, 2020

PLANET ROT, 2021

These three novels exist within the same world. Though there is an overarching narrative throughout them, they are still self-contained stories that can be ready in any order.

PLANET ROT, by H.J Bennett, 2021.

Inspired by Mary Shelley's "Frankenstein".

Cover art by Davi Go.
@constant.risk.of.fire
@seedavigo
https://artstation.com/davigoart

Spine art by Joe Gro (Joseph Grotesque), and Davi Go.
@joegrotesque

This trilogy explores an alternate version of the world we know where Dr. Frankenstein was real and reanimation of corpses is possible. Each story addresses grounded social and moral conflict related to reanimation's practice, with some supernatural undertones that are open to interpretation. Characters in each story fight to overcome their personal demons and learn what it means to do the right thing, no matter the cost. This is a timeline of overarching events that connect each of the separate, self-contained novels.

Trouble in Undead Detroit

This novel explores a world conflicted by the rise of reanimation. By the early 1980's, reanimation around the world was fairly commonplace. *Trouble in Undead Detroit* illustrates the impact of reanimation on one poor community in the United States. Though reanimation had become much more common, it was still heavily resisted by radical anti-reanimation protesters and the religious community at large. The reanimated undead were still a minority, and were subject to discrimination and violence. Across the world, countries faced major moral dilemmas about whether or not reanimation should remain legal. The Undead Wars waged across the world as countries fought amongst themselves and others: undead versus the living, reanimation versus natural life and death as God intended. Despite major attempts by the U.S. government to criminalize reanimation in the eyes of its citizens, the practice continued to gain momentum.

Franken-Fatale

In this novel, the Undead Wars are over and the tides have turned. It is the 2010's, and the reanimated population far outnumbers that of the living. Consumer demand has shifted dramatically, and the economy has no choice but to accommodate. Food-processing and farming industries are largely replaced with cosmetic and surgical industries, since the dead don't require sustenance. The few living humans that remain are called 'warm-bloods' and are subject to the same violence and discrimination that the undead were victims of when they were the minority. Outnumbered and isolated, these warm-bloods must travel undercover in hopes of finding sanctuary. With any luck, the living might carve out a chance to ensure the preservation of humanity in a reanimated world.

Planet Rot

The concluding novel in the trilogy follows after the events and characters from *"Franken-Fatale"* and explores a future where reanimation is just a way of life. Based in the 2030's, reanimation has continued to see regular practice and innovation. Scientists learn new ways to make reanimation safer and cleaner, and the undead have better options than ever before. The rotted body parts of other corpses are replaced with better prosthetics to match any need or personality. Full synthetic body-replacements are gaining popularity, where all that's left of the original person is the brain. At the same time, there exists a new sanctuary for the last remaining warm-bloods. This is a place where the living can thrive and rebuild. Though the living are still vastly outnumbered, their population is growing and they are not subject to the same discrimination and violence they once were during the Undead Wars. Still, they remain an anomaly. While the warm-blood sanctuary fights for its rights and needs, the rest of the world explores new ways to profit from reanimation and improve the nature of their immortality.

Reanimation has other pressing consequences as well. It is becoming evident that the undeads' abandonment of most agricultural resources has had a negative impact on major ecosystems. Additionally, the rapid increase in dead bodies through reanimation over the years has been quietly raising nitrogen and ammonia levels across the globe. These high levels endanger the health of the environment and make the air harmful for all living creatures. Despite the evidence, most of the undead population refuses to believe these effects on the environment. However, the time is coming where these threats to the planet's health can no longer be denied. The living and the undead must find a way to overcome their differences and fight for their continued survival before an unseen apocalypse purges humanity and resets the planet.

****

Dedicated to awesome mothers everywhere. Thank you for putting up with our shit and somehow loving us anyway.

***

In loving memory of Lynn

****

PREFACE

It goes without saying that the year 2020 was very challenging for everyone. Like so many others during the pandemic, I lost my long-time job and was forced into isolation to keep myself and others safe. Political unrest grew. Protests. Fear-mongering. Social division. A massive spread of dangerous misinformation. All the while, people across the globe were dying from a new threat we were ill-prepared for.

"Planet Rot" is more than the concluding novel in a fantasy/horror series about a reanimated world. It is the product of a tumultuous and uncertain time unlike any most of us have seen in our lifetimes. Written mostly during the height of the pandemic, it explores themes of fear, isolation, depression, and suffering on a large scale. Throughout all my personal and private struggles, I have been keenly aware of the fact that I am not alone in my suffering. Though it isn't new for me to address real-world issues and politics in my stories, *"Planet Rot"* does so on a more intimate level for me personally.

Indeed, *"Planet Rot"* was a means of coping with my own fears during this troubling time. In my isolation, I was forced to reflect on experiences and feelings that I had long buried. In order to finally move on from trauma I never wanted to process, I had to acknowledge its existence. Certain things have been holding me back long before the pandemic. Exploring these painful memories proved necessary for me to overcome my own fears, both past and present. That being said, it was highly therapeutic writing this novel.

Certainly I wanted to explore difficult themes so many of us can privately relate to. However, it was also important that I explore such themes in a safe, fictional environment: one full of monsters and magic. I have always been heavily inspired by monster movie classics and pop culture in general. I consume movies, comics, video games, and books like an alcoholic. Pop culture is as much of an escape from reality as it is a means of exploring challenging topics that remind us of our shared humanity.

We may not know what the future holds for us. However, it is my hope that by facing personal trauma/fear and understanding our shared suffering that we can slowly forge a more empathetic world. One where we focus less on our own suffering, and are hindered less by our own fears.

Maybe that all sounds like a cheesy Miss America contestant's speech. Maybe it's idealistic. All I know is that I'm tired of hiding behind my own insecurities and letting fear control me. It's time to take charge and be brave. Oh, and suspend your disbelief for a ridiculous story about ancient-soul-reaping monsters, reanimated corpses, and a psychological apocalypse. If you leave this story entertained and nothing else, I consider that a success in itself.

Thank you for reading. I truly hope 2022 offers you more peace and a better future than the years before it. You're stronger than you think.
H.J. Bennett

PLANET ROT

H.J. Bennett

PROLOGUE

Dry cement cuts at my bloodied bare feet as I run.

Hands still tied behind my back. Tears of terror streaming down my face, leaving streaks through the grime. I am no longer the person I was less than twenty-four hours ago. In this excruciating moment under the oppressive lights of an undead metropolis, I am an animal. Nothing more than prey to a hungry predator. Survival is the only thing on my mind. Full speed down a dim alleyway, desperate for the eyes and ears of anyone who will listen.

But he's fast. I hear the familiar crack of his whip, and my ankle snaps. It's too late. A split-second later I'm yanked backwards and face-to-face with cold concrete.

It would be easier if he spoke. This thing, whatever it is. He might be as famous as the other woman in his captivity, only for very different reasons.

I'm being dragged back into the sewer by a humanoid monster covered in staples and stitches, the gruesome amalgamation of his victims. As he looks over his broad shoulder at me, I see a face worse than any nightmares could concoct. Pieces of flesh both living and undead, male and female, human and animal. Like the rest of him, there is little sense to his handiwork, and even less of anything resembling an actual...person.

Vision blurs. My screams fall on deaf ears as once more I am pulled beneath the streets of Dead Vegas. All I can hope is that someone out there heard my cries for help. That they will send cops out here to rescue us before we end up as this asshole's next accessory.

Clang. Another blow to the head, this time as I'm thrown into the bars of an occupied cage. Inside is a woman, crying and reaching out to me. An eerie lamplight casts her shadow down upon me as I lay at her feet. A fitting metaphor. Always under the shadow of the woman enduring this nightmare beside me. The great Dayanna Morales Cordona, co-founder of THE sanctuary island for warm-bloods. Traveler of oceans, destroyer of Dr. Frankenstein. Immigrant. Survivor. Warrior turned humanitarian. But also...

"Mom, I'm so sorry! I'm just so scared, I tried finding help, but I couldn't...I couldn't...."

I see the tears shining in her eyes as she feigns a comforting smile. Her angular face and voluminous hair glow in the pale yellow light. Even now, after everything she suffered through, she's still absolutely gorgeous.

"It's okay, mi hija," her voice trembles, betraying her facade. "We will survive this. I won't let him hurt you."

"Mama, I'm so sorry for what I said to you, I didn't mean any of it! I was just so angry, because -"

"It's okay, we have - " My mom interrupts herself as she stops to yell hoarsely at the towering monster behind me. I'm too afraid to look back. "Take me and let my daughter go!"

No answer. His heavy boots slosh closer, closer, until he's upon me once more. The bits of flesh exposed under his gloves and heavy cloak are full of cuts, bruises, and burns. A bizarre and evil entity that has no doubt suffered countless deaths. A defiance of God's will, the worst example of what Dr. Frankenstein's reanimation can do to a person who's existence brings only suffering.

Immortality for monsters, disconnected from what it means to be alive. Or human.

"No!" I scream. "You're not hurting her! I'M the one who ran! I'm the one you want!!'

We do this, back and forth. Bartering with a madman who hasn't listened to a word since he kidnapped us. He clicks his fingertips, jitters his head like a broken bobble head. There is no interest in my mom. The collection of eyes behind that black veil fall squarely upon me. Well, most of them: the nonfunctional ones stare blankly into the middle distance, bloodshot. Those bore into my soul the deepest.

He forces me to sit up. I can barely hear my own voice over the sounds of my mother's pleading screams. From his cloak rises one of his extra appendages: the pale arm of a woman half his size, wielding a fucked-up scalpel. As he struggles to hold me down with his bigger arms, I see that scalpel rise above me with unwavering conviction. It's obvious what he wants. He's going to cut off a piece of me, and he wants to make sure my mom sees every second of my slow death.

Shit.

Is this…

How it ends?

My heart stops. Shrieks of terror in unison. I close my eyes. I'm going to die.

For the first time. I'll be dead.

Maybe they'll reanimate me in time. Besides, life after death has been the new normal for centuries. If somebody can bring my mom and I back to life, then maybe we can survive this hell...even if we don't.

But it's a long shot. This monster is known not only for what he takes from his victims, but also for what he leaves behind.

…

Bye, Mama. Hopefully it isn't forever…

Maybe I'll get to meet Dad and Dante...

A loud crack echoes through the sewer. Metal scrapes across cement. I open my eyes to a bizarre sight. My would-be killer is taken back, sharing the bewilderment of his captives. Indeed, there is more than one monster beneath the city tonight.

Standing between me and this psychopath is this...thing. Watching with unwavering eyes that glow like fireflies, planted in a bulbous head pulsating with veins and wiggling with tentacles. Bat-like wings peeling and stretching from a huddled form best described as a miniature prehistoric alien. The weapon that would be used to tear me up is in pieces across the floor.

Shit. I've seen this creature before! And not just in sci-fi flicks!

What...the hell is even happening?

The killer seems to be staring at it too, frozen in shock.

Is he, though? Maybe this is just a hallucination. A near-death thing. That's what I tell myself. Regardless of what it is, one thing's for sure: this is my chance to act. I kick evil incarnate as hard as I can in the shin, eliciting a muffled scream from the holes of his face. Then I pounce at the biggest piece of the scalpel and attempt to cut my restraints. Wincing through the pain, I manage to release my binding. But before I can plan the next attack, I'm in for more retribution.

Pain unlike anything I've ever felt. I blip out of consciousness, no doubt from the shock. My left leg is beneath a...

...Sledgehammer?

A fourth arm?

I...

In and out.

    In and out.

        Fading.

Heart racing. Once more, the monster looms above me.

Not the killer. The other one.

Is this real?

....

What is real?

Must...act...

The woman in the cage acts first.

A lantern ripped down and...and..

Oil all over. The three of us, we're doused in it. I'm confused for a moment, on the verge of fading out again. Through the agony and my failing vision, I hear my mother's desperate voice.

"More fuel!" she cries. "Your guardian will protect you!"

What is she...saying?

No time to question anything. The killer is winding back for another blow. It's now or never.

With my other leg, I kick over the killer's lantern. More oil pools around us. The killer isn't phased.

I turn back to my mom as we share this very powerful moment. Perhaps our last together. I can't hear anything now - just a ringing in my ears. She mouths the words 'I love you', and pulls a match from her blouse.

No.

Is she crazy?!

In and out...

      In and out...

No! Don't you dare fade out now!

"Mom!!" I scream. "Don't!!"

"It's the only way. You must survive, Isabella. Run, and don't look back."

"Mama!"

One final forced smile as the match is lit...and dropped.

CHAPTER ONE

BEFORE

"Mom, you know that nobody does PowerPoints anymore, right?"

"Just because they seem irrelevant to you does not make them irrelevant to everyone else, Isabella. Now, humor me."

I sigh and lean forward in my seat, attentive. "Alrighty. On with the show."

My mom is adorable when she's nervous. I watch her fumble with her papers and check her hair and clear her throat like ninety times before she finally picks up her clicker and begins.

"Hello everyone, and thank you for making it today. My name is Dayanna Morales Cordona, and I am the co-founder of the sanctuary island for warm-bloods."

"Everyone already knows who you are, Mom. It's only been like 19 years since you and Aunt Maggie founded the place."

"The islanders know, but not the outside world. Mi hija, I understand you've been nervous about the sanctuary going public. However, we cannot remain a secret any longer if we wish to survive."

"I'm not nervous. Carry on."

Click. Slide showing Earth from space, with poorly photo-shopped lightning bolts shocking the entire planet.

"Life as our ancestors know it was forever changed during the late 18th century, when Dr. Victor Frankenstein invented reanimation. From that point onward, death would no longer mean the end for anyone unconcerned with the sanctity of life. Anyone could rise again."

Click. Next slide. People that look like zombies walking in droves down the streets of some city, accompanied by a few statistics splashed over with blood-dripping effects. Heh.

"My dear daughter said it best: 'In the beginning, reanimation was a very rare practice as most people still doubted its safety and morality. However, the practice picked up mainstream momentum during the Third Industrial Revolution, in 1969. Religious entities ran campaigns against its practice continuously ever since its invention, but their efforts were in vain. Consumerism and capitalism had already shifted individual values. The United States played a critical role in transforming worldwide perception of reanimation. What was once reviled and viewed as unnatural was quickly becoming commonplace and glamorous. Celebrities and politicians began reanimating themselves publicly. By the mid 1970's, only 13 percent of the world's population was undead. However, by the mid 1980's, that number skyrocketed to 48 percent. Soon the practice would be officially adopted by most countries, and laws would be made to govern and monetize it.'"

"Geez, mom. Is it necessary to include an excerpt from my old history report on reanimation? It's awful and clunky."

"You are GOING to be a part of this. Either I include your beautiful report in MY speech or you do a speech yourself."

...

"Nevermind, the report's good. Go on, Mom."

Click. A famous photo taken during The Undead Wars, showing a warm-blood mother clutching her baby and crying as a reanimated soldier points a gun at her face.

"'As the undead population grew, so did general unrest. Conflict escalated worldwide as populations experienced moral and religious divides over reanimation. The Undead Wars were the result of this unrest. For nearly thirty years, nations across the globe experienced civil wars where the undead fought against the living. Needless to say, the warm-bloods did not win that fight.'"

Click. Slide page-wipes to an aerial view of South America, looking positively apocalyptic.

"Colombia was my homeland. Like so many other countries in the aftermath of The Undead Wars, it was completely destroyed. Indeed, the world's warm-blood population was decimated and forced into hiding. By the late 1990's, only 20 percent of the world's population was still living. Nearly 98 percent of the United States' population was reanimated at this time."

"Fast forward to the part where you co-founded a warm-blood sanctuary and we ask for money."

"This is serious, Isabella. And not all people are as bad as you think. Our cause is just. Anyone who hears the whole story will believe in our cause too. Your father and I - "

"I know, Mom. You and Dad traveled the world to make a future for me. Dad died for it. You believed in Aunt Maggie and together you survived all kinds of scary shit. You put your faith in others and the sanctuary was born. Don't think I take that lightly. I'm aware of the sacrifices you had to make, and the chances you had to take on people."

"Then why can't you take this seriously?"

I had to pause for a second on that one. Why was I being so stubborn and irritable about all this?

...That's a lie. I know the reason why, there's just no way I can say it out loud.

...

"Well?"

"I'm sorry, Mom. I do take it seriously. You're right, our cause is great. What I'm concerned with is whether or not a bunch of stuffy undead donors will recognize that. People may die and come back, but they don't change."

"People CAN change, Isabella. I've seen it. Reanimation has divided us, but it has also given a lot of people a second chance at life. Chances to fix their mistakes and to make the world a better place. That's what this sanctuary is all about: second chances."

That familiar hope. Boundless faith. I've always seen it in my mother's eyes. It's as infuriating as it is heart-wrenching.

"I'm sorry, Mama. This fundraiser needs to happen, and all we can do is hope for the best. I realize that we're gonna need to take chances on people to make this sanctuary work. I'm proud of you."

My mom cracks a smile, but I can tell she's still upset. I am exceptionally good at taking the wind out of her sails, and I hate it. I jump up out of my seat and give her a big hug, big enough to get a little giggle out of her. Then I plop back down and sit up straight.

I only hope that the frazzled woman before me doesn't lose that hope if things go poorly at the fundraiser. We still have each other, and that has been more than enough so far.

"Please continue, Mama. I'll keep my loud mouth shut this time, promise."

***

Wind in my hair, whipping at my patch-ridden bomber jacket. Watching the cliff-side mansion I call home shrink into the distance as my bumblebee yellow Vespa carries me and my worries away, if only for a moment.

Another day in paradise.

The sanctuary island, located in the Pacific Ocean: my home for the last 19 years. Tropical climate, the kind of place most folks would love to spend a vacation. But it's not fun that's got me on this ride. As the daughter of the island's co-founder, I've got some important work of my own.

Mostly delivery services.

"Mreow?"

A reanimated cat pops its little head out of my backpack. His whiskers are hanging on by a couple stitches and a prayer. He won't stop kicking at 'em.

"We're not there yet, Eckerd. Don't worry, I won't forget about you."

It's my aunt's cat. Run over by a truck, the punishment for his fascination with fast cars. Nine lives down and half a synthetic body later, Eckerd was eager to feel the wind in his whiskers again...And I was more than happy for the company on my errands.

Most of the local kids my age think I'm anti-social and too sheltered.

But I'm not not anti-social. I like people. And people totally like me.

And I'm not too sheltered. Everything I need to know about the outside world I learned from absorbing the stories of our people and watching movies with my aunt.

Take the corner, a hard left at the end of a dirt road. Drive by mile after mile of farmland, waving to the friendlier farmers along the way. Mostly root crops: yams, taro, cassava, and sweet potatoes. I think every meal I've ever eaten involved some combination of the four. However, my business today isn't with the farmers: it's with the fishers.

Our only source of animal protein is fish - tuna, mostly. We've got fisheries on every corner of the island. The people here have argued a lot over whether or not to open up trade with other countries, knowing how much our community needs assistance. But like me, most of the warm-bloods here are suspicious of outsiders. Given what they had to endure just to get here, I can't say that I blame them.

Farther down the dirt roads, leaving row after row of humble housing. Past our small cemetery, with that pair of crosses I've visited more times than I can count.

We've made due with what we have here, for the most part. Lots of volunteer work, and a little help from my rich aunt and her rich friends. What we have here...it isn't a lot, but it's something to be proud of. A triumph for a block of humanity that was already fighting against all the odds.

And so far, we've been plenty successful on our own. We can count on each other here. But out...there?

Who knows.

I ride by my peers as they're doing laundry outside. My eyes stay firmly planted on the road ahead as I increase speed.

They're not Dante. They would never understand.

People come and go. I've got Mom and Aunt Maggie.

"Mrrrreow!"

And you too, Eckerd.

Eventually, we reached the southern fishery. I park my Vespa and take a load of bags with me down to the port.

"Morning!" I shout out to the fishermen once they notice me coming. "¡Buenos días!"

Young and old. All kinds of different languages and cultures. The only thing the folks on this island had in common prior to starting new lives here? They're warm-bloods. What we have here now is something entirely new and beautiful. I'm proud to be a part of it.

I'm greeted with smiles and waves. One friendly older gentleman waves a fish at me. We laugh and make small talk, mostly about the palpable change in the air quality the last few days.

"Damn cold-bloods pollutin' the air," grumbles old man George. He grumbles about everything. "Givin' me one helluva migraine."

"Same here," I offer, "but don't complain too loudly or else you'll scare the fish away!"

We yuck it up. I give them bags full of supplies, and in exchange I'm given a new list of things the fishery needs. I let Eckerd out of the backpack so he can stretch his legs and smell the fish while I talk to Cho-Hee, the lady in charge. Before I leave, she offers me a small crate. It's full of big tuna, Yellowfin by the look of them.

"For your mother," she tells me with a gracious nod. "Bless her."

Gratitude and farewells are exchanged. Eckerd is returned to the backpack - to his disappointment - and the crate gets strapped to my bike. Away we go, the rumble and patter of my Vespa down the road as we head back home.

It isn't a bad life. It's peaceful. Predictable. And Aunt Maggie's got one hell of a DVD collection.

But that's all I've ever known. Here, I'm not much more than the daughter of Dayanna Morales Cordona. It's a title that has gained me a fair share of advantages on the island, but it's not without its pitfalls.

Anyway.

In a few short days I'll be leaving the island for the first time ever. We'll be going to the so-called 'undead capital of the United States': Dead Vegas. City of Perpetual Night.

So many movies and so many books about the outside world - I've absorbed them all with healthy cynicism. These fun tales are purely fictional and cathartic: the polar opposite of the stories my fellow islanders and I share. Warm-blood or cold-blood, it makes no difference. People suck.

"Mrrrrreow!" from behind my ear.

"Not you, Eckerd. You're the cat's meow."

***

A menacing mass of towering structures wearing a crown of smog. Way bigger than it looks on TV.

Dead Vegas. A symbol of mankind's overindulgence, revealing itself through the dense smog as we descend. My face is pressed against the window of Aunt Maggie's private jet. My mom is talking to me, but I can barely hear her. I'm practically mesmerized by the view below us.

The city stretches as far as I can see. Giant electronic billboards flashing commercials for undead cosmetics and ESTRID Industries. Casinos as far as the eye can see. Dancing holograms the size of our home back on the sanctuary, depicting reanimated celebrities with their own products to sell. Cars are everywhere - so many of them, backing up wide city streets. A concrete jungle and a sea of shameless advertising.

People...live here?

In the movies, Dead Vegas is always getting attacked by thugs, monsters, and aliens. Oh, and demons. In real life, there isn't much of a difference. This place is dangerous.

It's terrible, this city. Impossible, really. No thanks.

So awful, that...

I want to see it all.

"Isabella?"

My mom's familiar tone of irritation snaps me out of my thoughts. I pull my head away from the window to see her sitting beside me, rolling her eyes.

"Did you hear a word of what I just said?"

My fumbling and feeble attempt at dodging eye contact gives her the answer she wasn't hoping for. She sighs and mumbles something in Spanish under her breath.

"Aww, give her a break, the girl's excited."

It's Aunt Maggie, coming to my rescue yet again. She's got a glass of champagne in hand, sitting across from us. Pop star turned philanthropist, first reanimated at age 27 back in the early 90's. She hasn't aged a day...well, technically. She definitely has the skin of somebody who's been walking dead for awhile. She continues in my defense.

"Can you blame her? First time leaving the sanctuary, AND seeing one of the biggest cities in the U.S. I'd be losing my shit, too."

"Excuse me, I'm not losing anything." *Act cool, Izz.* "So, Aunt Maggie...you've been here before, right? Is it like the movies?"

I see a smudge of purple lipstick on her teeth as she grins wide at me. "I've visited a few times, and hell yeah it's like the movies. Some trips for business, other trips for the Lavender District."

"THE Lavender District?"

My mom pipes in with that mom tone. "Mi hija, how do you know about tha-"

Aunt Maggie to the rescue….again.

"Oops, nah, that isn't real, it's a Hollywood thing. The point is, Dead Vegas is a fucking blast. So much to do and to see."

I play it cool and shrug it off. "A city so polluted that you never see the sun? Insane crime rate? Massive target for invasions? Not interested in dying yet. We're here for the fundraiser and that's it."

"Isabella, don't you want to explore the city? We can find some fun things to do."

"Like gambling!"

"Not THAT kind of fun, Mags. Please. Maybe we can go shopping or hunt for an actual movie theater. I know you want to watch a real movie."

"Fuck yeah, we should explore." Aunt Maggie finishes her glass and leans forward. "I'll show you the sickest locales. The headquarters for ESTRID Industries. The undead roller-derby - I mean, those girls hold nothing back! You gotta see it to believe it! Plus all those street performers everywhere, sporting all kinds of crazy body modifications. Oh, and - "

"All of that sounds…pretty rad, not gonna lie. But we can't get too ahead of ourselves. Mom and I are gonna get a lot of unwanted attention as living females. It happens all the time on the news. We need to be careful."

"Isabella, things are a lot different now than they were before you were born. The world is changing."

"Yeah, that we can all agree on," blurts Aunt Maggie, before promptly remembering that her glass is empty. "Ah, more champagne. Do you girls want any?"

"Sure!"

"No, you're only 19."

"Yeah, that's right, listen to your mom. I'm gonna get some more bubbly."

Aunt Maggie swaggers off to the back of the cab, leaving me alone with my mom just long enough to attempt another warning.

"I know how huge this trip is," I start, "but I don't want you to get your hopes up on outsiders. We don't even know how they'll react to finding out we exist."

"Is it because they're undead? You should know -"

"No, Mom. It's because they're people, and people suck."

"Certainly that's true, at least 60 percent of the time," my mom smiles. "But if the sanctuary island is to thrive, we need to take chances on people."

"You keep saying that, but - "

"I took a chance on your Aunt Maggie, and look what we accomplished together?"

"Yes, Mama. All I'm asking is that you don't waste your chances on people who aren't worthy of them."

"One can never stay properly hydrated with a glass half empty. Oh, how you remind me of myself at your age... You MUST learn to trust sooner than I did."

"Oh, is that all? Because - "

"What did I miss?"

Mom and I look up in unison to see Aunt Maggie walking back to her seat with a fresh glass of bubbly in hand. "You girls are looking a little intense. Should have said yes to a drink, huh, mom?"

Aunt Maggie giggles and starts sipping away. My mom shifts back into her seat, looking as uncomfortable as I feel about where that conversation was going. Our landing will be a quiet one.

***

Jet lands. Us three girls file out, luggage in tow. Aunt Maggie has the most, of course. Paperwork, small talk. Signatures, photographs. Shuffled off into a taxi cab, and shuffled into our hotel after a slow ten minutes in Thursday afternoon traffic. I'm quiet most of the time, just taking everything in and trying not to puke.

You can't help but feel so microscopic on the streets of a city. Like a car beneath a kaiju's foot. A lone survivor in the apocalypse. Though it's only 2 PM, the sky is dark as night thanks to all that smog. It is utterly surreal, actually being in it. And I see dead people...everywhere. More reanimated folks than I've ever been around, ever. Though I'm curious and mildly starstruck, I reject all offers to explore. I'm not ready for that. Straight to the hotel room we go, to the dismay of both the women in my life.

So we sat in that big hotel room, talking over the itinerary for this weekend. We argue over who sleeps in what bed and who gets stuck with the sofa by the window. I sort out my clothes for the conference and talk shit about the garish floral blankets and curtains with Aunt Maggie. Dead Vegas feels like something out of a sci-fi fever dream. So many lights, signs, sounds, and spectacles. For being the country's most polluted and dangerous city, it's surprisingly...lovely.

My mom brought her record player, and I'm glad she did. She plays some of her favorite albums, ones I can't recall the names of but have heard a thousand times growing up. Music always calms her nerves, and that's something we have in common. The three of us dance around our hotel room, singing poorly and laughing at each other. The levity is more than welcome. But it doesn't take long before the flight takes its toll on us. We're bushed, and ready to call it a night early.

But even though my body's exhausted, my mind is still racing. I venture over to my mom as she lay in her bed, whispering one last question the moment it crosses my mind.

"Hey, Mom?"

"...Yes, Isabella?"

"What do you think Dad would have thought of Dead Vegas?"

"I think...your father would have loved the city for what it represents: opportunity, and what the future might hold. He loved science-fiction. Such a grand place as this...it would be like a page from one of his books."

I wish my dad and Dante were here to see my mom now. To see me.

"...Goodnight, Mama."

***

Woke up around noon the next day, feeling like I had slept for a thousand years. This perpetual night thing is gonna screw with me the entire trip, I'm sure of it.

Tossed down instant pancakes and child-sized cartons of orange juice with my mom before heading with her and Aunt Maggie to check out the venue for the fundraiser. And man, I gotta admit: seeing the civic center in person makes everything feel more real.

A couple of friendly old reanimated people greet us in suits, shaking hands and introducing themselves. Mom and Aunt Maggie talk business with them: the guest list, seating arrangements, itinerary, fliers, and so on. The joint is a little lavish for my taste, looking fit for a masquerade ball in the Victorian era or something. But there's no doubt that the kind of folks attending a place like this would have some pretty deep pockets.

"Everyone is quite excited to learn more about this warm-blood sanctuary of yours," says one of the old folks showing us around. Her posture in that Maude dress is so perfect that it's almost robotic. "It is a very brave endeavor. I believe your request for donors will fall upon compassionate ears."

My mom smiles and nods enthusiastically. Her bright personality is so unlike that of the woman walking alongside her. I doubt my mom feels as out of place as I do, even though we stick out in more ways than one. But I know my mom. If she's got any fears, she's hiding them brilliantly.

By the time we're done, us three girls are feeling a mutual excitement for the fundraiser. My mom and Aunt Maggie are gonna kill it Sunday night. We shake hands with our venue managers and event planners, each hand colder than the last. Say our goodbyes, accept their best wishes for the big day, and head back out for another taxi.

I spend the car rides glued to the window, watching city life unfolding all around us. Dead Vegas is somehow getting more interesting the longer I'm stuck in its traffic. Undead folks with synthetic or mechanical replacement parts at every corner. Fiction in real life. Some with skin flawless enough to catfish a warm-blood, others with the patchwork complexion of Frankenstein's monster. It doesn't seem to matter what time of day it is, the streets are always packed and full of energy. Nothing at all like home.

Maybe a little exploration wouldn't hurt.

"Hey, uh, driver," I prod from the back seat, "I'm starving. Any place to eat around here?"

Aunt Maggie hoots excitedly and my mom cheers. I turn beat red, and the razzing intensifies.

"Looks like our party pooper is coming around!" teases Aunt Maggie, shaking my shoulder. "Thatta girl!"

The driver just grumbles, tugging down his derby cap so it sits right above his pronounced brow. "I know a place."

***

It's only 9 PM and both my mom and Aunt Maggie are passed the hell out. I'm literally tip-toeing out of there, jacket over my shoulder, shoes in one hand, backpack in the other. *Slowly, slowly...Geez, these doors need a little WD-40...*

But I manage to sneak out unnoticed. Thank God. I do a little happy dance in the elevator ride down.

From the beginning, I found Dead Vegas 'holy shit' levels of intimidating. Fortunately, that's a feeling that has lessened with each passing moment here. I mean, I got to eat at a REAL diner! Sure it had a big hole in the wall and smelled like standing water, but it was a REAL restaurant! We were able to eat in peace, and most of the reanimated patrons paid us little mind. It was wholly unexpected. As I finished my food and walked out that door, my mind was made up. I was gonna give the undead city a chance.

"We should experience the city tonight. Aunt Maggie always talks about the nightlife. I wanna see it for myself."

Aunt Maggie was so excited to hear this, already running off possible itinerary for the evening. My mom? Less enthusiastic. I thought she would be happy to have me on board. Instead, she became increasingly uncomfortable.

"No. Nightlife can be very dangerous. We'll explore the city more tomorrow afternoon."

"When did you start worrying about the dangers of Dead Vegas?"

My mom sighed. "Evenings in big cities like this are full of mischief and temptation."

"Damn straight!" Aunt Maggie hooted, much to my mom's chagrin.

"Which is exactly why my daughter shouldn't be out there. She's too young and vulnerable."

"I'm not a kid, Mom. I can handle myself."

It was obvious that Aunt Maggie wanted to protest on my behalf. However, a death glare from my mom quickly changed her tone.

"Err, your mom's right on this one, kiddo. Sorry."

I swallowed my disappointment. I agreed with them and let the topic drop. But in reality, my mind was already made up. I was going out tonight, with or without my mom's approval.

I'm giving the city a chance. Isn't that what she wanted in the first place?

Maybe my mom's stubbornness is hereditary.

Fast forward to the present. Now is my moment. I'm outside and back on the sidewalk, overwhelmed with excitement. The city's lights glow brighter all around me, promising all sorts of possibilities. I can't make up my mind about where to go, so I just pick a direction at random and stick with it. I'll see what the city has to offer and be back at the hotel before anybody notices I'm gone.

Let's do this, Izz.

Crosswalk signal lights up. I follow behind a boisterous group of drunken undeads as they're telling jokes and arguing over what bar to hit next. The air is surprisingly dry for being so full of people. Definitely not like a room full of warm-bloods. Skyscrapers stare down at me through the smog, and a humility rushes over me not unlike the kind you get in church before the altar. My heart flutters and a tinge of anxiety strikes, but I keep moving on. One block after another, eyes all over the place.

A giant red hologram of a reanimated soccer player pops up out of nowhere on the corner beside me, and I jump. A couple of undead hipsters with cigarettes in hand chuckle at me, leaning against the side of a closed travel agency under a sign that reads 'No Loitering'. I play it cool and continue to loosely follow behind the intoxicated troupe. Certainly, they must know where the most fun can be had on a Friday night in Dead Vegas.

The lights are getting brighter. Heavy bass music blares out of bars as happy patrons pop in and out of their doors. Women hoot and holler from the backseats of passing cars, the drunkest of them spilling alcohol and flashing passerby. I see neon signs for businesses with names like The Velvet Casket, The Electric Hookah Lounge, Dead Fred's, Black Cemetery Tattoos, and, the most clever of them all, Cheap Booze N' Smokes. Fliers with crude police sketches of the so-called Skin Craft Killer are plastered all over, asking for information. Creepy, but I'm not buying it. Psycho murderers like that only exist in slasher movies. You'd have to be an idiot to fall for their tricks.

A couple of big, refrigerated trucks pass slowly by. They call 'em Slump Trucks...well, you're not SUPPOSED to call them that, but that's what everybody calls them anyway. I did a report on 'em once in school. Homeschool, that is. The United States Corpse Retrieval Service, or USCRS. Since dying is no big deal, everybody's doing it more than ever. Stupid, avoidable deaths. Fights over bullshit, failed dares, reckless thrill-seeking. Boredom, even. I see these Slump Trucks making rounds all over the city, picking up dead bodies to bring back to the reanimation chambers specified by their insurance. Guys in puke-green jump-suits dragging dead bodies into refrigerated cargo beds before driving off may seem like a scene out of one of those old gangster films, but around here it's perfectly normal. Besides, the dearly departed won't stay that way for long.

I stop under a stoplight's pale glow to watch one of the giant electronic billboards posted on the side of another skyscraper. It's playing highlights from an NBA game, and the players are sporting a variety of synthetic body parts as they dart across the court. Geez, it's hard to get used to sports involving reanimated people. There's always a body count at the end - the bigger the death toll, the happier the fans. I wonder how many times these guys have been reanimated throughout their careers...

There seems to be a bachelorette party a few bars ahead of me, and I hear them talking about the Lavender District. That's one of the places Aunt Maggie mentioned on the flight over! It has been featured in a bunch of action movies and TV shows, but I was always told it wasn't a real place. If that's where they're headed, I'm down to follow. I tug my hood farther over my head and continue on, hands tucked tightly in my jacket pockets.

Slowly, I see the crowd and landscape transform. The lights get dimmer, the streets get more narrow. There are some businessmen in expensive-looking suits talking in hushed voices, looking repeatedly at their phones as they walk ahead of me. I see the slumped bodies of homeless undead down even tighter alleyways. Some look like they're sleeping, others look like they might be drugged out. It's a little unnerving. I try to not think about it as I continue my loose trail behind the party girls. Smile awkwardly at the reanimated ladies in short skirts and sequined belly shirts standing on each corner looking for a bite.

Was this a bad idea? Following these complete strangers into who-knows-where? My mom would absolutely murder me if she knew I was doing this right now. I swear I can see a pair of luminous eyes staring back at me from atop a flickering street lamp. I've got to be imagining it in my growing paranoia...

Dad wouldn't be afraid. Neither would Dante.

Eventually, the streets widen and I find myself on a strip lit almost exclusively by purple string lights and neon signs. It's like an intimate festival of lights and mischief, a whimsical dream wrapped in a pungent reality.

It's real. The Lavender District.

Speaking of limbs, I see one come flying out the window of some bar on my left. One at a time, each girl in the bachelorette party steps over the broken glass and severed arm now lying on the sidewalk. They don't even skip a beat in their conversation. I guess this is normal? The owner of the arm hobbles out the door, grabs his recently departed appendage, and stumbles right back into the same bar, mumbling incoherently. Geez.

The Lavender District has always been portrayed as a fast-paced, seedy underground for criminal overlords, spies, and brave protagonists unafraid of getting their hands dirty for clues. But there are no sexy spies or dashing heroes fighting off gangsters here. It's clearly all about one thing: sex, the most down-played element in any silver screen depiction of the district. I'm surrounded by strip clubs, adult toy stores, porno theaters, and the like. There are bouncers and signs warning about age restrictions everywhere. The smell of cigarettes, booze, and sweat fills the air. I can't say that I'm too surprised, but I am getting a little uncomfortable.

However, like Eckerd, my curiosity is still getting the better of me. All of this is just so new. Apparently, there wasn't much actual filming in the Lavender District -I barely recognize any of the signage. Guess you really can't trust everything you see on TV.

I snoop around outside one club whose neon sign for "Hot-Blooded Nights" has only half the letters illuminated. An animated pin-up girl kicks her legs up and down above the crackling lights.

"ID, please?"

I'm startled, but I really shouldn't be. It's the bouncer outside, big as a refrigerator and as white as one, too. He literally has bolts in his neck! There's no missing him, or that look of doubt on his stern face.

"Um, sorry, I was just looking," and I try to shuffle away until he sticks one big arm out to stop me.

"Wait...you're a warm-blood, aren't ya?"

It's the first time somebody openly acknowledged that I was a living girl. I look for some kind of escape, but there are already other undead people gathering around. Shit.

"Sorry, wrong place, gotta get going."

"The boss is looking for new talent," says the bodyguard, and he starts looking me up and down without reservation. "He'll like you, no doubt about it. Come on in."

He opens the door for me, and the music inside pours out into the street. It's loud, and I can already see women pole-dancing inside under an eerie magenta glow. It smells like cheap booze and expensive cigars.

"No, I'm good, thanks."

I practically dash away, only garnering more attention. This was a stupid idea.

I'm moving faster through the crowd, feeling like all eyes are on me at this point. I swear I saw a huddled form in the darkness, taller than any normal human, staring me down with a wicked gaze. I'm darting down one street, then another as if I'm being followed. I make eye contact with a few strippers smoking behind another club. They're eyes and heads follow me in unsettling unison as I pull my hood tighter over my head. Does everyone know I'm a warm-blood now, or am I just paranoid? Maybe I was right all along, and all those stories I've heard are true. It's not safe for any warm-blood in the city. I might really be in danger.

Shit!

I have to go back. Check my phone, and I'm relieved to see I have no new texts or missed calls. After moving a little farther away from the clusters of undead, I decide it's time to head back to the hotel before my mom or Aunt Maggie notice I'm gone.

Carefully I turn back around, trying to keep as low of a profile as possible. I follow the signs and sights that brought me here, promptly leaving the Lavender District behind me only to realize that...

I can't remember the rest of the way back to the hotel. Not completely. Shit. I'm going to have to suck it up and ask for directions back to the hotel. But who can I trust out here, at almost 11 o'clock at night?

***

Shit, I don't know. Dante, what would you do?

Bam, I bump right into some tall guy in a trench coat.

"Watch it, lady!" His voice fades fast behind me as I pick up the pace once more. Make it to another crosswalk and wait uncomfortably, eyes everywhere.

Come on, Izzie. Stop freaking out and just think...You gotta know -

"The end is coming!"

Holy crap! I'm startled yet again, this time by the sudden appearance of a homeless man waving a giant cardboard sign that reads, 'THE END IS COMING - TRIUMPH OVER YOUR FEAR OR BURN - Isaiah 35:4'. His reanimated canine companion barks at me questioningly, sporting lackluster patchwork from snout to tail. The man makes eye contact with me beneath his matted red hair and utters something, but I'm too freaked out to hear it. I draw my arms closer around my body and move as quickly as my heart is pounding.

However, people aren't done trying to talk to the uncomfortable warm-blood. I hear a vehicle slow behind me, followed by a pretty voice in an Australian accent.

"A warm-blood in Dead Vegas, huh? You look lost. Need a lift?"

It's a red truck alongside the curb. The voice belonged to its driver: a super gorgeous undead girl with curly pink hair and pink eyebrows to match. She's rocking one of those expensive, synthetic bodies: perfect like a porcelain doll, albeit a little uncanny. A far cry from me, with my blemished skin and tousled hair that looks like I stuck my finger in an electric socket. Her skin looks so alive that the only giveaway for her being reanimated is the eyes: misty, like they're still lost somewhere in the great beyond.

Before answering, I lean forward to see if anybody else is in the truck with her. Nope. She's alone.

I'm not getting a creepy vibe. That's good...

"Yeah," I finally admit, "and I need to make it back to Cemetery Suites, ASAP. Um. Please."

"Well get your ass in here, girl," she simpers.

Why would someone like this stop for someone like me? What if I'm being recruited for some warm-blood prostitution ring? Is that...too extreme? I dunno. Kinda feel like I shouldn't look a gift horse in the mouth.

So I give in, and hop up into the passenger seat. The truck smells like cigarettes and vanilla. Death metal is playing low over the radio. Fuzzy dice are bouncing above a dashboard dotted with photographs and dragon figurines.

"I'm Olivia," coos the girl after I buckle up. She seems so earnest. "New to the city, huh?"

"Um...Yeah. That obvious?"

Olivia giggles and starts up the truck. "I've lived in this city ever since I was nine years old. I can spot a newbie from a football field away."

I'm embarrassed, but it's not like I can do much about it. She's right, anyways.

"Thanks. For your help. Dead Vegas is awesome, but...kinda..."

She giggles again. "Scary? Crowded? Pungent? All of the above?"

"Um...yeah, I guess so. No offense."

"What's your name?"

"Isabella. Friends call me Izzie."

"Alright, Izzie, consider us friends. I was actually headed to my auto shop to drop something off. It's on the way to Cemetery Suites. Do you mind?"

"Um...You have an auto shop? Like, for mechanics?"

"Uhh, yep, mechanics tend to work at auto shops. And trust, you aren't the first person to doubt it by looking at me." Olivia smirks, totally unphased. "And I wouldn't call myself a mechanic. More like a...paid tinkerer. That sounds kinda dirty actually, but it's not." She makes herself chortle. "I'm just really good at taking things apart and figuring out what makes them tick."

"That's cool."

'That's cool'? Really?

"So tell me, city newb, where ya' from? And what brings you to Dead Vegas? We don't see a lot of warm-bloods around here. Well...around anywhere, anymore."

My heart sinks for a second. I begin to consider the likelihood of survival if I just open the door, hop out, and tuck n' roll.

Olivia snaps me out of my panicked considerations of escape.

"Chill, I get it. If there's anything I understand, it's being different. You don't have to tell me anything you aren't ready to. We'll just focus on getting you back to that gaudy hotel."

***

"Boom. I am so fucking good at this."

The unlikely mechanic puts down her tools and grabs a rag with a smidge of dramatic flair. She told me all she had to do was drop something off, but somehow she ended up doing a little work on a customized motorcycle, too.

"Hey," I squeak out, "where did you...learn to do that?"

"My pops taught me, way back when." Olivia looks distant. "Side bar, I've been working on this junker for weeks. Hoping to get it road ready in a couple more. It just needs a little work on the engine, some replacement chains, new wheels...I mean, I don't wanna die in a blaze of glory, girl. Once was enough, trust."

"Must be fun, though...Um, not dying in a blaze of glory, but riding something fast enough to get you there. I love my Vespa, but its top speed is trash."

Olivia snorts. "You ride a Vespa, huh? Cool. Take it here some time, I can modify it. And if it's speed you want, no problemo. Nothing a little homemade rocket fuel couldn't fix, honey."

Is she joking? After that eyebrow wiggle, I don't think so.

I catch myself just staring at the Aussie with envy. She's taller than me, even if she wasn't wearing those pointy purple heels. Tube top and leather pants. Dude. She's unreal. Like a movie star. A far cry from Frankenstein's monster.

Olivia finishes wiping off her hands and tosses the rag aside. She struts on over to me and leans against the hood of a nearby car.

"Can I ask you something? Honestly?"

"Um. Sure. Of course."

"What's your deal?"

"Excuse me?"

"You are radiating this sort of negativity about yourself, and I don't get it."

I'm confused and caught off guard. Olivia continues a little more softly.

"All I'm saying is, you're gorgeous as fuck and you have this look like you should be in a comic book or something. I'm getting serious roller-derby girl vibes from you, like you don't take shit from any motherfucker."

I'm flustered, and it shows so hard that I might as well be glowing.

"See, that, right there." Olivia slinks closer and nudges me in the shoulder playfully. "You aren't buying what you're selling. But I'm a fucking great judge of character, and I recognize you've got that shit in you. Just gotta take some ex-lax and get it all out, you know?"

Olivia giggles, and I just stand there like the completely uncool doofus that I am. Plain and simple, I suck at taking compliments. I haven't allowed many people to get close to me. Like, ever. My mom had a boyfriend six years ago, and that was a shit show. Ever since then, it's just been the three of us: Mom, Aunt Maggie, and yours truly. And with the two of them so busy all the time, I've had no shortage of quality time with me, myself, and sweet potato pie.

I can't help but wonder how much more calm and collected Dante would have been. Or how much more social I would be if it were the two of us out here.

But I don't tell Olivia any of this. I just stand there, arms crossed, staring at my sneakers.

"It's okay, girl. I get it, trust. Just think about what I said, okay?"

All I can manage is a tight-lipped smile and a nod.

Suddenly we hear a door chime open in the rear of the garage. It's a tall and wide gentleman, wearing a greasy set of overalls and a tool-belt at his hip. Clearly reanimated in his forties, he's got this roughness about him. He stops in his tracks when he sees the two of us.

"This is private property," he grumbles. "Take your sorority somewhere else."

My new acquaintance raises a brow incredulously. "Nice one, never heard that before. I actually come here to work, like on a regular basis. I'm the one who put that scorch mark in the wall ages ago, testing out rocket fuel. We've seen each other before, lots of times."

The man just grumbles some more, clearly not buying it. What an asshole.

"Oh yeah? Does Tony know?"

"Yeah, he fucking knows. He orders the supplies for my experiments and I'm helping him rebuild a 1963 Ferrari 250 GTO on the weekends."

"Sure ya' are," he chuckles, setting his stuff down.

"Want me to call him up right now?" Olivia whips out her phone, and it's obvious she is getting progressively more pissed off as she repeatedly blows pink curls out of her face. "I can tell him some arsehole is in his shop insulting his apprentice."

The man says nothing, just prepares to work under some other junker car in the garage.

"It's late. Go home, lady. And take your doe-eyed girlfriend with ya'."

That's officially it.

The undead mechanic slides under the car to start working, humming to himself. What a jackass. Olivia angry-walks over and yanks the roller seat he's on, sliding him out until he's right at her feet. He's laying flat with tools still in hand and an annoyed look on his stubbly face.

"One last thing," she adds, her lips all pouty. "I am SO sorry about your dick."

"What in the hell are you - "

Bam. THAT...has got to hurt.

Olivia literally just put one pointy heel on this guy's crotch! He crunches up and starts howling in agony, tools clanging to the floor. He's down for the count. All he's got left is a slew of obscenities and sexist slurs too mangled by his pain to be comprehensible.

My new friend reacts only with a mischievous smile, stepping over the flailing gentleman and checking out her nails absent-mindedly.

That confidence. That 'take no shit' attitude, like Aunt Maggie's. Strong and unafraid, like my mom. I can't help but be drawn to Olivia. She's everything I wish I was.

But it is officially time to leave. Olivia grabs her keys and takes off. I follow her lead, listening to the geyser of dirty words and afflicted groans erupting from the garage fade behind a closed metal door.

***

A short drive and some shit-talking later, I'm back outside Cemetery Suites. Olivia and I say our farewells and exchange numbers after some initial resistance on my end.

"There's a party tomorrow, at my friend Hideo's penthouse. You should totally come."

A party implies lots of people. Already I feel myself wanting to retreat, but this time I fight it. New city, new opportunities to grow. Right? Besides, my mom is always encouraging me to give new people a chance.

"I'd love to go," I manage, and I'm grateful Olivia can't see how red I am under the moonlight.

"Righteous, I'll text the deets later."

And with that, Olivia gives me a wink and hops back into her truck. I'm alone again, but I feel so much better than I did twelve hours ago.

***

Saturday morning in Dead Vegas was nice and low-key. Dress-shopping, toy hunting for Eckerd, and another rehearsal of my mom's speech. The highlight of the day, however, was fast food delivery.

Not many places to get actual food these days, not when the majority doesn't require sustenance. But lucky for us, Aunt Maggie managed to have this miracle food delivered straight to our room. We finished up with errands by mid afternoon and returned to the hotel, where Mom and I threw down hamburgers and fries like it was our last meal on Earth.

God, fast food rocks. When Aunt Maggie told me this kinda stuff used to be on every street corner, I could hardly fathom the idea.

Slight vibrations in my pants pocket periodically. Texts from Olivia. I still haven't told either of my female companions about my impromptu late night adventures, and I'm not sure I will.

Speaking of, I was able to return to the hotel room without waking anybody. It's a miracle, really. Thank God both the ladies in my life are heavy sleepers. Aunt Maggie was still snoring on the sofa when I climbed into bed.

Another vibration. When neither lady is looking, I text Olivia back and promptly silence my phone.

"C U there," is what I told her. Yep, I'm sneaking out again tonight to go to that party. Cliche, I know. Stubborn curiosity is beating my cautious cynicism, but only barely.

Honestly, I had been tossing around the idea of staying at the hotel instead. The thought of being around a lot of new people my age in a new place makes me anxious. I managed to convince myself that going to the party will act as a warm up for going to that fundraiser, but I still feel like throwing up.

Despite my efforts to keep this to myself, my mom could tell something was wrong. Moms always know, I swear.

"Are you alright, Isabella?" she asks me with a mouthful of toothpaste. It's 9-ish and she's already getting ready for bed.

"I'm fine," I lie, "just feeling constipated."

'Feeling constipated?' That's my go to?

My mom doesn't skip a beat. "Have some yams. They will help, I promise."

Aunt Maggie stops messing around on her phone long enough to snicker and give me a look.

They make their jokes, we say our goodnights. Tomorrow is the big day: for my mom, and for the sanctuary she worked so hard to build. I rouse her before sleep yet again, with another question queued up.

"Mama?" I whisper from beside her bed.

"¿Sí, mi hija?" Her head's still buried under blankets.

"Are you nervous? About tomorrow?"

"Nervous. Terrified. Oh, yes. But there's too much at stake for me to let my fear win. A lot of people are counting on me to succeed, so I will."

She's so brave. Speaking to a room full of rich undead donors in a different country, trying to convince them that they should financially support the warm-blood minority that they used to discriminate against for decades? It's a tall order, to say the least. I may still be skeptical about those donors, but I have no doubt in my mom's drive and passion.

"You're gonna kick ass, Mom."

That finally makes my mom lift up the blankets just enough to see my face under the orange glow of the bedside lamp.

"Thank you, Isabella. You make me strong."

Turn off the lamp. Hop in bed. Pretend to be asleep until I'm absolutely positive that my family is. Then it's out the door to text Olivia and resist barfing.

***

Olivia was on time with bells on. Hop in the truck, and spend the next 15 minutes in traffic listening to my driver sing along with Madonna on the radio.

"She used to be pretty big in the 80's and 90's," Olivia starts with that lovely accent of hers, "but I didn't find out about her until her latest album, 'Unbeating Heart'. Most artists get reanimated and their best music comes post-mortem, in my opinion."

Can't help but think about Aunt Maggie, AKA Rita Venus back in the 80's and 90's. Guess I can't blame pop and rock stars for wanting to live forever.

A few more blocks of karaoke and vape smoke later, we show up at our destination: a towering skyscraper in upper Dead Vegas. Olivia hops out of the truck and flounces over to the big revolving doors, her perfect ponytail bouncing from side to side. She waves me over, and I can't help but become self-conscious. Olivia's dressed like she's ready for a cool clothing commercial with her long-sleeve, fitted crop top and puffy pants. In my favorite (and only) bomber jacket, holy tank top with the tiniest ketchup stain, and the same camo pants I've been wearing for the past couple days, I look ready for an intervention and a nap.

"Come on, girl!" She's all smiles as she waves dramatically towards the doors. "No chickening out now!"

Gulp. Away we go.

***

A stellar penthouse. Fancy shit, real expensive. Many stories up the skyscraper, complete with a balcony pool. The view is unreal from up here, overlooking a sea of flickering lights and glowing holograms that illuminate a rambunctious crowd parading the streets beneath them.

It's rad.

There are lots of people up here, too. All kids that were reanimated in their teens, full of energy and booze. Laughter and smoke fill the air. If these kids were all living, the room would be humid as hell. Instead, it's cold enough that I have to zip my jacket up. The stench of cheap liquor acts as an unusual contradiction to the very lavish household that contains it.

Lots of people are looking at me: the single warm-blood in the penthouse, maybe the whole building. I see them whispering. Or am I imagining it? Kids with bolts in their necks and body modifications that have them looking more cyberpunk than undead. I feel so out of place. I remember now why I'm no good with social gatherings, and I wonder why I even agreed to come.

"Don't worry about them," Olivia assures me, speaking over the loud music. "They're not used to seeing warm-bloods, but they're cool."

She introduced me to a few people, but I was too uncomfortable and distracted to remember names. Everybody around here seems to recognize who Olivia is, and she excitedly whoops for everyone who drunkenly calls out her name.

Not long afterwards, Olivia excuses herself for a second. That second turns into excruciatingly long minutes. Just like that, I'm alone in a crowd of undead teenagers.

I need some fresh air.

So I head outside, near the pool. There are lots of kids jumping in and flirting with each other.

"Feeling a little out of place, huh?"

I turn around to see a red-headed teenage boy with the body of a jock. Well, half the body of one - I see a whole lot of steampunk replacement parts peeking out under his tank top and heavily embellished jacket. Good-looking dude, albeit a little goofy. Must have died hard and young. Southern boy, by the sound of it.

"Yeah, I know I'm the only warm-blood here."

"No shit, Sherlock, but that ain't why I asked." He steps in front of me. "I recognize that look. The discomfort, the awkward lurch. You wanna hear a joke, am I right?"

"Um...not really?"

The teen crosses his arms and gets the biggest grin ever on his freckled face.

"Why is stand-up comedy such a good gig for zombies?"

"Um...."

"Because they're either dying out there or killing it."

He's smiling so big. Maybe my amusement isn't what he was after. He's fully satisfied.

"I'm Beckett," he offers finally. "AKA the 'Red Bastard'. Heh. I'm friends with

Olivia. Well. Friends with everybody, kinda."

He sticks his hand out enthusiastically. He's almost child-like in his self-satisfaction, and I hate to admit it but it's kind of endearing. I give in and shake his hand. Though it feels cold to the touch, his demeanor is warm and genuine.

"I'm...Izzie."

The two of us talk, and I tell him how Olivia and I met.

"Yeah, Olivia's one of a kind," he tells me, finishing up his beer. "Plus she totally digs me. Watch her get fifty shades of twitter-pated when she sees me tonight. Just wait."

Soon I'm introduced to the undead kid responsible for this whole party, and he certainly leaves an impression.

His name is Hideo, and he rises from the pool with a girl on each arm. High cheek-bones and platinum white hair, dripping with water. Handsome, and he knows it, too. I notice sutures around his entire neck, and everything below that is silicon and shiny aluminum. He's like 90 percent android! He's amped, like he'd keep on swimming and flirting if Beckett hadn't called him over to 'meet the warm-blood Olivia invited'. He poses for a quick selfie with his bikini-clad fangirls before breaking away. They're all giggling.

"Any friend of Livi is a friend of mine," he smiles. "Sorry you had to meet Beck though. Did he tell you one of his crappy jokes?"

"Screw you, pretty boy." Beckett smirks, sticking a toothpick in his mouth.

When Olivia finally comes back, I'm legit relieved. She's like my safe base amidst all these new people.

"Sorry for the delay, hon. Had some business to take care of."

Beckett leans down to whisper something in my ear...loudly.

"She means she had to finish a drug deal first."

Olivia shoves Beckett in the chest, a gesture that seemed equal parts playful and annoyed.

"Shut UP, dumbass."

Beckett simply chortles and looks down at me with a wink. "See? Told ya. Twitter-pated."

Olivia rolls her gray eyes loudly before turning them back on me. "I see you two have met. Did he already tell you one of his dad jokes?"

"Why is everybody hatin' on my jokes? They ain't THAT bad."

Hideo cackles, taking the vape pen from Olivia for a few hits himself. "We'll stop talking shit about them the moment they actually net you a girl."

We're together now, the four of us. Olivia properly introduces me to everyone and we make small talk. We haven't been here long, but I'm already nervously checking my phone for missed calls or angry texts. Hideo seems to notice, and quickly speaks up.

"This party's getting boring. What do you guys say we get out of here?"

The three of us agree. Hideo puts his shirt back on - I recognize it as one of those overpriced designer tank tops marked 'dead_meat.'. Heh. So eloquent. I snap out of it as he continues.

"You think the city lights look gorgeous from up here? Just wait until you see them from the rooftop."

***

I thought Hideo was teasing or speaking metaphorically at first, but no. He meant the actual rooftop. This guy is nuts!

But I'm glad I resisted the urge to say no and make excuses. Olivia, Beckett, and I followed after Hideo as he climbed out the window, up the stairwell, and onto the roof. The noise from the party was substantially subdued from up here. Nothing but a stunning panoramic view lit like a Christmas tree.

"Not bad, huh, newbie?" Olivia nudges me, giggling. I assume that my reaction is plastered all over my countenance.

"Where I'm from, we don't have anything like this. It's amazing."

Hideo hops down from the ledge, hands in his pockets. "I know an even better place to view the city. Just a few rooftops from here. Come on, let's boogie."

"But...isn't that YOUR party down there?"

I'm answered with a shrug and a smirk. "So?"

The kid takes a running start and literally bounds off the rooftop! I immediately fear the worst. Quickly I run past Olivia, ignore Beckett's hearty guffaws, and look off the ledge. Sure enough, Hideo was not a pancake on the pavement below. He's on the rooftop of the skyscraper across from us, waving.

Yeah, this kid is nuts!

But apparently, Hideo is in good company. Beckett makes another retort before dashing and bounding off the ledge himself. Olivia signals me over before following suit. I watch with still breath as Olivia leaps and lands on the next rooftop with a nice little roll. How she managed to hurl her petite self over and land so gracefully is beyond me. Must be the power of the puffy pants.

Now all three of them are waving and beckoning me to follow. Talk about peer pressure. I'd say I was immune, but that is woefully untrue.

I take a deep breath and back up for enough running room. Hop up and down a little, warm up. *Don't overthink it, Izzie. Don't think about how crazy this is. You used to climb trees and play outside all the time as a kid. This is a piece of cake.*

Time seems to stop. The moment lingers forever, with me suspended in the air between two buildings more than forty stories up. I swear I caught a glimpse of some demonic stalker for a second, fluttering in the air close by.

The next thing I feel is a jolt of pain in my knees and in my left wrist. Cold cement beneath me, and a rain of cheers above. I may not have stuck the landing, but at least I landed!

"Way to go, Izz!" Beckett cheers, helping me to my feet.

Olivia's next. "Oh my God, I didn't think you'd do it! You fucking rock!"

"Not bad, for a warm-blood," Hideo smirks.

"I know that look."

Hideo looks at Olivia, guilty as charged.

"What?"

"You're thinking about hitting on the new girl, I can tell."

"Livi, I'm hurt. I'd do no such thing."

Beckett chuckles, playing with the toothpick in his mouth. "Says the horndog who takes his pants off for every girl in a ten mile radius. You're worse than that playboy Viking douche-bagel who runs ESTRID Industries."

"His name is Frode Algar and he is literally a genius. Oh, and he also invented reanimation ages before Victor Frankenstein took a crack at it."

"Allegedly," Beckett sniggers.

Olivia nudges me and rolls her eyes as the two continue arguing. She proceeds to walk past them, towards the rooftop's edge. "Are you boys gonna stay here and bicker over our shared man crush all night, or can we get back to showing Izzie here a good time?"

Before either Hideo or Beckett can make a retort, the girl darts and leaps off the rooftop to the next building! The boys are quick to follow, with Hideo even quicker to take the lead. They seem pretty competitive. Apparently our misadventures aren't over yet.

Hideo leads us from one building to another. The kid's a natural at parkour. He's got us hopping across buildings, swinging off stairwells, climbing up windows. The three of them are cracking jokes as they're performing these crazy feats, like it's just a normal Saturday night for them. Meanwhile, I'm just trying to keep up and wondering what my mom would think if she knew I was doing this.

We finally got to the building Hideo talked about, and he was so right about the view. The horizon is covered in flickering neon signs and dazzling lights, and the smog above is illuminated by their glow. I take a selfie with all my new friends, using the cityscape below as our backdrop.

It feels so good to be a part of something. To feel normal for a change.

The gang chills out a bit up here, where we get to talking more. Turns out all three of my new friends had found something meaningful through reanimation.

For starters, Hideo had lived his whole life paralyzed from the neck down. It wasn't until after he died and was reanimated that he was able to change that. Started with a biomechanical spine and ended with a bunch of other cool upgrades that rendered him far more metal than man. Finally, he could walk. Hell, he could do anything.

"Ask him why he didn't change his mug," teased Beckett. Hideo's face shifted into that familiar grin.

"Because I'm too handsome."

We yucked it up, but Hideo was quick to elaborate.

"ESTRID Industries changed everything for me. I could finally get a new body and a new chance to live the life I always wanted."

And then there's Olivia. While Hideo chose to keep parts of his original body, Olivia opted for a total overhaul.

"All that matters is the brain," Beckett piped in, pointing to his temple with a shit-eating grin. "Scientists found out you can change everythin' else, as long as the brain is intact."

"I spent the seventeen years of my life in a body that wasn't mine," Olivia told me, "and it wasn't until after my death that I was finally able to be who I was meant to be."

"Amen to that." Hideo purred cheerfully, and Beckett hooted loudly in agreement. He pulled a flask out of nowhere and took a swig.

Speaking of Beckett, his story was a lot different than I expected. Party animal who died drinking too much lager? Poor fool who made the wrong joke in front of the wrong person? Nope. He was a U.S. soldier stationed in post-war South America. He died from a grenade blast.

"Took my arm and most of my torso, as you can see. The government didn't have much of a plan for us reanimated veterans, so my grandpappy had to step in and put his tinkering skills to the test. Built me these replacements with his own hands. Pretty nifty, huh?"

Beckett flexes his robotic arm and twiddles his mechanical fingers. I see gears turning, random pieces ticking and rotating. It's like looking at clock pieces, everything so small and precise. But also very...outdated.

"Why not get replacements from ESTRID Industries, too?" I ask before my brain can edit the thought. "They're supposed to be pretty affordable these days, from what I read."

The red-headed vet just shrugs. "Reckon I'm a little sentimental."

"What's it like? Being reanimated?" I ask out of nowhere.

Stifled laughter from the gang answers that question.

"It feels like...I have this insatiable need..." Beckett stands up and sticks his arms out. "For braiiiiins!"

The brawny redhead comes at me, and Olivia and Hideo react with a cocktail of amusement and annoyance.

"Come on, Beck. She's serious." Olivia rolls her eyes and takes another hit off her vape pen. It smells like pineapple. "And you shouldn't make zombie jokes. Not after what happened in '84."

Beckett just grumbles to himself. "Sensitive much..."

Hideo is a little more helpful. "It's hard to explain. Mostly it feels the same. Maybe a little hollow sometimes."

"Are you a social media fuckboy or a twelve year-old emo kid? It's one or the other, my dude."

"Shut up, Clockwork Hillbilly."

Olivia gives my question a little more thought. "Hideo's right. When you're reanimated, you're still you. But at the same time, it feels like occupying an oversized shell."

"More like overpriced."

"Way better value for my suit than that rusty junk you call 30 percent of your body."

Beckett puffs out his mostly metallic chest. "Better than the fancy place where you got your tits, so I suggest you promptly calm them."

"No, you're right. I'm sure it was very magical when your 'grandpappy' whittled you together like trailer trash Pinocchio."

As the two go at it, Hideo just laughs it up. Is this how brothers and sisters talk? They're so charismatic, chill, and totally confident in themselves.

Everything I'm not.

"So what's Izzie's story?" pipes in Hideo after passing the flask. "A warm-blood in an undead metropolis. Inquiring minds want to know."

I'm conflicted, unsure what I should disclose.

"Business trip with family."

"What kind of business?" Beckett is the one who asked, but all three of them are staring at me intently for the answer. I'm finding myself getting uncomfortable under the spotlight.

"Fundraising for our community."

Olivia is passed the flask, and after a hearty drink she asks me yet another question.

"A warm-blood community? Here, in the United States?"

"Nah. Overseas."

This answer only serves to ignite their interest further. I'm bombarded with questions, more than I can keep up with. Part of me is flustered and eager to get out of the spotlight, even if I have to bound off another rooftop. But the other part of me? Excited at the pure notion of being...special.

Just maybe.

Together we swapped stories and bad jokes. That is, until a pocket vibration snapped me out of my newfound comradery. It's a text from Aunt Maggie, asking where I am.

"Fuck!" Everybody stops laughing and looks at me. "I gotta get back to the hotel. Now."

Beckett chuckles. "What, mommy's got a curfew for ya?"

I am so screwed.

Olivia seems to pick up on my discomfort. "She's serious, guys." My hand is clasped in hers. "Come on. I'll take you back."

***

Climbing back down and getting to Olivia's truck felt like an eternity. Driving back to Cemetery Suites felt even slower. The Aussie hugs me goodbye and wishes me luck.

I'm gonna need it.

Once I finally get out of the elevator and back to our room, I'm greeted by a very stern Aunt Maggie outside the door. Her arms are crossed, cigarette in hand despite the sign nearby that reads 'No Smoking'. I approach her slowly, with my head down.

"So," she asks inevitably, quietly, "where were you sneaking off to?"

There's no bullshitting the former pop star. I spill the beans nervously, avoiding eye contact.

"Does Mom know?" My voice is so quiet, I can barely hear it.

"No. She's still out cold."

"Are you...gonna tell her?"

Aunt Maggie sighs and puts out her cigarette. "Not my place."

Relief rushes over me, but the shame is still there.

"Listen," my aunt continues softly, "I get it. And I'm happy you're warming up to the city after all. But it can be dangerous out there at night, Izz. She's not wrong about that. You better promise me you're gonna be more careful from now on. Leave the dumb decisions to me, alright?"

"...Alright. I promise."

Conversation over. The two of us quietly enter our hotel room. My mom stirs but only for a moment, and Aunt Maggie is quick to cover for us.

"Sorry, needed a smoke," she whispers as I quietly hop back into bed. Mom just mumbles and covers her head again. I give Aunt Maggie a look that says it all. I'm grateful, albeit embarrassed as hell. I mouth the words 'I owe you big time'. She mouths right back, 'I know', before smiling tiredly and climbing back onto the sofa.

***

Sunday, the big day.

Fessing up to Mom this morning about my extracurricular activities led to the reprimanding I had anticipated. Fair enough. Her response to me making friends, however, was less expected.

"You can't trust them, Isabella."

That tone.

"Excuse me? You're always telling me to make friends and try trusting people! Aren't you happy I'm actually taking your advice?"

"Not like this. It isn't safe."

"A little hypocritical, don't you think? I'm almost 20, Mom. I'm not a child. You should have a little more faith in me."

"Those cold-bloods you met might look your age, but you have no idea how long ago they actually died. They could be over 100 years old."

"All three of them died between 3 and 6 years ago."

"Is that what they told you?"

"Yeah, and I trust them."

"You shouldn't, mi hija. They could be lying about everything they told you."

"Didn't you say you wanted me to start trusting people earlier than you did? I'm NOT stupid, mom! When will you ever trust my judgement? Seriously?"

My mom sighs loudly. She's as frustrated as I am. Her tone shifts for a new approach.

"This is our last day in the city. I want it to be a good one, with the three of us all together. But to do that you need to promise me that you won't see those reanimated kids again. No more sneaking off, either."

Still frustrated, I give in and make that promise. Hug it out and get ready for one last eventful evening in the city that never dies.

***

Worst part of events like this? The attire.

Strapless bras. Pantyhose. Uncomfortably tiny shoes that clink loudly and announce your presence everywhere. No pockets, so you gotta carry around a stupid little purse. And the dresses. Man, I hate dresses. They make you have to move all stiff like a preppy robot or else you'll flash your business some way or another. Give me a tank top, shorts, and sneakers any day.

But tonight isn't about me.

"Would you like a drink, miss?"

Earth to Izzie. It's a tall waitress with a platter of champagne glasses. I politely decline, not so eager to add underage drinking to my list of offenses this trip. The undead waitress smiles and goes on her way.

Standing in the corner. Listening to the sweet and dulcet tones of the piano, played by a rather lively undead fellow as white as his suit. The foyer is packed full of reanimated rich people and I can feel their eyes on me from every which way. They seem as uneasy around me as I am around them. Sizing me up, trying to decide if an investment in the living is worth their time and money.

I hate it.

There's a heavy pat on my back. It's a miracle I didn't just tip over in these heels.

"Having fun playing the uncool kid at the party?"

It's Aunt Maggie. She's got a half-empty glass of champagne in hand, wearing a slinky dress that even Jessica Rabbit would be jealous of.

"They're just staring at me. Like they want me to do a little dance for them or something. I hate it."

Aunt Maggie chuckles and pounds her glass. "So do I, Izz. But it's a big night. We're gonna secure the future of your mom's sanctuary. Happy ending for everyone."

My aunt is greeted in passing by a few of the donors, who call her by her former stage name: Rita Venus. She greets each one of them in turn, smiling and making a show of it, just like always.

"You sure look like you're hating this too," I razz her, only slightly annoyed.

The former pop star takes another sip of champagne then quickly embraces me before I can protest.

"Buck up, buttercup! I get it that you feel outta place, but you gotta give yourself more credit. Your the daughter of a fucking hero. People stare because you're basically a celebrity. Trust me. I'm familiar with that stare."

Aunt Maggie teases with a wink, pounding the rest of her bubbly before giving the empty glass to some random guy I'm 90 percent positive doesn't even work here. "Now, let's make some friends with thick wallets, huh?"

"Do you really think this will work?" My sudden inquiry stops the woman in her tracks.

"It better," my aunt simpers. "Seriously though, with your mom involved, how could it fail?"

The undead pop star prances off. I remember again just how out of place Aunt Maggie is here. She's rich and undead like the rest of these goons, but she sure as hell doesn't act like them. If she can mingle here...then so can I.

Besides, this is important. I'm not even speaking tonight. The least I can do is suck it up and make nice with the donors.

***

It was the same thing all night: pleasantries with the rich and douchey. Introductions to white undead assholes I forgot the names of the moment they extended their hand for a shake. Weird hand kisses from a few fellows who looked thirty but had been dead for twice as long. Comments about how good my skin looked, how lucky I was to be the daughter of such a brave and influential woman, so on and so forth.

That wasn't that bad compared to the other shit. On separate occasions, three older white women asked if they could touch my hair. Really? It's not gonna grant your fucking wishes. But again, I just smiled politely and lied, telling them I spent a lot of time fixing my hair and didn't want it to get messed up. And I can't count all the times I had to correct people about my ethnicity.

"Afro-Colombian, actually."

"Oh, we're from Colombia."

"No, um, we aren't drug runners."

Racist assholes.

"Colombia. Yes."

"It's in South America."

Wow. Really?

"Nope. Not a U.S. state corrupted by 'the Radical Deep Left-Wing Vampire Conspirators'."

Fucking really?

I was right. These reanimated people are nothing like Olivia, Hideo, or Beckett. They're so haughty and elitist. It's almost like we're just wasting their time. Once the novelty of talking to a warm-blood wore off, they seemed quick to check out.

Which leads to the most contentious thing of the night thus far for me. When I regrouped with my ladies before the speeches started, most of the people we talked to ignored my mom completely. They addressed Aunt Maggie like she was the brains behind the whole operation, the sole founder of the sanctuary and the one making all of this happen. They treated my mom like she was the help.

After Aunt Maggie left with one group of snobs, I nudged my mom and whispered something.

"They're being totally rude to you, Mama. Screw these guys. You don't need their help."

But my mom, like always, maintained her cool and told me not to worry.

"I don't like it either. But Maggie is right. We need them. I will change all their hearts with my speech, just you wait."

"...I sure hope you're right, Mom."

"You need to have faith. Now, wish me luck."

She kissed me on the head and went on her way. She's nervous, I can tell. But she'll kill it.

I'm alone again, but before I can nervously check my phone five times a minute, more unwanted attention is headed my way.

"Oh MY GAWD, another living girl!"

Twist around to see the dictionary definition of a bimbo headed my way on loudly-clacking heels. She's wrapped in diamonds and an expensive club dress, but her demeanor is slightly less...sophisticated?

"This must be the daughter of that chick who's talkin' tonight!" Her breath smells strongly of champagne, and I'm 80 percent sure I see a little white powder in one of her nostrils. She examines me with enthusiasm, tugging her dress down every time it rides up. With one hand she squeezes my cheeks until I must resemble a fish.

"You're pretty for an immigrant girl."

I smack her hand off my face, and she looks genuinely insulted.

"Fuck off, trainwreck."

Oops.

The woman is aghast. I'm already walking away when she starts calling for backup.

"Frodoh!! FRODOH!!"

A tall man is coming quickly to her rescue. And holy shit, he's got this air about him. Confident and poised in an expensive - albeit one size too small - Armani vest. A walk that says 'king of the jungle', and an undercut/beard combo that says 'Viking wannabe'. If you could package the essence of "bear taking a shit on a pine tree" and turn it into expensive cologne, that would be the odor he was drenched in.

Holy crap. It's that undead playboy from TV, the one my new friends wouldn't shut up about! That inventor dude, the founder of ESTRID Industries. Frode Algar, Viking warrior turned immortal inventor - allegedly. Super famous, the Tony Stark of zombie upgrades. He's the only rich, undead adult here who's skin isn't chalk white, and hands-down he's got more bling on him than anyone else in the building.

As soon as Algar arrives, his lady friend starts pawing at him and crying about how mean I was. He looks down at the evil adolescent in question, and rolls his eyes.

"How about you run along to the lady's room and cool off? I'll handle this."

Little Miss Trainwreck concedes, shooting me the stink eye before click-clacking off.

Algar's eyes fall back on me. He seems unphased.

"'Frodoh', huh?"

"Pleasure to meet you, Isabella Cordona, " he says with this deep voice, extending his hand to me. " Dayanna has so many good things to say about her daughter. Frode Algar, founder of ESTRID Industries."

For a guy who sells synthetic bodies and parts for a living, I'm surprised to see how many scars and imperfections he's got on him. I snap out of it and cross my arms, the coolest cool.

"I know who you are. I watch the news. Your new gal pal is a real piece of work."

"Be nice. I think I might actually like this one."

"Yeah? What's her name?"

He pauses, and I can see the sparks fly as he contemplates my question.

"...Nikki? Or is it Trinity?"

"Good luck with that. Is it true that you're literally the oldest tightass in this building? That you found a way to reanimate yourself way before reanimation was invented?"

Algar sniggers. "Yes. Adversity breeds innovation, and my first life was nothing but."

"Nice. Steal that one from a website with inspirational quotes for boomers?" Needless to say, I'm unimpressed.

"Well, the old adage is true: with age comes wisdom."

"But mostly unwanted body hair."

"Charming, but not inaccurate."

"Enough small talk. I heard you're in a legal battle to take control of land intended for farms in California. Land you wanna take from warm-bloods and drop more factories all over."

"I'm sorry you feel that way. However, I am merely following the flow of demand and supply."

"Yeah. At the cost of everything that still lives and breathes on Earth. Body part stores on every corner, zombie skin cream being sold everywhere from super-malls to Amazon. But just a few farms or food-processing plants? Some fucking cans of beans for us living folks? Nah, too much."

"Statistically, demand for produce and processed food is at a historic low, accounting for less than 8 percent of the world's economic output. This trend appears - "

"Oh, can it with the statistics, artifact. We've established that you don't give a shit about warm-bloods. What are you doing here, for real?"

"Your mother invited me."

What? No way my mom invited this guy.

"If I find out you're here to mack on my mom, I swear to God I'll find you and kick you in the dick so hard that you forget how to use it."

He lets out a chuckle, a flick of gold lighting up that big white row of wolf's teeth in his stupid face.

"If I didn't know better, I'd think you were the daughter of Rita Venus, over there," and he sluggishly points one ringed-finger off at my aunt, who is currently dancing and singing one of her own songs with an empty glass in her hand. A few donor couples watch on: husbands with dumb smiles on their faces, wives with disdain or embarrassment. At least SOME people are enjoying this event.

"How do you know my mom?" I ask assertively, getting straight to the point.

"I am a friend, believe it or not. Just a friend, so no...'dick'-kicking required. "

"Oh yeah? How come she never talked about you then?"

"I'm sure she has her reasons, but those aren't mine to share."

Can't help but scoff. I feel some kind of way about my mom being friends with a reanimated, playboy inventor. Not sure if it's jealousy over sharing my mom with outsiders, me simply being overprotective, or a combination of the two. Maybe I AM just overreacting.

I should apologize.

"Sure. Satisfy your warm-blood fetish with some other living girl. One who has less self-respect and loves Viking roleplay as much as you do."

That...was not an apology.

Algar reacts with little more than a smirk. "I will take your suggestion into consideration. Now, find your seat. The main event is about to begin."

With that, Frode the Chode gives me this snotty bow and swaggers back into the crowd.

What an asshole. Gotta keep an eye on him. He's gonna regret the day he was born if he tries getting cozy with my mom.

***

The fundraiser went about as well as to be expected with 'Rita Venus' involved. I've gotten used to my aunt's shenanigans at this point, but not these poor folks.

My mom, though. She did great. At the beginning of her speech she was all stiff, doing that nervous thing with her hands. But slowly, as she continued, I saw that woman's confidence blossom.

"I believe that we are constantly reshaping our future. Reanimation has taught us that we are the writers of our own fate. We are not deterred by the impossible. We are not paralyzed by our own fears. It is true that warm-bloods and cold-bloods have long been at odds with one another. However, our painful past of violence and discrimination does not have to be our future. It must not be our future. I speak to you all now, not only as a warm-blood humbly asking for your help, but as a proud immigrant and mother. Whether alive or dead, do we not share the same hopes, dreams, and desires for ourselves and for the future of our loved ones? Do we not understand that the human condition transcends all superficial differences between us?"

Her final plea for assistance is equally heartfelt and moving. She went off the cuff at times, and her speech was better because of it. At the end, after a controlled bow to the crowd and a round of applause, she gave me that look. Every mother has her own, and every daughter just knows it. She was so proud. I couldn't cheer loudly enough for her.

Before my aunt took the stage next, I surveyed the crowd for their reaction to my mom. Maybe I had imagined their response. Was the blaze of applause mainly my own? I was witnessing a lot of bored faces and half-hearted claps. Undead assholes sipping their fancy champagne and checking their fancy watches.

Feeling mildly good about themselves just for being here.

I was pissed. And just in time for an intoxicated 'Rita Venus' to finish her introductions and start with her speech.

This one was different. My mom spoke slowly and with intent, choosing every word carefully. Fighting against her own discomfort, her own history of violence at the hands of undead assholes like these. Every word, every pause, and hell, every click of that clicker for her PowerPoint was a triumph. But not Aunt Maggie. No speech in hand, nothing scribbled on her palm. She was talking freely, humorously. Sometimes it was like a comedy roast.

"Look at you. Most old guys would already have a life sentence in prison if they had spent that many years inside a teenager's body."

The crowd was yucking it up, at least up until the QnA bit of the night.

For this one, my mom and Aunt Maggie came out together. All smiles at one another, real smiles. Two people that endured some crazy shit to make all of this happen. Two people who weren't just blowing smoke out their asses about making the world a better place. They were really doing it.

The QnA took a very distinct turn early on. Every question submitted by the crowd was aimed at Aunt Maggie. Questions about why Rita Venus did this, what plans Rita Venus had for her 'pet project', aka the sanctuary island. Even inquiries about when her next damn album was coming out.

"Taking a long hiatus from the pop star bit," she corrected politely for the fourth time tonight. "Much more important shit to worry about, am I right?"

As for my mom, she was talked over repeatedly. It was almost like they were making a point to ignore her.

Shit. I really wanted to be wrong about this fundraiser idea. I was about to stand up and make a stink, right then and there.

But my aunt beat me to it.

"Hey, dickshits," she shouted loudly, silencing the murmurs across the crowd.

She had their full attention. My aunt continued, throwing one arm around the very bashful lady I call Mom. "Y'all need to show this fucking badass woman right here some goddamn respect. She's the whole reason this sanctuary exists. The reason humanity is gonna have another fucking go. And the reason you're all sitting on your asses right now sipping champagne that's even older than you. You're welcome, by the way."

A silence to end all silences. It could have ended there, but it didn't.

"So I have to respectfully ask that you take your hands off your dicks and dig them into those wallets. Part of your families' legacy is to pretend you gave a shit about humanity, so start pretending. This is an amazing cause and you all fucking know it."

An uproar in the crowd. A cocktail of cheers, jeers, and confusion.

That's the moment I'm in now. Clapping, cheering for my mom and Aunt Maggie with tears in my eyes. Regardless of what happens tonight, we're gonna be okay. We'll find our way.

Suddenly I noticed someone peculiar in the crowd. Was he here the whole time? If so, how did I not see him? A very tall figure in a black cloak, wearing some weird... mask, is it? Hard to tell. Nobody else seems to pay him any mind as he watches my mom on stage. Slowly, he diverts his attention over to me, across the crowd...

"She's quite a character, isn't she?"

An unfamiliar voice behind me. I turn to see a very dashing undead dude in a tux. A quick double-take at the crowd and the masked dude is already out of sight.

The other guy is still here, unfortunately. Like so many other rich dead-heads, he got himself killed in his prime and has been a teenager for the last forty years plus. Hair dyed the same howdy-doody red it was when he was living. Jawline like Superman, eyes like Lex Luthor.

He senses my confusion and distrust as he smiles this wicked smile. "Rita Venus, that is."

"She's got plenty of fans, so get in line, buddy."

He stands in front of me, blocking the way. The crowd is standing with us now, talking and shuffling about.

"I'm actually more interested in your mother and her cause."

"Oh yeah? Then what's her name, you remember that?"

He smiles again, and it seems sincere. "Dayanna Morales Cordona. I'm going to need that name if I want to write a check for her, am I right?"

It's tough. When people die for the first time and get themselves reanimated, they are stuck forever in the body they died in. I mean, die and get reanimated as a kid and you'll stay in the body of a kid forever. You get how confusing that can be? Talking to what looks like someone my age, who I know has been walking dead for almost seventy years?

I'm getting some warning signs from this guy. Yet he keeps talking with that calm, soft voice and that pretty face, so I keep listening.

"Your mother's words have moved me, I confess. And your aunt's words, though harsh, remind me of what is truly important. I want to help. Please, come with me as I locate my pocketbook. I will give the check to you directly."

That's it. I'm officially freaked out. This guy is a total creep.

"No thanks, I should be catching up to my mom now."

I try to move around him. He blocks the way and grabs my wrist tightly. The moment he lays hands on me, a rush of tormented flashbacks come pouring in.

"I think you should come with me."

No. Please, no. Not again.

Panic. Fear. Just as it starts to rush over me, someone unexpected comes to my rescue.

"Can I help you?"

The predator lets go of my wrist lightning fast when he hears that familiar voice. Frode Algar is suddenly towering over him. The asshole has little to say besides a low mumble, guilt all over his face.

"I think you should leave," adds Algar, unwavering.

The piece of shit is quick to do just that, a fraction of the man he thought he was moments earlier.

"Are you alright?"

"Yes...Um...Thank you." My voice is so quiet, I can barely hear myself. I feel so small and afraid all of a sudden, like it's just now settling in. I look across the crowd, numb to all the noises around me. "I just...want to leave. Now."

There appears to be a sincere form of concern on the playboy's face. It's unexpected.

"Of course. I will let your mother know."

My heart sinks. "No. Don't. Please. It's her night. I don't wanna ruin it. I just...can't be here right now."

Algar's brow furrows. "Yes. I understand. My assistant can give you a ride."

My vision begins to blur with tears. It's as if this incident brought something else back to me. Something I've buried for a long time, and I'm not anywhere near being ready to process it.

"Can you walk me out?" I ask before my brain can filter out the question.

"Of course."

Algar's true to his word, walking me down through the foyer and back outside. I'm introduced to his assistant, an undead lady in a maroon suit and pencil skirt, who doesn't look a day over twenty-five. Super pretty, with a smile that would make a dentist jealous. But she's really nice. And she doesn't ask questions, at least nothing about what just happened. Thank God. I just wanna go back to the hotel and disappear for a little while.

***

Texts from Olivia and Hideo, asking how my mom's fundraising event went. Missed calls from Mom and Aunt Maggie. At least Algar covered for me and told them I left because I was sick. I don't answer any of it. I feel too small and I don't know what to say about anything.

Right now, I just need to be...

Alone.

So I leave the hotel and end up finding myself sitting on the rooftop of the laundromat a few blocks away. I barely even remember walking here, or climbing up. I'm just here.

Alone.

Again.

My distrust of everyone bubbles back up to the surface. Things would be better if my twin brother were here with me. Maybe everything would be better and I wouldn't feel so goddamn alone all the time.

***

An uncertain amount of time passes with me curled up on a cold rooftop under the moonlight. My phone continues to beg for my attention, and I finally give in. My mom left the fundraiser early just to get back to me at the hotel, only to find our room empty. She's worried. I feel even worse at the thought of putting a damper on her big night. I didn't even get to tell her how proud I was of her yet. Gotta suck it up and respond.

I text. She calls. We talk.

She worries. I say I'm okay. It's a lie. Just needed some air. That much is true.

I tell her I'll be right back to the hotel. She says she will come to me and we'll go back together. I tell her that isn't necessary. She insists. I focus on wiping away all evidence of my despair as I wait.

She shows up in a cab. I meet her outside under a streetlight. An overwhelming sense of dread washes over me, like a bad omen. I'm prepared to make more excuses, but the distressed woman in the champagne-colored dress speaks up first.

"Are you alright?"

"Yeah. Let's go."

"Not so fast. You promised me you wouldn't sneak off again, and what do you do? Sneak off into the city alone once more. It's for those reanimated kids again, isn't it?"

That was it. I'm not sure what came over me, but the very suggestion made me snap. The exact words that spewed out of my mouth? I can't recall most of it. My mom's countenance changed abruptly, parental anger turning to pure shock. Did I think that unleashing on the poor woman was going to make me feel better about myself? Was it going to offer me the peace I needed right now?

No. Without a doubt, my temper tantrum only made things worse.

So I yelled. Accused her of never trusting me.

She didn't trust me THAT night either...

And I declared that she had no respect for her only daughter.

"Maybe you just wish it were Dante who survived and not me."

The mere mention of his name visibly tears her to pieces. What's wrong with me? We don't talk about him for a reason. Passersby on the street were definitely watching now, but I didn't stop.

"Please, mi hija," she pleaded with me. "Let's just go back to the hotel. We can talk about things more calmly there. Please."

She was embarrassed by the spectacle I was making, and though I pretended not to care, it actually made me feel more guilty. Eventually I agreed, and my mom waved down another cab.

Only we didn't make it in.

From the shadows appeared a tall form dressed in black, face shrouded by a veil. By the time we saw him, it was too late. Shots of some kind of tranquilizer directly into our necks, and the world would soon fade away...

That feeling of dread moments earlier: I didn't understand it at the time. Only assumed it was the byproduct of re-sparked nightmares. I thought I would be solely responsible for the evening's despair, but fate had already decided its leading role in the torment to come.

CHAPTER TWO

AFTER

Three weeks. At least that's the amount of time they tell me has passed. I'm not sure. Living in a haze, my concept of time isn't what it used to be.

Parades of people coming to visit, offering support. Asking what I need, what they can do for me, etc. But the truth is, I'm unsure what I need. I just feel...lost.

Why...me?

The whole thing screwed with me, bad. My leg was so fucked up, it had to be amputated below the knee. I was in a coma for five days, hearing people talk at my bedside about how much they pitied me and marveled at my survival. How they were afraid of what I would think when I woke up and heard the news.

Little did they know, I heard it while I was out. And the revelation just made my coma more nightmarish.

I was the only known survivor of the Skin Craft Killer. Not only that night. But....ever.

The only survivor...again.

Fucking why?!

When I finally woke up, the first thing I asked the nurse was if my mom had been reanimated. I was told that a distressed Aunt Maggie gave the permission for Mom to be taken to a reanimation chamber, ASAP. Her body couldn't be saved, but her brain could. A synthetic body was quickly lined up, and shock docs went to work. However, after numerous failed attempts to bring her back, those same doctors had to give up.

...Give up?!

I argued about it. Blurted out choice words to some poor nurses just doing their jobs. Blamed this person and that. I mean, how could it be possible? Modern reanimation works every time as long as the brain is intact and the procedure takes place within 24 hours of death. It should have worked! I demanded to see the shock doctors who tried to bring my mom back, and I immediately regretted it when I understood that familiar look on their faces.

Pity. They had no good news to share with me. Only their condolences.

"Instances of intact brains rejecting reanimation are exceptionally rare," began one doctor carefully, "but they do occur. We are very sorry, Miss Cordona."

A 'miracle'. There's that word again. I'm told it's a miracle that I survived at all, as if that's supposed to make me feel better.

What DOES make me feel better? At least that fucker didn't get to wear my mom like a trophy. She denied him that and died on her own terms. A badass to the end. It's not much, but...knowing that helps a little.

As for me?

The girl who cheated death as a newborn.

The girl who crawled out of a furnace, unburned.

The girl who somehow survived a serial killer known for his success rate.

I'm fucked up for sure.

But...alive?

Why...ME?!

I don't understand it. Any of it.

It still seems like some cruel joke. I'm neck-deep in denial. Yet every day since I woke up, people are constantly reminding me that the most important person in my world is gone and she isn't coming back.

And I've got some really, really big shoes to fill.

Rehabilitation. Funeral.

Hugs. Tears. Rain.

Reporters. Aunt Maggie shielding me from questions I wasn't prepared to answer and literally fighting off paparazzi. She's got a mean left hook.

What was to become of the daughter of Dayanna Morales Cordona? What would happen to the warm-blood sanctuary her mother worked so hard to build? How did a teenage warm-blood survive The Skin Craft Killer's final attack?

Everybody wants to know, and I get it. But every time they ask, and every time I see stories about it on the news...I just feel worse.

Before that psychopath came into the picture, my mom's final moments were with a petulant teenage girl who made her feel disappointed and unappreciated. It's a nightmare. I'm full of all these regrets. I'm lost in them, battling with my anxiety over the future and a self-loathing that threatens to swallow me whole.

Why did I get to live? What do I even have to offer?

What's harder: losing someone dear before getting the chance to meet them, or losing someone you've known all your life?

Loss is something you think you understand. You can try to be there for somebody who lost someone, and I mean REALLY lost someone. You can think you get what it feels like. But until it happens to you personally...you can never quite anticipate the extent of that hollow feeling. There is no Band-Aid fix. No waking up one day and feeling better. It's a battle everyday to find some sort of peace and process what it means to move on.

If moving on is even an option.

***

Click.

"I say, the end is coming. An apocalypse of our own creation. Damnation for the transgressions against our fellow man and God's green earth if we do not repent

for - "

Fire and brimstone, huh? Nah, too early in the day for that. Click.

"ESTRID Industries CEO Frode Algar continues to address conservative critics about his recent investment in the warm-blood sanctuary - "

Click.

"The autopsy of The Skin Craft Killer was made public this week, providing more questions than answers. Though the killer was thought to be responsible for ten murders across the Midwest over the last three decades, salvageable DNA from his alterations linked him to more than twenty different victims."

...

"I have never seen anything this horrific in my twenty years in the business," recalled the coroner to UBC News earlier this morning, moments after resigning. "Something straight out of a horror movie. I will see that thing in my nightmares."

"The killer's actual identity could not be determined, as his body had been burned beyond - "

...That's enough. At least that fucker's dead. Click.

"The newly public warm-blood sanctuary is still reeling from the loss of its beloved co-founder and humanitarian, Dayanna Morales - "

Nope. Next channel.

Click.

"-now and get a second tube of 2nd Chances for half the price. We guarantee your skin will glow like you're alive again. 2nd Chances: You got a second chance at life - shouldn't your skin get the same?"

So sick of these undead cosmetic commercials. I hear them in my sleep.

Click.

"Here's the hard truth, Katie. The rapid increase in dead bodies through reanimation over the years has been quietly raising nitrogen and ammonia levels across the globe. These high levels, paired with record-breaking smog worldwide, endanger the health of the environment and make the air harmful for all living creatures. The National Wildlife Federation has already confirmed the extinction of 11 more species in the past two years alone. These include once prevalent species of both flora and fauna."

"How awful."

"And that's not all, Katie. Since the undead don't require sustenance, enormous industries that once fueled nations economically have become practically non-existent. Restaurants and supermarkets are a thing of the past. Farmers everywhere are out of work as demand continues to plummet."

"Oh, my."

"I know, Katie. I know. However, humanity has always been good at adapting. Millions of jobs were lost, but millions more took their place. New markets have grown and flourished as demand for undead cosmetics, reanimators, replacement parts, and surgery steadily rise. Not to mention a rise in tourism thanks to wealthy, reanimated thrill-seekers."

"That doesn't sound so bad, then."

"Maybe not, Katie, but the damage has already been done. The undead might endure, maybe even for eternity. But the toll our selfish desires have taken on the environment cannot be undone. Less and less farmland, more concrete jungles filled with bodies far past their expiration dates. Complex ecosystems decimated, forgotten. The simple fact is that we are destroying the planet at the cost of our own immortality."

Blip. TV turns off. I poke my head further out of my blanket cocoon to see Aunt Maggie in the bedroom doorway.

"That guy is full of shit," she grumbles, cigarette in hand. "Corpses have been walking around all over the place for centuries. Still no apocalypse."

She's trying to add levity, something she's good at. But I don't feel like anything can pull me out of the mental state I'm in right now.

"You have a visitor, Izz."

I sit up in bed and really look at my aunt to see if she's joking. Like me, she is pretty disheveled. Since we've been back on the sanctuary island, Aunt Maggie has been working full time to keep everything running. Between the loss of my mom and all the extra responsibility on the island, I can really tell it's taking a toll on her. I would normally bring up my 'no visitor' policy and bury my head back in the blankets, but a quick clarification changes my mind.

"It's Frode Algar. He's kinda hot."

An uncontrollable grimace spreads over my face as I sit up straight. "Ew, don't be gross, Aunt Maggie."

She just giggles, and I find myself mildly disarmed.

Frode Algar. I can't stop hearing about this guy even if I tried. Last time I saw him was at the funeral, but we didn't speak. He tried reaching out a few times since then, but I always had an excuse not to see him. I remind myself that he was a friend to my mom, and one of three new benefactors for the island. Maybe I can't hide forever.

"Tell him I'll meet him downstairs," I give in, strapping on my prosthetic leg.

Aunt Maggie seems relieved. She's always encouraging me to go out or see other people, warning me about the dangers of too much isolation during depression. She's right, but it's easier said than done sometimes.

"That's good, Izz. I'll tell him. Do you want me to stay with you down there?"

"Nah, I'll be fine. Thanks, Aunt Maggie. For everything."

She gives me this tired smile. I don't think I ever saw Aunt Maggie without makeup before that awful night. Now she rarely paints that pretty mug.

I barely remember getting dressed and heading down. All I see next is a tall and vaguely menacing figure in a gray petticoat, standing by the lobby fountain with his hands in his pockets. He came alone. The warm-bloods filtering in and out of the lobby stare at him with such disbelief that I can't tell whether it's because he's a celebrity or the only reanimated man in the entire building.

"Nice petticoat, you get that at the Big and Tall store for leprechauns?"

"Isabella," Algar starts hesitantly, broaching the distance between us. He totally ignores my snide comment about his fashion sense. "How are you holding up?"

"Pretty shit, to be honest," I say hoarsely, arms tucked close to my body. Did I say something else? I can't remember.

His next few lines are not so different from what I've heard a thousand times already. Sincere condolences, statements about my mother's character and wishes. But every time I hear those words, I'm forced to face reality again: my mom's gone, and I have no clue where to go from here.

As the former Viking continues, I notice the cuts on his right knuckles. Healing's a bitch when you're undead, I guess.

"Thank you," I heard myself say, and I'm certain I interrupted him. But Frode isn't offended, nor is he his usual confident self. He seems uncomfortable. Now THAT I can understand. "What happened to your hand? Got in a bar fight?"

Frode looks at his knuckles and shakes it off.

"Not quite. You left the fundraiser early that night, but our unwelcome guest did not. He required a little motivation, which I was happy to provide."

Mumble mumble. That's my eloquent expression of gratitude as my face turns beat red. Algar smiles ever so slightly before cutting the silence with welcome small talk.

"How do you like the new leg? It's a very special prototype made just for you."

I look down at the prosthetic again. To be honest, my new appendage has been the last thing on my mind. It's a constant reminder of The Skin Craft Killer and what he took from me. I look a little closer and see that it's got that fancy

ESTRID Industries logo etched into the metal.

Memories flash across my brain. The sound my bones made when that sledgehammer made contact...

...

Bury it with the rest.

"It's nice. Really nice. Thanks."

More silence between us. Frode scratches his beard uncomfortably and lets out a deep sigh. Apparently, I'm not the only one who's bad at this.

"I saw them talk about us on the news," I finally blurted out of nowhere. "Paparazzi caught you escorting me to your assistant's vehicle, the night of the fundraiser. People seem to think you're hooking up with a warm-blooded teenager now."

Algar rolls his eyes and rubs his temples in irritation.

"Yes. I heard."

"Doesn't that bother you?"

"It's frustrating, yes. But par for the course, considering my reputation. If I were caught watering a plant, people would think I was screwing it, too."

I can't help but chortle at that. Frode seems to view this as an opening as he continues.

"I understand the pressure you must be feeling right now. The loss, anger, fear. I was there myself once."

Kidnapped and tortured by a serial killer? Unlikely.

However, I say nothing. Just stand there, uncomfortable, trying to ignore the attention of those around us.

"I had a daughter, long ago. Estrid was her name. To be honest, I see much of her in you."

"I'm not your daughter."

Why do I say stuff like that? I realize he means well. *Stop sabotaging yourself, Izzie. This guy saved your ass and kept your secret. Right? Hear him out.*

"Heh. Indeed, you are not."

I'm afraid he's gonna leave, and that once again I'll ruin any chance I have at getting the support I need right now.

"Wait!" He places those gray eyes squarely on me, hands still in his pockets. "I'm sorry. I suck at this. You were important to my mom. The least I can do is hear you out before I hide away again."

"No apology needed. I understand your skepticism. I simply...want you to know that I'm here for you, Isabella. If you need help or guidance of any kind, please contact me."

Frode finally pulls a hand out of his pocket, and he's holding a business card. Hesitantly, I take it from him.

"My personal number is written on the back. Don't share it with anyone else, understand? Should you ever need me, call. Whether it be man or monster that vexes you, there is nothing too strange for me to handle."

That last sentence is odd in itself. Is he talking about my little monster stalker, the one that appeared in the sewer? The thing that kept me alive, somehow? Or am I just reading into this way too much?

I tuck the card in my jacket and try to ignore the next wave of despair that rolls over me.

"Your handwriting sucks. But...thanks," I manage oh so gracefully.

The celebrity engineer gives this nod, and apparently that's that. If he muttered anything else, I didn't hear it. He's halfway to the exit already. Fiddling with the embossed card in my pocket, I give in to the urge to retreat to my bedroom and sort out my feelings about all this later.

***

50 miles per hour on the back roads my mother helped build. Wind in my hair, hands clenched so tight to the handles of my Vespa that they're sweating. Watching miles of farmland go by under a crescent moon blanketed by eerie clouds. It feels like a dream.

Still numb. Lost in my thoughts, I just want some kind of escape.

Investors in the island want to talk to me. Reporters fight for an exclusive interview with the 'girl who survived The Skin Craft Killer'. Calls on my phone nonstop from sanctuary elders despite my aunt's attempts to hold them back. Worried texts from my friends in Dead Vegas, who learned about what happened and who I lost over the news.

I'm not ready for any of this. I just want to hide away. Hell, I'm only 19 years old and I don't have my shit figured out at all.

...Dante would have known what to do.

60 miles per hour. The cold air stings my face. Maybe I should wear a helmet. Or maybe...I just don't care what happens to me right now.

And I don't. I'm apathetic, and it scares me. I don't know what the hell I'm doing, or who I really am now that my mom is gone...

Who am I? The daughter of Dayanna Morales Cordona, the girl who survived a serial killer. The 'miracle baby'. But when all that is stripped away, can I stand on my own?

65 miles per hour. The roads are empty this time of night. Nothing like Dead Vegas. I kind of miss the city, even though it's intimidating as hell. So much distraction everywhere, easy to take your mind off shit that threatens to destroy you.

I see the towering mansion I call home on the cliff side above, melting into the distance in my rear-view mirror. Empty. Someplace I definitely don't wanna be right now.

70 miles per hour. My grip tightens. My heart pulses rapidly. My eyes begin to blur, and I'm not sure if it's because of the stinging air or unwelcome tears.

It's not fair. I realize it sounds childish, but...seriously. Why?

Why me over Mom? Or Dante?

Fucking why?!

It's survivor's guilt, yet knowing that doesn't stop me from feeling this way. My mom had so much to offer the world. She didn't deserve to die. In a cage beneath the street, like some kind of animal! It wasn't her time, not by a long shot. And I get to live so I can do...what exactly? Run away from everything and push everybody away?

78 miles per hour. I'd be going faster if I could. I'm losing it. My apathy grows. I don't care where I'm going, or if I get there. Maybe I'll die tonight. Maybe I won't.

And then I see him. The winged monster that always seems to appear when I'm in danger, fluttering in the air above me doing his best to keep up. His eyes glow like fireflies as they narrow in on me. Maybe it's in my head like everything else, but I swear I detect a hint of frustration in my stalker's gaze as he follows.

Fine. Who knows what this thing really wants. He did nothing to save my mom when those flames rose up. Whether he's real or not, screw him.

But if he's waiting for me to die next, it just might be his lucky day.

Heart beating out of my chest. I take another turn fast, faster than I should. I keep an eye on my mirror, and the demonic thing that occupies it as I speed forward.

If I die tonight...it's okay.

What am I saying?

Suddenly I spot something big ahead. It's a bat, I think, flying low and straight at me. Apparently I'm not the only one with a death wish tonight!

Snap out of it, Izzie!

I panic and swerve hard. Shit, I'm losing control!

Burning rubber. My Vespa slides at top speed across the dirt road, directly towards a ditch.

This is it. Close my eyes tight, brace for whatever comes next. Game over.

Time for a family reunion...

Something like warm tree bark wraps tightly around me for a second. What? The smell of smoke fills the air. Am I alive? Afraid to open my eyes, I anticipate pain all over, mangled in the wreckage of my poor Vespa. Or maybe no feeling at all, another lost limb or something.

But...my dumbass is still here. Still caught up in my own thoughts. Did I survive the impossible...again?

Why??

Finally I open my eyes. The Vespa is a goner, but...me? I'm fine. Not a scratch.

How?

It feels cruel. Even when I think about ending things, just playing with the thought...I can't do it. It's like I'm not supposed to die.

But...fucking why?? I'm nobody!

I stand up and watch the bat flutter nervously away, unharmed. Twist around to find my monster stalker perched on a tree behind me like some creepy gargoyle that has come to life.

"What do you want from me?!" The words spew from my mouth, and I'm so pissed that I'm shaking. "Why won't you let me just die already!"

A blink and he's already gone. No answers for me.

And I'm sick of it.

Maybe I'm crazy, maybe I'm not. But I decide something right then and there, before I dial my aunt for a ride home.

I'm gonna catch that monster. Somehow, I'm gonna catch him and figure out why he's so insistent on keeping me alive. Find out why my mom knew about him, and why he did nothing to protect her. Maybe it's all as crazy as it sounds, but at this point...I'm just desperate for answers. For some sense of hope or purpose after all the trauma. Hell, even just a little distraction to save me from insanity.

But before I can chase ghosts, I need to escape the ghostly memories haunting me on this island.

Dead Vegas, hope you missed me.

CHAPTER THREE

Admittedly, I had been dreading telling my aunt about my plans to leave for Dead Vegas. I prepared for any and all arguments she might have against it. My mind was made up.

But when I told her, I didn't get the response I expected. Guess I need to remember that my aunt is most definitely not my mom. She sighs deeply and takes a seat beside me on the bed.

"I was younger than you when my dad died. I felt lost. I left home and tried starting fresh. Had to clear my head, figure things out on my own, you know?"

Empathy, from the once famously self-centered 'Rita Venus'? No way. I'm caught off guard.

"You never talked about your dad."

"Well, in case you didn't realize, I kind of suck at getting in touch with my...feelings."

Aunt Maggie makes this expression like she just ate something gross. I can't help but snicker.

"But...what I'm trying to say is that I get it. You need to do what you gotta do for yourself right now."

No resistance at all? Her lack of argument has me feeling more guilty than if she fought my departure outright.

"But what about you? Handling everything on this island yourself...It's a lot. And with Mom gone and a reanimated woman taking the lead, you're bound to deal with more prejudice from the warm-bloods."

The woman beside me just shrugs, and for a moment I see the exhaustion weighing over her. In no time at all, she replaces it with her signature smile and wink - acting like everything is just fine. Maybe it is.

"Come on, it's me we're talking about," she simpers. "I've handled much crazier shit. Trust me."

I force a smile, but it doesn't last long. Clearly, I'm not as strong as my aunt.

There is a silence between us. At first Aunt Maggie does nothing, just looks around the room uncomfortably. But after a few minutes, she gives in and puts a hand on my upper back.

"I miss her," I hear myself say. "So much."

Aunt Maggie pulls me closer to her. "I know, babe. So do I."

"I just don't understand how Mom couldn't be reanimated. It's wrong. All of it."

"I agree. But there's a lot about life after death that we don't understand, no matter how hard we try."

"Maybe. How did you move on after your dad died? I don't know if I can do this."

"To be honest, I never really got over it. Losing him, I mean. He was my hero. I wish I could tell you some easy, bullshit self-help way to move on, but it doesn't work that way. It's gonna suck for a long time. Maybe forever."

That doesn't help. But she's being honest, and that's something I do appreciate.

"What you do next," she starts, leaning her head against mine, "that's what matters. Loss like this, it can paralyze us. Make us pissed off at everything, and make us wanna shut off from the rest of the world. You can't let it do that to you, Izz. I'm aware of what happens when you allow it. Shit road you don't wanna go down, trust me."

"So what should I do?" I feel so small right now, like a child.

"Ask yourself that. I don't have the answers. Fuck, I'm still winging it. Do what you gotta do for yourself right now. Get your fresh start and clear head. Just promise me you won't do anything to hurt yourself, and that you won't go it alone. I'll track your ass down if you do anything stupid, got it?"

"Got it."

Aunt Maggie gives me this big hug. I'm not prepared for it.

"Take it one day at a time, Izz. And remember that I'm always a phone call away if you need me to kick somebody's ass for you."

I wanna thank her, but no more words come out. Still, it's gonna be alright. Aunt Maggie remains with me, as I sit in despair for what feels like a very long time.

I'm just glad I still have some family left, even if she isn't by blood. I may not be able to move on, but at least I can try moving forward.

***

Landing back in Dead Vegas was more unsettling than I had anticipated.

The mixture of distrust and awe I had on our first flight here is replaced with melancholy. It's a blend of memories both optimistic and traumatizing. I swapped the private jet for a commercial airline, comfortable chairs for a seat in coach, and offerings of champagne for really old bags of peanuts. Aunt Maggie had offered for me to take her jet, but I've been told I'm spoiled enough times that I insisted on doing this myself. It felt like the right thing to do, and even though I'm stuck next to a guy who snores like an ancient dragon, I don't regret it at all.

This is the first time I've gone this far away on my own, without any family. It's a little intimidating, but I'm used to being by myself and I trust my judgement. I won't make the same mistakes this time around.

However, I wouldn't be by myself in the city for long. The somber cloud surrounding me dissipated a little upon landing, when I was unexpectedly greeted by some familiar faces. Olivia holds a glittery sign with my name on it, shaking it like a cheerleader when she sees me. Hideo is close by, flirting with some pretty undead girl who was waiting for someone else. And Beckett, with that gravity-defying toothpick hanging off his lip, staring off into the middle ground. Olivia elbows him to get his attention, and he promptly starts waving that mechanical arm back and forth enthusiastically. Though I had texted Olivia that I would be landing back in the city today, I wasn't expecting the warm welcome.

"Sup, celebrity!" Hideo changes gears and holds up a bag of something. "Figured you'd be hungry after the flight, so we looked up some grub for ya. Hope you like potato chips!"

"Missed you, babe," offers Olivia with a big hug. She still smells like vanilla and cigarettes. "Kickass new leg, by the way."

"Welcome back, LIFE of the party!" On-point puns from the red-headed vet.

I'm bombarded with greetings and questions about The Skin Craft Killer. I'm quickly offered condolences over my mom, but I ask to avoid the subject just as fast. I'm not here to relive anything. Thankfully, the gang respects my wishes and doesn't dwell on it. What IS fair game, however, is the question of my relation to celebrities living and undead alike: a humanitarian mother, former pop star aunt, and the billionaire...wannabe dad? They act like my life must be glamorous, but it sure as hell doesn't feel that way.

We spend the walk out and back to Olivia's truck talking about my allegedly exciting existence. They're chomping at the bit to ask how I survived The Skin Craft Killer, I see it all over their faces. Although I can't blame them for their curiosity, I do feel a tad disappointed that my new friends seem more interested in who I know than in who I am. Still, I decide that pouting over it is not an option, and instead accept the attention with whatever grace I can muster. Besides, they seemed to like me before they knew about my 'adventurous' life.

So we talk, and laugh, and take our minds off everything else if only for a couple hours. I answer all their inquiries about life on the sanctuary island between mouthfuls of sour cream potato chips.

"It's a lot of pressure," I admit, "You know. Trying to live up to all the expectations. Living in my mom's shadow. I'm not sure how to handle it."

It's a sentiment I immediately regret sharing. However, the revelation was met with compassion across the board.

"Sore na! Tell me about it."

"YOU decide your worth, hun. Nobody else."

"I wish I could stop comparin' myself to my old man. That shit will drive you crazy."

Knowing I'm not alone? It helps, if only a little.

Olivia inspects my prosthetic leg with contagious enthusiasm, expressing on multiple occasions the desire to make alterations. But despite all the comradery, I'm absolutely bushed from the flight. I decide to call it and head to my newly-booked room at Motel Macabre, but only after getting teased endlessly for falling asleep mid-conversation.

Olivia drops me off at the motel and we make plans to hang out tomorrow when she's off work. I make a quick retreat to my room, a far-cry from the spacious suite I stayed at last time. Good. It has a bed, and that's really all I need right about now.

Why is flying so exhausting? Geez. You'd think I flapped my arms and flew here myself.

Flop on the bed, face down and ass up. Big sigh into the pillow. Can't help but wonder what my mom would think about me returning to Dead Vegas and back to the reanimated kids she told me to avoid. I feel a little guilty for it. But at the same time, I trust these people and I need the company desperately. I gotta follow Aunt Maggie's advice and at least TRY looking forward. Because if I don't, I'll shrink away into myself until there is nothing left of me.

I decided to forget about the business card in my pocket for now. I trust my new friends - they feel like siblings. I just gotta figure out how to tell them that I need their help catching a literal monster, one who may or may not have saved my life on multiple occasions. Without sounding crazy. That might be harder to do than forcing myself to socialize.

Crazy lady, out.

***

"So how do we make your little friend appear?" Beckett questions, somewhat humorously while playing cards with Hideo. He's losing badly.

"Well...I need to be in danger. Or at least afraid, I guess. That's when he shows up."

"So we just gotta scare you, that's it?" Beckett puts his hand on the table, and a very proud Hideo follows up with a hand twice as good. "Hell naw, you cheated!"

"Yeah, right. My penthouse, my rules." Hideo rakes in more cash and looks over his shoulder at me. Dressed head to toe in baggy designer clothes, I can't imagine him needing the extra dough. "It's scary how bad Beckett is at blackjack. Does that help?"

"Nah, screw you, man. Mr. Good At Everything." Beckett stands up, still grinning. "It's more like...THIS kinda scare!"

And Beckett just lunges at me, howling like a werewolf. I jump a little, but that's it.

"You're an idiot," I snicker. "That didn't work at all."

"Scare you, huh," pipes in Olivia from the couch, without taking eyes off her illuminated phone. That smile says she's texting that new boyfriend of hers, no doubt. Beckett won't shut up about him. "How about this: high-waisted mom jeans are making a comeback this season."

"Closer than Beckett got to scaring me, but nah. I mean 'afraid for my life' kind of scary. Fight or flight."

"So what do you suggest then?" Hideo leans forward in his seat, still counting his winnings. It's obvious he isn't sold on my story.

None of them are. They're just being polite after what happened to me, and I get it. However, that won't stop me.

"I'm thinking that we need to manufacture a situation in which I feel afraid for my life. Real fear. Then that...thing should appear, and we can catch him."

Olivia's turn to protest.

"I love you babes, but this is all sounding kinda batshit. Monsters? I thought you were just being funny when you texted me at work about it. Are you sure you aren't a teeeeeny bit high?"

Yeah, yeah. I spilled the beans about my little monster via text message. There may or may not have been little bat wings and octopus emojis involved. What can I say, I have tact in spades.

"Yeah I'm sure! That thing is real - both my mom and the Skin Craft Killer saw it too! Hell, I think even Frode Algar is a believer!"

Beckett and Olivia double take in unison. Hideo slaps his cash down on the table mid-count.

"So you DO know Frode Algar?" the fanboy asks in awe. "As in, you actually KNOW him?! We saw the pictures of you guys together on the news, but we thought it was photoshopped or something. Didn't believe it."

"Scandalous," giggles Olivia, not helping.

"Not like that, Olivia! But yeah, I met him that night at the fundraiser. He's friend's with my mom, apparently."

All at once, they start asking me lots of questions.

"Did he say when he was gonna release his new line of synthetic bodies?"

"Did he really try hitting on you at that fundraiser?"

"What was it like talking to him?"

"Is he single?"

"Olivia, does your ugly hipster boyfriend know that you wanna jump that playboy's - "

"Shut up, Eugene!"

On and on. I'm equally amused and frustrated.

"He's cool I guess, nicer than I expected. But that isn't the point. The point is, this monster thing is real and I'm gonna catch it tonight whether you guys help me or not."

"Chotto matte," Hideo pipes in, pocketing his winnings and ignoring Beckett's middle finger two inches from his face. "Adrenaline. Maybe that's all you need to see this thing. Don't scare yourself shitless. Just get adrenaline levels high enough."

Wait a second. I think Hideo might be right. The night I first met him and Beckett, when we were hopping buildings like stuntmen, I witnessed my monster. I'm sure of it. It might really be as simple as that.

"Hideo...I think you might be onto something."

He beams and kicks back in his chair, flipping the bill of his trucker hat backwards. "Yep. I'm pretty brilliant. Everybody hear that?"

"But if I wanna catch this thing, I need to trigger fight or flight in a confined space. A space where we can control where and how the creature comes in. Set the trap, and boom. Interrogation time. Find out what it wants from me and what it knows about my mom."

I'm feeling more relieved already. I seem to have people on my side for once. Sure, I can tell they're skeptical. But I get it, a certain level of skepticism is healthy when you're talking about catching nightmare monsters. As far as they know, I'm having a mental breakdown post-trauma.

Heh. Maybe I am.

But I'm not imagining this. I'll make believers out of my friends soon enough, I'm sure of it.

"Ladies and gents, this is absolutely batshit," declares Olivia, putting on her oversized shades, "and I am so fucking down for it. Plus I think I have just the thing to get you in the mood for a monster sighting."

***

Feeling clammy even though my heart is thumping. Faster, faster.

Operation: Monster Snatch is officially underway as the adrenaline drugs Olivia gave me begin to kick in. I'm sitting in the middle of Olivia's auto-body shop after-hours on a quiet Thursday night, the perfect bait for our unsuspecting catch. The plan? Lure my demonic little stalker close enough that Beckett can take a shot with his tranquilizer gun. Monster goes 'night night' before he can try another one of his disappearing acts. BAM, proof I'm not nuts and finally a chance to confront my personal demons. Literally.

So there I am, sitting on a rather creaky swivel chair with my arms in my lap, eyes all over the garage for signs of my boogeyman. Muscles tightened, sweat dripping down my throat.

I'm ready, all right. Ready to catch this asshole.

"You sure about this, Izz?" asks Beckett. He has this look that loudly proclaims 'I think you're nuts'. So does Olivia, looking mildly concerned as she stands beside me with arms tightly crossed. Hideo is obviously bored, playing with his hair and taking selfies in his 'Planet ROT' designer hoodie more than he's watching the door.

They look like they're ready, all right. Ready to have nothing happen.

Just wait, guys. You'll see.

"Positive," I reassure them, offering a thumbs up. Maybe that's not entirely true. I have horrible jitters, like I just drank an ungodly amount of coffee. Still...I trust myself.

My wish is soon granted, and thank God for that. I resist the urge to spring out of my seat when I see that familiar pair of gleaming orbs appear, floating in the air above an El Camino in desperate need of TLC.

"Over there," I announce with a hushed voice, "Right above the El Camino. Hurry."

Whenever I see him appear, it's like I can't look away. He flutters down and lands on top of the car, rocking it ever so slightly. My friends definitely noticed that. His eerie gaze pierces right through me: menacing and...skeptical? Tentacles writhing like worms as he looks at me curiously, ticking those creepy little claws against his new aluminum perch. My friends definitely heard that.

"Where is it now?" Beckett's voice pulls me back. I look to the far corner of the garage to see Beckett peeking out from behind a silver SUV, tranquilizer gun still propped and ready. Hideo and Olivia express similar excitement now, looking every which way for the very obvious monster directly in the middle of us.

"He's right there, sitting on top of the El Camino!" I'm getting frustrated now. "He's looking right at me!"

Beckett grimaces behind the telescopic sights of his dart gun. "I don't see shit!"

"Come on, Izz!" Hideo joins in nervously. "Stop messing around."

"Izzie, babe," Olivia speaks gently behind me, "are you sure - "

"Yes I'm fucking sure!" I'm over it. I'm not sure what the problem is, but I'm ready to take matters into my own hands. Out of the chair I leap, pushing past rolling tool boxes until I'm by the hood of the El Camino in question. The prehistoric asshole sitting on top flicks his wings out and falls off balance. I think my rush might have caught him off guard. Good. These undead kids may be scared stiff, but it's alright. This is MY time to act.

My arms slip through the air comically as the creature narrowly escapes my grasp. He's up in the air again, flapping those little wings as he looks down at me.

"Get back here, asshole!" I'm still leaning up against the El Camino as I shout over my shoulder to Beckett. "Just shoot him, Beckett! Take the damn shot, hurry!"

"You crazy? There's nothin' TO shoot!"

My heart feels like it's gonna burst out of my chest. I take the nearest thing I can find to throw - an oily wrench will do. Hurl it up into the air for what would have been a perfect hit. That is, if my fucking monster didn't just disappear on me. Again. The wrench spirals through the air and clangs against the roof of another car, setting off its car alarm. Great.

A scream of pure rage leaves me. I pound my fists on the car like a spoiled brat. As the boys chatter and Olivia rushes to disable the car alarm, I'm left feeling like a complete dumbass.

"What's wrong with you guys?" I holler, attempting to hide my own embarrassment with blame-shifting. Classic move. "Beckett, you totally let him get away! Do you need glasses or something?"

Beckett drops his dart gun and raspberries his lips. "That's what the doctor told me, but glasses are for dorks."

Hideo's next. "Livi, what drugs did you really give that warm-blood? I want some."

"Firstly, glasses are not for dorks. They're actually kinda hot. And secondly, I can't take credit for the show. That was all our girl Izzie right here."

Olivia giggles and that's it for me. They're already talking amongst themselves and laughing. I whistle loudly and demand their attention.

"You guys think this is some joke?! That creature could be the key to everything I've survived!"

The three of them are altogether now, giving me this mutual look of pity.

"Um, babe, you've been through a lot. We understand that. You need more time to recover..."

"Yeah, from the roofie you clearly gave her."

The boys cackle while Olivia tries to keep a straight face. Clueless and hurtful, the three dead-heads seem as though they were unable to see my little stalker at all.

"Is freakin' out about invisible monsters tryin' to kill you a warm-blood thing, or a sheltered island girl thing?" Beckett smirks.

"Whatever it is, I'm pretty sure it's treatable."

"Come on, boys..."

More laughter. I can hardly believe it. Am I completely crazy after all? My mom saw the creature, and so did The Skin Craft Killer. So why couldn't these guys see it?

I'm pissed and embarrassed. Suddenly I feel small and insignificant all over again. That weird, spoiled kid, 'making stuff up for attention'.

"Aww, sweetie, we didn't mean to hurt your feelings."

I look up to notice I'm being stared at by my three hecklers. Olivia might be playing nice now, but the damage is already done. I don't need their pity.

The other two knuckle-heads are backpedaling too, but I don't hear a word. Olivia reaches for my shoulder and I shove her hand off. I was right all along. I don't need anybody.

"Fuck you guys," I spit, reaching for my backpack. "I don't need your help. I'll handle this shit on my own, like always."

And I'm outta there. I don't look back. Blood still pumping, body trembling. I blame it on the adrenaline, but my defensive attitude had a leading role as well. I don't need them to believe me. I'll catch that monster myself and find out who he is and why he insists on keeping me alive.

Me, myself, and I.

Team Izzie.

It's cool. Totally cool.

Maybe some people are meant to be alone, anyways.

***

Turn the shitty hotel TV on. Plop on the bed, face first into teal bed covers.

No luck, no leads. I'm crazy. It's official.

"ESTRID Industries CEO Frode Algar survived what onlookers have described as an 'impossible accident' last weekend when an angry ex-girlfriend rammed into Algar's limousine..."

Great, can't stop hearing about this guy either.

Wait...What?

"One witness described the scene to EMZ."

"The car was like BREEEE, and the limo was like AHHHHH, and then SCREEECH, and BAM, you know, like right into each other, bad, bro. That limo was thrashed, bro. I saw the blood. Nobody could survive that, bro. "

"The USCRS promptly arrived at the scene, only to discover Algar completely unharmed..."

That's when I saw it. On TV. That's the famous engineer alright, but paramedics and nosy onlookers aren't his only company.

It's a monster. Huge, descending on beetle-like wings the color of crude oil, touching down on the street with cartoonishly long arms. Insectoid face, save for those creepy lips and horse teeth. The entity fidgets from arm to arm as it eyeballs the hell out of the oblivious people surrounding the crash site.

I sit up straight instantaneously. It's true, then. I'm not crazy. Not only is my monster real, there's...more?

Frantically, I pull Algar's business card off the dresser. My gaze fixates on the pixelated image before me on TV as I hold the card so tight that it crumples.

"Motherfu--"

CHAPTER FOUR

The tallest, newest building in Dead Vegas. A sore thumb, sandwiched between an aging law firm and yet another run-down casino.

I push past security at the glass doors and help myself in. There's something fantastic about this place, so full of modern marvels and white-collar workers riding glass elevators up and down like clockwork. My eyes go directly to the large sculpture five times my size, maybe bigger: a precarious balance of geometric shapes, upon which floats the holographic words, 'ESTRID INDUSTRIES'. Grand displays of limb and body replacements here and there throughout the building at every visible level. A robotic-sounding voice over some mysterious intercom, bragging about the various accomplishments of the company. And last but definitely least, the smug face of the company's figurehead looming overhead in a gently flickering hologram, as tall as the windows on the opposite wall.

Alright, maybe I'm a little impressed.

Now's not the time, though. Ignore the guards, storm my way up to the receptionist. I address a tiny woman sitting at an enormous desk, who is currently looking me up and down suspiciously over round glasses.

"Can I...help you?"

I'm sure I look massively out of place here: a warm-blood dressed like it's casual Friday at boot camp or something. But none of this matters. I know what I'm here for, and it's an emergency.

"I'm here to talk to Frode Algar," I tell her, out of breath.

"Um...Do you have an appointment?"

"Do I look like I have an appointment? I gotta speak to him, it's an emergency."

"I'm sorry, but Mr. Algar is very busy right now and he cannot be seen without an appointment. I have to ask you to leave, ma'am."

Walk up to the giant desk and slam my hands down on it. Pretty receptionist chick barely reacts, aside from slowly reaching for her desk phone.

"Are you calling security?"

She just stares at me, not breaking eye contact as her hand inches slowly closer to the phone.

"Don't you call security on me. Don't you do it."

Her little hand moves closer.

I'm too fixated on her to realize that one of the front door security guards is already upon me. He's ready to carry my ass right outta here, but no way. I'm not leaving without getting what I want.

"Tell him it's Isabella Cordona! Dayanna's daughter! I need to speak with Frode, ASAP! Please!"

No response. Lady just joins everyone else in watching the crazy living chick get carried outside the building.

I resist the urge to kick the security guard in the balls and fight back in. Don't need to be getting myself arrested. So I sit and pout on the corner outside.

But not for long.

Maybe ten minutes or less later, the same security guard that so politely escorted me out shows up with a message.

"Our apologies, Miss. Cordona. Mr. Algar will see you once his meeting has concluded. Please, come with me."

Hell yeah!

I make sure to stick my tongue out at the receptionist when I pass by her this time.

***

Frode asks his assistant to leave us be. He looks frazzled. White boards behind him are covered in mathematical scribbles, diagrams of prosthetics and marketing statistics. Not sure if it's my random appearance that has him so clearly frustrated, or if it was the busy meeting he had right before letting me in. I'm gonna assume the former and make my case quickly.

"Why are you here?" he inquires quite flatly. There is no compassion in the man's voice, not this time. Just irritation, the kind you would have with a stubborn child.

"For your cheery attitude."

"Really now?"

"Of course not, I'm here to talk about fucking monsters."

One scarred eyebrow raises.

"You have my number. You could have called." He pushes a button and the curtains in the room close slowly. "You're a teenager. You do own a phone, don't you?"

"Cute. It's super important and confidential, so I had to see you in person, okay?!" The following is a whisper. "Don't play dumb, either. I'm aware that you have a monster stalker too, I've seen it on TV."

His eyes get bigger. Algar takes a look around the room, just in case somebody is listening in behind a potted plant or something.

"Oh, that. You have questions, I'm sure."

"Yeah, no shit. I tried to catch mine with the help of my so-called friends, but they couldn't even see it. I need to know why it's there and what it wants from me. And why some people can see it and others can't."

The former Viking sighs and leans back against the conference table with his arms crossed.

"Very few people can see our 'monsters'. You're special."

"I don't feel very special," I whine. "I don't even know what it wants with me."

Algar grunts. "It's an Eldritch creature, a servant to Earth's oldest inhabitants. Yours is a guardian-reaper, and its job is to watch over you until your time is up, so to speak. Your friends couldn't see it because they haven't had any exposure to arcane magic. Only those who make deals with the Old Ones can see them."

'Guardian-reaper'? Yeah right. I thought guardians were supposed to have feathery wings and pluck harps or something. And reapers were supposed to wear black robes and wield giant scythes. I'm not buying it.

"But I've never made any deals with Eldritch monsters or whatever. I don't even understand what that shit is."

"That is because someone made a deal on your behalf, I'm afraid. Very special case." He's holding back. I can tell.

Someone made a deal on my behalf? My mom? No way. Maybe Aunt Maggie. I love her, but she's definitely more of the 'Hail Satan' type...

"So why do YOU have one of those creepy monsters hanging around? Did someone make a deal for you, too?"

I see the ever-confident Frode look around for a second, a little unsure of himself. I assume this is a subject he's used to keeping to himself. He's debating whether or not he should tell me, but he gives in.

"No. I made a deal myself, a long time ago, for immortality."

"Wait a second. I thought you were the so-called 'original inventor of reanimation'. Are you telling me that's a lie?"

The deepest sigh ever is his response.

"Technically, I suppose. My resurrection was thanks to powerful arcane magic, not science."

"Hmmph. Why lie, then? Not famous enough, are you?"

"I tried the truth, many times. But oddly enough, most people have a hard time believing in magic and monsters. The truth is what people feel most comfortable with."

Couldn't argue that.

I sit down in a nearby swivel chair and lean forward. I have...SO...many questions.

"So what is this arcane stuff anyway? What kinda deals are we talking about? Are they with the devil?"

"Slow down. We're talking about ancient beings with many names, whose true nature is unfathomable to human minds. But I can tell you this much : the Old Ones have nothing to do with heaven or hell. God or the devil. They live beneath the sea, beneath the earth itself, on a parallel plane called The Penumbra. They have been known to share their magic with humans brave enough to summon them, but at a price."

"And what price would that be?" I chortle. "Human souls or something?"

The inventor says nothing, just scratches his beard and shrugs. Shit.

"You're telling me these monster things...they make deals with humans for their souls?!"

"Circle gets the square."

Smartass.

"So you sold your soul for immortality?" I cross my arms. "Doesn't make sense. Call it what you want. It sounds like a deal with the Devil to me."

"The Devil was murdered a long time ago."

I start to chortle, but stifle it. He stated this absurd thing so plainly, like it was a pure and simple fact. He isn't amused by my outburst either. He sighs and continues.

"All cosmic planes are fueled by life forces. Souls happen to be especially potent."

This is without a doubt, the weirdest conversation I've ever had.

The playboy looks at his extremely expensive watch and cracks his jaw.

"I have another meeting to attend shortly," he begins, "but we can continue this fun little conversation later."

He can't bail yet! I still have a buttload of questions!

Clearly he senses my frustration.

"You said you wanted to catch your monster? I can help." He pauses to grab a pen and piece of memo paper from his desk. Scribbles something down and hands it to me. "If you are absolutely sure this is what you want, then meet me at this address tomorrow night. It won't be easy, but I promise that this difficult experience shall be as temporary as it is worthwhile. Endure, and you will receive all the answers you seek directly from the source."

I take the paper quickly and nod. Countless questions are still floating around in my head, but I suppose they can wait until...

"Tomorrow it is," I grin from ear to ear. I can hardly wait.

"Now, I'll have my assistant escort you out. Be safe out there, Isabella. And learn how to pick up a phone next time."

***

Total darkness. All I can hear is my own hurried breath. Panic. The onset of madness.

"Are you sure about this?" Algar had asked. I arrived at the private address he scribbled down for me, fifteen minutes early even. A three-story estate in a petrified forest outside of Dead Vegas.

He asked me if I was sure about going through with this. I told me yeah, I was sure. I signed some papers and was given a pocket knife and a cup of tea. I had to learn how to control my fear. I had to confront the monster that saved my life. To understand why I was the sole survivor that horrible night beneath the city. It felt like the key to everything.

But as I lay here, six feet under the ground in a coffin fit for Dracula himself...I realize just how wrong I was. About confronting fear. About Frode. About me.

Still woozy. That asshole drugged me. Shouldn't have drank that cup of tea. I don't even like tea! Was this the 'difficult experience' he insufficiently warned me about?

Start thumping on the wooden wall only inches from my face. Total darkness. I cry out for help. For escape from this box, this ever-growing madness about to consume me. For a chance at making it out alive, and the chance to make Frode the Chode pay for burying me alive.

I'm scared.

My cries are unanswered, unsurprisingly. Knuckles are bloody from banging on the coffin lid. I smell the dirt packed heavy above me. Resist the urge to scream. Betrayed again. I must be the biggest fool ever. I feel like I need to remind myself how to breathe.

Is this for real? Am I...gonna die down here?

Breathe in, breathe out. Gasps for air, choking on tears. The mad urge to flail my body, but no space whatsoever to do so.

I'm...gonna die.

As if on cue, a set of beaming, bulbous eyes appear down by my feet: the single source of light here in my prison.

It's him. He's coming for me again. It's hard to see a guardian when I look at the prehistoric beast before me. I feel no comfort, only fear.

"Leave me alone!" I cry out, or something along those lines. Those weren't the words I had in mind for the creature that saved my life. Everything is a blur.

Adrenaline rushing. Feel like puking. "You can't take me, asshole!"

Those bulbous eyes blink at me inquisitively. I feel warm, meaty claws grip onto my legs and begin climbing up my body towards my chest. How did he even get in here? Hell, how does he fit? Is he phasing through me now? I'm losing it. I gotta be.

Shit! I can't reach my knife. Kick my legs, wiggle around helplessly, exclaim incoherently between terrified sobs. But the monster doesn't stop. He's taunting me now, just like he did when he appeared in front of my friends. Just like he always has.

There's no way this thing is some kind of protector. Right? He wants me dead, no doubt about it. And I hate to admit it, but this time...

No, Izzie. You can't think that way. You gotta fight.

"Leave me the fuck alone!!"

He doesn't listen. Just sits on top of me now, or is it through me? Tentacles wiggling right in front of my face but just out of reach. Sitting there. Watching me. Like he's waiting for something. My last breath, no doubt. I'm seeing less 'guardian' and more 'reaper' right now.

"I'm not gonna die here! You can't take me!" But my voice betrays my empty threats. Clearly I'm terrified, trapped. Running out of oxygen, and fast. All the while that creepy little monster just...stares at me.

"Why are you here?! What do you know about my mom?!"

The Eldritch monster takes a moment, head still at an inquisitive tilt as he observes me. Suddenly, he tries grabbing one of my arms with his tentacles. I try to pull away, but I'm running out of strength already. I thought he was gonna bite me, or maybe rip my arm clear from my body. But what he does instead is much...weirder.

Tentacles assume a physical presence and wrap around my bare arm, tight. I feel those gross little suction cups all over me, and my skin immediately turns numb. I scream, but within seconds my own voice sounds like it's underwater, someplace far, far away.

I'm slipping...

Into some strange world between worlds. Hard to explain.

Feels like I'm falling...No, more like getting yanked down into an abyss within the deep recesses of my own mind. Seeing a world of memories flash and fall around me. Washing over, shaking me to my core.

Yep. That little fucker is in my head.

But it's almost like he's showing me something. These memories and moments...I view them like a spectator in a dream, even though it's me that they're happening to. Well, kind of happening to me. Am I officially losing it?

It's my mom in labor, alone. Her screams are full of agony, and even like this, with her hair all matted and sweaty and tears streaming down her face, she's still just as pretty as I remembered her growing up.

Flashing by, falling around me like I'm barreling down through layer after layer of moments and synapses.

Another quick moment. My mom is crying with twins in her arms. She's the only one crying, though. Her babies are perfectly still, perfectly silent. It's unnerving. I had always heard stories about the miracle that brought me back to life, how my mom's prayers were answered. But actually seeing it...

Wait.

More flashes. More falling, spiraling down deeper, deeper. Mind pulsating, I swear I can hear my own blood pumping faster and faster.

Candles in the dark. Otherworldly symbols painted in a circle on the ground. Unfamiliar words strung together with urgency and desperation. My mother's body heaving, drawing blood, dancing almost in some sort of trance. Strange lights, stranger voices. I wait for it all to stop, but it doesn't.

Something dark and terrible, I feel it all around. Or is it just in this memory that doesn't quite belong to me? Promises made. Blood and tears shed. Desperate pleas. Glowing red eyes in the dark. Then suddenly...

I fall through more abyss, twisting about like I'm stuck in an endless falling dream.

But I can hear it. The slow and growing cries of one of the newborns. Breath. A heartbeat. Something beautiful gained, but something terrible lost.

A rush, I can feel it, numbing every part of me. And suddenly, I just know everything.

Fuck.

Dante and I DID die at birth.

And...

Shit.

It wasn't a miracle that brought me back to life.

It was...

...

***

God. My head hurts. I imagine this is what hangovers must feel like.

I wake up lying in the grass, drooling. I can taste my own blood. My nose, it's bleeding. Where am I? What time is it?

Birds chirping, cool air on my skin. Air! I shake my head and rub my eyes, trying to ease the blur. I'm not in that coffin anymore! It's morning and I'm above ground, right beside the spot that asshole buried me. The ground is all torn up.

How did I get out??

Cough. Dust and dirt all over me. Dryest mouth ever. God, I need a drink. Manage to set up, but still too disoriented to stand. Drag myself to the edge of the hole and look in. It's partially caved in now, but I can still make out pieces of the coffin. It looks like I busted straight out of the top of that thing and clawed my way out.

Did I really do that? I check my hands, but...no. There's no dirt packed under the nails. Knife never left my pocket either. So how the hell did I get out of here? Did Algar save me?

No. That isn't the answer either. My brain is still buzzing, like deep inside me I already have the answers.

And I do. My savior...it wasn't me or Frode. It wasn't Aunt Maggie. It sure as hell wasn't Olivia or the others.

It was him. My so-called guardian-reaper. To my rescue...yet again.

I whip around, looking for the little guy. But of course he's long gone again. I'm alone.

All the memories from last night come rushing back. Everything the creature showed me. I dry heave on the spot. There's just...so much to process. Algar's car is gone already, that dick. I'll deal with him later. In its place is his assistant's car, and I assume she's waiting for me. However, I don't want her help. I'll take a cab back to my hotel and give my aunt a very important phone call.

Well...after I lay here for just a little longer.

Fuck.

***

Everything right now feels like a wicked fever dream. No piece of new information gives me the comfort I so desperately need. Clarity just makes it worse.

My call to Aunt Maggie proved less than fruitful. She knew little about my mom's 'extracurricular' activities, and even less about the nature of my birth.

"I was in captivity when your mom gave birth," she tells me with a volume much too high for the phone. "And she didn't talk much about it after we escaped Frankenstein's island either. But as close as your mom and I were, there was a lot of stuff she didn't tell me. I kinda got used to it and stopped prying. There's shit I don't like to talk about either, so I get it."

However, I DID get an answer when I asked where my mom learned about this magic stuff. Thank God for that. But like I said...clarity did not bring much comfort.

"I know this sounds crazy," she started, "but I guess 'crazy' is just par for the course right now. A very old undead pirate named Madame Ching introduced your mom to arcane magic. I saw what it could do myself. Brought a dead person back to life without a reanimation chamber. Did some other scary shit, too."

Should I be more afraid? I'm pissed off for sure. Confused. But...I have no clue what I'm really dealing with here.

"Where can I find this Madame Ching?" I need more answers, ones that don't involve an undead playboy assclown burying me alive. "I need to know everything."

If there is even the tiniest chance I can bring my mom back with the same magic that brought ME back, I need to take it. No matter how batshit crazy it sounds.

"She's hard to find. Not exactly in the yellow books. Sorry, kiddo."

One fist clenched in my lap at the edge of my bed, the other hand gripping my phone so hard that it's sweating. I get the horrible feeling that my mom couldn't be reanimated because of the bargain she made with her soul to bring me back. I feel even worse. I NEED to fix this. Somehow.

"Izz?"

"...Yeah?"

"Whatever your mom did...she did because she loved you. I can't imagine what you're feeling right about now, but you need to remember that YOU were the most important thing to Dayanna. More than the sanctuary, more than me, more than anything."

....*More than Dante?*

"...I know."

"Love you, Izz. Sit tight and I'll stay in touch."

***

Standing on the ledge now. Looking down immediately gives me vertigo. The cars below look like they're the size of hot wheels. I can barely even hear the horns of angry drivers below. Partially because I'm so many stories up, and partially because I'm just so angry.

It feels like my life is a lie. I thought I was the 'miracle baby', the one who survived out of pure chance. Instead, it was my mom sacrificing her own soul to bring me back from the dead, and for what?

So she could die in a cage, sacrificing herself yet again?

For what?

Why me? Why not Dante? Could she only revive one of us through this...magic? Was it random, or did she have to choose? Neither option makes me feel any better at all.

Why me?!

What's the point? My mom had so much more to offer this world than I do. And I'm sure Dante would have grown up to be smarter, more courageous, and more charismatic than I. I'm just a brat, another spoiled rich kid too damaged to make any real difference.

The whole thing is nuts. I mean, blood rituals? Alchemy? Magic? Is this for real right now?

What the actual fuck?

Step closer to the ledge. I'm at my wit's end. All I can see in my head right now are those luminous eyes, watching me. Waiting for the next moment I'm afraid for my life.

The next moment I'm about to die.

"You want me, asshole?!" I shout into the still air at nothing, no doubt looking crazy to anybody who might be watching. "I'm right here! You want me so bad, come and get me! I have nothing left to lose!"

I should have thought of something after that. But I didn't.

Instead I just took a step right off the building. No turning back.

Am I totally insane?

Air whipping around me as I fall. Cold air like a bunch of tiny daggers, ripping at my skin and pulling at my jacket as I cut through the night sky. Those tiny cars are getting bigger, bigger. Close my eyes.

I'm sorry, Mama. I'm not strong enough. I'll see you and Dante sooner than you thought.

Suddenly a whoosh of air below me. Open my eyes to see my Eldritch stalker has returned, and just in time. Dinosaur flesh surrounding me, bat-like wings flapping at max speed as the monster grabs me from behind and around the shoulders like a scaly backpack. Unlike last time, the little guy is physically all there. I can feel him and all his weight.

My body yanks up, and his claws dig into my skin. How he's managing to carry my heavy ass I have no clue. He pulls up and carries me off into an alleyway out of sight from the main street. We're descending rapidly.

The ground must be within 15 feet or so now. A disturbed rat pulls his head out of a toppled trash bag and makes a run for it as we come flying in like an asteroid.

Claws digging into me, deeper. I have no clue where my head is. I just feel Algar's pocket knife in my hand, even though I don't remember taking it out.

And I remember making a very rash decision. Still not sure if it was the right one either.

One quick movement. A weird, otherworldly howl of pain above me and inside my brain. A squirt of blood darker than the sky above. And I go falling even faster, straight into a dumpster.

Clang.

Everything hurts. Grab my shoulder, try to stop the bleeding. Ignore the ringing in my head, the smell of overly-fragrant cosmetic byproducts keeping me company in the dumpster. Pull myself up, look around the alley for my stalker.

And there he is. Curled up like a scared animal, bleeding. A deep puncture wound in his left shoulder is dripping black blood to the cement, where it glows red before bursting into green flame. This WTF little fire quickly dissipates, and I swear I feel something different in the air. Like something's changed.

What have I done?

CHAPTER FIVE

I hop out of the dumpster, still unsteady on my feet. Stumble over to the monster a few feet away from me, still releasing these eerie, discordant howls as he lay there. I'm reminded of Eckerd after his accident, and I can't help but pity the beast. Is that weird? Standing over him now, he doesn't look so scary. In fact, he actually looks...afraid. Afraid of me?

Well duh, Izzie. You kind of just attacked him while he was airlifting your dumbass to safety.

Admittedly, I still don't get it. He's a little winged nightmare, but how many times has he actually hurt me? I'd be dead twice over if it weren't for him.

What have I done? I tell myself it was self defense - protecting myself from magic and monsters I can't begin to understand. But what if it was just cruelty instead?

I come within reach of the monster. He sees me and tries to escape. Wings all over the place. He's trying to fly away, but he can't. Clearly, the little asshole isn't accustomed to fear. That shit will paralyze you.

"Hey, easy, easy," I tried to soothe him, dropping the knife and raising my hands. "Don't be afraid. I'm not gonna hurt you again."

He isn't buying it. Paws me away like an angry cat, little wings every which way. And can I blame him? Somehow I just gotta do something. I need to make this right.

"I'm sorry I hurt you." He looks at me again, unblinking. "Can you...understand me?"

No response, just more pained sounds. He won't let me touch him, but he's not breaking eye contact either.

"You saved my life...again. Why?"

Nothing.

"What are you? Who are you?"

Radio silence.

I remember when he grabbed me in the coffin. How he showed me things. Maybe that's how he communicates?

Roll my jacket sleeve up, and thrust my exposed arm right in front of the creature's wiggling tentacle face.

"Show me. Show me who you are. What you want from me. Show me!"

He just looks from my face to my arm, back and forth. Then he makes his decision.

Another attempt at escape by air. But once again, he doesn't get far. He's screwed, and he knows it.

I bridge the gap between us. His big eyes don't leave me as he sits there, clutching at his shoulder.

"Please...I'll help patch up your shoulder if you just show me what all this means."

The creature watches as I thrust my arm out once more. He thinks on it one more time, as if weighing his other options. And finally, he narrows those ember eyes and yanks my appendage in with those slimy, skin-tingling tentacles.

And I fall. Faster than I fell from that building. Faster than you can slip from one thought to another. Faster than light itself.

Deep. Deeper still. Hurdling through pain, utter confusion. Collapsing into one fragmented synapse after another. Brain lighting up. New synapses firing. And I feel my eyes open. A rush of knowledge, memories, and powerful emotion. Something old. Something new. Something about...an apocalypse? Altogether, all happening at once. Feels like madness is about to swallow me whole, right up until...

I know.

I know.

I know.

I....

***

"Hey lady...you alright?"

Eyes flutter open. There's the scruffy countenance of that familiar homeless dude inches away from my face. His breath smells like beef. He's still got his apocalypse sign, too.

Sit myself up. A massive migraine ensures I don't rush to my feet. Look around for my little mind-scrambling stalker. And to my surprise...he's still here. Sitting near some tattered newspapers in the alley, nursing his shoulder and keeping an eye on me.

Why is that thing still here? I wanna freak out.

"I'm okay," I manage to spit out, wiping drool from my chin. "Thanks."

"Don't go drinkin' alone next time," the good Samaritan warns me, grabbing his cane and drawing his coat around himself closer. "Not safe for pretty girls like you. Especially with the end of the world comin' and all."

"End of the world. Right. I'll be careful."

And he's on his way, walking right past my monster with his sign hoisted over his shoulder. His dog companion huffs and follows after.

I let out a big sigh. New day. New outlook.

The low whining of a wounded monster pulls me back.

New problems.

"We gotta get out of here. You're coming with me. I'll see what I can do about that shoulder."

***

I thought things were bizarre before. But after this morning...they just got a whole lot weirder.

Lots of bonding time, just me and my monster. Led him back to the motel I was staying at. Bought some cheap stitching at the corner store - they sell this shit everywhere, it's meant as quick repairs for reanimated folks. He still wasn't sure what to think of me, or any of this. But I was determined to make up for what I did. Especially after what I understand now.

Just like before, I felt this flood of knowledge. The monster had downloaded some serious exposition into my head, and it was returning in waves.

For starters, what Frode the Chode told me was accurate: this creature is indeed my guardian, here to protect me from a premature death.

Weird, I get that. But he showed me. He's saved my ass a few times, and I have the scars to prove it. Hell, so does he! I don't know what kind of contract my mom signed to bring me back, but at least I got a sick little bodyguard out of it. If only my dad could see this thing!

It's in the fine print of my mom's contract. It's a lot to process, and Mom's not here to fill in the blanks. I'm still so conflicted, but it's time to focus on everything else that has come to my attention. Be lonely again, but with someone else for a while.

Or maybe, something else. Not sure yet.

He's right in my face. Sitting on all fours in the cactus-patterned chair in front of me as I sit myself on the edge of the bed. This is the first time I've seen him unobscured by darkness. He looks like something ancient, uncovered as a fossil somewhere. The iPod Mini of monsters. I look at the vein patterns in his wings. The various markings on his reptilian skin, like ancient tattoos or something. Scars and scratches all over. Claws the size of shark teeth. This guy could definitely hurt me if he wanted. I'm glad it isn't in his job description.

What the hell?

I was all ready to stitch up that wound when my hand passed right through him! Like he's some kind of ghost, or creepy celebrity hologram! I guess I wasn't imagining it when I was six feet under!

Snap out of it, Izzie. More knowledge from the tentacle brain cocktail emerges. It feels like I've always known...

I can only have physical contact with my little monster when he allows it. Apparently, one of his nifty arcane tricks is the ability to phase between reality as he sees fit. Typically only visible to those exposed to arcane magic, and only in the presence of heightened adrenaline. Intangible to all living things unless he chooses otherwise.

Yeah...it's bizarre. But it's what he showed me, and it makes sense in its own messed up way. That's why he can physically interact with me when I'm in danger. He chooses to become material when I'm in need of his help.

"I'm trying to help YOU right now, tough guy." A rogue wing slaps the desk and knocks my phone to the ground, hard. "Mind putting those things away and letting me touch you for a second?"

Watery grumbles beneath those tentacles register as childish complaints. Shortly after, though, he begrudgingly complies. I watch in disbelief as those wings clasp onto his back and fuse along a pronounced spine. They blend so well into his back, you could barely tell he had wings at all.

Cool.

"Thanks. Now let's try this again..."

Whoosh. Hands pass right through him yet again, like butter. Ghost butter. Apparently, he still doesn't trust me enough to let me touch him. Fair enough.

I put down the needle and thread.

"Fine. Patch yourself up."

That's rude. Even Eldritch monsters have feelings. Right?

Gladly. Human only make things worse.

What the hell? It's a different voice than my own, but I definitely heard it in my head. The discordant sounds start out in some foreign tongue, but it's as if they're being translated inside my mind in real time.

Well, I'm fresh out of sanity. Still, I can tell by what the monster showed me that he is definitely...real. I have the claw marks to prove it. Thankfully, he's on my side. Here to protect me from a deal made without my consent. I guess even monsters can be sticklers for rules.

Sigh. I feel like such an asshole.

"Hey. I'm sorry for what I did to you. But can you blame me? I didn't know shit about anything. And people don't exactly see demons every day."

He shoots me this glare. He's still pissed. Clearly he understands more than I think.

"Um...Sorry. You're not a demon. You're..."

More revelations return to me. I see flashes of strange characters in my mind. Like some sort of old language lost to time. Slowly the characters shift and mold into something I can comprehend. I read it out loud, as if it's written on my brain.

Checcachecchunderayonus.

Um...Is that his name? Yeah...It is.

"I think I'll just call you...CheccChecc. Is that okay?"

He stares at me with this bob of his head. After a moment to think about it, he shrugs.

This is the weirdest shit ever.

"Um..It's nice to meet you then, CheccChecc. Officially, I mean."

I put my hand out for him to shake it. His tentacles float around closely, observantly. He looks up at me, and I'm sure he must think I'm an idiot.

"Oh yeah, sorry. I forgot. Hologram monster doesn't trust me."

Stare off into the wall.

"I just tried to shake hands with a hologram monster. I'm nuts. Crazy."

All humans crazy. No wonder planet needs Penumbran intervention.

Yeah. I'm nuts.

"So, uh...Are you hungry?"

He seems to react to that question. I sense that he likes to eat, but doesn't need to. Not the way I need to, at least. Thank goodness he seems to understand my language. I wonder if they have English classes in the underworld or if spending a little time in my brain is to thank for that. I'm thinking it's the latter.

"What do you eat?" It's a question I'm afraid to get an answer to. I'm not prepared to slaughter a sacrificial lamb, or some virgin. Way too early in the day for that. I look out a window overlooking the city below, contemplating a trip to that diner from last time.

Ah, wait a second! Aunt Maggie brought me some fast food before my flight, but I stuffed it in the hotel mini fridge and forgot about it. What, with being buried alive and told I was revived with arcane magic. Kinda got a little side-tracked.

Rush to the mini-fridge and pull out a crumpled, greasy bag. Ah, fast food, how I love thee.

Alright. Breakfast time.

I clear the little coffee table and open the bag. Take out the strawberry milkshake, that one's for me. Then, in a nice clean row, I lay out French fries and a hamburger, disassembled into two piles: meat only and veggies only. As my hands move carefully, CheccChecc watches with the mildest of interest.

"Now, what do you like to eat?"

Step aside, and let my imaginary friend make his choice. I'm secretly hoping he picks the vegetables, because a vegan monster makes a tasty human feel a little safer.

Those enormous eyes bounce from one pile to the next with an almost cartoony level of curiosity. Tentacles wriggling everywhere, all over everything on that table. Gross. From one to the next he goes, until his gooey suction cups have been over literally everything...including my milkshake.

"Nah, dude, that one's mi - "

CheccChecc made his choice, I suppose. He's already half-way through sucking down my strawberry milkshake. Yeah. This is some cartoony bullshit, right here.

Aaand he's done. A plastic cup that once contained the nectar of the Gods now rolls across the carpet, completely empty. Also on the floor is an especially excited monster from the underworld.

I wanna get annoyed, but he's just so happy with himself. Like, it's almost adorable. Almost.

"Yeah, this human stuff isn't so bad, huh?"

Before, CheccChecc only appeared when I needed rescuing. Now I see him all the time. Oddly enough, I didn't get an answer to that in the brain cocktail.

"Hey," I ask abruptly, "why do I see you all the time now? Is it because I hurt you or something?"

CheccChecc seems confused by the question. Maybe his telepathic English needs work?

Hmm. Sure. Stuck topside because human hurt CheccChecc or something.

"Well, don't sound too sure about it." *Don't be rude, Izz. How many people can say they have an actual, real-life monster companion looking out for them?*

"Um, what I mean is, sorry. I'm sorry for hurting you."

Neither I nor CheccChecc have a clue what to do, or where to go from here. It's a predicament neither of us were prepared for.

It's uncomfortable.

"You've always been around, haven't you?" He lifts his head from the empty cup on the floor and zeros in on me once more. "Showing up to save the day time and time again. And I had no clue. God, this is crazy."

I plop back down on the bed, suddenly aware of how exhausted I am. But there's no way I can sleep right now. Apparently, I have a prehistoric pet that may or may not be high maintenance.

"Invisible to pretty much everybody...That must be so lonely."

Listen to yourself, Izz. Maybe you got a concussion from your dumpster landing last night. You're acting like this isn't completely batshit crazy.

You've watched waaay too many movies. That's the problem here.

Real, not real...What's the goal from here? Or do I just need more distraction?

Right on cue, my mind goes back to my mom. I feel like I'm gonna puke. I'm not done being pissed, but there is literally nothing I can do about it. I can't ask my mom why or how she used arcane magic to bring ME back and not Dante. I'm angry, confused, and horrified all at once. It sucks. And I'm not done being pissed at Beckett and the others for treating me like I was crazy either.

Wait a second.

I grab a pillow from the bed and toss it at CheccChecc. He catches it in one claw with surprisingly good reflexes, investigating it with those tentacles he calls a face.

"We're stuck together, right? If this shit is actually real, how about we have a little fun?"

***

"I'm still pissed at you guys for acting like I was crazy the other night."

Pitiful attempts at dismissal from the class. I didn't tell them to meet me at Hideo's penthouse for half-hearted apologies. Nope, not here for that.

Cross my arms. Look as serious as possible. Coolest. Cucumber. Ever.

"You guys didn't trust me."

I give CheccChecc the signal behind my back.

"But I knew I wasn't making shit up."

"Aww come on, Izz," whined Beckett, "we didn't mean to hurt your feelings. We thought you were playin' around, that's all."

"Yeah, girl, we didn't mean anything," cooed Olivia, playing with her blue hair absentmindedly as she stares into the glow of her phone.

"Forgive these dumbasses," teased Hideo as he makes a drink for himself from the bar, "they're just scared of what they don't understand. They fight fear with humor and..."

"Valium?"

Olivia's joke makes the guys erupt into snickers.

Yeah, yeah. Yuck it up, guys.

It's showtime.

"I suggest you all shut up and show me some respect, or else I'll have to use my newfound powers on you..."

Hmm. That didn't sound as corny in my head. But whatever.

Final signal. Wait for the big reaction. Wait for it...

Um...CheccChecc?

"I said I'll have to use my newfound powers on you..."

Sneaking a quick look over my shoulder, I notice CheccChecc is distracted watching sports on the giant, curved TV mounted on the wall.

I clear my throat and cough. Ignore the skeptical looks of my so-called friends. Finally get my monster's attention, and give him the signal once more.

Okay. Showtime for real.

Raise my hand like I'm using some kind of magic. Watch CheccChecc in my peripheral vision as he quietly scurries into the middle of the room and grabs Hideo's hat off the coffee table. Close my eyes, and wait for the gasps of disbelief.

Ahh, yes. Music to my ears.

Fighting back a self-satisfied smile, I keep my hand raised and focus on the hat carefully tucked into CheccChecc's tentacles. I watch as my assistant hops around with the hat, swaying my hand to match his movements. Olivia watches with mouth agape, hands frozen on her phone. Hideo looks like he's ready to sprint for the nearest window.

"How you doin' that?" questioned Beckett, now standing on top of his chair and pointing like a little kid. "I don't see no strings. How? How you doin' that?"

"Are you telekinetic or something? Oh my freaking lord, hun." Olivia starts trying to snap pictures of my magic act. Not so bored now, are ya?

Yes, my hecklers watch on as I perform magical feats of levitation. Call me petty, but I suppose it pays to have an invisible friend after all.

"Yeah, I'm telekinetic," I warn, and just as we rehearsed, CheccChecc lifts the hat higher and starts spinning in circles with it. "And if you disrespect me again, I might just have to...."

Snap of my fingers. CheccChecc crumples the hat and tosses it away.

Cue the eruption of shock and awe.

I'm bombarded with apologies...and then requests.

"Can you move this?" Olivia grabs a potted plant, and CheccChecc watches curiously right in front of her. "I wanna film the whole thing."

Hideo pulls out a bowie knife, seemingly out of nowhere. "Can you catch this mid-air?"

"Move me!" Oh, Beckett. Less 'Red Bastard', more 'Red Doofus'.

Heh heh. All humans this gullible?

"I'm not a circus act, guys. With great power comes great responsibility. I can only use them when I really have to. Just don't push me. We clear?"

Everybody nods in unison. Hideo puts the knife away with a genuinely disappointed expression plastered on his mug. After a little more protesting, they finally give in. And I gotta admit, the look on their faces - that absolute attention, that utter amazement aimed directly at ME - did feel pretty good. I relished the moment, but I couldn't take the credit. I would give CheccChecc a pet on the head if he'd let me.

"We're going out tonight," offers Hideo, "to that new club that opened up on the strip. You wanna come?"

I kinda do, but I'm still pissed at them. Plus I'm exhausted. One of the things Aunt Maggie taught me was the importance of 'leaving the audience wanting more'.

"Actually, I gotta practice my telekinetic powers some more. Lots of meditation, you guys wouldn't understand. See ya around, kids. It's been real."

I stop in my tracks. I've got this fire in me, and I realize I'm not done here after all.

"Actually, you know what?" I whip back around, arms crossed. "A few more things, for each of you assholes."

I turn to Beckett, whose eyes are as big as the space between us. "Beck, you like jokes, so here's one: what's small, blue, and regularly found under the same five nails? Beckett's balls every time Olivia rejects him."

Hideo lets out a loud snort, and Olivia's gaze darts over to Beckett. I swear the veteran would be red from embarrassment if he wasn't undead.

"And you, Hideo. Do you pay your stylist in fruit cups? Because it looks like a toddler dresses you."

He bashfully looks down at his outfit, a collection of tacky jewelry and mismatched clothes covered in zingy one-liners that barely make sense. I can't believe that stuff is so expensive.

I don't know where I'm going with all this....but I'm still not finished.

"Last but not least, there's Olivia. I thought I saw you the other night back in the Lavender District, standing in the window of an adult toy shop. I knew that welcoming expression, that warm presence as undeniable as my mommy issues. But I was wrong, it was just a blow-up sex doll."

Beckett cracks up and starts pointing at Olivia.

"I told you!" he teases.

"Shut up, Eugene."

"And Olivia, girl," I go on, "you're not fooling anybody. The sexual tension between you and Beckett is thicker than the walls I hide my social anxiety behind. You guys need to stop pussy-footing around and just hook up already."

Olivia is literally hiding her face now, and Beckett is looking every which way but Olivia. Hideo is still just cracking up and enjoying the show, apparently. I wasn't trying to be funny. CheccChecc stares at me with that familiar head-cock of his, just trying to make sense of me and my bullshit.

Where did all that come from? I used to only say dumb stuff like this to my mom, or to other adults when I'm uncomfortable. So why am I saying this now? I barely pay attention to their actual responses after this moment. I'm almost embarrassed I let loose, but at the same time...it just felt good. Having this sort of confidence around people my age for a change, and saying what I really think without it being a nervous reaction. It's unexpected, but oddly welcome. To me, at least.

I wrap things up with the most ungraceful parting words I can manage. "Anyways. Moral of the story is don't mess with me and my magic mojo. Okay bye."

And I'm outta there, with my invisible friend close behind. The conflicting murmurs of the audience fall behind me as they're forced to watch my early departure. I almost feel bad for conning them, but they had it coming. And besides...maybe it's okay to feel a little exceptional. Having an invisible monster guardian? I'm starting to think it IS pretty special after all.

...Dante would have loved him.

Take the elevator all the way down, head back out onto the street outside. Wave down a taxi. My partner in crime hops into the vehicle behind me. His wings are everywhere.

"Watch the wings, dude," I whisper.

"Whuh?" The hardened taxi driver looks at me in the rearview mirror, her voice devoid of patience.

"Um, nothing, sorry." As I respond gracelessly, I watch CheccChecc draw his wings into his back again. It's such a creepy flex, and utterly alien.

Yep. So cool.

"Know any good places around here to get sweets? Candy, chocolate, anything?"

The taxi driver grumbles and turns up the radio. "Yeah, I know a place."

Turn back to my partner in crime and whisper a little more quietly. "Good work back there, little guy. We're gonna get you something sweet, as promised. Then head back for a nap. Sound good?"

He thinks for a moment, then nods.

Humans funny little things.

Hell yeah we are.

Off we go!

***

It's the day after. Feels like...the day after an acid trip.

By the time I woke up, it was like 7 PM the next day. Popped two aspirin to help with the killer migraine. Drank some water. Scanned the motel room.

Nothing in here but me, myself, and migraines. Maybe I really did imagine all that 'monster being real' stuff.

What IS real? Maybe all of that crazy stuff was in my head. Just a bad trip. Frode must have given me some really strong drugs. Maybe I am just a regular chick. That's a good thing, right?

I don't really know how to feel. Check my phone, and notice that it's super dead. Plug it in, get it charging. I'm sure Aunt Maggie has called me like five times by now.

Go to the bathroom. Turn on the light, and...

"Holy fucking duck farts!" Why did I say that? I dunno, but it's what came to my mind the second I witnessed the monster from my dreams sitting partially in the toilet. He looks perfectly content in there.

"What are you doing, you little weirdo?"

He looks at me, almost irritated.

Obvious. Bath.

Wait. Is he...really talking to me telepathically? I didn't imagine it last time?

Way cool.

"You don't take baths in toilets. You can use the shower, right there."

CheccChecc looks over at the tiny shower right next to him, then back to me.

No water there. Silly human. How bathe without water?

This weird sound emits from his tentacles, and I swear he's laughing at me. Like I'M the weird one.

I walk on up to the shower, pull back the curtains, and turn on the faucet. CheccChecc is visibly startled when he sees water come out.

"See? You've been dropping in on humans long enough that you really should've known that already."

Humans spend loooong time in these rooms. Looking at self, talking to self. CheccChecc get bored and wait outside door.

"Oh really? I thought your job was to protect me. What if I die in a bathroom? Say I slip and fall, break my skull? Knifed by a killer, slasher movie-style? Makes you kinda negligent."

Though I'm snickering at my own joke, my monster seems far less amused.

CheccChecc die from boredom first.

My monster familiar has clearly spent enough time around me and Aunt Maggie. He's full of piss and vinegar. Not sure what I was expecting...but not this. Color me thoroughly amused. He seems satisfied with the shower option and hops out of the toilet and into the shower, dripping and flipping toilet water all over me as he does so.

I stand outside the shower with arms crossed, failing to stifle a smile. He's got such a cute little attitude, like Eckerd when he's feeling sassy...

Snap out of it, Izz! As weirdly amusing as all of this is, I can't just drop my guard! And now that my monster can communicate without mind-scrambling me, there's no time like the present to ask my burning question.

"The night you saved me from The Skin Craft Killer. Why didn't you save my mom, too?"

Only the white noise of running water.

"I know you can hear me."

Not part of deal.

My skin crawls. "That is some heartless bullshit. Take some responsibility. My mom deserved better than to die in a cage. She…Well, her soul…I understand that you monsters make deals for souls. That's why you didn't save her, huh? You wanted her dead so you could eat her soul or something. Am I right?"

Mean.

"What?"

Human. Mean.

You gotta be kidding me. Am I getting scolded by an ancient pint-sized beastie for being 'mean'? When this little guy is literally in the business of dark magic and human soul exchange?

I yank the curtains back and turn off the faucet. CheccChecc just freezes and looks at me, eyes narrowed.

"You don't get to judge me, not after what I've been through. Give me a break."

My guardian responds by shaking himself off like a wet dog. I'm completely splattered all over with cold water, and I wish I could say I didn't have that one coming.

Humans judge first. Always. Not think. Always.

Geez, this guy's more cynical about humanity than I am.

"Alright then, fine. Explain to me why you didn't save my mom."

CheccChecc guardian of Izzie alone. Another Penumbran reaped soul of mother. CheccChecc could not interfere.

"Oh, so your buddy just appeared and killed my mom, huh? Is that it?"

Reapers not kill, only appear when death is near to collect souls. Nothing personal. Just doing job.

I'm angry. Having someone else to blame for what happened to my mom...it just feels like it would be easier.

Easier than blaming myself.

"Give it back, then!" I cry out behind gritted teeth. "Her soul, just get it back and we can be done here!"

Souls returned to The Penumbra. Contracts final. Mother aware when making deal. Accepted consequences for survival of Izzie.

CheccChecc hops out of the shower and walks right past me. He's getting annoyed, I don't need another tentacle brain-cocktail to perceive that.

I'm furious and utterly crestfallen at the same time. He's so matter-of-fact about it. I want to spit and scream and protest, but deep down...I realize that he's telling me the truth. It just sucks.

Silence fills the motel room for a while following our argument. It's way too uncomfortable. Being angry...it's exhausting. And fruitless. Yet for some reason, anger is one of my default emotions lately. I find the strength to compose myself before confronting CheccChecc once more.

"Look, you're right. Maybe I'm being a little...mean." He stops licking his wound, but doesn't look back. "You put yourself in danger every time you have to save me. I appreciate that. I really do. So. Um. Sorry."

My Eldritch familiar stops at the foot of the bed and at last faces me. More words filter through my mind and find themselves translated.

Maddening. Easier when human not see CheccChecc.

What? I'm apologizing!

I'm missing something. Clearly, I am. A few shared tours of my brain, a harmless prank on ex-friends, and several helpings of high fructose corn syrup. I thought we were bonding. 'Getting each other', so to speak. I thought the little guy was secretly cuddly, but instead he's moodier than I am.

"Alright, so I'm a stupid human who doesn't understand shit about arcane magic or underworlds or whatever. You got me. But I want to learn, okay? You could tell me all of it. I want to soak up everything there is to know about this...weird world my mom got herself into. Everything about the magic that brought me back and gave me natural life. Then the next time I try being a judgmental asshole, I'll understand what I'm actually talking about."

He just stares at me. God, CheccChecc would be undefeatable at staring contests. He's a total pro.

"Will you just tell me? Please? I'll take a taxi across the city for another milkshake if you do. Promise."

CheccChecc doesn't say anything. His big eyes avoid mine. He's shifting weight from leg to leg, wings jerking out with a hint of annoyance. He's pondering something, alright. He'll make the right decision, especially with another tasty milkshake on the line. Got 'im.

Finally, CheccChecc looks at me and seems to emit a low sigh under those face worms of his.

Fine. CheccChecc will tell. Come closer.

Good boy!

I get closer to the little guy, ready to take a seat on the edge of the bed and listen in for more exposition. But instead, the mini monster starts reaching those tentacles out towards me.

"Nope, nope, nope!" I protest, pulling back. "Use your words, not your tentacles!"

He keeps coming at me, tentacles extending further, pulling in closer...

"Seriously, big nope, my brain can't take another - "

Tentacles wrap around me. Tangible once more, alright. Slimy wetness, cold suctions, all up my arm. Oh God, I'm not ready for this again -

...

Lights out. Migraine of the century incoming.

Guess I have...

To learn...

The hard way...

***

Rush to the toilet. Puke out leftover French fries. Drink a glass full of tap water. Wait for the next information dump.

God, I hate it. I need to reiterate to Checcs which method of communication works best for me. Ideally, the one that leaves my poor brain out of the playing field.

Take a seat, look for my monster. I don't see him anywhere. Must be on a rooftop again, brooding like I used to when I was a kid.

Ah. It's coming back. This revelation is less essay and more bullet-point.

Turns out my Eldritch monster held back on me in a pretty big way. He's not just tasked with protecting me. Sure, he's keeping me safe for now. But the contract my mom signed has got me stuck with a deadline. After all, I'm living on borrowed time.

The short of it? Checcs is here to ensure I die at the EXACT time specified by my contract, no earlier. And he's gonna be the one to collect my soul too, once my time is up.

Shit, dude.

"Strategically left that out, didn't you?" He's still not here, but I'm saying it anyway. "Saving your own ass, making me think you're my protector and that's it. You had me thinking I was special, asshole. Instead I'm just walking meat, and none of it's even my fault."

I'm scared, pissed, and legitimately hurt. Guess the term 'guardian-reaper' literally said it all.

Damn, I'm stupid.

As crazy as it is, I wanted to believe this creature was my lifelong partner in crime. I felt alone all my life and when I finally found out I never was, the whole thing gets shredded to bits by this new revelation. I wish I didn't know. It felt good thinking that I had something really special looking after me.

I'm over it. Once more I get the answers to my questions before I ask them.

CheccChecc wanted me to comprehend this. I hear his peculiar voice inside my mind, this time like a memory implanted with everything else.

Not friends. Only doing job.

Those five words get recycled in my mind. It sounds so cold, but I sense something else underneath. Guilt, maybe?

"Your job, huh? If your 'job' is to protect me, then why didn't you do anything when I was assaulted? Where the fuck were you then?!"

Rage. Scream into a pillow before hurling it across the room. Resist the urge to punch a wall. Glance at myself in the hanging mirror and see nothing more than the scared little girl I'm always trying to forget.

"Pussy," I say at last under my breath. The whole thing sucks. He wants me to be angry. I get it. He doesn't wanna befriend the cow when he plans on eating the burger.

Will I always only be prey?

No, Izz. Bury it.

No brother, no mom, no friends, no monster companion. Guess that's the universe's way of telling me I'm supposed to be alone.

"Breaking news: the mortuary holding the Skin Craft Killer's body was broken into earlier this morning..."

....What?

My attention is immediately thrown to the story unfolding on the motel TV.

"NMPD encourages everyone in the city to remain vigilant and share any information they might have regarding the suspect."

An extra pale sheriff appears on the screen, speaking before a crowd of journalists and cameramen.

"The suspect in question broke in early this morning," he grumbles. "CCTV footage from 2:30 AM to 4:00 AM was deleted from cameras on the premises. If anyone has any information on who might be responsible for this crime, please come forward immediately."

My heart sinks. As the report goes on, it only gets worse...

"Coroners confirmed that the only thing stolen from the mortuary was the brain of The Skin Craft Killer, which had been preserved for the ongoing investigation."

...

The sheriff continues.

"We are uncertain whether or not we are dealing with multiple suspects..."

He keeps talking, but his warnings against panic fall on deaf ears. It sounds like I'm underwater.

As if one monster floating around wasn't enough.

Panic is inevitable. All of my fear returns in powerful swells.

I'm not free.

My nightmare is not over.

The Skin Craft Killer has an ally. Someone who is gonna take that psycho's brain and get him reanimated.

Heart pulses faster. Thump thump.

I gotta do something!

Thump thump thump thump.

I've gotta stop him.

Thump thump thump thump thump thump...

I...I...

CHAPTER SIX

Everything.

Everything there is to know about The Skin Craft Killer.

I consumed it. All of it.

From the internet. From interviews, police reports, crime journalists. Hell, even hearsay across the city.

Here's what I found out.

Though the exact identity of the Skin Craft Killer is unknown, he IS a U.S citizen, originating somewhere in the Midwest. Great. That really narrows it down. It is believed that he has a medical background and a fetish for lace.

He tortures and kills in pairs. Often two people who know each other in one way or another.

His first reported killings were in 2009. Two female prostitutes. As it was a crime against sex workers, the murders were barely investigated. The killer wasn't taken seriously until two businessmen were found murdered the same way a few weeks later. His kills were periodic throughout the next two decades, but always in pairs.

All crime scenes were relatively the same. Two victims were disproportionately tortured, one confirmed dead hours before the other. Animal cages and homemade restraints were frequently used. Actual cause of death was usually either blood loss or blunt force trauma, but the head was always smashed post-mortem with a sledgehammer to prevent reanimation.

I'm familiar with that sledgehammer.

...Anyway.

Random body parts were carefully removed from his victims. Though the parts of over twenty victims were found grafted to The Skin Craft Killer's body, he did not take parts from every victim. This makes his actual kill count difficult to confirm.

Thorough. He always covered his tracks, left no DNA or footage of himself behind despite committing most of his crimes in public places. The FBI was tracking a ghost.

Sporadic. His murder spree brought him from one state to the next without any discernible pattern. A killer on tour. How a monstrous entity with multiple limbs wearing a lace veil was able to move about unseen is a mystery in itself.

Speaking of patterns, there were none when it came to his selection of victims. No preference for social class, age, or gender. Reanimated and warm-blooded victims alike. Paired victims ranged from relatives and friends to coworkers. None of his crimes were sexual in nature. He appeared most interested in observing the behavior of the pairs he selected, before choosing his trophies.

Then there's what I learned from experience.

He's methodical. A little OCD. All of his tools and weapons were perfectly lined up. He's got this neck twitch, almost like a tick. It happens more when he's frustrated, when things aren't going his way. If he can speak, he chooses not to during his killings. His interest in lace and his use of restraints and whips lead me to believe he might have been a customer at adult toy shops. Maybe. He's got skin grafts everywhere, but his favorite body parts seem to be eyes, arms, and fingers.

It's a lot, but not as specific as I'd like.

Aunt Maggie has been trying to contact me, to make sure I'm okay after hearing the news. I manage a text back: *'I'm fine. Love you.'*

I'm not.

However, researching The Skin Craft Killer made it easier for me to talk about him...temporarily. I used my courage to address the cops, who had been itching to talk to me for information after the break-in at the mortuary. Paparazzi and journalists filmed and photographed my walk to the Dead Vegas Police Department. They waited outside as I talked to authorities for an hour or so.

They thanked me for my cooperation and offered me protection, should the killer come back for me.

I told them no. Because I'm not running or hiding. Not this time.

More concerned calls and texts from my new friends. My aunt thinks I should come back home. They're all afraid I'm going to break down. That I'll be a victim again.

I won't.

Not anymore. I refuse.

The cops told me that they'd find this asshole. That they've got eyes on every reanimation chamber in the city. That there's no way The Skin Craft Killer will come back and kill again.

I smile and thank them, but I can't shake the feeling that it's all empty platitudes. Somehow, I just know it has to be me. I'm the one who's gonna find this psycho and stop him for good.

Somehow.

All I know is that I seem to have one little advantage that others don't: a reluctant monster whose job it is to protect me.

If you do come back...It won't be for long. Someone will stop you from hurting anybody else. Even if that someone has to be me.

***

After an uncertain amount of time lost in my own thoughts, I throw on a hoodie and head out the door. Leave the lobby so fast I can't even remember my interaction with the receptionist. Look over my shoulder, see CheccChecc perching on a neon sign like a gargoyle. He's watching me wait for a taxi and pace around the sidewalk. I imagine he'll just be keeping watch from a distance now, fork in hand.

But...what if The Skin Craft Killer is watching me, too?

...

Shit.

Climb into the first cab that stops, looking over my shoulder every few minutes. If I look paranoid, it's because I am. I don't even know where I'm going, I just need to go. Ever since coming back to Dead Vegas, I've been looking to other people to solve my problems and make me feel better. Maybe I just need to refocus myself and think about what I need to do next. Peaceful. Zen.

Yeah. Zen.

***

Well. Tried the whole Zen thing. Sat on a park bench as bicyclists and joggers sped by the well-lit path, pretending not to see or care about that soul-hungry monster babysitting me from a distance. Tried blanking everything out of my head, but nope. Too much unfinished business. Not enough resolution. Well, at least not the resolution I had so desperately hoped for by returning to the city. In fact, if I'm being perfectly honest...

This trip has been a shit show.

And now I'm sitting here, staring at everybody like they might be out to get me. If the Skin Craft Killer is getting reanimated, that means his brain could be inside anybody. Who knows what body the serial killer will be sporting this time around?! Whenever a passerby makes eye contact with me, my skin clams up. Is that jogger the new Skin Craft Killer? That cop? That dog walker?!

Listen to yourself, Izz. You're completely paranoid. It's not like you were the killer's sole survivor and partially responsible for his untimely demise. He won't come back to finish the job.

...

I am SO screwed.

The hours I thought had passed 'being Zen' ended up being closer to minutes. How can I calm myself down?

A call to my aunt for love and support?

Reading and answering a text from Olivia? Even just one?

Another shot at peaceful self-reflection?

That's a 'no' to all of the above. An arguably better idea came to mind.

Confront that asshole Frode for burying me alive. Maybe punch him in the dick.
Yep. Much better...

Right?

Just agree with me on this.

***

Red. That's all I see. The receptionist at ESTRID Industries had no chance of
stopping Hurricane Izzie. Not this time. I was inevitable.

"You fucking buried me alive, you asshole!" I'm right in his face now, but he
doesn't even twitch. Just looks at me with tired eyes, and it makes me even more
pissed.

"I did."

"Are you some kind of psychopath? I could have died!"

"You could have, but you didn't."

Standing in his lab, he's so nonchalant about it. Like I'm complaining about
something benign.

"You didn't know that! I was horrified!"

"Exactly," he utters smugly, standing his ground with his hands behind his back.
"You feared for your life, and your guardian-reaper came to your rescue. They
always do."

Somehow, that isn't good enough. I'm not done being angry, and CheccChecc isn't close enough to try and stop me from being careless. I shove Frode hard, but he doesn't budge. Doesn't even flinch.

At this point, I just want something out of him. SOME kind of reaction, anything. I've been waiting to confront him about this, thinking over all the things I would say. But he clearly doesn't give a shit, and it's making me feel worse.

"Yeah, some hero. That monster's only around to nab my soul when the time's right. And you didn't have to go so extreme! Burying a teenage girl alive? Are you fucking out of your mind? Or does scaring girls a tiny fraction of your age get your rocks off?"

Having those words screamed out in his lab has got Frode the Chode looking nervous. Yeah, don't need anybody hearing about THOSE extracurricular activities of his. I react to this by repeating the same thing, only louder.

"FRODE ALGAR BURIED A TEENAGE GIRL ALIVE ON HIS PRIVATE PROPERTY! FRODE - "

He shushes me quickly and puts a hand over my mouth. Finally, an actual reaction!

"Are you crazy?" he whispers.

His hand gets shoved out of my face. "Hilarious, coming from the asshole who buried a FUCKING ADOLESCENT IN THE GROUND."

"You signed the waiver. Didn't you read it? I literally told you what was going to happen, and you agreed."

I pause. "Um. Okay, maybe I didn't read it exactly."

He scoffs. "A bad rower blames the oar." Between his bullshit response and my own embarrassment, I find myself more fired up.

"That doesn't make it okay! How many people are you burying alive to need an actual waiver for that shit anyway?"

"Enough. I help when I can."

I freeze, and just in time to feel tears well up. I hate angry-crying. It's so counter-productive when you're trying to show you're pissed and in charge.

He leans in, voice real low. "Listen to yourself. You sound like a child - impulsive, indecisive. You asked me to help you confront your fear, and I did exactly that. You wanted to catch your monster, and I told you how to do so. Meanwhile, you couldn't be bothered to actually prepare yourself or even read a couple pieces of paper. Clearly, you weren't as ready as you pretended to be."

"Shut up!" I try to shove him again as he stares at me with those intense gray eyes.

"You try to act tough. But you are no more than what you believe yourself to be: the spoiled, scared child of a woman whose shoes you could never hope to fill."

"Shut the fuck up! You don't know the first thing about me!"

"Do YOU even know the first thing about yourself?"

Frode takes a step closer to me, and instinctively I take two steps back.

"What do you want to do, then? Hit me? Blame me for everything else that ails you?"

Another step closer to me. Then another. I didn't think it was possible to feel so absolutely enraged and simultaneously terrified at the same time. I wanna hide in a tight ball and fade away. Become invisible to everyone, like CheccChecc.

"Listen to me closely," he presses, looming over me. "What you believe about yourself manifests. You might have been a victim in the past, but you absolutely cannot continue to view yourself as such. Otherwise you will always be the version of yourself that you fear the most."

I do nothing. I can't look Frode in the eyes, not even after he backs up.

"If you cannot bite," he sighs, "never show your teeth."

I'm still beyond pissed, yet at the same time...He's right.

If only I could admit that to him.

"Is this how you treated your daughter?" I snort, wiping my snotty nose like a little kid. "You must have taken Father of the Year home regularly."

Algar's expression shifts, and it's almost a 180. Suddenly he's looking a little uncomfortable himself.

"I...apologize if my methods seem...extreme. It's how my father raised me, and it was a...very different time, to say the least. What you need to realize is that my goal is to help you grow and become strong. It's the only way you can survive in this world. And I want you to survive, Isabella. I owe it to Dayanna to help you in any way I can."

There is a sincerity in those pale eyes that betrays this asshole's cold exterior. My mom trusted this guy. THIS guy. I keep thinking Algar's gonna be like the other adult men that managed to get close to me and my mom. Though I catch glimpses of authenticity that I never saw from the others, this rich asshole doesn't exactly have a spotless record.

"How do you know my mom then, huh? Tell me the truth and make it quick."

"Your mother knew about my past. It was my familiarity with the Old Ones and their magic that brought us together. She had scant knowledge of this secret world, so I served as her guide. There aren't many practitioners of arcane magic left in the world, so we must stick together if we wish to preserve our sanity."

Anger boils up in me. Higher, higher. It's just beneath the surface now.

"You knew?!" I yell, my tears betraying my tone. "You knew what happened to me? What she did to bring me back?!"

"Yes. I'm so sorry."

"And you didn't tell me? Didn't think to share why my mom couldn't be reanimated?! I thought I was going crazy, seeing monsters and imagining shit! And you buried me alive to give me answers that you could have just fucking told me?!!"

 "Your mother did not want you to have the burden of knowing about these things. I had to respect her wishes and keep my promise. If you were going to learn, you had to learn it on your own."

"Bullshit," I whine. But it has to be true. It sounds exactly like what my mom would do. "But you learned arcane magic. You could have made a new deal or something to bring my mom back after she died."

It's evident that Frode is treading very carefully now. His next words are halted, picked carefully as if they were precious stones.

"I'm afraid you already know the answer. It's true that Dayanna's inability to be reanimated was due to the contract for her soul - without it, the body is nothing but an empty shell. And of course you want to reverse that contract and bring your mother back. So do I. However, I'm telling you from experience that there is no going back on pacts made with the Old Ones. We must live with our choices and the choices of others, no matter how painful or unfair the results may seem. I am sorry."

"...and Dante? Why me and not him?"

"One soul for another. She made the offer and the Old Ones handled the rest. Isabella - "

"Stop. Just stop."

I'm at a loss for what to do. I'm angry, yes. I feel lied to, absolutely. But between what Frode just told me and what CheccChecc already showed me? It's all true. Despite all my rage and denial, I understand it's the truth. It's an acceptance that only makes the pain worse.

"I get it."

I'm done here. I'm about to stomp off, but I backpedal for one last thing before I get the hell out.

Slap! Right across his face. I always wanted to do that. It stung more than I expected, but it still felt good. He seems shocked.

"Honoring my mom's wishes, fine. But burying me alive? Hell fucking no. Waiver or not, you don't get to put me in dangerous situations like that again. Ever. Understand me?"

Did I do that for real? Holy crap, I could only ever dream of doing that to the people that hurt me in the past. My heart sinks and I half-expect retaliation, but instead I'm greeted with a surprised grin. Pride, maybe? Or just amusement?

"Yes, ma'am."

Not another word is spoken between us as he walks me out the door. From there I am greeted once more by his well-dressed assistant, who escorts me outside the building before an uppity security guard can.

"I know he seems harsh," she offers on the way, "but Mr. Algar really does care about you."

"Defending him, huh? He must pay you really well."

"I understand how you feel, Miss Cordona. And I can't tell you it's wrong, not after what he has done. All I ask is that you consider giving him a second chance. Just don't tell him I said so."

And for the first time, Algar's assistant smiles at me and it's not Stepford Wives-ish.

"Um...I'm sorry. I never asked. What's your name?"

"Claudia," she nods, opening the door for me. "Have a lovely day, Miss Cordona."

***

When my phone started vibrating at midnight, I almost threw it into the thin walls of my motel room.

It was Frode the Chode again. Stupid asshole with his stupid Viking quotes. He can fuck right off.

But while I watched the low glow of my phone as it shuffled across the bedside table, I made another decision.

I answered the phone.

***

"Sup, my name is Paul and I..."

"...heard about what happened to the Skin Craft Killer's brain..."

"Yo, lady?"

"Um...sorry, yes?"

"Can I take your order or what?"

"Yeah, sorry. I just..."

"...realize how angry and scared you must be feeling right now."

"You're holding up the line, lady. Order something or get outta the way."

Snap back to reality. It's the morning after my phone call with Frode. Right now I'm in a fast food joint, starving and holding up the line like an asshole.

"Um, yeah, sorry again. One strawberry milkshake, please. Actually, make that two."

A very disinterested undead teenager rings up my order, and I swear he's half asleep. Undoubtedly, if he could see the Eldritch monster with his face pressed to the window outside, his day would be a tad more interesting.

That's one thing I definitely took for granted back on the sanctuary island: the abundant access to food. We had so much rich farmland and all the fish you could eat. Out here? Different story. Though ninety percent of this menu consists of alcoholic beverages, cigarettes, and other things for reanimated folks to enjoy, there are at least a few actual food items for us rare warm-bloods.

"Forty dollars?? Seriously?"

The guy working the register just gives me this look that oozes disdain.

"Yeah. Dairy's exported."

"That's robbery. Can I talk to the manager?"

"Carl!" shouts the undead kid over his slanted shoulder. I can see the stitch marks around his discolored neck. "Caaaarl!"

"The dairy is exported!" hollers back another undead guy from the kitchen. Carl, I presume.

The undead kid turns slowly back to me, a smirk spreading over his pale and pot-marked face.

"Forty dollars, please."

Whatever. But I notice I'm the only living person in the building right now, so I don't need more attention on myself.

I fork up the money and take a seat in a corner booth, far from the other customers. I make sure I'm near a window, so that the monster staring in at me can see what I've got for him: let's call it a peace offering. He's been tailing me from a distance ever since he showed me his true nature. We can keep it strictly business, just like he wants. But I just can't take another bungled, strained relationship propelled by my big mouth.

That second milkshake is bathed in sunlight. It might as well have a ray of heaven floating over it. The Eldritch creature outside stirs. He sees it. There can be no ignoring the deliciousness that awaits. I give the cup a little shake, and those big eyes follow every movement from directly outside the window now.

I practically jump out of my seat when the monster that was outside only seconds earlier suddenly phases right through the glass. I'm not sure I can get used to...that. He is suddenly seated beside me, tentacles wiggling inquisitively. I get the feeling he's trying to act cool and not show just how excited he is.

"Nothing wrong with a little drink on the job, right?" I offer very quietly with a forced smile. "Sorry for being an asshole. A judgmental, mean asshole."

CheccChecc eventually changes that surly expression, his willpower no match for 16 ounces of cream and sugar. He sighs and hops up into the seat opposite me in my booth.

"Be easy with it," I whisper, passing him the milkshake. "Can't be drawing too much attention, alright?"

My guardian-reaper nods before removing the plastic lid off his beverage and slurping its contents. Not as discreet as I would like, but I can tell he's trying to have some degree of restraint.

Me? I sit there with mine, twirling the straw absent-mindedly. My conversation with Algar lit a fire under me, and now it's all I can think about.

"I contacted NMPD on your behalf," he had stated calmly, *"but they said there were no leads on the suspect responsible for the theft. Whoever they were, they covered their tracks well. I'm so sorry."*

I was furious. Still am. But I can't say that I'm surprised. Crime is a little easier these days when a different identity is only a new body away. Tracking people? It's harder than ever. The federal government's trying to get everybody microchipped to solve the problem, but most folks are waaaay too distrustful of that technology to ever agree to it.

Bottom line? There's no way police can catch The Skin Craft Killer in a new body, let alone the person responsible for getting him reanimated. It's a lost cause. Somebody else is gonna get killed and it feels so helpless.

At least it did. Things changed a little, once I told Frode about my interaction with the killer that fateful night in the sewers.

CheccChecc's final slurps shake me out of my thoughts again. Those tentacles are covered in whip cream and milkshake. Damn, he's messy. I slide a napkin towards him, but he's too busy burping and slurping up every last drop of his favorite snack. Finally, he looks at my milkshake and then back at me. As if to ask 'Are you going to have that?'. I put both hands around my milkshake and started slurping mine as well. Sorry, little guy. I'm gonna need this.

"If the killer indeed saw your guardian-reaper, that means he too has Enlightenment. Therefore, he is connected to The Penumbra and its arcane magic like we are. Was he accompanied by an Eldritch creature?"

I look up to see everyone staring at me, all around the dining area. Undead folks, sipping on alcoholic beverages and tapping away on keyboards, staring at me without reservation. I notice CheccChecc is still making a lot of noise trying to get every last drop out of his cup.

"What are you looking at?" I challenge them, slurping my own drink even louder. I attempt a burp, but it's a pathetic one. Everybody turns around in a clumsy sort of unison, pretending they weren't just burning holes in me.

"Gotta be more quiet than that," I whisper to Checcs. "Please?"

He looks at me intently, not breaking contact as he attempts one final, defiantly loud slurp from his empty cup. Cheeky.

I saw no monster with The Skin Craft Killer. It was just him, me, my mom, and CheccChecc. I thought that unfortunate news would deter Frode's new lead, but I was pleasantly surprised to witness the contrary.

"No matter," he told me. *"If you're absolutely positive that he perceived your guardian-reaper, then his connection to The Penumbra is still intact. Let me ask you this: what is it that you intend to do next?"*

I had pondered that question for a moment. Do I forget about all this? Leave Dead Vegas and return home, where the Skin Craft Killer can't get me?

No. I was done running. Done being a victim. If there was one good thing I could do, as the sole survivor of the murderous psychopath who took my mom from me, it could be this.

"I'm going to find him," was my answer over the phone, *"and I'm going to stop him before he can hurt anybody else."*

Frode did his best to change my mind, but it was made up in stone long before he opened his mouth.

That choice was only further cemented moments earlier, when I noticed the headline on the newspaper folded up in the corner of my booth.

SKIN CRAFT KILLER STRIKES AGAIN - FIRST DOUBLE HOMICIDE SINCE REANIMATION

...

It's just as I feared, only it happened far sooner than I could have imagined. Everyone in the diner is mumbling about it like it's vaguely inconvenient. What's worse? These new murders took place out of state. He's already on the move again.

Going after this serial killer might be crazy...but somebody has to do it. Frode must have understood this, because somehow, he actually ended up giving in.

"If this is what you must do," he muttered at last, reluctantly, *"then I can help. I know of a place where you can convene with Penumbrans without having to make a deal or learn arcane magic."*

I shove the newspaper aside and fidget with the crumpled note in my pocket, recalling his words.

"This location is home to lost Eldritch creatures incapable of phasing back into The Penumbra. It is headed by Udolthra, a powerful Old One with a unique compassion for humans. She can search your memories of The Skin Craft Killer and use them to discover his true identity. Then you can tip law enforcement off on the investigation."

I had found it: the motivation I was looking for. If I could stop The Skin Craft Killer before he struck again, then maybe - just maybe - I could make my mom's sacrifice worth something.

"Oh, and bring Udolthra a gift. Anything will do."

One final slurp of my straw and the milkshake is toast. I grab CheccChecc's empty cup as well and toss both in the trash. Out the door I go, with CheccChecc loosely behind on his hind legs. He still hasn't uttered a word to me, but I feel like our shared lunch is a step in the right direction.

Oof! *Snap out of it, Izz!* I bumped into somebody right outside the door. Really need to save my deep reflection over exposition for when I'm NOT in public.

"What the - "

It's Olivia! And she's not alone! Hideo is beside her, and Beckett brings up the rear with that damn toothpick still hanging off his lips. He's wearing glasses now, and it's a surprisingly good look. Guess his opinion on them changed after hearing Olivia's.

"Easy, girlfriend," teases Olivia, fixing her platinum white curls. She's rocking a neon jumpsuit better suited for the runway than a fast food joint on a dirty street corner.

"What are you guys doing here? How did you find me?"

Beckett crosses his arms, almost as smug as the kid at the register. "Warm-bloods gotta eat somewhere. It was either here, the diner, or that snack shop at the airport."

"There's also that donut stall in the Grand Gate Casino," pipes in Hideo as he nods at an undead hottie jogging by. Ever the flirt. "But you don't have to taste those pastries to know they're as stale and dry as Beckett's love life."

"Screw you, pretty boy."

They're acting just like they did the night I first met them. But there is a huge elephant in the room: our last interaction, where I showcased my magical new abilities...or something like that.

"Listen, babe," starts Olivia, almost nervously, "we came here to apologize. Laughing at you and treating you like you were crazy the other night...it wasn't cool. Like, at all. If there's anybody who gets what that feels like, it's me."

"Yeah, I laugh at Livi all the time."

"Shut up, Eugene. This is serious." Olivia grabs my hands in hers and looks me straight in the eye. "We were wrong. Forgive us?"

I can't help but be skeptical. By the look on Checc's face, he's feeling the same way.

"What if I promise to take a look at your leg and make those alterations you wanted?" Those doe eyes aren't gonna work on me, Olivia.

"I seem to recall that being YOUR idea. And are you guys sure you aren't just apologizing because you're afraid I'm gonna throw you across the street into traffic with my mind?"

"The magic tricks were pretty dope," Hideo admits, "but the truth is, we all understand the feeling our girl Olivia described. We've been there. Maybe not over capturing some invisible monster, but...we get it."

"Forget the floating hat, you read the shit out of us back there," Olivia smirks. "You didn't spare yourself either. It was hilarious."

"Didn't know you had it in ya, warm-blood." Do I detect a hint of pride in Beckett's voice? "Whatever you need, we're there."

I'm somewhat surprised. I thought I wouldn't see these guys again, period. And the thought of any one of these beautiful, talented, and charismatic assholes feeling picked on? It's just hard to wrap my mind around. Popular people can't possibly comprehend what a habitual loser goes through. But they seem earnest. Maybe they really do mean it.

"Alright. Apology and leg upgrade accepted."

I pause for a moment. I've been consumed with one revelation after another. It feels important that I allow myself to stop over-thinking and just be present for a change.

Cold air on my skin. White noise of steady traffic, passing conversations, and repeating advertisements playing over electronic billboards above. The ever-present darkness looming over the city somehow feels less oppressive right now. A nostalgic curiosity washes over me.

The note in my jacket can wait. It has my anxiety to keep it company.

"My aunt told me there were roller derby games in the city," I say out of nowhere. "I think I want to see one. You guys wanna join me?"

Raised eyebrows and mischievous grins all around. I'll take that as a yes.

CHAPTER SEVEN

The floor rumbles beneath our feet. I feel it in my bones. An exhilarating feeling, watching those fearless athletes glide and grind around the circular track.

Cheers. Jeers. Sympathetic groans as players hit and hurl each other across the ring. Plastic cups spilling beer across the bleachers as excited viewers rise to their feet in unrivaled enthusiasm. It's contagious, even if I don't know all the rules to the dangerous game that occupies this auditorium.

Hideo's friends with some of the roller derby girls. Naturally. He's got us front row seats, right behind the glass. Every turn and tumble into the barrier, we feel it. I'm not sure who's more excited: me or Checcs. His gaze is fixated on the ring, unblinking.

Aunt Maggie was right. These girls hold nothing back. They're all reanimated, wearing surprisingly minimal protective gear considering the sport. Fearless, crazy, or a dangerous combination of the two. Some have mechanical limbs spray painted with logos and sponsors. Others have old-school Frankensteined bodies held together with nothing but stitches and a few prayers. One girl has actual spike attachments jutting out of her flesh, which she uses to shred another competitor's back in a brutal blitz. BAM, she's on the ground, tripping up a few other girls as she groans in discomfort.

Is that even legal? Guess so. The referee saw it but didn't say anything.

Another derby girl uses the temporary chaos to take the lead, gliding ahead on her wheels. She doesn't have feet - just wheels. It seems like anything goes in there. An instant replay on the jumbotron above recaps the accident that got her the lead. More cheers.

"Get it, Jade!!" hollers Hideo beside me. The wheel feet girl looks up as she rolls by us, giving Hideo the thumbs up. Her wheels are the only new things on her: the rest of her body is a patchwork of human parts only recently reassembled. Beckett chugs beer from his plastic cup and whistles so loudly that it startles the invisible monster in front of him. Olivia's puffing away on her vape pen, hurling insults at Jade's competitors. And I thought I was the Shit-Talking Queen.

Thunderous twist through a curvy tunnel, bobbing and weaving between course obstacles like table saws and pits. I'm on the edge of my seat.

Humans seek harm for fun?

"Yeah," I lean in and say, barely audible above the sounds of the crowd. "A lot more often these days than you'd think."

CheccChecc turns away from me and resumes his face plant against the glass.

Fascinating behavior. Crazy humans, so crazy.

The little monster winces in unison with the rest of us as one girl is tripped into a saw blade.

Shit! It's stuck in her chest! The rest of the athletes either race by or hop over her body as black blood oozes out. The crowd erupts. Paramedics move out on roller blades, pulling the poor girl's body off the course once the coast is clear. Lucky for her, reanimation chambers are on site.

And that's just the thing. This roller derby isn't just dangerous - it's deadly. Olivia noticed my obvious discomfort and was quick to remind me that death in sports these days is the norm. Hell, the girl's death blow is being replayed in slow motion on the jumbotron. Announcers revel in it just as much as the crowd.

I can't help but wonder...How did this ever become normal? How could death ever become so...

"Awesome, ain't it?" Beckett calls out, shaking my shoulder.

"Batshit crazy, is more like it," I try to say, but I don't think the red-head heard me. The audience is already cheering for another accident on the course involving a girl missing a jump over a pit of nails. Paramedics are headed back out.

Batshit crazy indeed.

Final lap. The racers are getting especially mean now. Shoulders, feet, elbows, and fists everywhere. It's a dirty free-for-all.

Jade is still in the lead, dodging and hopping around racers as they fall and fight one another. She drops low through another tube, doing a full 360 before dodging a moving beam on the other side. BAM, the girl behind her takes the metal beam to her face. My nose hurts after seeing that.

More falls and tumbles out of the tube. Girls fight to crawl over one another, some getting into fist fights. One girl rolls out and gets yanked by the ankle, falling face-first to the floor in one second flat. Another slips on a pool of blood and slides into a wall.

Jade has it. Only a handful of girls remain now, pushing hard to catch up. Jade is heading towards our side of the ring, and she offers us a smile and a wink.

Maybe just a little too soon.

One of the other girls takes the turn tight and low, catching up to Jade before she could even notice. The large woman shoulder checks Jade, sending her flying into the glass in front of us. Her body literally tears apart at the seams! It's gruesome.

Everyone groans before cheering even louder. I'm just standing there in shock, watching parts fly across the rink as Jade's wheels roll off unattached into another wall. Big girl wins it.

I look to Hideo, expecting an equal amount of shock and dismay for the fate of his friend. However, I witness no such thing. Hell, he seems proud, almost. He's whistling and howling even louder, taking pictures with his phone.

"Fucking glorious exit, Jadey!" he hoots after high-fiving Beckett. "You got it next time, girl!!"

The excitement continues. Announcers recap the events on the jumbotron as paramedics roll out once more to collect Jade's parts. Blood and scraps are all over the course. This is all new and slightly terrifying for me. But for everyone else here? It's just another Tuesday night.

Am I being lame? Maybe it's just because I haven't died yet. I mean, I get it. Reanimation has been around for a long time. Death isn't a big deal when you can just come right back. This shit is normal to everybody, but it isn't normal to me.

If humans have no value for planet, and no value for own lives. Then what do humans value? Anything?

It's like CheccChecc is reading my mind. There's no doubt the little guy was entertained by the sport, but apparently through the lens of a morbid curiosity not unfamiliar to most humans. And I hate to admit it, but despite all my discomfort I was still thoroughly entertained myself. What does that say about me? I feel a slight sense of shame as I reflect on Checc's sincere question. I don't have an answer for him.

"Hey," I nudge Olivia, "remember that new club you guys talked about last time?"

"Yeah? You wanna go?"

"You bet I do. Let's get out of here."

***

Absolutely surreal.

The thunderous rumble of athletes on wheels is replaced with a deep rhythmic beat propelling an array of synth tracks over enormous speakers. Neon pinks and blues light the space, flickering and pounding to match the DJ's music. It's like hearing, seeing, and feeling the music all at once. Multiple stories housing crowds of drunken patrons: flirting on the balconies, playing poker by the bar, dancing everywhere. Droves of people so full of life, you forget they're all reanimated.

Hideo got us in without issue. We weren't even carded. Beckett orders shots for everyone, and in no time at all I've got a tiny glass of something orange and sweet in front of me. I ignore the parental glare of CheccChecc as I throw down my drink in unison with my friends.

It was disgusting.

But it's working.

"Hideo?" asks one of the female waitresses, fast-approaching our friend with her arms at her sides in balled fists. Oh, no.

"Oh, hi, Annie."

SLAP! The brunette's hand right across the boy's face, so hard that he spills his booze all over himself. Beckett's laughter trails Annie as she stomps away, clearly satisfied.

Now Olivia is dragging me through the crowd by hand, towards a packed dance floor. I pass by glass boxes containing warm-blooded gogo dancers wearing six inch heels and spiky lingerie. They're absolutely gorgeous.

The patrons themselves are jaw-dropping in their own way. As I hesitantly join Olivia in dance, I can't help but notice all the many different faces surrounding me. One athletic girl with a big pink mohawk, and over half of her body composed of mechanical implants. An androgynous person taller than Beckett, with a synthetic body so flawless you'd think they were a god. Bikini girls with cat ear implants and tails. WORKING tails, it's so weird. Buff guys with stainless steel arms the size of tree trunks. Supermodel ladies with leg implants for days. A patchwork fella my age with body parts in multiple shades, sporting tattoos that used to belong to other people before they found their way to him.

Is that a weird sentence? Heh. I'm a little tipsy. I think.

I'm afraid they're all looking at me. The way I felt back in the Lavender District, before I freaked out and ran away. What if they know I'm a warm-blood? What if I'm a target here, too?

"Relax, girl!" Olivia razzes me, pulling in closer. "You're safe here with us!"

And it's true. Nobody is watching me. There's nothing but laughter, flirting, and dancing. Here, I'm not a victim, a celebrity, or some morbid curiosity. I'm just another body in the pit.

It's...nice.

For a moment, I allow all the noise and distraction to fade away. It's just me and Olivia and CheccChecc, standing in the middle of a crowd that is living only for this very moment in time. Maybe I can follow their example, just this once. The Skin Craft Killer, all this monster and magic business...maybe it can wait for just one night.

Just one night.

So I give in. The music flows through my body, and I'm dancing like I'm by myself. Lights flickering and casting shadows all around me, illuminating my silhouette. I don't care what anybody thinks. I don't care if anybody cares. I feel free. It's the most fun I've had in a long time.

***

Sweaty and exhausted, although my brain didn't get my body's memo. I'd keep going, but Olivia is ready for a break. It's time for another shot with the boys and some quality time in one of the upstairs booths.

Second shot goes down a little more smoothly. Still tastes like spicy wood, though.

Does that even make sense? Hee hee.

"Where'd you learn to dance like that?" Olivia asks me as she sips some fruity drink.

"My mom. Music has always been important to my family."

Just mentioning my mom has got me feeling melancholy. Maybe another shot is necessary.

Olivia seems to notice like always, and puts a gentle hand over mine on the sticker-covered table.

"You miss her. I still miss my mum, too."

"....Yeah." I'm floating, resisting my guardian-reaper's attempts to infiltrate my mind. Right now, my thoughts need to be my own.

That is, until I share them with someone else for the first time ever.

"...After my mom died. I never cried. Not even once. Does that...make me a bad daughter?"

Why did I say that? My eyes dart away from Olivia's at all costs. I'm getting that urge to run away and hide again.

The Aussie sighs and grabs my hand tighter. "No. It doesn't. Girl, there isn't some rulebook on how to grieve. We all do it our own way. Just as long as you don't bury it, alright? Process it. Face it. Control it or else it will control you. Trust."

My heart lightens. The drunk girl in front of me is echoing the words of the other important women in my life. But before I can stop while I'm ahead, another unfortunate truth leaves my liquored lips.

"Um...The night it happened. When the Skin Craft Killer had us. He left us alone for a moment. I managed to escape. But when I did...I made a run for it. Alone. I told myself it was okay, 'cause I was gonna go get help. But...I was fucking terrified. If he didn't catch me...I'm not sure I could've gone back. Does that...make me a bad daughter?"

All the noise of the club seems to dissipate for a painfully long moment. I can't look Olivia in the eyes. She sighs.

"Izz...You were terrified. Fear can make us do some shit we aren't proud of. It doesn't make you a bad daughter. It makes you human."

That wasn't the answer I was expecting. She's trying to help, but it feels like an excuse. One I don't really deserve.

By the way, being drunk sucks. I thought it was supposed to make me feel better, not worse.

"But people do horrible things to each other out of fear. It's what kept my mom in hiding for all those years. It's what got so many warm-bloods killed, and so many cold-bloods before that. We gotta be better. We have to be. I have to be."

Izzie smarter than Izzie looks.

Cheeky monster.

No answer from the human sitting across from me, though. Olivia is getting uncomfortable and so am I. *Bury it again.* Some levity is more than welcome now. So I finally find the strength to look Olivia in the eyes and smile weakly.

"Anyway, I'm good," I lie. "We're supposed to be having fun tonight. So how about another shot?"

"Hell yes! Wait right there, and I'll be back with more go go juice. Hee hee!"

The girl in the tube top and cargo pants swaggers off towards the bar, leaving me and CheccChecc to ourselves at the booth.

What is go go juice? Same liquid humans ingest and spill while having seizures together?

I wipe my eyes and snicker, turning my attention to the little monster sitting patiently beside me. His eyes have an innocence in them that contradicts their menacing glow.

"For starters, we're not having seizures together. It's called dancing. And yeah, 'go go juice'. It's got a lot of different names, but it's basically a drink for adults to help them relax and have fun."

As if on cue, some girl pukes in the booth ahead of us and falls flat on her face, ass up. After watching the incident quietly, CheccChecc rolls his eyes and turns back to me.

Huh. Looks fun. But Izzie not adult. So no drink for Izzie.

"What are you, my mom?"

Protecting human is job. Go go juice make Izzie forget?

I'm equal parts amused and annoyed. "Whatever. Besides, I can legally drink in ten and a half months. Close enough."

If human say so.

Shaking off the attitude, I resume my scan of the club. The familiar hoot of Hideo brings my gaze straight to him: evidently, he just won a match of poker at another booth. He's raking in more cash to the evident chagrin of his opponents, a pair of well-dressed gentlemen sporting an array of tattoos and stitch-work. I suddenly notice someone else at the booth I didn't notice before: Beckett. While everybody else emotes, the red-head just sits there, arms crossed, staring off into the crowd with a vacant gaze. It's like his mind is elsewhere, and it's not the first time I've seen him look like that between cheesy jokes.

"I'm baaaack, girl! What did I miss?"

Olivia slides back into the booth, two shots in each hand. She slides me half before plopping back in her seat heavily.

"Hey," I ask cautiously, "what's wrong with Beckett?"

"Hmm?"

"I mean, I saw him across the room. He's all distant again. Something's clearly bothering him."

A sigh escapes Olivia's lips. "Yeah. Beck tries to act cool, but he deals with PTSD from his time in the Undead Wars. Sometimes he just slips away for a bit."

"Poor guy. Is there anything that can help him?"

"He used to go to therapy, but I'm not sure if he still does. He's kinda private about it and his past, so don't mention that I told you any of this. We just do our best to be there for him. You know, laugh at his bad jokes from time to time."

It's written all over Olivia's face. I'm not the only one at this booth who sucks at hiding their feelings.

"Anyway," she sighs, feigning a smile, "time for shots, baby!"

1...2...3...

Down the hatch!

Cough. Gag.

My nose stings!

Not adult, Checc echoes in my head.

"Party pooper." That's what I'd say, if I wasn't too busy coughing and chugging down water. Olivia already pounded her shots like a champ, which is convenient since it gives her more time to laugh at me.

"Sup, ladies!" It's Hideo, looking mighty drunk and mighty full of himself. "Drinks are on me!"

Olivia gets this wry smile as she brings her attention to the returning boys. "The winning streak continues, I presume?"

"Bingo," joins Beckett in the enthusiasm. He's back to being his usual self, yucking it up as he grabs Hideo by the shoulders and shakes him roughly. "Well, more like a winnin' marathon. Those boys were none too happy 'bout it either. Should'a seen their faces!"

As Becket mimics the reactions of said sore losers, I recall Olivia's candid revelation about the red-head. My laughter at his joke ensues, perhaps a tad more enthusiastic than necessary. I even got an eyebrow raise from Hideo.

However, our celebration is short-lived.

"You fucking cheat," spits one of the tatted sore losers as he leads his entourage to our booth. "Give me my money or else I'll kick your fake ass back to China."

Hideo pulls away from Beck, fixing his hat and chains. "I'm Japanese, you racist dickbag. And I've spent more time in the U.S. screwing your mom than you've spent losing trust fund money."

An array of giggles and guffaws emerge from the entourage, only infuriating their leader more. He shoves Hideo in the chest, eliciting 'oohs' and 'ahhs from the growing crowd of onlookers.

"Says the asshole who lives off his parents' inheritance," interjects the other sore loser as he pushes through the crowd. Hideo double-takes at this revelation. "Yeah, I'm familiar with your history. Used to be some saint before you got the fake body. Now you're nothing but another spoiled rich kid people love to hate."

"I have over 1.5 million followers on Instagram who would disagree with you."

"Sure, and how many actual friends?"

Olivia stands up. "Enough, Darius. Matthew. Take the 'L' like real men and go home."

The racist loser scoffs. "Yeah, because you know all about what it means to be a man, don't 'ya?"

"I wouldn't talk that way to the dealer you have on fucking speed dial, arsehole." Olivia isn't having it.

Beckett's attempts to hold Hideo back are fruitless. He succumbs to the heckling entourage and gets up in the sore losers' faces.

"You leave her out of this," Hideo demands. "Your beef is with me, so let's settle this outside."

"Only if you tell your fake girl and fake friends to mind their own business."

Now Beckett is riled up, too. He's quickly in the antagonists' faces, chest puffed out. I find myself sinking lower and lower in my seat.

"You don't talk that way about her!" the red-headed boy yells vehemently. "A man who talks that way about a lady don't deserve any respect."

"You get your ugly ginger mug outta my fa - "

Boom. Gasps from the entourage. Cheers and video recordings from the surrounding crowd.

Beckett just clocked that loud-mouthed loser square in the nose. With his mechanical hand, no less. Now THAT had to hurt.

And just like that...it's officially on.

Fists and beer glasses everywhere. People slipping on spilled booze. Random girls pulling each other's hair and shrieking like angry banshees. Hideo and Beckett are right in the thick of it, exchanging blows with the shit-starters to the exuberance of their newfound audience. I look to CheccChecc, who appears as alarmed as I am. I expect Olivia to remain the voice of reason, but by the time I spot her again she's already breaking a beer bottle over the top of one asshole's cranium. Ouch.

It's a stereotypical bar fight. The kind you see in old western movies or something. And as I sit here, moderately drunk dodging flying bodies and booze, I ask myself something.

What does one do in a bar fight involving friends? Especially when the fight is against assholes who are literally blocking your way out?

Um...You join in. I guess?

I stand up, ignoring the warning glare of the monster beside me. Grab an empty beer bottle from the booth behind us and hop over an unconscious lackey. Sneak up behind another goon with flying fisticuffs and...

Bonk.

No shattered glass. I thought this was supposed to be easy. Instead I'm still holding a fully intact bottle as it vibrates from the impact of my ineffective attack. My victim shakes it off and gives me this look of surprise and disgust.

"Um...Sorry?" I offer. Oddly enough, he doesn't accept my apology. I find myself scurrying and hopping over booths to avoid his liquored wrath.

The rest? Just as messy or worse.

Beckett throws a sloppy left hook at one guy, who promptly ducks. His fist meets the head of the guy behind him, who's too busy flirting with his date to notice the fight he's suddenly in the middle of. Said dude joins the battle.

While the red-headed vet is keen to tanking hits and relying on fisticuffs, Hideo falls back more on his agility and clever use of props. Another beer bottle meets its doom on the back of the asshole who initially provoked the Instagram star. An empty metal tray from one of the booths is turned into a frisbee of pain. DING, right into another dude's cranium. That guy hits the floor hard, eliciting near equal gasps and chuckles from the girl posse. After a confrontation with yet another angry ex-girlfriend, Hideo is back to dodging blows and pitching beer in his attackers' faces.

"What the hell is wrong with you guys? Are you really gonna beat on a war veteran?!"

It's Olivia, trying her best to save Beckett from the heart of the bar fight. When that doesn't work, she tries a new technique.

"Hey, micro dicks!"

That got their attention. As I poke my head up over a broken jukebox, I see the wall of guys nearest Olivia turn and face her with their chests puffed out. She slaps Dude #1 across the stubbled face, kicks Dude #2 in the dick, and delivers a mean right hook to Dude #3.

Poor, poor, Dude #2.

Angry human coming this way! Time for saving!

Huh?

I turn around fast and see that guy I hit with the bottle. He looks confused, and he's headed this way...Only he doesn't seem to be looking for me. But before I can do anything, a certain little monster decides to intervene.

A bottle goes spiraling through the air from below, clunking the poor dude right in the head. Now THAT one broke.

"What are you doing?!" I ask Checcs, panicking.

My monster familiar just nods at me and raises his head proudly.

Saving Izzie. Good job, yes?

Checc's victim starts looking around frantically until he spots me. Unsurprisingly, he thinks I'm the culprit yet again and comes charging.

"Bad job, bad job!" I cry out, trying to make a run for it.

One little slip is all it takes. The guy is on me in a flash, with a fistful of my hair!

Bad idea.

I fling my head back and hit something hard, presumably his chin. He curses at me and eases his grip enough for me to escape it. Running would probably be a better idea, but instead...

BAM.

I palm the back of his bald head and shove his face into the jukebox. The vintage electronic whirls and lights up, playing some random British pop song. Guess I fixed the jukebox.

"Sorry!" I yelp. I mean it, but I don't think he'll accept that apology either.

NOW it's time to make a run for it. Hideo's still handling his new frenemies, but Olivia is fighting her way through the crowd to Beckett by herself.

"Olivia!" I declare, though I can barely hear myself over the energetic chorus roaring from the jukebox. "I'm coming!"

Or not. A giant bouncer in black blocks my path, looking none too pleased with my rescue attempt. Giving in would probably be a better idea, but instead...

WHOOP.

I shove the behemoth of a man backwards. The move would have accomplished nothing at all, if it weren't for the puddles of booze all over the floor. Big guy loses his balance and slides right off his feet, crashing into Beckett's attackers like the first domino. A really big, heavy, angry domino.

"Sorry, officer!"

'Officer'? Really?

Down they go!

Whoever isn't knocked down runs for the hills, no doubt freaked out by the sudden presence of security. The crowd is thinning quickly, revealing a berserker Beckett stuck under the remaining pile up. He's hooting and cackling, a comical contrast to his bloodied face and matted hair. It looks like he was losing, but apparently the Red Bastard himself didn't get the memo.

"Party's over!" announces a second security guard as he hurries to his partner's aid. Right on cue, three cops rush up the stairs to join them. Everybody freezes, including Olivia mid-throw of one of her heels. The security guard I shoved brushes himself off and gives me the stinkiest stink eye I've ever seen. I smile stiffly and offer a weak wave. Checcs freezes too, but only after throwing another bottle at one of the cops.

Well, shit.

***

"Tonight's your lucky night, kids."

Collectively, we hobble over to the bars. We're all a mess. Missing shoes, twisted ankles, liquor spilled all over our clothes. Olivia and I are sporting hairdos that make us look like we've survived a hurricane. I bite my lip nervously and grip the bars until my bloodied knuckles whiten. I'm bracing for Aunt Maggie's appearance through those doors. Her scorn is less abrasive than my mom's, no doubt about it. But she's gonna nail me for breaking my promise. The promise to not do anything….stupid.

I think underage drinking and bar fights qualify as stupid.

Door swings open, and a click clack of high heels follows. Only it isn't the former pop star I was expecting.

"Claudia?" For some reason I'm extra embarrassed. It seems like Frode's personal assistant only gets to see me at my worst. In her charcoal pencil skirt and matching top, she carefully steps over the ugly stains between the guard and the bars that highlight tonight's poor choices.

I force an awkward grin. I can taste the lipstick on my teeth.

"Hi." That's all I can say. Claudia hides the faintest smile.

"Time to go home and sober up," she offers placidly.

Drunken grunts and groans from my friends. A warbled snigger from Checcs, who no doubt will rub this in my face later.

Guard lets us out. Take all our shit with us, sign some paperwork, and do the walk of shame back to Claudia's car.

It's a painfully long drive back. Claudia drops us all off at Hideo's penthouse, but not before some light scolding.

"When Mr. Algar pressed you to be fearless, he wasn't talking about adolescent debauchery."

I scoff. "Is that what he told you to tell me? Remind your boss that he isn't my dad, no matter how hard he tries."

Claudia's smoky eyes remain on the road. "He only cares about you, that's all."

Cross my arms and lean back in the seat, pretending not to hurt everywhere. Pretending I don't appreciate the concern. "Well, the 'adolescent debauchery' is out of my system now, so he doesn't have to worry about me anymore."

For the first time, Claudia actually looks back at me in the overhead mirror. I'm the only one in the back of this car besides Checc that isn't passed out.

"You're an important person, Miss Cordona. Your mother's legacy lives on in you."

"So I've heard."

"You need to believe in your worth, Miss Cordona. You can't run away from who you are."

"Your boss give you that line for me, too?"

Claudia smiles sweetly. "No. Simply sharing a thought, if I may."

My fruitless defiance wanes. I smile back, and I can't help but laugh at the hot mess looking back at me in the mirror. The ever patient woman driving us joins in, and the tension dissipates. No matter what I might say, I'm thankful. It's a nice feeling to have people believe in me, even if I'm not quite there myself.

But holy crap, does my head hurt. And I need to pee.

***

So I told them everything. As everyone cozied up at the bar in Hideo's penthouse, hungover and sore as hell, I shared a host of information that no doubt made them think I was still deeply inebriated.

My twin Dante and our untimely demise at birth. The ritual and magic my mom used to bring one of us back. The likelihood that my mom's death and inability to be reanimated had to do with the deal she made: her life for mine. And I told them about CheccChecc: why he's here, and why only I can see him. Despite their very evident disbelief and confusion, or the extra shots of booze that were very necessary to get through my bizarre story, they didn't tease or say anything until I was finished.

"Is that monster reaper thing with you, right now?" inquired Beckett, a tall glass of water in his mechanical hand.

"Yeah. He's always here now. Right beside me."

I gesture to the spot my invisible friend is occupying. Without warning, Beckett steps over and dumps his entire glass on top of CheccChecc. His guffaws and my startled yelp are quickly replaced with horror.

Sure enough, they can see the water as it drips down CheccChecc's frame. As I observe a very vexed monster shake off like a wet dog, I can only assume what my friends are seeing: a ghostly form whose volume and nature is only vaguely informed by the patterns of drips coming off of....well, nothing.

"Sweet God almighty!" Beckett hollers, dropping his glass and hopping over the bar to join Hideo. The Eldritch monster charges, eliciting girlish screams from the Red Bastard himself.

"You could have used a blanket or something for the same effect, you know." That stunt only served to prove the truth of my outlandish story. There is no doubt on any one of those pretty faces now. They are in it.

"Can we touch it?" Olivia asks cautiously, hiding somewhat behind me at this point.

"Only when he lets you. Mostly that's when I'm in danger and need my ass saved."

"What is a guardian-reaper, exactly? He looks like a baby kaiju or something." Hideo is nervously pouring another glass for him and Beckett. His eyes are so glued to the dripping monster that he over-pours both drinks and makes a mess. I guess I didn't have all of his attention the first time I told him.

"I don't exactly have the rule book on me. But from what I learned so far, he's here to keep up their end of the bargain. Eldritch beings are kinda like demons, making deals for souls."

Demons? Again? Really?!

"Life given by these monsters is only ever borrowed. So this little guy is here to make sure I don't die until my pre-determined expiration date. It's freaky, I get that."

"Freaky is an understatement. So you're aware of when you're gonna...you know..." Beckett emulates a shot to the head, closing his eyes and sticking out his tongue.

"Nope. I'm not allowed to know that. But when it IS my time to go..." I pause and gesture towards CheccChecc, who is almost entirely invisible to my friends again. "He's gonna be the one to take me."

"So the same fun-sized hellspawn who saves your ass regularly is also gonna be the one to kill you? Um...No offense at all, sweetie, but what's stopping him from just getting it over with now? How can you...well, trust him?"

Humans always so distrustful and destructive. Proof planet needs Penumbran help to stop apocalypse.

And I'M the judgemental one? Sheesh. Plus I'm tired of hearing about the supposed end of the world from preachers, transients, and monsters alike. Needless to say, I understand Olivia's confusion. Hell, it's still confusing to me, too.

"The Old Ones are bound to the contracts they make with humans."

Hideo finally notices his mess and starts soaking it up with a kitchen towel. I've never seen him this flustered. "I second Olivia's question. How can you trust him? Being around the thing that's gonna kill you someday, any day...I dunno, man. Sounds morbid as shit."

I look down at CheccChecc, who is still shaking his wings out. He seems to sense my attention and stops to shoot me a look. Tentacles wiggling, big eyes blinking inquisitively. Maybe he wonders what my answer is, too.

"Honestly...I don't know. This is totally crazy, and I'm still trying to wrap my head around all of it, same as you guys. CheccChecc and I, all we can do is try to trust each other. I'm already living on borrowed time anyways. Just gotta make the most of it and keep an eye on this little guy."

I reach out to pet my monster instinctively, but my hand passes right through him, as usual. Still, he's giving me that look I've seen before. An expression that seems to say so much without him muttering a word into my cranium. And I don't tell my friends, but I'd like to think I detect a hint of compassion in those bulbous eyes. The same ones that observed me during all my darkest moments. I've gotta believe that. The alternative is too depressing.

"I admire your courage, girl." Olivia gives me a slight hug. "I don't think I could live with an actual demon. My inner ones are bad enough."

She chortles, and the others join in...nervously. They are trying really hard to be cool about all this, and I've no clue how much they truly believe. But they aren't laughing at me this time, and it's a good feeling.

"So what's next for Isabella and her traveling circus monster?" Beckett is definitely getting hammered now. I don't blame him.

"I'm sure you guys saw the news. The Skin Craft Killer was reanimated, and he's already killed two more people out of state. I need to stop him before he hurts anybody else."

"You?" Hideo asks inquisitively. "No offense, but how?"

"The cops are already on it," adds Beckett with a raised brow.

I reach into my jacket pocket and pull out a folded brochure.

"The cops don't have shit on The Skin Craft Killer. Let's say I have a unique perspective to offer the investigation. And I've been told that somebody here could help me ID that asshole."

Beckett and Olivia reach for the brochure in unison, but Olivia snags it first. Her face twists in confusion as she reads it aloud.

"'Grady's Haunted Mystery Mansion'?"

"A tourist attraction in bum-fuck nowhere?" Hideo chortles. Beckett isn't having it.

"Hey man, my momma took me there when I was a kid. It's kinda cool, actually."

"I'm not gonna lie, babe. This is...a lot to take in. But we believe you, and we're here to help any way we can. Right, guys?"

Hideo and Beckett look at each other with comically synchronized timing. Another shot down the hatch.

"Yeah, of course."

I start to feel that doubt creep in again. That negative voice in my head, telling me that the closest I'm gonna get to being cared about is having people pity me. But I gotta stay strong, and I have to fight those negative thoughts. Maybe every day for the rest of my life, even. And perhaps learn to accept a little kindness once and awhile without questioning every ounce of it.

Besides, can I blame them for being skeptical? Olivia was right, it is...a lot.

"Nah, I gotta do this alone. But...thanks."

And when I look at Olivia, I really mean it. She feels like the big sister I never had. Not totally sold on my shit, but determined to be there for me anyway. I hope I can see her and the others when I get back from my trip.

But I don't say that. Somehow I never manage to say the things I wanna say. I just smile nervously and take my brochure back. I attempt a graceful exit, but after leaving I realize that it probably seemed a little abrupt and premature.

"Checcs, does it get old watching me sabotage myself all the time?"

My guardian-reaper gives me side-eye as he trots by my side. He's gotta be tired of my bullshit. Hell, I'm tired of it.

Izzie overthinking constantly. Living in different reality. Spending too much time in own head.

I snort. "You spend more time in my head than I do, buddy."

He's right, though.

I'm going to make you proud, mom. The murderer who stole you from the world is gonna pay for his crimes, and this time he won't come back to hurt anybody else ever again.

CHAPTER EIGHT

The delightful scent of apple cider in the air. Exuberant tourists sitting on hay bales and taking corny photos in front of cardboard standees covered in bird droppings. Comic sans font sprawled over a rusty metal sign, cradled in the plastic arms of a googly-eyed mansion wearing a cowboy hat. Friendly-looking ghost animatronics so old that they're falling apart right in front of the entrance.

Yep. I'm here. A four hour flight paid for by my gracious (and incredibly insistent) friends, a thirty minute bus ride, and zero sleep later, I'm standing right outside my destination in Backson, Wyoming. And thanks to Olivia's obsession with disregarding the warranty on my bionic leg, I'm stepping foot on small town ground with a few upgrades up my sneaker.

"I do my best work while I'm sobering up," she had told me coyly as she returned my appendage before the flight. *"Better flexibility and mobility. A few other little things too, no big deal. Don't worry, I included a user manual. Thank me later, Izz."*

"Howdy, and welcome to Grady's Haunted Mystery Mansion!" hollers a voice over the very aged intercom above. Sounds like an old-timey prospector. "Come on in and experience the horror, magic, and darn-tootin' buffoonery of the Midwest's wackiest haunted mansion!"

Another voice quickly interrupts the friendly and boisterous one before it, speaking far quicker and more monotone. It's so fast, I almost miss it:

"Tickets are non-refundable - Senior discounts available under certain conditions, restrictions apply - Do not urinate on the Malcolm Mansion standee. Urinating on the Malcolm Mansion mascot will result in a $1000 fine and a permanent ban from the mansion. Grady's Haunted Mystery Mansion is not responsible for lost or stolen property."

The happier greeting replays afterwards without skipping a beat.

Um. Was Frode messing with me, sending me here? This place...it isn't exactly oozing a 'prehistoric monster orphanage' kind of vibe.

But as I stand there with brochure in hand, CheccChecc shakes his head and trots ahead of me.

Don't be scared. Ghosts not real.

"Smartass," I grumble under my breath as I follow.

Step into line, fiddle with the straps of my backpack. 'Kids Day', says a crude sign taped to the ticket booth. There's a reanimated mother and daughter ahead of me, talking casually with a person wearing a full-body ghost costume. They're laughing and smiling as the daughter gets showered with compliments. The mother pays admittance and is promptly funneled along into the mansion. My turn.

Face to face with Admittance myself. The softball-sized googly eyes on that weathered plastic is weirding me out.

Oh shit. There's a face behind that gaping mouth of the mascot head, barely visible behind the black screen. I just happen to make out the face of an old lady, so stern that the crinkles of her brow would have to be counted with both hands.

"Um, Hi, one ticket, please. Adult."

The old lady who was laughing and pinching cheeks a second ago is now grimacing at me without restraint. Maybe she thinks I can't see her behind the screen? She's looking me up and down with obvious disdain. I wanna ask her what her problem is, but instead I force a smile.

"First time here," I say light-heartedly, flashing my brochure. "I'm...um. Super excited."

No response or reaction at all. It's so bad that the Malcolm Mansion mascot waving to visitors ahead stops and stares at me too.

"We don't like trouble-makers here," she grumbles at me.

"I'm no trouble-maker, ma'am."

"Where did you come from anyways?"

"Um...Dead Vegas."

"Warm-blood from Dead Vegas? No prostitutes allowed here. It's a family establishment."

Bitch, much?

She's reaching for a phone with those goofy blue gloves. I'm pissed, but I gotta get inside this stupid building. *Think fast, Izzie...*

"Not a prostitute, ma'am. I'm actually here with my daughter, she's been dying to see this...uh, mansion. On Kids Day, and all."

"Daughter, huh? I don't see any daughter."

I look down at CheccChecc beside me. He doesn't know what he's in for. Sorry, little guy.

"She's at her grandma's right now," I lie. Poorly. "I'm going to pick her up and surprise her. Be back in a flash."

I force another smile and get my ass out of there. A confused monster tags behind me.

Wrong way.

"I'm gonna need you to do something for me, Checcs," I whisper, "and you aren't gonna like it."

***

Twenty minutes and thirty dollars later, I'm back outside the stupid haunted mansion. Walk myself right back up to Admittance and make eye contact with the grumpy old ghost again.

"Two tickets, please. One adult, one child."

Child? Izzie is child. Stupid.

The woman begrudgingly leans forward over the counter to observe my 'child': a certain invisible monster wearing full-body, pink bunny pajamas from the costume gift shop around the corner. CheccChecc has the posture of a cat protesting clothing.

"What's your name, sweetie?" she inquires at last, leaning in more to get a closer look at the face behind the cheap rabbit mask. She's not going to find anything back there.

"She's shy," I pipe in quickly, and Checcs takes a clumsy step back from the weary eyes of Admittance. "Her name is Sandi, with an 'i'."

Sandi? Stupid human name. Stupid ugly disguise.

Geez, big baby.

"What's with the costume?"

"She...um, feels safer when she's wearing her favorite costume. Being shy and all. You know how kids are."

Bad liar.

I attempt a giggle and try to channel my inner mother. I get a dead-pan stare in return.

"Why is her head so...bulbous?"

"Sshhh, don't be rude. She's got a tumor. And, uh, a skin condition, too. Very sensitive about it."

Really bad liar.

Worm face over here needs to can it.

An odd silence follows as I smile nervously at the old lady. Checcs does this cute little hobble from leg to leg, followed by a head tilt. I watch those limp bunny ears flop from side to side, and it's enough to make the old lady soften. Good thing she can't hear what he's saying.

"Alright. Two tickets, coming up."

Thank God. Finally, we're in.

***

The actual mansion is clearly old, sporting some really cool ornate architecture and old-timey paintings. But whoever came up with this weird, prospector-meets-Boo Berry marketing campaign must have been high as balls. The strange elegance of this mansion is competing with the tasteless marketing juxtaposed throughout: posters, photo-ops, mascots, and booth after booth of souvenirs as cheap as they are overpriced. They even sell Malcolm Mansion branded barf bags.

CheccChecc is already getting restless in his disguise. I get it.

"Sorry, little guy," I whisper, eyeing those tentacles as they writhe outside the mask's cheesy simper. "You can't get out of disguise. Not yet."

"Well howdy, little girl! Need a brochure?"

Damn it, it's that stupid mascot. Sounds like a prerecorded message from decades past. My head begins to pound, as if something or someone is trying to break into it and it's not CheccChecc. Maybe that atmospheric music over the intercom is messing with my head.

Malcolm Mansion hobbles on over, waving those goofy gloved hands at us.

"She's shy. And we have a brochure already, thank you."

"Want a picture with Malcolm Mansion? Only fifty dollars!"

Fifty dollars is highway robbery, unless that price includes a manicure from Malcolm Mansion.

Strange. Familiar almost. What? Smells like old humans.

"No thank you. Come along, um, daughter."

The enthusiastic stranger keeps dancing in front of us, wearing cyan tights under an over-sized box with fake windows and googly eyes. A cartoony cowboy hat is attached to the top of the mansion costume, illuminated by an LED light shaped like a ghost. The more I look at him, the harder my head pounds.

CheccChecc and I excuse ourselves and make a run for the staircase ahead. According to Frode's directions, the library is where I need to go.

"Third floor, library," I repeat under my breath. "That's where we're gonna find Udolthra and get a chance to ID our psychopath. We've got this."

No, we don't.

An exuberant woman fit for a Tupperware party blocks our path. She's in a bright cyan uniform, complete with a cornball mansion-shaped hat. Her ghostly name tag reads 'Darthy, Tour Guide'.

"Well, howdy, visitors! This way is off-limits without a guide. Luckily for you, I'm a - " she stops to point at her name tag and giggle - "tour guide! Yaaaay!"

Great.

"Actually, my daughter and I just want to see the library."

"Even better! The tour of Grady's Haunted Mystery Mansion covers all of this fantastical building's most impressive rooms. We will be visiting the library on our little tour, so buckle up, buckaroo! And don't worry, the fright won't bite...much! Hee hee!"

Silly big blue lady. Fear has no teeth to bite with. Most of time anyway.

I'll pretend that isn't a weird-ass statement.

Suddenly I'm aware of the small crowd of people around me. Undead tourists as pale as milk wearing Hawaiian shirts, hand in hand with children laden in souvenirs. They all seem genuinely exuberant as Darthy the tour guide rounds us up.

"Well, howdy, boys and girls! My name is Darthy and I will be your ghoulishly good guide today. Are you ready to experience the horror, magic, and darn-tootin' buffoonery of the Midwest's wackiest haunted mansion? Don't answer that, of course you are! Yaaaaay!"

***

Whatever our new pal Darthy is taking, I want some. Her energy levels are ridiculous, and she's peppy enough that I considered jumping out of a window once or twice to get away. But alas...jumping out of the mansion is 'not part of the tour'.

We're shown the foyer in great detail, which showcases a bunch of historic pictures, documents, and handwritten letters from ol' Grady himself. Nothing spooky so far.

"Grady Wilkins was a poor prospector who built this mansion back in 1820, shortly after striking it rich during the gold rush." Darthy has got this flare as she recalls the history. I hate to admit it, but it's almost enough enthusiasm to make me give a shit. "Folks have no clue how he managed to find gold up in these hills, but gosh darn it, he did!"

These human heroes? Strange greedy humans destroying planet for fame and make rich?

"Not my heroes," I whisper to the hooded-monster beside me. "Not my mom's either. But yeah."

"Ahem."

Eyes up. Darthy is giving me this cautionary glare. Guess I'm interrupting. Clear my throat and return my focus to the display ahead. The tour guide relents and goes back to work.

Darthy points to a giant black and white picture of the mansion. The only thing that's changed since then is the welcome lack of Malcolm Mansion branding.

"Things were good in the beginning, and nobody could tell anything was wrong with Grady's mansion. But it didn't take long before straaange things started happening on the property."

Our tour guide leads us forward, down a very old hallway. Eerie atmospheric sounds pour out of newly-installed intercoms, eliciting 'oohs' and 'ahhs' from the eager flock around me.

Next are such exciting locales as Grady's guest bathroom, an 'especially haunted' broom closet, and a billiards room that smells like dust bunnies and cottage cheese. I've yet to see any ghosts or monsters - only an abundance of unwarranted excitement, khaki shorts, and knee-high socks.

"Grady became aware of a mysterious presence in the mansion. Strange noises, objects moving on their own, the whole sh-bang. It was right here in the billiards room where he first witnessed supernatural activity."

Darthy says the last few words louder, like it's a sound cue. Sure enough, a mechanism visibly pops out on the center pool table, knocking the balls every which way. Everybody gasps, and the energy is raised as the group moves on to the next room. I shoot CheccChecc a quick look, curious what he thinks about all this. I'm positive I detect a glowing eye roll behind the eye holes of that pink plastic.

Kitchen's next. Ugly yellow wallpaper. More Malcolm Mansion the mascot. More exposition. Grady ate here, Grady sat here, Grady cleaned dog shit off his shoes here, etc. etc. We watch a chair get knocked over and pretend not to see the string attached to it. The group claps. Darthy keeps cheesing and shaking her fists excitedly.

"Excuse me?" Darthy seems surprised by my interruption, so I raise my hand just in case. "Um, can we see the library next?"

Our tour guide raises one pencil eyebrow, unamused by my impatience. "We'll be visiting the library soon enough. Now, tuck them tails and follow me upstairs to the study. Come on now, come on!"

Good lord.

The crowd shuffles up a narrow winding staircase, still bustling with excitement that I clearly am not understanding. Before I head up after them, I notice that

Malcolm Mansion mascot is just standing still and staring at me from behind the kitchen counter. No dancing. Just staring into my soul with those...googly eyes.

Creepy. Onward ho.

We find ourselves in a spacious study fit for Sherlock Holmes. Cue more atmospheric music overhead. Most of the furniture in this room is roped off. Stacks of paperwork and the scribblings of a madman, beside giant signs that read 'DO NOT TOUCH'. One closet is missing its door, as evidenced by the broken hinges and the caution tape blocking its entrance.

"Grady spent most of his later life studying the paranormal. He became consumed by his research and rarely left the mansion. Most folks called him paranoid, delusional, and, well heck, darn-right cuckoo! But no doubt about it, Grady was right about one thing: something was very wrong with his estate..."

A low evil laughter emits from another intercom, turning heads all around me. People grab their loved ones and point at other objects being 'mysteriously' moved: the rotating arm of a fake stone statue; the yank of a tablecloth; and the subtle slide of a roped off chair. More applause follows.

"Excuse me?" My arm rises up high again, this time stopping Darthy short mid-monologue. "Are there any actual ghosts here? Or just cheap gags?"

The tour guide's expression changes so fast that it's the scariest thing in the mansion thus far. She looks like I just kicked her dog or something. Everybody else in the group turns and glares at me in unison. Am I...crazy for asking that?

Darthy storms straight towards me, the crowd making a clear path for her. I'm legit freaked out as she whispers in my ear with a highly uncharacteristic tone dripping with disdain.

"Listen, princess. You might think you're hot stuff on account of being a warm-blood and all, but I ain't impressed and neither is the group. This is MY fucking tour, and I've been doing it for the last fifty goddamn years. So I politely suggest that you shut that big mouth of yours and let me do my fucking job. Got it?"

I get an angry finger to the sternum. CheccChecc watches closely, and I wish he would just tackle the big girl then and there.

He doesn't.

Heh. Big blue lady scared Izzie.

"I'm not scared, asshole," I whisper to Checcs just as Darthy is stomping back.

Shit. She heard that. Time for one more earful.

"Another word from you and I'm calling security. You'll be banned from Grady's Haunted Mystery Mansion for life. For LIFE, you understand? So shut...your GODDAMN MOUTH."

Okay, maybe I'm a little scared.

"Y-yes, ma'am."

Darthy narrows her eyes at me once more before switching her 'I'm gonna kill you' demeanor back to 'cheerfully wholesome' for the group.

"Sorry for the slight interruption, buckaroos! Let's get the group a'movin', and see what mysteries Grady's master bedroom has in store for us ghouls and gals! Yaaaay!"

***

It's like some kind of nightmare. An eternity of cheap jump scares, gullible tourists, and feigned enthusiasm. It's hard for me to understand how people could believe any of this ghost stuff, let alone be so interested in the daily activities of a crazy old prospector in his dusty old mansion. The only memorable thing so far was seeing some bratty undead kid insult CheccChecc's costume and try taking his mask off. That look of absolute terror when the kid saw nothing at all underneath? Worth the price of admission, right there. Checc's warbled laugh as the kid ran crying to his mommy told me that he shared my sentiment.

"Grady Wilkins enjoyed the fame and attention the mansion brought him, and turned no interview down. It came as a great surprise, then, when Grady fell completely silent. Authorities went looking for old Grady. Heck, the whole town went looking for him. But Grady could never be found. It was as if he had disappeared without a trace."

Hmm. Perhaps old man Grady was a practitioner of arcane magic? I don't share that thought with the class. Wait a second. Am I actually getting invested? Well played, Darthy. Well played.

"Ever since ol' Grady disappeared, the mansion started seeing far more paranormal activity. Moving furniture, disappearing objects, strange noises, the works! If y'all are lucky, you just might hear straange voices in the walls..."

A massive ringing in my head. Is this another one of Darthy's parlor tricks? It feels like something is trying to get inside my brain. I throw CheccChecc a look, but he's preoccupied with the attention of a giggling undead girl exactly his height. She waves at him and hides behind her mom again, while Checcs stands there awkwardly and waves back. Cute, but that crosses my guardian-reaper off the list of brain-intruders.

Spin around until I see Malcolm Mansion, again. This time the mascot is standing by a pop-up booth that's selling Malcolm Mansion plushies, in the same den touted as being 'unchanged since Grady's disappearance'. Sure. The mascot approaches and waves at me with those big goofy gloved hands. The assault on my brain resumes just as that recorded voice booms out of the mascot once more.

"Want a picture with Malcolm Mansion? Only fifty dollars!"

I can't help it, but I'm getting a little annoyed.

"Look, dude, I don't want a picture. I can think of a lot better ways to spend fifty bucks. And seriously, a mansion mascot for a haunted mansion? Not a friendly ghost or something? It's kind of weird."

A G R E E E E D.   N O W   F O L L O W   pretty please. Follow follow follow follow.

Wait a second! That voice. It isn't Checcs. This sounds kind of androgynous and fussy. All this time...is it...

As the group shuffles towards the next room full of fake scares, I slip behind to get a closer look at Malcolm Mansion. I'm looking into those vacant googly eyes like they're gonna reveal something to me. But there's nothing out of the ordinary.

"What did you...say just now?" I ask finally, low enough that the sleepy guy working the plushie booth doesn't stir.

Malcolm Mansion says nothing. Just turns around and starts hobbling away with a little less pep than he had earlier. I'm either crazy and wrong or extremely dense for not noticing sooner. But I decide to take my chances on this one. Checcs and I follow after him loosely, keeping an eye out for Darthy in case she realizes her favorite visitor left the party. I'm not sure even CheccChecc could save me from that woman's wrath.

Down another musty hallway, around a corner, up another flight of stairs. It looks like we're taking some kind of shortcut, judging by the lack of production and ambiance found on this route. But sure enough, we find ourselves in what is very clearly a library.

Thank GOD. I was gonna lose my damn mind.

Tall rows of bookshelves, almost as high as the dome ceiling itself. Stained glass windows in the shape of peacocks pouring colored polygons of light onto the hardwood floor. It's gorgeous, but I can tell the library is only a shadow of its former glory. Everything in here is so dusty and aged, reflecting what I can only assume is the public's overall lack of interest in seeing a room full of books.

No time for daydreaming. Move move.

Fine. I continue after Malcolm Mansion and Checcs, looking every which way for signs of arcane monsters. No dice. I decide I'm not gonna protest anymore at this point.

But it isn't the library that's our final destination after all. Our new tour guide leads us into what appears to be...a janitor's closet.

Um. What? I take back that bit about not protesting anymore.

Malcolm Mansion unlocks the janitor's closet and swings open the door like he's revealing a new car. But nope. Just a small room with a mop bucket and a rack of cleaning supplies.

"You want us to go...in there?"

Malcolm Mansion does another little dance and points once more to the closet.

Follow follow follow. Time is ticking, tick tick tick tick tick

"Alright, alright, white rabbit. Take a chill pill and lead the way."

"Come on now, buckaroos!" goes the pre-recorded voice box as the mascot steps into the closet and closes the door behind him.

Um...what? Following a dude in a mascot costume into a supply closet...Yep. Nothing creepy about that.

A full minute goes by with me standing outside this closet door, waiting for something to happen. Checcs shakes his bunny-eared hood in what I can only assume is impatience. He hops up to the door and twists it open with his tentacles.

Malcolm Mansion, he's gone! All that I can see in there are four walls and a bunch of cleaning supplies. My guardian-reaper is braver than I am. He steps into the closet and closes the door behind him. I listen in for some kind of sound. Maybe a 'ding' like an elevator, or the heavy roll of a moving wall. But nope, I hear nothing. Only my own nervous breathing as I stand alone in the library.

And any reservations I had about locking myself in a dusty closet are quickly replaced by a sharp discomfort at the thought of being alone again. So in I go...

Door creaks open. No CheccChecc, no mascot. Hardly enough room for one person to fit in here. But if there's anything the past few weeks have taught me, it's that sometimes you need to suspend your disbelief. I've got important questions that need answered, ASAP. And nothing left to lose. It all comes to this.

So suck it up, buttercup, and get in the damn closet.

***

Holy crap. Not exactly sure what happened once I closed that closet door, but the best way I could describe it was like taking a magic-powered elevator through time and space. Serious Alice in Wonderland vibes. Swallowed in a puff of red smoke that smelled like sulfur, consumed by what felt like an out-of-body experience. Shifting through floors at a nauseating speed, until all at once it just...stopped. I think I puked in my mouth a little.

But once I was sure it was over, I hesitantly opened that closet door and took a peek outside. Sure enough, I was in a totally different space that I could only assume was under the mansion. A space very unlike the outdated estate I left behind.

A large area as organic as it was carefully constructed. Like being in the belly of some kind of tree monster...if that makes any sense. Purple roots everywhere in between, pulsating and vaguely luminescent. I step out into the area fully and close the closet door behind me. That man-made door looks woefully out of place down here, surrounded by walls of trees and otherworldly roots so tightly interwoven that you couldn't tell where one ended and the other began. Ceiling so high that its exact height was obscured by darkness. Ground like gray moss that felt extra spongy beneath my feet. Primary light source? Glowing blue-green leaves, all over the tree walls. It's as gorgeous as it is eerie.

Am I dreaming? This new place I find myself in...It can't be real. It's just like in those sci-fi movies I used to watch with Mom. The walls and floor seem to be alive, rising and falling ever so slightly like they're breathing. Is that even possible? I regret not buying a Malcolm Mansion barf bag.

Before I can consider stepping back into the closet, a familiar little bunny hops over to me on all fours. It's CheccChecc, still in full costume minus the mask. I've never been that comforted by the sight of my little stalker.

"What the hell is this place?"

Place between places. What Izzie came for. Obvious. Hurry up.

And he's running off. No time to turn back! Take a deep breath and follow after my monster guide.

The farther we go, the more the space reveals itself. Tunnels on either side, large enough to drive a bulldozer through. Strange runes marking the walls here and there. The weirdest thing, though? I'm noticing random human artifacts, and I mean random: a toaster here, a Malcom Mansion plushie there, some shoes of different sizes, and so on. It's almost like a junkyard. Checcs takes a hard left down one of the tunnels, and he's going fast enough that I need to jog to keep up.

The tunnel's bountiful leaves glow so bright that I'm blinded for a second. By the time my vision returns, I find myself in a space even larger and better lit than the first. Only this one is filled with monsters!

All kinds. Large and small. Weird and creepy. Crawling, flying, or slithering. Bipedal and quadrupedal. Skin like bark, skin like stone. Most of them share combinations of human and animal characteristics. Just an array of monsters a child might draw up, shuffling about their business like it was some kind of otherworldly monster airport.

Everybody looks busy until they notice the only human walking amongst them. Their reaction is mixed: chittering teeth, raised brows, a couple menacing grins. Hell, even a few throaty guffaws. I don't understand what's so funny. They're clearly communicating with one another by the shared looks on their faces. It's enough to make a girl feel like she's the butt of a joke in high school or something. I might as well have a "KICK ME" sign on my back.

But in the middle of them all, I see that Malcolm Mansion mascot. Gotta stay focused on that. He's leading us forward, dancing and waving at passing monsters along the way. It's the strangest thing I could imagine. But CheccChecc seems confident about following the costumed stranger, so I try to stay focused and keep up.

"Oof!"

Not focused enough, apparently. It's another monster, one I happened to bump into. He's twice my height and width, with a face vaguely reminiscent of a mummified cat.

"Um, sorry, excuse me!"

Creepy dude just grumbles at me and lumbers off on legs that look like tree stumps, swinging that club-like tail back and forth as he goes. I have to step aside quickly to avoid being clobbered by it. The weirdest part? I swear I can feel his thoughts. Maybe intentionally, maybe not. But I definitely hear it faintly in the recesses of my mind...

ALL DEAD SOON ANYWAY.

Geez. And I thought humans were rude.

We end up in a smaller place that could best be described as a waiting room of
sorts. It's populated with more man-made furniture and objects, which I can only
assume were taken from the human world above. They are woefully out of place
down here, but their arrangement hints at an appreciation for their design and
use. I find the familiarity oddly comforting in this strange space. Hell, there's
even a TV hanging in the corner. Sure, there's no electricity and the screen is
cracked. But whoever put it there at least understood its use, considering all the
rows of chairs facing it.

And for the first time since I've been down here, I see other humans: one
businessman; one pretty, middle-aged woman covered from head to toe in pink
and rhinestones; and one little boy with glasses seated beside an Eldritch
familiar. Everybody is in their own world.

T A A A K E   a seat.   Anyyyy seat!

And at last, Malcolm Mansion takes off his head and reveals the stranger
underneath.

Wow. I'm not sure what I was expecting, but it wasn't that. It is a bipedal
humanoid that looks like it belongs in the movie Pan's Labyrinth. And to think
this thing has been waving at visitors and taking pics with kids all day...Holy
crapballs.

It's something both beautiful and horrifying, barely more monster than human.
Skin like marbled rock. Aging supermodel vibes radiate from the creature's bare
shoulders, across her banded throat, and up to a prominent jawline. Painted lips
stretch over vampiric fangs in a sincere smile. The remaining 60 percent of her
face and head is composed of...well, a stone tablet fit for The Ten
Commandments. Finding little solstice in her Stepford Wives smile, I avert my
eyes to the gaping blast crater in her tablet face.

Shit, that's not helping.

Humans with Enlightenment are so so so rare these days! Children of the First Mercy, extra special! Lucky lucky, had to escort human personally!

"Um, are you...Udolthra?"

Though she has an actual mouth, this creature isn't using it. Maybe she can't? She continues to speak telepathically, grinning at me the whole time.

DING D I N G -I N G! Udolthraronrhra is speaking to you, but humans get tied-tongue so they name me Udolthra. Your name is Isabella Cordona. Yes?

"Um...Yeah. How did you know?"

Udolthra V E R Y   G O O D with names. If human has Enlightenment, Udolthra can identify them. Yes yes!

She tilts her head and sticks a hand out for me to shake. She's still wearing those oversized mascot gloves. After a pause, I give in. The monster shakes my hand like she understands the concept, but not the execution.

Isabella, you wait here. Make friends with other humans, yes yes! Udolthra see you soon, after finishing little bitty meeting, alright!

Geez, this Udolthra is kinda off her rocker. Maybe it's just an Eldritch monster thing? Before I can ask one of my hundred other questions, she hobbles off through one of several man-made doors built right into the organic walls. I suddenly wonder if this is where the missing doors in the mansion ended up. Now I've got a hundred and one questions.

I take a look at my watch. Barely after noon. I awkwardly clutch my backpack and survey the seating. Most of the chairs are unusable: busted, horribly uncomfortable, or intended for toddlers. The undead lady in pink eyes me suspiciously before sitting her purse in the seat beside her. Alright, fine. The businessman doesn't acknowledge me, only keeps his eyes on his phone. Next to the button-nosed little kid it is.

Upon getting closer, I notice that the little boy is definitely reanimated. That creature must be his guardian-reaper? Not exactly sure how all of this works.

This entity looks like a cross between a toad and a well-fed bear. Toad on the top, bear on the bottom. They both look at me with mild disinterest as I sit down and try to get comfortable ten different ways. I can feel the disdain radiating off the both of them. I attempt to break the ice.

"I like your monster."

Did it work?

HELLO. FOLFRAKKA HERE. NICE TO SEE A LIVING HUMAN.

What? Is this one actually talking to me?! Her voice is like a bass instrument reverberating in a cavern.

"Folfrakka here is not a monster. You should know that. Why is your guardian-reaper wearing that stupid costume?"

Okay. Maybe it didn't work. This kid isn't having it.

I look to CheccChecc, who has hopped up into the seat beside me. He awkwardly shakes the droopy bunny ears out of his eyesight.

"It's called a disguise. Made it easier for me to get in here."

"You DO know that they're invisible to normal people, right?"

ICARUS ALWAYS TALK ABOUT BEING INVISIBLE.

"Well?"

Now the kid's getting on my nerves a bit. "Do your parents realize you're down here?"

The dark-haired boy shrugs and pets his companion. "They're dead. So probably not."

Geez, kid. I change the subject.

"I see your companion lets you pet him, that's pretty cool."

ICARUS ALSO PETS FAVORITE STUFFED TOY EVERY NIGHT.

Not sure if I should be amused or confused by these telepathic revelations of a total stranger. The kid, on the other hand, doesn't react at all. He scrunches his face and looks up at me with what I can only imagine is disgust. "Folfrakka is a 'she'. And yes. What, yours won't let you touch him?"

I'm a little embarrassed to admit it. So I don't. Heh.

"Me? Yeah, totally. Of course, duh."

Folfrakka and her little buddy swap looks with each other. Icarus snickers and shakes his head. They're talking some telepathic shit, I know it.

"Sure, lady," he says at last.

The little boy sighs and goes back to petting his companion. His body language says he's done talking. I can feel my mom's stubbornness coming through me.

"We've bonded telepathically lots of times," I brag nonchalantly. Checcs is looking at me now, and I can tell he's amused.

Do tell.

"He shows me things and we talk together all the time. No big deal."

The kid shrugs loudly, looking extra pretentious in that preppy, oversized coat he has on. "So? Can you shift your consciousness at will and see through his eyes?"

"I... think so?"

"Can you read and speak in their native language?"

"Um..."

"Can you phase between realities together?"

191

ICARUS MUCH CREATIVE.

"Alright pipsqueak, if you're so smart, then what are you doing here? Clearly you already know everything."

"There's always more to learn about the Old Ones and their magic," he answers immediately, ignoring my attitude. "It's kiiind of the oldest civilization of all time ever. So yeah. Learning is good. You should try it."

I'm annoyed and fighting with myself over it. Am I seriously gonna let some freckle-faced kid get the best of me?

HUMANS SAY LEARNING FUNDAMENTAL. OFTEN WHEN FOLFRAKKA TEST ICARUS ON HUMAN MATHS, ICARUS FALL ASLEEP. LEARNING VERY VERY HARD SOMETIMES.

Hearing Folfrakka's shameless secret-sharing about this twerp, I decide to take the higher road.

"You realize your buddy here is gonna tear your soul out eventually, right? Maybe even tomorrow."

Okay, so maybe that wasn't the high road.

"The Old Ones never reap the souls of children. They're not monsters. You, though....You're old, you probably don't have much time left."

VERY TRUE. FOLFRAKKA AGREE. WARM-BLOOD GIRL MUCH OLD.

Now I've had it! I just want to give the brat and his over-sharing mutant pal a little scare or something. Show both of them that I'm way cooler than they think.

"Teach this kid some manners, Checcs."

Checcs visibly shakes his head, and I detect a hint of amusement in his glowing eyes.

No. CheccChecc like the smart tiny human.

Gee. Thanks a lot.

We sit in an awkward silence for a while after that. Checcs gets up and starts interacting with the little brat's companion, and the two are sniffing each other curiously like dogs meeting for the first time. It's kinda cute, and I think to myself just how much cooler my guardian-reaper is compared to this weird bulky mutant thing. Maybe that's the butthurtness talking, but whatever. Checcs is better, end of story. Even if he is a little dick most of the time.

Don't tell Folfrakka any of my secrets, Checcs. She's a bonafide blabber.

"The world's gonna end soon," the kid says out of nowhere, twiddling his thumbs in his lap. "That's the word around the water cooler, anyways."

"Being funny, huh, kid?" I scoff and cross my arms. "Clearly you watch too much TV. Religious nuts have been talking about an apocalypse for a long time, but the world's still rolling."

Brat shrugs again and scrunches up that button nose. "People don't understand anything. The Old Ones know lots of things. The world is gonna die. But the Old Ones won't let that happen. They are going to save the planet themselves."

"Are they, now?" I look to Checcs for confirmation, but he's too preoccupied with his new ugly friend. "Well, hallelujah. The people of Earth thank them their service."

The boy rolls his eyes so hard that I'm amazed they don't fall out of his head. "They aren't doing it to save people. The Old Ones don't like people, and I don't like them either. So I don't really care."

"Neither do I, so we have that in common. As long as the world waits to end until after I stop the Skin Craft Killer, I'm good."

His eyes seem to light up behind his glasses.

"You're going to stop that serial killer, huh? How do you intend to do that?"

MY turn to brag.

"Oh, just some very critical, one-of-a-kind information in the ol' noggin that Udolthra might be able to do something with. Nothing a kid like you has to worry about."

"I'm not a kid, I died for the first time decades ago."

ICARUS GREAT AT TELLING JOKES.

Moments later, the door opens and out pops Udolthra. She holds the door open for another monster to exit. This one looks made out of stone, with no discernible features aside from long limbs and beady eyes peering out of its disproportionately small torso. It sounds like it's grumbling. I don't see a mouth to grumble from, but it is definitely complaining from somewhere as it stomps out of the waiting room.

Next up is the loud-mouthed pipsqueak. The kid hops off the chair and walks with his companion, side by side. My brain scrambles for a clever quip to end our conversation with me on top.

"Good luck with your stuffed toys and your math, Icarus." Not good, but that's all I could think of.

It was enough. Heh.

Icarus turns on his furry companion so fast that he must have gotten whiplash. Folfrakka immediately shifts into the expression of a guilty dog.

"Remember? Boundaries?" The boy sighs and turns his attention back to me. "Don't listen to her. Good luck with your mid-life crisis."

Bonafide jerk, fun-sized. I just sit and watch as the door closes behind them and Udolthra, looking dumb I'm sure. Checcs hops back up on a chair beside me, and the two of us are left to wait with the others. I glance at my guardian-reaper, cautiously extending my hand in an attempt to pet him. Woosh, right through the little guy. Again. The only thing I make contact with is the fluffy costume he's wearing.

Fine. Maybe we're not besties like that brat and his guardian-reaper, but everybody is different, right? Checcs just has higher standards and is slower to warm than some cartoony toad bear.

I'm not bitter. Nope. YOU'RE bitter.

"Hey, Checcs?" I manage to get half of his attention. "You didn't share anything personal with that monster, did you? You know...about me?"

The other half of his attention flies out the proverbial window.

Calm down. CheccChecc never share boring stories with new friends.

***

After an hour or so of falling in and out of uncomfortable sleep, I'm finally summoned by Udolthra. I feel like I won the lottery! I low-key wipe the drool from my chin and head into the office room at last.

What's on the other side of that door, though, was not what I was expecting. Same organic walls, but what's inside them is nothing but human artifacts being re-purposed in odd ways. A Barbie doll hung on the wall upside-down. A pair of headphones hanging from the ceiling by its cord. A shelf stocked with shoes, jewelry, flashlights, and empty toothpaste tubes. A busted-up computer monitor screen-down on a suitcase, with a frying pan full of comics on top. A mannequin torso with a bunch of random knick-knacks nailed into it. It's like a really weird, abstract art exhibit. Everything seems so comically wrong, yet every element was meticulously placed.

In the center of the room is an actual desk, most likely taken from the mansion upstairs. Udolthra walks around to sit on the bean bag behind it, and for the first time I see my host fully out of costume. Her body is very slim but mostly humanoid, save for the talon feet and creepy pair of T-Rex-like arms protruding from her back. She looks like something that would be eating children in the woods. But as she plops down on her bean bag and enthusiastically gestures for me to sit across from her, all I see is a harmless - albeit slightly crazy - ancient hoarder.

"What is this place?" I ask my host quietly, settling into a plastic folding chair. "I mean, what is it really?"

Udolthra throws up one long, bony finger to stop me.

Payment F I R S T!! Yes yes!

"Oh, right."

Reach into my backpack and fumble around its contents until my hand lands on the 'gift' Algar instructed me to bring. I pull it out and present it to my host, watching her expression nervously.

I guess you could say that her face is...hard to read.

Heh heh.

Long fingers clasp the small black disc carefully, delicately. The strange creature examines the object closely, flipping it around in her hands and searching its grooves for answers.

So B E A U T I F U U U U L. What is flat circle named?

"It's a record. A 45 RPM LP record, to be exact. 'What's New, Pussycat', by Tom Jones."

Udolthra holds the record up to her face and licks it! I flinch. That's not sanitary.

"It's music. You listen to it."

I watch as an exuberant monster shakes my least-favorite LP and presses it to the side of her head.

"Um, you need a record player to listen to it." Maybe I should have thought about that first. Like some ancient monster is gonna have a record player on hand.

However, my gracious host seems perfectly happy with my gift as is. She questions it no further, only clutches it to her sunken chest before slipping it under her desk.

Udolthra will cherish 45 New Pussys by TumJons. Find G

O O O D place for it on the wall. Yes yes.

"It's called 'What's New, Pussycat'...nevermind. I'm happy you like it."

S O! Isabella's first question. This place. Udolthra
took MANY years and MUCH magics to create safe space
for topside Penumbrans.

"So all those creatures back there...what are they here for?"

Penumbrans can only phase topside if a contract binds
them to a human soul. S O O O, soul contracts are
bridge between human world and The Penumbra. When
contracts are broken and souls not collected, bridge
between realities collapses. Penumbrans stuck topside,
no longer capable of travel between worlds. Stuck in
world that doesn't see them, doesn't want them.
Udolthra make home for them here.

Checcs. I can't help but feel a sting of guilt for hurting him. Quickly I look to
either side of me for my guardian-reaper. He's nowhere to be found. Had I seen
him at all since waking up in the waiting room? Maybe he snuck off? I feel
guilty once more for not even noticing before now.

"Is that what happened to you?" I'm genuinely curious. Her response confirms
my suspicion.

Udolthra tasked with collecting soul of Grady Wilkins.
Human made deal for F A M E and F O R TU N E. Eager to
enjoy benefits, less eager to pay. When time came to
collect, and Udolthra appear to Grady, human was
ready.

The eccentric creature takes both hands and imitates what I can only assume is a
shotgun. She then puts it up to her face.

Clickity. Click. B O O O O O M.

Fingers click like they're on a trigger. Udolthra sells the recreation of that fateful
event with a throwback of her head, tongue hanging out. It's as comedic as it is
awful, since everything about this monster is making a little more sense now.

Grady Wilkins wanted to kill Udolthra before Udolthra kill him. Didn't realize that Penumbrans nooooo come to kill humans, only come to collect souls when death is near. B O O O O M to Udolthra, go night-night. Wakey wakey, find Grady Wilkins dead from heart attack. Can't collect soul, too late. Brain different. Stuck topside. Hide body. Start over. The end.

Udolthra ends that note with another creepy yet well-intended grin. I smile back at her nervously, wondering what this poor creature was like before shrapnel embedded itself in her brain. Stupid Grady and his stupid non-mystery mansion.

"Humans can be real dicks," I tell her, leaning back and crossing my arms. Thinking about those who mistreated and misjudged me. Thinking about those I mistreated and misjudged, too. "I'm...really sorry for what happened to you."

The creature before me just waves it off like it's nothing. I wish I were that forgiving.

N O O O O biggie biggie. Human Isabella did not come all this way to learn about Udolthra. Your original question. Ask ask ask.

Right, the whole reason I came here!

"I wanna get a soul back from The Penumbra. How do I do that?"

Why did I say that? That wasn't the reason. Right?

A confused head tilt begins my response. Udolthra assuuuumes Isabella is talking about the soul exchanged for her resurrection? Dayana Cordona?

"I mean, it sounds a little weird when you put it that way, but yeah. It's my mom. She just recently died in an accident and doctors can't reanimate her. It wasn't her time and she's way too important to the world to just disappear. Please."

My eccentric host sighs heavily. Great. I suppose even monsters struggle with breaking bad news.

E V E R Y human ask this question in here. Answer

always always always same. Like humans say: all deals
final. No takesy-backsy. Eyeballs better kept on
future Isabella can change than on past she cannot.
Yes yes.

My heart sinks at this revelation. It's what I was afraid of. What Algar and
CheccChecc tried to tell me.

Reanimation means that nobody has to lose the people they love for good
anymore. My mom brought me back her own way. Now, when I need to bring
her back MY way...it's impossible? All because some stupid contract says so?

It's not fair.

I refuse.

Without another thought, I drag my arm across the desk, knocking space clear.
Udolthra watches with mild surprise as I roll up my sleeves and stretch my arms
out over the sticky surface.

"Prove it. Do that thing you guys do where you download information directly
into the brain. Show me what you're saying is true, otherwise I'm calling bullshit
and walking right out this door to find answers on my own."

W O W Z E R S S S   bad words and SO dramatic.
Humans just like in movies. Okey dokey pokey.

Not another word. Udolthra turns around on her bean bag chair so that her back
is facing me. Damn it, I forgot about those creepy little arms she's rocking back
there. She extends them across the desk, and I'm glad she can't see me wince as I
feel those leathery little appendages make contact with my flesh.

***

A cacophony of mental discord. A painful injection of impossible revelations,
worse than any previously experienced at the hands (or should I say tentacles?)
of my Eldritch familiar.

Worse than the worst hangover imaginable.

They say knowledge is power, but in this case it's more of a nauseating roller-coaster you can't wait to get off of. If I subject myself to that again, I might come out with a liquefied brain. No thanks.

Anyways. I got my answers, only they weren't abridged.

Millennia of contracts made with the Old Ones. Most humans traded their own souls for fame and fortune. Others traded the soul of another for power or immortality. And a rare few traded their own souls to give a loved one a second chance at life. However, no matter the nature of the contract, the soul bargained with is always claimed by the Old Ones in the end. As Udolthra so eloquently said, "no takesy-backsy". All sales are final.

However, most of the knowledge Udolthra gifted me had nothing to do with my actual question. It is very clear that she wanted to show me something else. Images, memories, feelings. A horrible sadness swells inside me in waves. Loneliness and suffering, caused in nearly equal parts by humans and the Old Ones running The Penumbra.

An otherworldly landscape. Shackles. Green fire. The silhouettes of Eldritch creatures larger than Dead Vegas's skyscrapers, sitting upon thrones of throbbing root. It isn't hell. It's something else entirely. It has to be...The Penumbra.

While Eldritch slaves tend to every need below, and reapers risk their lives for souls above, their bloated leaders reap all the benefits. All of them. I'm eerily reminded of a similar dynamic...

But I also feel something else. It's powerful. A great resentment towards mankind in general, one that has lasted since humanity's creation. And a promise that the world will be saved from destruction, no matter the cost.

Wake up. Sleepy human, Always so sleepy.

Eyes wide open. Wipe the drool from my mouth, pretend it didn't happen. Sit up straight, and survey my surroundings.

Back in the waiting room, slumped over uncomfortably in a chair. I guess Udolthra carried my brain-fizzed meatbag back out here to make room for another visitor. A look around the room seems to confirm this, as there is nobody else in this strange space besides myself and CheccChecc. Oh, and that asshole kid with the glasses creeping in the doorway, apparently.

"Checcs! Where have you been?"

The Eldritch monster in bunny pajamas only shrugs.

CheccChecc spoke to others. Made friends. Sort of. Learned things, too.

"Ah yeah, that's right. All those other creatures. That's good. Yeah."

God, my head is pounding so hard I can hear it.

It's a lot to accept. I'm still wrapping my head around the idea that monsters exist, period. Let alone some weird alternate world powered by soul bucks. Then there's all that talk about the end of the world...

"Hey. Checcs? I keep hearing about some end of the world. I thought it was a joke, but it keeps coming up. What does it mean?"

The little guy pauses for a moment, like he's carefully considering his answer.

Old Ones know planet is dying and will save it from destruction.

"No offense, but is that based in religious scripture? Or are these actual plans?"

Both. Happening soon. Sooner than CheccChecc thought.

"Really, now?" I'm still a little skeptical. But how skeptical can you be when you're already talking to an invisible monster? "How will you guys save it, then?"

Stop coming apocalypse. Planet thrives again. The Penumbra can survive on life force of planet instead of human souls. Like in beginning, before humans arrived.

"Hmm. Keeping our souls out of the equation sounds nice. But that's more of a goal and less of a plan. Does that make you the good guys?"

CheccChecc hesitates for a moment, big eyes lost in the middle-ground.

CheccChecc hopes so. Saving planet is good thing. Agree?

Is he looking for approval? Validation? It's the first time I've heard my cheeky guardian-reaper sound unsure of himself.

"Yeah. Saving the planet is a good thing." I feel so..awkward. "Go green! Err..right?"

Silence. My Eldritch companion is back to looking bored with me. I sit there for a moment, looking down at the white knuckles in my lap. What Udolthra showed me: all that resentment for humankind. I wonder...does CheccChecc resent me, too?

I don't wanna hear the answer to that.

"Oh...shit! The Skin Craft Killer!!"

How did I forget to ask? It's only THE reason I flew across the United States and endured that stupid mansion. It's what I CAN change, not what I can't.

"Shitfuck!"

Checcs watches me with mild curiosity as I stand up and stumble to the office door. I don't even knock - just barge right in.

Udolthra is sitting with a different businessman now, and they both turn to look at their uninvited guest. I assume that if Udolthra had eyes, they would be narrowing at me too.

"My original question," I start with a slur, "I still haven't asked my original question."

An uncomfortably long pause. The businessman mumbles something in what I believe must be German. I don't need to speak it to understand he's talking shit.

Time's up. Busy busy B U S Y.

"Please! I'll give you another gift, too!"

Udolthra freezes right there and tilts that tall cranium at me. Frantically, I dig through my back pocket and grab the first thing I find. The creature promptly takes the item from my hand before I can change my mind.

OOH. Hmmm. WHAT IS THIS?

The businessman double-takes at the item and slumps back into his chair. If he could blush right now, he'd be as red as Udolthra's lipstick.

"It's, uh, a spongy napkin to soak up drink spills."

Our monstrous host reflects on the tampon, twirling it in her fingers curiously.

OOH YES. Very HANDY. Udolthra will cherish drink holder.

"So I can ask my original question now?"

A S K   A W A A A A A Y. Quick, tick tock tick tock.

Geez, how do you say this without sounding wacko?

TICK….TOCK...

"Can you do the little arms thing again and go back into my memories to locate a specific person?"

Udolthra thinks on it. The German businessman is getting more impatient, looking at his watch frequently and mumbling under his breath.

DEPENDS. This specific person share connection to The Penumbra? Enlightenment?

I nod emphatically.

P O S I T I V E?

And keep nodding.

Then yes. QUICK. QUICK.

Hello again, t-rex back arms.

Okay. Let's do this.

"The memory - or, the person I wanna locate is - "

H U S S S H H H. Isabella's mind will reveal the human sought. Enlightened minds, tethered. If there is connection in time, Udolthra will find it. And FO L L OW FO LL OW.

Deep breath.

The second my fingertips make contact with her grasping claws, my mind slips miles away again.

...

...

It's different this time.

The air gets knocked out of me, or so it feels. I'm falling into myself, slowing gradually as my blood pressure skyrockets.

Oh God...I hope I don't come out of this as a bigger vegetable than the sweet potatoes back home.

***

"Mom, I'm so sorry! I'm just so scared, I tried finding help, but I couldn't...I couldn't...."

...

"It's okay, mi hija...We will survive this. I won't let him hurt you."

It's a dream within reality. An out of body experience. Watching my final moments with my mother over again, it's more than I can take.

I was horrified then. And as I watch the experience over again, a fragmented memory behind a red filter, it hits me harder. The nuances of my mom's body language. Her tears and mine. Her bravery and my fear. The only peace I have in reliving this moment is the chance to see her face again.

"Leave her alone! Take me and let her go!"

He's back.

Pushing through time and space in slow motion, I watch The Skin Craft Killer approach. Every heavy step of his booted feet echoes through the sewer, through my mind. The functional eyes beneath his black veil fixate on me with a fury mixed with madness. Bloodshot, tormented.

…

"No! You're not hurting her! I'M the one who ran! I'm the one you want!!'

I wasn't wrong. He was going to kill me that night. He was going to kill me right in front of my mom. And who knows what trophies he would have cut from her afterwards.

I can't watch.

…

Please, Udolthra. Make it stop...

That loud crack echoed through the sewer. Metal scraped across cement. I open my eyes once more to that familiar sight. My would-be killer was taken back, sharing the same awe of his captives. Indeed, there was more than one monster beneath the city that night.

CheccChecc.

The moment freezes. It's surreal. Dead silent. Hesitantly, I walk around The Skin

Craft Killer and observe his reaction in the exact moment he saw my guardian-reaper. His expression is obviously hard to read after all those...alterations. But there's enough in those eyes and in his posture. He saw CheccChecc, alright. And he almost appears...scared?

The remainder of the memory continues to play out at rapidly fluctuating speeds. It's like somebody is rewinding and fast-forwarding the memory around me.

"Mom!! Don't!!"

"It's the only way. You must survive, Isabella. Run, and don't look back."

Flames engulf the sewer, so bright that I'm rendered blind momentarily. Good. I don't wanna see this. Not again.

"Mama," I say voicelessly, choking back tears, "I'm so sorry. This was all my fault. It should have been me. It should have been me."

A strange silhouette appears amidst the flames. It's my disfigured body, cradled in the arms and wings of the creature half my size. His little body trembles beneath my weight as he presses on, ignoring the flames licking at his hardened flesh. How I escaped with no burns whatsoever is still a mystery to me, even in this moment as I watch our radiant ascension from the sewers.

I wonder if it hurt him. The fire. The heat.

And I wonder if he was afraid, too.

But I'm still standing there, in the sewers. Watching the Skin Craft Killer flail and burn. My eyes are glued to him and him alone, and for good reason. There are some things you can't see without them destroying you forever.

"It should have been me," I repeat meekly. "It should have been me."

The Skin Craft Killer falls to his knees, most of the flesh burned off his deformed figure. I return my full attention to this psychopath, planting both feet firmly before him. Though I'm surrounded by flames in this hellish memory, I feel no heat. No physical pain. My despair is replaced with rage as I watch the piece of shit responsible for my mom's death suffer before me.

"I'm gonna find you, motherfucker." My whole body is trembling. "And this time, you'll stay dead."

In his final throws, he freezes. His eyes lock in on me - wait, how is that even possible?! Am I imagining it?

I'm staring...into bloodshot eyeballs on the verge of bursting. All the rage I feel in me, I see it in his collection of eyes as they peer into my soul. It's as if he's challenging me right back.

Bring it on, asshole. This time, I'm the predator and YOU'RE the prey.

Suspended once more in time. Sucked into the eyes of the serial killer so fast that it feels like my insides are getting pulled out. Falling through spaces inconceivable. Rising and sinking all at once, pulsating through my own mind until...until…

***

WAKEY WAKEY.

...Huh?

A long nail flicks against my forehead. My eyes roll back into place, and I promptly wipe the drool from my chin as discreetly as possible.

Udolthra's creepy grin is inches from my face. I startle enough that I fall backwards onto the spongy floor of the office.

"How long...was I out?" I'm utterly disoriented. A quick pat down of my person brings some comfort, revealing that my guts are indeed inside my body.

H m m m m. THREE SECONDS. Maybe F O U R ?

"That fast? Shit…"

Under the watchful glare of the German businessman and the blank stare of the estate's monster host, I help myself up to my feet.

"Did you...find out - "

EMERY FARROW.

"...What?" My heart skips a beat. No, multiple beats. All the beats. Shit!

The H U M A N sought. Connected to The PENUMBRA AS ISABELLA PRESUMED. Called EMERY FARROW, and his name is written in B L O O D.

A name! An actual name! I can't believe it!

"Holy crap, you're amazing!" I have this urge to hug Udolthra, but my step towards her is met with a step back and a lip curl. "Um, sorry. Did you see anything else about him? Where he is now, who brought him back?"

The ancient monster takes her seat on the bean bag once more. **Nopes. Human brain is not like fortune teller ball. Udolthra only sees through memories and contracts humans make with Old Ones. They show Udolthra N A M E S. Names are everything. Yes yes.**

"That makes sense...I guess. Thank you. So much."

The businessman clears his throat loudly and crosses his arms.

"Easy, dude, I'm leaving, I'm leaving."

He talks more shit in German, and I'm glad I don't understand it.

I'm halfway out the door when the Penumbran reaches out to me one last time.

UDOLTHRA offers many condolences for Isabella's LOSS. CRUEL FATE. Very different, humans and Penumbrans. Yet both understand S U F F E R I N G, injustice, and isolation. Find the PEACE you need. Okay? Bye-bye.

The Penumbran host waves at me with the same excitement I saw when she was disguised as Malcolm Mansion. I return the wave and make my exit before the businessman can throw any more bad words my way.

"Bye-bye."

That's the last thing I said to a rare being older than the oldest human civilization. A poor creature who suffered at the hands of humans and her own kind alike, and somehow managed to still have compassion for both. As I close the crooked door behind me, I can't help but wonder what she thinks of me. Am I really just like every other human that stepped into that room?

Anyway, I'm done feeling sorry for myself, and I'm sure you're done hearing inner monologue packed with self-doubt. Maybe I should actually listen to Udolthra: focus less on what I can't change, and more on what I can.

Emery Farrow. The Skin Craft Killer.

I was going to find out who you were and leave the rest to the authorities. Let them sort it out.

But after reliving that memory of you and my mom...I think I've had a change of heart.

Is it crazy? Definitely.

Am I equipped for the job? Unlikely.

But this shit is personal. I have a lot to prove and not much else to lose.

Emery Farrow. I'll find you. And I'LL be the one who ends you once and for all.

CHAPTER NINE

"I'm coming with you," the pipsqueak says matter-of-factly, blocking my exit from the bizarre waiting room. It's like I don't have a say in the matter.

"Hmmph. I don't see why you would need to tag along with me. Sounds like you and your bosom buddy have everything figured out already."

"You're going after The Skin Craft Killer."

"Nothing a kid like you should worry about."

OH, ICARUS MUCH WORRIED. TALK ABOUT SKIN CRAFT KILLER ALL OF TIMES.

...Do tell?

Kid crosses his arms and rolls his eyes. His monster familiar follows suit in an almost comical fashion.

"I'm no kid," he complains. "I've been dead longer than you've been alive."

ANOTHER GREAT JOKE. ICARUS MUCH CLEVER.

Gotta stifle a laugh over that tidbit.

"Good for you," I say at last. "Listen, what I'm going to do is dangerous. It's something I have to do alone, plain and simple."

The boy immediately protests, but I've already made up my mind on this. My risky quest for revenge is best suited for me, myself, and I. Besides, I'm really not feeling the company of a pretentious reanimated child and his big-mouthed Fairy Frogmother.

"Sorry, kiddo," I start, "but it's a no. If I'm getting anybody killed with my batshit plan, it'll be me and me alone. See ya."

And away I go, the protests of a pint-sized cold-blood falling behind me. I don't look back. CheccChecc grumbles, and I'm certain he has an opinion on the matter. However, he says nothing. My guardian-reaper simply follows me out the door, plodding away on all fours with his eyes on the ground.

No way I'm gonna feel guilty for telling that kid to back off. It was the right call and I don't regret it.

***

Fluffy. Golden brown. The perfect drizzle of syrup, topped with juicy strawberries.

"Do you guys still sell pancakes here?"

I slide the dusty menu across the table, where a heavy-set woman in a pink apron grabs it with manicured nails. The stitches above her temple crinkle as she furrows her brow.

"You're about ten years too late, sugar."

Can't help but wonder why they haven't changed the menu then. The rumbling of my empty stomach stops me from saying something sassy about it.

"Do you have anything else with calories?"

"We got coffee."

I force a smile. "That'd be great, thanks."

"Anything for your little one?"

Turn and look at the pint-sized monster sitting beside me in his bunny pajamas. I want his opinion, but his face is once more obscured by that goofy-looking rabbit mask.

"Yeah, can I have some sugar packets with it too? If you have some?"

The undead waitress looks like she's judging my parenting approach. Eventually she nods with a smile about as forced as mine, and she's off.

Sigh deeply. Twiddle my fingers on the wooden table, vaguely following the tune of the outdated country music playing from the speakers. Look out the window, see nothing but power lines and dead grass, uneven road and a 2nd Chances billboard that looks decades old.

12 hours to go before my flight back to Dead Vegas. Apparently, time worked a lot differently in Udolthra's magical monster sanctuary. I got what I came for, but what lies ahead feels heavy and uncertain. I have a name - more than anybody has had on The Skin Craft Killer before. I thought I could look up everything on this asshole in a few minutes of internet searching, but I was woefully mistaken. It's like this Emery guy doesn't exist. Well, unless you count the dozens of Emery Farrows across the country with incomplete LinkedIn profiles and dead Facebooks. Nothing seems suspicious about any of them. This might be harder than I thought.

The clink of a ceramic cup on the table. The rush and pour of steaming coffee accompanied by a polite 'thank you'. The waitress drops a few packets of substitute sugar beside my beverage. She seems like she wants to ask me something, but she doesn't. She just nods again and walks off with coffee pot still in hand.

"Here you go, kiddo." I slide the sugar packets in front of CheccChecc. "They aren't milkshakes, but at least they're still sweet."

Checcs finally raises his head slowly. I show him how to open the packets and get the sugar out. He's hesitant at first, but eventually he grabs a pack with his tentacles and shreds it open. Sugar is everywhere, but some of it makes it down his throat.

He spits it out, bringing a little unwanted attention to our booth.

"Um, sorry...It's a sugar substitute. My bad."

Checcs pushes the remaining packets across the table back to me. He seems bored, or maybe just tired.

With a sigh, I take one of the packets and start pouring it into my coffee. The silence between us is deafening. I reflect on what Udolthra showed me regarding Penumbrans and how they feel about humans. I still wonder what Checcs thinks about all this. Ever since we left Grady's mansion, he's been...different.

Waitress pops back over with a big smile on her face.

"Look what I found," she says all sing-songy. Checcs and I watch as the undead woman pulls a lollipop out of her apron. It's old candy, still in its crumpled plastic wrapping. "For the little one."

The ancient lollipop is extended towards a very surprised monster. I wish I could see his face right now. He seems hesitant to take it.

"It's okay," I say in my sweetest, most motherly voice. "You can take it. It's sweet like milkshakes."

Not like foul pellet bags?

Resisting the urge to chuckle, I just smile and shake my head 'no'. Checcs takes the lollipop at last to the delight of our waitress. I thank her and she busies herself once more.

I clear my throat. "As soon as we leave this place, we can get you out of that costume. I know you hate it."

Maybe not so bad. Soft. Also being seen by others is new feeling. Not bad either. Makes humans nicer, too.

Slight pause as Checcs collects his thoughts and I reflect on what he just admitted. Having a chance to be seen by everybody when you're used to being invisible? I get it.

Still stupid costume, though.

I wonder if he's messing with me, but I'm uncertain if he's capable of sarcasm to begin with. It was a lot easier when nobody saw him, but if he really does like his new digs I can't take them away. Not yet. I just wonder what he thinks will happen the next time he tries popping his wings out. A flying 'child' in bunny pajamas miiight bring unwanted attention, if those wings don't tear his costume to bits first. We'll cross that bridge when we come to it. Heh.

A new song on the radio starts to play. A song by Elvis Presley. Not really my thing, but my mom loved his music. Waves of nostalgia wash over me. I remember how Mom would make anything fun, no matter how boring it seemed. God, I miss her.

At that very moment, I made a decision. These 12 hours before the flight would not be spent moping around a rundown diner after reliving my worst memory. I was gonna spend it showing CheccChecc a good time and strengthening our bond. Make something positive out of this trip. It's what Mom would've done.

I wave down our waitress as she walks by and ask her what kinda stuff there is to do in this town. She's quick to give me an answer. Short version? Not much. Not compared to Dead Vegas, anyway.

But I thank her regardless and leave a tip after my cup's empty. I'm already making plans.

"Alright, Checcs," I say optimistically, patting his bunny hood, "we're gonna have some fun, just you and me. You're gonna see how awesome human stuff can be, baby!"

My guardian-reaper takes off his mask and gives me this look. Someone is feeling a little skeptical.

Operation: Monster Party is officially underway.

***

Cue the montage music.

Chasing ducks by a cloudy lake. Checcs is scared of them in the beginning, but by the end he's just upset they won't let him tentacle their faces.

Feathered long-necks mean. Want to eat CheccChecc but have no teeth.

"They won't eat you," I chuckle. "But yeah, they can be little assholes like us sometimes."

Hopping the middle-school fence so we can mess around in the playground. Hopping right back over after a maintenance guy catches Checcs and I on the swings.

Humans get in trouble for hurling bodies around on string chairs?

I pant, safely out of range and out of sight. "Only if they're not your string chairs. Heh. And not if you don't get caught."

Throwing rocks at billboards. I learned my guardian-reaper is a southpaw right before one of his rocks broke the window of an old pickup truck parked outside a gas station. That's when CheccChecc learned what 'Oh shit, let's get out of here!' meant.

Izzie must love trouble. Find everywhere.

"I grew up on a remote island, my dude. Gotta be creative when it comes to entertainment. And besides, I saw your face. Don't pretend you didn't have a little fun."

...Quiet, human.

Dancing to muffled music on the roof of a bar. It's not my favorite genre, but it's got a beat and I'm determined to show Checcs how fun moving to it can be. He was confused at first, staring only at my feet with that curious tilt of his head.

More seizures? Izzie okay? Need saving? His voice echoed through my brain as he stared at me nervously, contemplating rescue.

"No, asshole. It's called dancing, remember? People do it for fun. Don't overthink it, just move your body to the rhythm."

CheccChecc protested a little longer before my peer pressure crushed him. Halfway through the third song, I saw my monster start wiggling his butt and stomping his feet. Proud, I used the opportunity to teach him something else: high fives.

Suddenly my eyes are drawn to a familiar, monstrous bulk on the street below. Next to it is that Icarus kid from Udolthra's waiting room. They're both waving, trying to get my attention.

Not gonna happen, kid.

The faintest reverberations in my temporal lobe. It's that Folfrakka, trying to tell me more things I don't need to hear. Gotta block it out...

Check my watch. Holy crap, only five hours have passed?! Operation: Monster Party is going slower than expected, but it isn't over yet!

"Hey Checcs." He looks over his shoulder at me, bunny ears flopping backwards. "What do you wanna do next?

Little guy just stares at me, unblinking.

Don't understand.

I stoop down so that I'm near eye level with the monster. "We're having fun, right? I've made all the decisions so far, now it's your turn. What do YOU wanna do?"

He seems totally lost, like he's looking for some kind of answer. Either he is utterly unfamiliar with the concept of fun or we're having a communication issue. I hope for his sake it's the latter.

Only job. CheccChecc protect human, fulfill contract.

Sigh. There's my answer.

"Look, I get that this is all foreign to you, thinking outside the job. But I wanna have a good day with you. We got what we came for on this trip, so we ought to celebrate. You like milkshakes, right?"

That makes him perk up! Tentacles rise, eyes widen. Hopping from one clawed foot to the other.

"See? That's what I'm talking about! Milkshakes are, uh, like fun. It's something you enjoy, apart from work. It makes you happy. So think real hard, and tell me what else makes you happy."

216

After a pause, I get my answer.

Fluffy things. Here.

He pets his pajamas again. It's not much, but it's a start!

Also waves.

"Waves?"

Checcs demonstrates with a wave of his hand, well-suited for the back of a parade float.

"Aww I get it. Attention. You need more of that too, huh?"

No. Humans need attention, not Penumbrans. Definitely not CheccChecc. Attention only nice. Like milkshakes. What Izzie said. Understand?

I'm hiding a smile, pretending not to notice the Eldritch pipsqueak getting all defensive.

"Sure, Checcs. Like milkshakes."

Now entering Phase 2 of Operation: Monster Party - Checc Yourself Before you Wreck Yourself.

"Alright, I think I have just the thing for you. Time to make some friends."

***

With only a few hours left before our flight, I can confidently say that Operation: Monster Party was a success!

Phase 2 took us to an animal shelter, where CheccChecc got to meet some friendly cats and dogs. He got his 'waves', alright. The good folks working there were eager to allow a young mother and her 'shy child' to check out the animals, and they showered my bunny-hooded companion with high-pitched greetings and more old candy. The dogs freaked Checcs out a little, but he liked the cats and the cats liked him. Nothing but purrs, face rubs, and curious stares.

Like Eckerd, he told me while letting one young calico sniff his extended mitten. I had no clue he even knew Eckerd! Maybe he was more present back home than I realized?

"Hey Checcs," I asked as we left the shelter, "how do you say 'hello' in your own language?"

Hmm? Why does Izzie want to know?

"There are all kinds of different languages back home on the island. It's awesome. Come on, teach me some phrases. Maybe throw a bad word in the mix too. It'll be our secret."

Still patting cat hair off of his pajamas, my guardian-reaper seems unprepared for my request. He shakes his head and raises his brow at me.

CheccChecc can't teach. Penumbran language inconceivable to humans. Hearing it can drive humans mad. Turn brains to goo.

"Well, shit, dude. Nevermind."

I was, however, pleasantly surprised when Checcs opened up and shared something else he wanted to do: watch sports.

Like roller derby. Much action. Excitement. CheccChecc wants to watch again.

This request was easier said than done. Dead Vegas was full of live sporting events and venues, but this little town? Not so much. However, our continued trek through town led us to the next best thing: a sports bar.

Checcs and I slipped into the back of the rustic establishment, behind a very animated bunch of fellas spilling beer everywhere. A giant TV surrounded by team flags was broadcasting a live football game. Together we watched as reanimated athletes went balls to the wall. The crowd ahead of us hooted and hollered even louder whenever a dead body from the opposing team needed to be carted off for reanimation.

I encouraged my Eldritch companion to join in the cheers and jeers, to which he soon obliged. It's hard to tell sometimes, but I think he was enjoying himself. Those big eyes got wider and those tentacles twitched whenever he witnessed a gnarly tackle or exciting touchdown. It was completely adorable. Well, it was for a while, anyway. One time I got up to use the bathroom, and by the time I came back to our table I saw Checcs guzzling a pitcher of beer he snagged from the distracted fans ahead. Had to make a speedy exit once the tall guy working the bar scolded me for letting my 'child' drink alcohol. Guess I'm not cut out for being a parent yet. Heh.

Potent go go juice, the words slur in my head as we hurry down the street. **CheccChecc feel funny. Fuzzy. Want more.**

"Yeah, I don't think so. It's for adults. Remember?"

Ahhh. Okay. Oooooooh. Kay. Izzie good friend. Izzie should know that.

"Sure thing, buddy."

Trektikzt.

"Um...Gesundheit?"

CheccChecc grabs me with his fluffy mitten and looks me straight in the face holes. I think he's mostly holding me to keep himself steady.

Izzie wanted to learn word in Penumbran. Trektikzt. Bad word. Use when MUCH angry.

I can't help but laugh. "Trektikzt, huh? I like it. I'll save it for when we catch the Skin Craft Killer."

It was a good day. Full of firsts for both of us.

I wonder...are those the sorts of misadventures that Dante and I would've had together?

Now we're waiting at the airport, where I find myself utterly exhausted. I text my friends and Aunt Maggie finally, letting them know I'm alright. Slump into my chair, watching the weather warnings on the overhead monitor as I fidget with my ticket.

"You ready for the long flight back to the city, little guy?"

No answer. I glance over to the seat beside me, expecting to see CheccChecc hungover. Instead, I see a very pensive monster seemingly lost in thought.

"You alright, Checcs? You look a little blue behind the face worms."

Finally, my guardian-reaper gives in. He doesn't look at me, only speaks directly to my mind once more.

CheccChecc heard things at Penumbran sanctuary. New things. Bad things.

Hmm? I sit up straight. "You did, huh? From the other monsters? What did they tell you?"

Old Ones making first move to stop apocalypse. Sooner than expected.

"But that's...not so bad, right?"

About that. Apocalypse not what Izzie thinks.

"Don't tell me you haven't sobered up yet. You're officially weirding me out, dude. Spit it out already."

He leans forward with tentacles out, ready to grab me again. I pull my arm away quickly.

"No. Don't take the easy way out. Just tell me."

An uncomfortably long pause ensues. CheccChecc holds himself and sighs beneath his tentacles.

Planet dying. Last chance at saving. Apocalypse Penumbrans will

stop is...

"Hey, lady."

Hmm?

I turn around and sure enough, a familiar pair is back on my tail: Icarus and his Penumbran pal, Folfrakka. I have to give it to him: he's definitely persistent. Stomping up to me like a petulant child, arms crossed.

"Listen, I already told - "

"His far right eye, middle row," he says out of nowhere.

"Excuse me?"

"That's what he took from my brother."

It takes a moment for me to register what I just heard. Suddenly, I'm hit with the gravity of those words. My skin grows clammy as I stop and look at Icarus wearily.

"You're not the only one who lost somebody to The Skin Craft Killer."

He's right. Over twenty victims, that was the count. That's a lot of suffering for the families of those victims. Sadness. Survivor's guilt. And rage. Plenty of rage.

...

PLEASE. ICARUS NEED FRIENDS MUCH BADLY.

Heh. Really, how could I say 'no' after that?

"Alright. But it'll be dangerous. If we confront him, ya know, for real...Will you be okay?"

Icarus holds his head up high with a confidence that contradicts the subtle trembling of his tiny hands.

"Will YOU?"

Honestly? The answer to that question presently eludes me.

"I'll be okay when that fucker's in the ground for good."

My new partner nods, extending his hand towards me enthusiastically. The firmness of his handshake is startling. His resolve rivals my own. Maybe this will be a fruitful partnership after all.

"It's a deal, then. But I'm in charge. And I don't do babysitting, so try to keep up."

Or maybe I spoke too soon. Cheeky little bastard.

***

"Welcome to the RezCity Digital Archive, a subsidiary of the National Digital Archive for Historic Research. Please state the reason for your visit."

"Research."

The robotic librarian rotates at its waist with a faint buzz. It focuses those disc-like eyes on me and my pint-sized partners, issuing another default answer through the speaker in its grinning face.

"Please be more specific."

"We need to research The Skin Craft Killer."

"I'm sorry. SPIT CAT FILLER is not a permitted reason for visitation."

Icarus and I exchange eye rolls.

"SKIN CRAFT KILLER," I try again.

"I'm sorry. SKIN CRAB PILL HER is not a permitted reason for visitation."

Heh. Izzie bad at own language.

"Oh, shut up, Mr. Use Complete Sentences Only When You Feel Like It."
The robot flips those disc eyes as if to blink at us.

"Hurtful language is not permitted at the RezCity Digital Archive."

Icarus pushes me aside and stands toe to wheel with the oh-so helpful librarian.

"We're here for a school project on cats."

Pivot pivot. Those discs glow green as they flip with increasing frequency.

"Reason for visitation - POOL ROCKETS ON BATS - is approved. Access to Study Room 10020 B is granted. Please enjoy your visit to the RezCity Digital Archive: your portal to infinite learning. And fun."

The librarian rolls back into the wall, where its body seems to power the heavy doors directly to its left. A deep rumble sounds beneath our feet. The digital sign above the door changes names rapidly before stopping on 'STUDY RM 10020 B'.

Ding. Doors slide open.

WOW! HUMAN MAGICS! Folfrakka claps excitedly, but slows to a stop after noticing nobody joined her in applause.

My little monsters and I hurry through and...into total darkness. Not for long, though. Once the doors close fully behind us, the temperamental lights of the room power on.

The study room is uncomfortably small. Two touch-screen computers on opposite walls, with full-length monitors on the others. A decent size for a party of two but a little cramped for two kids and two monsters. Good thing at least half of us can phase through dusty chairs.

Directly to work we go.

My flight to Dead Vegas had been canceled. Maybe for the best. When I told Icarus my internet searches for Emery Farrow were fruitless, he immediately had another solution.

"You can't always trust the internet. Duh. Look him up the old-fashioned way."

Lucky for us, just out of town was RezCity. It's one of the nation's fully automated cities, a little older than me and home to a variety of outdated services.

So we scour public records. Birth certificates. Death certificates. Anything that can possibly bring us closer to finding the man behind The Skin Craft Killer. Thankfully, Icarus had been doing his own research as well. Together, we were able to narrow down the Emery Farrows of the country until we were sure we found our guy.

Born in North Carolina, in 1967. He had a fairly normal life, fixing watches and working as a doctor in his small town. He married the daughter of a preacher and had two kids: a son and a daughter. Was drafted into the early Undead Wars as a combat medic. Survived it and came back home, different. Reportedly asked for help from the government and his community, but his requests fell on deaf ears. There was no help. No support. It's enough to almost make me feel bad for the person he once was.

Multiple failed suicide attempts. Eventually he abandoned his family and fell off the grid. The last official record of his existence was a mental health report in 2002, right before he was admitted to an insane asylum a couple states over. He complained about "voices in his head". Classic crazy stuff. A search into the asylum went nowhere - the place was demolished decades ago.

Naturally, attention falls on his family. Icarus and I couldn't help but exchange our excitement. We might actually be narrowing in on something here.

His wife remarried and moved the kids out of state. She never looked back. His son was eventually drafted into the Undead Wars as well, where he died a permanent death. His daughter followed her father's footsteps and became a doctor in Seattle. A career woman: unmarried, no kids. She died a natural death and was reanimated by colleagues. By the look of things, she's still practicing on Illaria, one of several environmentally friendly cities built on airships above the heavy smog that covers most of the United States.

"Those airship cities are real?" I'm floored. I've seen them in movies, but they sounded too fantastic to be true.

Icarus sighs and rolls his eyes. "Uh, yeah. They are. A bunch of rich people built them, thinking they were the future of humanity. Undead people against reanimation and its impact on the environment. Lots of people hate 'em. Mostly conservatives who think they're all a bunch of hippy dippy liberal hypocrites."

"Heh. Wow. What do YOU think of them?"

The boy shrugs. "My parents hated 'em, too. But I don't feel that way. If those people wanna try and do somethin' good for the planet, that's a good thing I think. Plus the airships are kinda cool."

"Yeah, you'd think that. You probably see stuff like that in your favorite Saturday morning cartoons."

I chuckle at my own crappy joke, plenty amused. Ignore the fact that I also think airship cities are rad as hell. My dad would've loved them. Dante probably would've loved 'em, too. Icarus throws a crumpled piece of paper at my face in response.

"Again, not a kid. Cartoons are for kids and sheltered island warm-bloods who type like cavemen."

"What?! Are you insulting my keyboarding skills?"

The pipsqueak returns his attention to the glow of his own monitor. "You're doing your best. That's all that matters."

NOT BEST. ICARUS TELL FOLFRAKKA THAT IZZIE IS MUCH TERRIBLE. COULD BE BETTER.

...Thanks, frog face.

A warbled laugh emits from underneath CheccChecc's tentacles.

I whip my head around and give him a warning finger. "Don't you say anything, Checcs."

CheccChecc not say anything. Only enjoy good conversation.

They yuck it up a bit, and it's very evident that the mood has lifted. We're actually on to something here. We finally have someone we can go to for more answers: The Skin Craft Killer's daughter. After a minor debate, we agree that our best bet is to pay a visit to Illaria and talk to the doctor herself. If we're lucky, she just might give us valuable intel to help us catch our killer.

Or she's the one who stole her dad's brain and had him reanimated. And she'll kill us on the spot for asking about him.

Fifty-fifty, really.

***

"Holy crap, tickets cost $5,000? Each?!"

"We could just fly up there."

Icarus gives a lazy thumbs up while leaning all the way back against a park bench. His monster pal looks at him and mimics the thumbs up in my direction. I'm skeptical that Folfrakka can even fly, until I remember how well CheccChecc can hide his wings. I give up trying to figure out how these monsters work.

I put my phone down in my lap, defeated. "Says the guy who weighs under 60 pounds. I don't think Checcs can carry my fat ass all that way up."

Bunny ears flop back and forth as my guardian-reaper shakes his head.

No chance.

"Besides, those airships fly with big engines and propellers or something, right? Wanna get sucked into one and turned into human confetti?"

HUMAN CONFETTI SOUND FUN! LIKE BIRTHDAY PARTY!

That finally gets his attention. He's sitting up straight, one eyebrow raised.

"That's inappropriate," Icarus tells me. Heh.

"Then what do you suggest, smart guy?"

"Your family's loaded, right? Plus you're famous. Just buy tickets. Duh."

"Dude, I'm mostly famous for surviving The Skin Craft Killer. If they know I'm coming, his daughter won't wanna talk to me. Especially if she's the one who got him reanimated."

"Then you don't have to go. Folfrakka and I will handle this ourselves."

Icarus hops onto his little loafers and tries walking right past me. A deep sigh and an arm out in his face stop him fast in his tracks.

He sniffs. "You've got B.O."

"YOU are B.O."

"That doesn't even make sense."

"Listen, twerp. You're the one who begged to join me. BEGGED."

"No, I didn't."

ICARUS DEFINITELY BEGGED. DESPERATE AND LONELY CHILD.

"Yes, you did, and Folfrakka agrees. If you don't need me, then why did you pester me to bring you along?"

The boy's gaze darts away from mine. The bulbous eyes of his monster companion seem to look right through him, concerned.

"You looked a little lost. Like a scared puppy. So Folfrakka and I thought we would help."

"Sure," I scoff. I'm over it. Whatever's on his mind, he's not gonna share it with the class. "CheccChecc and I are fine on our own. Good luck, kiddo."

Now it's HIS turn to act like the scared, lost puppy. His exclamation as I turned my back on him was priceless. I hide my smile as I turn around.

"There's another way we can get there," Icarus interjects, "ticket and human confetti-free."

"And that would be…"

A sinister smile crosses that munchkin face. Almost in unison, Folfrakka grins this creepy grin and puffs out her chest along with him.

"Mind control," Icarus proudly announces.

…I'm listening.

***

Sometimes the vastness of a place can feel so powerful and profound. I felt that way the first time I was down on the streets of Dead Vegas. And now, standing in this Colorado airport a long bus-ride south from RezCity, I'm feeling that sense of awe all over again.

Everything is so perfect and clean and…expansive. The ceiling is taller than the cliffside my home was built on. Escalators and glass elevators everywhere. I've never seen anything like them in person before. Flashing signs and holographic ads dotting ivory walls. People shuffling in and out all around us, but with an order that is almost robotic compared to the sporadic flow of travelers at the Dead Vegas airport. It all feels so surreal.

A nudge to my ribs pulls me out of the daydream.

"Come on, we gotta hurry," my annoying new companion reminds me before scurrying ahead with Folfrakka. "Take-off is in less than thirty minutes!"

I tug at the straps of my backpack and hustle onward. A quick glance at CheccChecc tells me that he is equally focused on the task at hand, moving to all fours at an energetic pace. It's almost weird seeing him without his bunny pajamas right now. He wasn't exactly excited to get out of costume, but he understood why we needed him invisible. At least for now. I assured him that his pajamas would remain safely tucked inside my backpack.

A few confused stares and security checks later, we reach the line for airship boarding. With the mass amount of security guards and cameras here, it's safe to assume that random guests to Illaria are highly uncommon.

Um. I'm getting sweaty.

I'm not sure how we're gonna make this work. Mind control? Am I crazy to believe this kid or what?

As we fast approach the tall gentlemen working the desk, Icarus shushes me needlessly and grabs my hand.

"Follow my lead," he whispers. I wanna pull my hand out of his little gremlin paw, but now's not the time. Not with a bunch of wrestler-sized security dudes watching our every move.

An old lady dressed like a politician finishes her transaction and gets her shiny golden ticket, hassle-free. We're next.

The guy helping us furrows his brow and cocks his head. A muffled voice can be heard in his earpiece.

"Excuse me. Are you two...lost?"

"Nuh uh!" says Icarus in his cutest little kid impersonation. He grabs my hand tighter and shakes it playfully. "My stepsister and I are here to board the airship Illaria."

"Really, now? What organization are you affiliated with?"

I have no clue what to say. Thankfully, the energetic boy beside me seems to have all the answers.

"We're here on behalf of the Noah Jake Jackson Foundation."

The two men behind the desk look at each other incredulously. It's more than obvious that they aren't buying it. One of them leans in closer and really looks me over.

"You look familiar. Are you that girl who survived - "

"Nope," I'm quick to answer and take a step back. "But I get that a lot."

"Last name?" Suspicious Guy #1 asks at last.

"Troponski."

"Spell that, please."

As Icarus spells out the name he obviously just made up, my heart starts racing. I feel everyone's eyes on us, and it's making me want to escape again. I'm trying so hard to keep my cool and put my trust in the miniature liar clutching my hand. Thankfully, my guardian-reaper is there to save me from myself again.

Nothing to fear. Human minds fragile. Folfrakka handle with strong magics.

I sure hope he's right.

Click click click, tap tap tap.

Suspicious Guy #2 looks up from the glow of his computer monitor and narrows his eyes at us.

"I don't see any Troponskis on this list."

The other guy talks into his headpiece as if we aren't there.

"I have a black warm-blood adolescent and a white reanimated child here claiming to have tickets to Illaria."

Security guards are closing in! Shit! Whatever this kid's monster is gonna do, she better do it quick!

"Aww, there must be some kinda misunderstanding," Icarus says with pouty lips. "Check again."

The boy signals to his monster pal, and she nods. It's showtime. As the two men look from us to their monitors, the invisible Folfrakka clammers around the desk so that she's between them.

"Hey hey hey! Sorry for the misunderstanding, fellas, these two are with me!"

What?

Folfrakka freezes and tilts her head, confused. Icarus and I toss a suspicious look over our shoulders in unison.

Right behind us in line is an overly enthusiastic guy dressed like a geeky tourist. He's gotta be in his mid-twenties, with an average height and build. Clark Kent-lookin' face, complete with slick hair and thick-rimmed glasses. He struggles to push them up while adjusting the strap of his disproportionately large backpack. The most interesting thing about him? He's an actual warm-blood!

"Name, please?"

"Mikal Forrenson," he replies promptly. He looks to me for permission to step ahead. Icarus and I exchange glances. The boy furrows his brow before shrugging. Folfrakka appears genuinely disappointed that she couldn't use her powers yet. I am, too.

We wave this guy in, and he nervously hustles forward to the desk. Apparently, the dude's name is immediately located on the list.

"Oh, a sponsored guest, I see," says one of the receptionists with wide eyes. "Congratulations. Please, right this way."

"They're comin' with me, too," Mikal gestures towards us exuberantly.

"You know them?"

Mikal snorts. "Only of course! You recognize THE daughter of Dayanna Morales Cordona, right? THE founder of the warm-blood sanctuary? Huh?"

I wanna shrink away. Both guys working the desk examine me closely, and I hear some murmurs from the nearby security guards.

"If so, then why did she give us a fake - "

"Aww, come on now!" Our unexpected supporter waves it off with another snorty laugh. "She's being shy, and can you blame her? She's only a celebrity! Hah!"

Without a second thought, I shush the guy. He continues with a degree of forced reserve.

"Oh, sorry!" The rest is a low whisper. "I mean, can you blame her? Daughter of a humanitarian, survivor of the Skin Craft Killer? I wouldn't want all the attention either!"

Mikal continues to chat with the receptionists a little longer, keeping it low. I can't make out everything he's saying, but it appears to be working. The guys at the desk finally give in. Folfrakka lets out another sigh before returning to her incredulous companion's side.

"Alright, you're all clear," we hear at last. "Enjoy your visit to Illaria."

Our unexpected supporter waves us after him energetically. He's quickly heading through the unlocked doors, whistling to himself. Icarus and I look at each other again. I've got no clue what to think of this new development, but there isn't much time to contemplate it. We got our free ticket to Illaria, and that's good enough.

***

Once we're down another hallway and past another security check, we have a brief moment of silence before boarding for Illaria.

"Why did you help us back there?" I ask out of nowhere. Maybe I shouldn't question it, but I've learned to be skeptical about random acts of kindness. For better or worse.

"Are you kidding me?" Mikal snorts, shifting his weight from leg to leg beneath his heavy backpack. "I'm just stoked to meet you! Your mom did some super amazing things for us warm-bloods. You deserve a visit to Illaria more than I do! Hah!"

The guy seems...sincere. He's dorky and more awkward than I am, but there's nothing threatening about him. Even the grumpy Icarus has to give in a little.

"So, uh...have you been to Illaria before?"

"Nope!" Mikal shrugs. "Always wanted to visit, though! Illaria is one of a handful of airships promoting alternative living to improve the planet's health. If it's successful enough, these airship cities might become the way of the future! Floating cities over the vast blankets of smog! Pretty crazy, right?!"

"Yeah, pretty crazy."

"So what is a fancy 'sponsored guest' like yourself doing in Illaria exactly?" Icarus's voice is full of skepticism. He is definitely no longer playing the role of 'doe-eyed little boy'.

But we don't get the answer to that. The floor trembles slightly as an enormous elevator lowers to the platform ahead of us. The few others waiting ahead of us are allowed on by a set of well-dressed guards. We're last in line, and we shuffle onto the elevator and take a seat in one of the corners. Everybody is instructed to belt themselves in. Folfrakka and CheccChecc watch as we belt up, and Icarus gestures for his companion to hold on to something. Folfrakka does just that, grabbing onto the handrail that wraps around the length of the elevator. CheccChecc, on the other hand, ignores the warning and flaps his wings proudly, as if to say he doesn't need any support.

After several rounds of seatbelt checks and safety guidelines, we're finally ready for take off. I'd be lying if I said I wasn't a little bit nervous.

An automated voice over the intercom echoes through the large elevator chamber.

"Now departing for Illaria in 5....4....3..."

Deep breath. Sweaty hands gripping my seatbelt.

"2..."

Icarus isn't even scared. He's almost bored. When I notice how unaffected he is, I try to act bored, too.

I don't think I'm pulling it off, though.

"1. Enjoy your ascent."

***

Ding.
The great glass doors of the elevator open up at last, revealing a large dock platform miles and miles above the city below.

Mikal and the others pour out of the elevator with luggage in tow.

Me?

I need a moment.

We just spent a few minutes blasting hundreds of miles into the air at frickin' warp speed. At least it sure as hell felt like it! My stomach shot up into my head and back down into my foot. I had to talk myself down from barfing and screaming, not necessarily in that order. I thought the transportation of the future was supposed to be...I don't know, peaceful? That took a few years off my life, that's for sure. Icarus attempts that familiar poker face as he exits, but I can tell that he didn't enjoy the ride either. He's got sunken eyes behind those glasses of his as he leans against Folfrakka for support.

"You alright, Checcs?"

CheccChecc not want to talk about anything.

Yeah, I bet he doesn't. Mister tough guy spent the whole flight up bouncing around the walls of the elevator, his wings doing little to save him. The other passengers heard the racket and worried that the elevator was breaking down. Nope. Just one arrogant monster who probably should have heeded the safety guidelines.

At the end of the platform ahead is the floating city itself. It's gotta be half the size of the sanctuary island! Eclipsed in the shadow of a blimp, an enormous mass of fiberglass sitting atop row after row of propeller blades. Adrift in a swirl of clouds, a city as likely to be plucked from the earth as it is from a dream.

I hesitate a moment, my heart pounding from my chest like it's trying to escape.

I want to run towards Illaria as much as I want to run away from it.

But I'm not running anymore, damn it! Dr. Farrow awaits!

After a deep breath, I press forward with the crowd. Checcs is ahead of me now, but Icarus? He's still with Folfrakka on the platform. The kid is grimacing almost, and I wonder if he even realizes he's doing it.

"Yo, Icky Sticky! Time to go!'

"Don't call me that."

The boy's swift and stern response throws me off. I stop mid step to toss him a concerned look over the shoulder. He's pouting hard, and I can't resist.

A mischievous grin crosses my lips. "Icky Sticky, Icky Sticky, Icky - "

Icarus stomps his foot. "I said stop it! Never call me that!"

At that moment, I realized the kid wasn't joking. Folfrakka pats his shoulder comfortingly. I feel like an asshole already.

"My brother used to call me that."

"Hey. I'm sorry. You and your brother...you guys were pretty close, huh?"

The boy crinkles his nose and puts his hands in his pockets, all nonchalant.

"You said we have to go, right? So let's go."

Fair enough.

Humans hard to comprehend. Say one thing and mean another. CheccChecc can't keep up.

Checcs sighs under those tentacles and follows after Folfrakka and Icarus as they quickly pass us. As I take up the rear, I can't help but agree wholeheartedly with my companion's assessment.

CHAPTER TEN

"Ladies and gentlemen, welcome. To our beautiful home in the clouds, Illaria!"

'Oohs' and 'aahs'. Flash photography. Note-taking and pocket-book fondling.

I'm reminded of the tour of Grady's Haunted Mystery Mansion, only this time the crowd strikes a greater resemblance to the donors at my mom's fundraiser in Dead Vegas. Nothing but snobby undead assholes, only most of them are lodged inside expensive synthetic bodies. It's like being surrounded by androids in Armani suits.

Our host for the afternoon is none other than the founder of Illaria himself. Don't ask me what his name is, because I already forgot it. There's something about him I just don't like. He's more uptight than the crowd surrounding us. A tall white dude with immaculate blond hair, and a stupid bluetooth in his ear. His lack of charisma is enough to make me actually miss Darcy. He goes on and on for a while longer about his dream for a better future being realized, his accolades, his upcoming autobiography, blah blah blah. I only tune back in after Icarus elbows me.

"Illaria is one of three prototype communities built on groundbreaking aerial technology made possible through the cooperation of ESTRID Industries and the Federal Aviation Administration. We pride ourselves in building one of the world's most sustainable communities, with a carbon footprint 65 percent lower than the average U.S city alone. The air quality up here is between 70 and 80 percent cleaner than the nationwide average. Additionally, Illaria is crime-free, solar-powered, and self-sufficient." The founder pauses for a moment, fixating on me and Mikal before an arrogant grin spreads across his thin face. "I see that we have a couple warm-bloods joining us today. It is my honor to welcome you to our fine city. You will find it is equipped to meet the needs of the living and the undead alike."

The remainder of the crowd turns to face the only warm-bloods of the group, a mixture of awe and confusion in their layered voices. Mikal and I share a similar discomfort under the attention, but it's gone only moments later. Thank God for that. Besides, there are way more impressive things to see around here.

And no doubt about it, Illaria is impressive indeed. Everything looks expensive, avant garde in some areas and utterly minimalistic in others. Spiral fountains several stories tall, bizarre art installations made of metal and glass, and buildings composed of white boxes stacked on one another like houses of cards. Ornate street lamps, minimal advertisements, and a variety of foliage that looks too perfect to be real. I hate to admit it, but the illustrious city in the sky might just live up to the hype.

We continue through the city in an orderly fashion. I've already seen an art gallery, a law firm, a library, a tailor, a hospital, and a variety of high-end fashion stores through downtown Illaria alone. The city's founder is rambling the entire time, mostly about himself. Everyone around me is enthusiastically taking notes, including Mikal. I wish I could say I shared the same interest in pompous ego-stroking.

"Since the dawn of life itself, mankind has looked to the sky and dreamt about what lies beyond the clouds. Now, my friends, we have fully realized what the sky holds for the future of humanity. Nay, for the future of planet Earth itself. By investing in groundbreaking new civilizations like Illaria, we can continue to dream about a future beyond the clouds. A brighter, safer, and more sustainable life for all. It is MY dream, that one day humanity will forsake its failures on the surface below and build a new future for humanity amidst the clouds. Together, we can make our dreams a reality."

Mr. Bluetooth concludes his corny speech with a bow, and he is met with poised applause and a few more photographs. While most of the crowd stays behind for questions and handshakes, Icarus and I slip out and on our way. Our monster companions aren't far behind, equally in awe of the expansive city surrounding us.

Air city impossible, Checc pipes up at last. **Hard to fathom humans capable of creating such place.**

"Right there with ya, little dude," I reply with a dreamy sigh. "This place really is something else."

No doubt about it. I'm a loooong way from the island I call home.

What would my mom have thought of this place? Aunt Maggie? They both saw all sorts of crazy things in their adventures. Maybe I'll finally have my own crazy stories to share, too.

Doctor Farrow's office is much like the rest of Illaria.

Extra.

It looks like an expensive spa at some vacation resort. Zen music playing from integrated speakers. A cube-shaped fountain under a skylight. A few potted plants, acting as the only natural contrast to all the straight edges and plain walls everywhere else. The chairs of the waiting room look more like art installations than actual furniture.

Bonk. Crack.

Back to reality. Spin around and notice that an overly curious CheccChecc knocked one of the plants over. Everybody in the waiting room turns to look at who's responsible, only they're incapable of seeing the culprit. I'm left to right the plant and put handfuls of escaped dirt back into its pot.

"Easy here, little dude," I whisper to my klutzy companion. "Everything here looks expensive."

Then humans shouldn't put expensive everythings out to touch.

"You're not supposed to touch it in the first place. Claws to yourself."

"Can you guys stop bickering like babies?" Icarus, being oh so helpful. I ignore him and turn back to Checcs.

"Listen, you gotta wait back here. Icarus and I will handle this."

What if humans get killed by killer's spawn?

"Have you seen this place? That won't happen, I'm sure."

No way Izzie would survive. Child, maybe. Izzie? Not possible.

"Thanks for the vote of confidence. I'm perfectly capable of handling myself, believe it or not."

Okay. CheccChecc does not believe.

Icarus snickers and exchanges looks with Folfrakka, who has taken a seat by the fountain.

IT'S ALRIGHT! ISABELLA SHOULD NOT FEEL BAD. MANY HUMANS INCAPABLE OF TAKING CARE OF THEMSELVES.

"Oh, shut up, all of you."

I'm starting to get a few confused stares, despite my hushed tone. Geez. Gotta wrap this up.

"Listen, Checcs, we'll both be fine. Alright? Remember bathrooms? How boring you say they are?"

Hmm, yes. CheccChecc die of boredom first.

"Right. Well, this doctor visit is basically the same thing. Boring stuff. So chill out here and don't touch anything, alright? We'll be back."

CheccChecc shrugs and plops down on one of the empty seats. His little legs dangle off the edge, and he looks like he's already bored. Heh. Good enough for me.

Onward, ho!

"Can I help you?"

Focus my attention now on the petite receptionist behind a glass window ahead of me.

"Uh, yes, we're here to see Dr. Farrow."

"Do you have an appointment?"

"No. We just have to talk to her real quick."

The brunette receptionist finally looks at me over her glasses. One eyebrow is raised, and I'm not looking forward to the answer that's bound to follow.

"You can't see Dr. Farrow without an appointment."

"It'll be really fast, though."

"You still can't see her without an appointment."

"Mommy, the pretty lady doesn't want me to live?"

Holy crap, Icarus. Clearly, he has picked his plan of attack on this one. I look at him, and once again he is in full character. Doe-eyed, grabbing my hand tightly. If only this poor lady knew.

The receptionist leans forward to see the precocious child telling her sweet little lies. Icarus is pouting, on the verge of tears.

"Oh hi, little guy! Of course I want you to live! What's wrong?"

It's silent for a moment as the two of us think of a lie. We come up with a different one simultaneously.

"A brain tumor!" I attempt.

"Cancer!" Icarus cries.

We look at each other. I finish it up.

"A cancerous brain tumor. We've exhausted our options, and we heard Dr. Farrow is the best doctor around. Didn't we, son?"

Icarus nods his head emphatically.

"Poor thing," coos the receptionist, checking her computer. "But Dr. Farrow still can't see you without an appointment. I have an opening in....four weeks. How does that sound?"

The water works begin. I gotta hand it to Icarus. He could make a killing as a child actor.

"Mommy, I'm not gonna make it! I'll die before the nice doctor lady can save me!" Icarus starts sobbing harder and hugging my leg. "The brain tumor will eat my brain and I'll die for real! I don't wanna die, Mommy! Mommy!!"

The other people in the waiting room are getting concerned now. Some of them start urging the receptionist to have a heart. I play things up, attempting to calm my inconsolable child. Thankfully, the escalating scene and accompanying pressure break the receptionist down.

"Alright, alright, it's okay. It's okay. I'll let Dr. Farrow know you're here. One moment, please."

As the poor woman turns to phone the doctor, I give Icarus a little pat on the back for a job well done. Checc's warbled laugh can be heard behind me.

"She will see you now," sighs the receptionist behind a tired smile.

Shortly after, a nurse steps out of the door ahead, beckoning us to follow. I thank the receptionist and grab a handful of old candy from the swan-shaped dish beside her desk before following the nurse.

Here's hoping it's all worth it.

***

"What do you want? Money?"

Dr. Farrow isn't wasting any time. Her pale eyes are obscured by her tousled blonde hair and thick glasses, but I can tell that they barely leave the clipboard in her arms.

She wasn't especially pleased to hear our actual reason for meeting her. Even less prepared for what we knew about her pops.

"Um...What?" I'm caught off guard. "No, ma'am. We're not here for - "

"We aren't trying to blackmail you." Icarus is done with the kid act. "We're here for information, that's it."

"Well, I can't help you." Though the doctor is frail and whiter than a marshmallow, she's tough as nails. If she could hit a button and drop us through a trap door to be done with us, she would.

"But we came all this way, just to talk to you!" I whine, blocking her from opening the door for us. "I get that it's a tough subject, but we can't stop Emery without your help! Please!"

"I don't talk about my father for a reason," she says flatly. "I do not condone his actions and I want nothing to do with him."

"Then you must understand why we have to stop him!" Icarus joins in, his little voice dripping with conviction. "Don't pretend you didn't see the news. He got reanimated and he's already killing again! Don't you even care?"

"I've worked very hard to get where I am today," she continues with a hushed tone, scanning the room as if she were looking for spies. "And if anybody learns of my ties to this...murderer...then my very practice could be in jeopardy. All the trust I've worked to build up would be lost."

Icarus gets up close to her, puffs out his chest and stands on his tip toes.

"Do you think we care about your practice and your trust? Maybe YOU were the one who stole The Skin Craft Killer's brain and brought him back. Maybe people would be right to not trust you."

Dr. Farrow is having none of the pipsqueak's threats. She sits her clipboard down and stands her ground.

"Watch your mouth, child. I could have you both thrown out in a matter of seconds. Hell, I could throw you out of Illaria just as fast. It doesn't matter who your accomplice is, I will not be threatened in my own office."

I put a hand on Icarus's shoulder, urging him to back down. He shakes my hand off, but he does stop. The kid steps back and crosses his arms.

"Listen," I offer quietly, "we're both here because The Skin Craft Killer took someone from us. If he isn't stopped, he's gonna keep hurting more people. We need to find him, but we can't do that without your help."

Dr. Farrow sighs and blows a strand of hair out of her face.

"I can't help you. I have too much to lose here. I'm sorry. I really am."

"So you don't care if more people die, huh?"

Did I just say that? I'm supposed to be the voice of reason. Good cop, and all. *Calm down, Izz. You can talk your way out of this and convince the good doctor to help. Just keep your cool and try this again...*

"As long as you can keep living your pretty little life in the clouds, you don't care at all!"

Oops. Take Two...

"Oh, I'm the Skin Craft Killer's daughter, and I don't give two shits who gets their heads bashed in! La la la, I don't hear any of it, la la la, nothing can hurt me in the clouds, la la fuckin' la dee dah BULLSHIT!"

...Wrong again. Good job, brain.

Silence. Icarus uncrosses his arms and raises an eyebrow at me.

Gulp.

Dr. Farrow grabs her phone and storms between us. She dials someone and throws the door open.

"I want you both out of my office. Now."

So that's that. Mission utterly failed. We're rushed out the door and escorted out. I want to protest, but a little elbow to the leg from Icarus keeps me in check. Making matters worse, it is abundantly obvious that CheccChecc did not listen to my instructions. While Folfrakka minded her own business by the fountain where we left her, CheccChecc managed to knock over another potted plant and a few golf magazines from the coffee table. When I first spotted him, he was rifling through some lady's oversized purse as she slept in her chair.

"AHEM!"

Checcs snaps out of it and hops back to my side, Folfrakka close behind at a docile pace. My guardian-reaper is acting innocent. Nice try.

But there's no time left to fix anything we fucked up. I hand off some waiting room candy to CheccChecc and jet for the exit before Dr. Farrow and her receptionist can retaliate any further.

***

"Now what, big mouth?"

Strumming my fingertips upon the patio table outside a winery. I smell lemon cleaner. Hard to miss, with my face firmly planted on the resinated wood.

The crunch of candy can be heard beside me. Checcs, no doubt.

Izzie great at making friends.

"Shut up, both of you," I grumble. "Not like either of you helped the situation. Folfrakka is the only sensible one here."

I raise my head just in time to see Folfrakka nod with that contented grin of hers.

MUCH TRUE. FOLFRAKKA FULL OF CENTS AND ABILITY!

"It's not like we can just bail," I continue, brushing matted hair out of my face. "Next stop is in two days."

"Unless you get us kicked off the airship," mumbles the pipsqueak as he tinkers with his watch.

Slam! Both hands on the table. My dramatic reaction manages to get another single eyebrow raise from Icarus. Checc freezes for a second before popping another candy in his tentacled mouth.

"I'm done with the negativity, alright? What's done is done. We'll have to ride this one out. Figure out a new plan of attack. So we don't have Doctor Farrow. Big deal. We have the internet, right? The internet has the answers to everything."

"And like a billion conspiracy theories. And fake news. And Skin Craft Killer fanfiction."

"Good point, I guess."

"Face it, genius," Icarus sighs, "Doctor Farrow was our most reliable source for a real lead, and you botched it."

SOUNDS LIKE ISABELLA HAD EXCITING FAILURE. FOLFRAKKA SORRY FOR MISSING IT.

I hate to admit it, but they're right. Gotta keep that epiphany to myself.

"Wait. Weren't you gonna have Folfrakka use her...mind control, or whatever back at the airport? Can't you just mind control the good doctor? Make her tell us what we want?"

"We'd have to get to Doctor Farrow first, and it's unlikely we could even make it through those doors now."

"Then Folfrakka can mind control every last one of those assholes. Make them lay down the red carpet for us."

The kid's monster grumbles and rolls her eyes. Rude.

"It doesn't work that way," Icarus sighs, still tinkering.

"Oh really? I'm starting to think this whole 'mind-control' thing isn't even real. Just the product of an underdeveloped child's hyperactive imagination."

Ooh. That got him. Heh.

NOT TRUE! FOLFRAKKA POWERFUL PENUMBRAN. CAPABLE OF AMAZING

THINGS, ALL OF TIMES.

Got the Fairy Frogmother, too. Ha!

"For the last time, I am NOT a child! And Folfrakka's got more capability in her left toenail than you got in your whole stupid body."

Folfrakka strikes a pose. CheccChecc grabs at my jacket to get my attention and points at her.

"Yes yes, I see her, thanks, Checcs."

"Maybe I should make her use mind control on you. Make you jump off the airship railing."

"Give me a break, you little - "

"Heya, kiddos! Aren't you both a little young to be wine-tasting?"

Saved by our new friend Mikal. He's suddenly just there, still toting that backpack of his. Bright-eyed and bushy-tailed.

"Beat it, weirdo."

"My nephew doesn't mean that," I laugh. "We're just having a quick seat. What are you up to?"

Mikal raspberries and looks around. "Oh, just checking out the place. I'm still taking everything in. Quite an impressive city, am I right?"

"You got that right." I'm suddenly struck by a lightbulb moment. "Mikal, right? You're an expert on Illaria. What's there to do around here? That's, well, age-appropriate for us kiddos?"

"Let's see...I've heard they have a movie theater around here somewhere. Perhaps you two can catch a showing of a good family film? One with good family values, right?"

"Sure." I kick Icarus's shoe under the table to put an end to his overt eye roll, then continue. "Thanks, Mikal."

The nerdy dude salutes us with a cheesy smile from ear to ear.

"My pleasure."

"I need a glass of water." Icarus closes up his watch, hops off his seat, and strolls away. Folfrakka double-takes and follows after him.

And I'M the brat?

"Um, excuse me, Miss Cordona? Can I ask you something?"

"Yes?"

Mikal leans in close. "What was he like?"

"Who? My nephew? A nightmare."

"No, I mean HIM. The Skin Craft Killer."

My heart stops for a moment. I haven't been asked about my experience with that psycho in months. Aunt Maggie made sure to keep everyone off my back. Enough to make me forget sometimes how often people's morbid curiosity gets the best of them.

"I don't like to talk about it. Especially not to strangers."

"But we're not strangers! We're friends, right? You couldn't have gotten up here without my help!"

"We would have managed." Oh, shit. I feel myself getting defensive again.

"Could you?"

The warm-blood's tone catches me off guard. He continues.

"You want to hear something else I know about Illaria? The citizens don't take too kindly to unwelcome guests. Imagine that." Silence hangs for a moment, before Mikal finally snorts and laughs. "I'm only pulling your leg! You should have seen your face, though! Hilarious!"

But I'm not feeling the humor. It feels more like a threat to me.

Careful. CheccChecc can't save Izzie from some dangers.

He's right.

"You want to hear what the Skin Craft Killer was like?" Mikal leans in closer. "He was a fucking psychopath. Devoid of any humanity. Undeserving of all the fame he gets. He smelled like rotting pig, and by the time my mom and I were done with him, he smelled like rotting bacon. Happy?"

Mikal stands back. Crinkles his nose and pushes up his glasses.

"I apologize, Miss Cordona. No doubt the memory is still too fresh for you. It was wrong of me to press the issue. Please, enjoy your movie with the little one."

The guy's countenance returns to normal. He smiles and salutes before trudging in the general direction of Fuck-Off.

Head meets tabletop once again. I wonder if it'll ever get easier, talking about my trauma. Probably not.

Izzie alright?

"Peachy," I mumble into the table. I'd rather change the subject. "You ever see a movie before, little guy?"

Mooovy? Strange four-legged things that stand in field and eat grass?

...What?

"Of course you haven't. What was I thinking?" I manage to raise back up and force a smile at the curious monster seated beside me. "Well, neither have I. Not in a real live movie theater, anyways. You're in for a treat, buddy."

Buttered popcorn. The stuff of legends.

They stopped manufacturing this product fifteen years ago, according to Aunt Maggie. Apparently, it's THE complimentary snack for movies. I never really understood why it would be so critical to the movie-going experience.

Until now. Illaria is full of surprises.

Pure heaven in my mouth, shoveled in by the handful. My accuracy has got to be at around 87 percent.

"What's your deal?" Icarus whispered as we slumped down into our seats. Top row, very back.

"This stuff is freaking amazing, my dude."

"It's just popcorn."

"Just because YOU can't enjoy food anymore doesn't mean I can't."

"Enjoy it more quietly, then. The movie is about to start."

"It is?" I pipe in with a mouthful of fluffy, buttery goodness. "How can you tell?"

"Are you serious? The lights are dimming as we speak. Have you really never been to a movie theater before?"

"Uh, no."

"Geez, you really are a sheltered islander."

I stop and throw a piece of popcorn at the pint-sized asshole. It gets stuck behind his glasses, eliciting a warbly laugh from Checcs. A sideways glare from Icarus turns Folfrakka's snicker into a fake cough.

"Do you always have to be so rude?" I ask, stuffing more popcorn in my mouth and chewing as loudly as possible. "No wonder you don't have any friends."

Icarus removes the popcorn and wipes his glasses with a handkerchief from his pocket. "I don't need friends. I have Folfrakka."

MUCH TRUE. ICARUS IS FOLFRAKKA'S BEST FRIEND.

"Yeah, I have an invisible friend, too. Right, Checcs?"

Quiet! Something happening!

Boom. The giant screen before us lights up. I'm startled out of my seat for a moment as the sound of a brass section echoes powerfully from the speaker system. It's so loud I can feel my insides shake. I can vaguely hear Icarus laughing at me, but I don't even care. Whatever it is that we're in for, I am so ready.

A family movie we did not choose. Instead we picked Better Deader, a cult classic flick with as much action as there are cheesy one-liners. I hadn't watched it before, but I've heard all about it from Aunt Maggie. Better than any of the Oscar-bait alternatives the theater was offering on a Tuesday afternoon.

From the first explosion to the last roundhouse kick, it was the most fun I've had in a long time.

The cheers and painful cringes of the moderate crowd joining us.

The orchestral soundtrack pouring out of the sound system, periodically softened beneath ear-pounding gunshots and car chases.

I'm grabbing my seat. CheccChecc is standing up in his, those wings flicking back and forth excitedly. And even though the pint-sized party pooper seated beside me wasn't feeling the movie idea at first, it's obvious that he's enjoying himself now. Icarus is yelling at the lead characters when they make bad decisions and laughing his ass off at the fight scenes. It's the first time I've ever seen this kid smile, let alone laugh. I could tell I wasn't the only one sneaking peeks at the kiddo from time to time, as Folfrakka seemed to spend more time grinning at her companion's reactions than watching the film itself.

It was a blast.

The daring protagonist Jason Deadhouse, bloodied after his hard-met victory against the undead Nazi cartel, strokes the cheek of his love interest Maddie Moonbow, played by the reanimated Marilyn Monroe.

"They can't hurt you now, baby," he says in his most sultry voice. *"They're all dead."*

"For good?" she asks Jason with those big, doe-eyes.

"For good. And trust me, Maddie baby. Some people are just...."

Drumroll...

"...better deader."

Pure brilliance. Heh.

The two share a passionate on-screen kiss as the triumphant music reaches its crescendo. Fade to black, as the camera pans out on the expanse of ocean surrounding the pair's jet ski.

Everybody claps, but nobody enjoyed the experience as much as we did. As the credits roll and our fellow movie-goers filter out of the theater, the four of us excitedly share our favorite parts.

"I've never seen this one before," starts Icarus with a stretch, "but it wasn't half bad."

ICARUS LOVES BETTER DEADER. WATCHED TWENTY-THREE TIMES ALREADY.

Ha! I knew it! I didn't imagine him mouthing the words...

Incredible! Based on true story? Real life?

"Nah, definitely not," I chuckle, plucking bits of popcorn out of my shirt. Damn, I can feel pieces in my bra. How did they even get in there? I must have eaten like a wild animal. "Just a fun story. The product of some wild imaginations, and maybe a few drugs! Ha!"

Checcs seems to reflect on this information deeply.

Penumbrans love stories, too.

"Don't we all?"

Penumbran stories need more BOOM, though. And more Jason Deadhouse.

Icarus snorts, and it's evident that my awestruck monster companion shared this information with all of us. It's a nice moment, and altogether unexpected for our trip to the city in the clouds.

The credits stop rolling and the lights turn back on. We grab our things and head out. The fun was much needed, but reality awaits us outside.

"My brother's name was Michael."

Hmm? I stop in my tracks as Icarus continues to plod ahead beside Folfrakka. He seems to notice I stopped, and he turns around. He's got his hands in his shorts pockets, eyes on his loafers.

"He was two years older than me. He was my best friend. After our mom died, before we became aware of Folfrakka's presence, Michael took care of us. He cooked for us every night. He sucked at it. We would watch action movies together, build things, and eat burnt macaroni and cheese." Icarus pauses to sigh and push up his glasses. "Burning macaroni and cheese. How do you even do that?"

And with that, the kid turns on his heel and continues through the lobby.

"My twin brother's name was Dante." Icarus halts as I begin, although he doesn't turn around this time. "But like my dad, I never got to meet him. He was stillborn. I often wonder what kind of person he would be, if he were still here today. Maybe he'd have my mom's eyes, or my dad's love of science fiction. Maybe he'd be a little asshole like me, my partner in crime. Or he'd be something else, something better."

Icarus finally turns around. He's expressionless, his eyes obscured behind the glare on his glasses.

Admittedly, I feel a little self-conscious sharing this very private information. Not even Olivia knows about this.

"It's weird, I know," I backpedal, "missing somebody you've never met."

"It's not weird at all," he says at last, behind a smile so tiny I might have just imagined it. "Although I couldn't take two of you. One is bad enough."

And he's back on his way. Folfrakka nods at me before croaking and plodding after Icarus once more.

"Little asshole," I say under my breath, and I'm out the door with a little more pep in my step.

CHAPTER ELEVEN

The remainder of the day was largely uneventful. Citizens of Illaria keep to themselves and show little interest in me and Icarus. I get the vibe that they kind of turn their noses up at us, but I don't care. Laying low works best for us anyway, especially after our attempt at gathering intel from The Skin Craft Killer's daughter failed so miserably. There isn't much left to do besides wait out the trip. Still, trying the doctor again in the morning is a thought Icarus and I have been tossing around throughout the evening. So is the morality of just using Folfrakka's alleged mind control to get our answers forcefully.

"Folfrakka says it's out of the question," the kid keeps telling me. "She's got morals and standards, unlike somebody here. Besides, it was hard enough to get Dr. Farrow alone the first time."

Suuuure. He's not wrong about the latter, though. So we agree to sleep on it, and the four of us spend some quiet time overlooking the sleeping city from the clock tower.

As the night goes on, a chill air fills the compact streets of the city. Dark clouds spread over us. Before long, a foreboding storm begins to brew. It's time for us to stop sightseeing and make a run for our sleeping quarters.

By the time we make it back, we're drenched in rain. Folfrakka and CheccChecc shake it off like dogs, splattering water all over the ornately patterned corridor leading to our rooms. I slipped and fell on my ass. Icarus laughed and gave me shit before promptly being shushed by other guests sharing our quarters. Time to call it officially, I guess.

So we part ways for the night. CheccChecc and I make our way down the corridor to our room, hearing nothing but the heavy rainfall outside. It almost feels like a bad omen. Even my monster companion appears uneasy as he plods beside me.

Not far from my room, I see a familiar face. Mikal. He's leaning against the corridor wall, beneath one of the gently swaying art-deco lights overhead. He looks incredibly uncomfortable, fidgety as he stares blankly into the adjacent wall. It's impossible to avoid him, so I don't try.

"Hey," I whisper, "you alright?"

Mikal snaps out of it and looks at me. His pained expression quickly transforms into a feigned smile as he adjusts his glasses.

"Oh hi!" He seems utterly self-conscious as he regains his composure. "Yes, I'm alright, thank you for asking. It's this storm, that's all."

I nod. "Yeah, I get it. Feels like a bad omen or something. Try to get some sleep, okay?"

The warm-blood enthusiastically agrees. We exchange awkward farewells before CheccChecc and I continue to our room.

Hopefully the next day will bring something better for all of us.

***

The storm rages on. Sleep eludes me. A bad feeling persists. I venture out of my room, back down the corridor. A gentle sobbing can be heard ahead. I'm feeling nosy. Ignoring the parental warnings of my guardian-reaper, I sneak over to Icarus's room. Oddly enough, the door is cracked open. Glance at Checc, who quickly shakes his head. He doesn't have to read my mind to know what I'm thinking. I tip-toe around the molded door and take the sneakiest little peek inside…

Icarus is the one crying. Laid on his bed in the fetal position, eyes closed. Somewhere between asleep and awake. He's scared. Maybe it's the storm, maybe it's something else. But the kid mere feet away from me isn't the same confident asshole I met in Udolthra's waiting room.

But that's not all. Folfrakka is at the boy's side like a concerned mother. She's got a paw over his trembling hand. And…

What the hell?!!

Folfrakka's wide froggish face is split open like a Venus flytrap! As the halves of her face split farther apart, the mushroom-shaped core inside seemingly pumps out some kind of pollen substance. The pollen resembles purple fireflies as it rains down over the boy. As the pollen makes contact with flesh, it begins to gain a more solid appearance. Almost like glowing larvae the size of quarters. They latch on to Icarus and seem to crawl through him, into his body.

"HOLY SHIT!"

Did I think that, or did I say that?

Folfrakka twitches and starts to...uh, close her head?

Okay, so I definitely said it out loud.

Time to go before I'm next.

Clang.

My bionic foot bumps the door. *Great. Good work, Izz.* The noise seems annoyingly deafening. Icarus doesn't stir, but Folfrakka quickly finishes closing her head up. I don't see what she does next, because I'm already running back down the hallway.

Good job. Izzie much graceful.

"You're one to talk," I whisper, and I close my cabin door behind us as quietly as possible.

We're not alone for long. A slow knock on the door, only moments later. I'm positive it's gonna be Icarus, ready to act tough again and chew me out. I get an awkward excuse on the ready, but Folfrakka phases through the door before I can open it.

Shit!

"I-I'm sorry," I offer with my hands raised. The creature just stands before me staring with those enormous, unblinking orbs.

PLEASE, ISABELLA NO MENTION THIS TO ICARUS.

"Um...of course."

Should I ask? Can I ask? Nah, I probably shouldn't.

"What were you doing back there? Was that the mind control thing Icarus talked about? Were you...m-mind controlling him?"

Alright, guess I'm asking anyway. Can you blame me? That shit was disturbing.

NOT TRUE. ICARUS HAVE NIGHTMARES. FOLFRAKKA HELPS TO SOOTHE SLUMBER.

I'm somewhat taken off guard. I don't know what answer I was expecting, but that wasn't it.

"Wow. The kid's lucky to have such a good guardian-reaper in his corner."

Folfrakka shakes her head.

FOLFRAKKA NOT GUARDIAN-REAPER.

Huh?

"But you're always around him, keeping him safe. Isn't that literally your job? From my experience, Penumbrans don't exactly just hang out with humans for fun."

The Eldritch creature visibly sighs.

BOUNDARIES. FOLFRAKKA NOT SUPPOSED TO SHARE EVERYTHING. WON'T TELL ISABELLA. NO WAY!

"Hey, it's alright. I understand."

OKAY THEN. FOLFRAKKA WAS RESPONSIBLE FOR REAPING THE MOTHER'S SOUL AFTER TRAGIC DEATH. FOLFRAKKA REFUSED. SONS COULD NOT REVIVE MOTHER, NO ACCESS TO REANIMATION. FOLFRAKKA COULD NOT LEAVE SONS BEHIND. MORE DEATH SOON FOLLOWED. HELPLESS. FOLFRAKKA'S PURPOSE NOW IN HUMAN WORLD IS TO PROTECT ICARUS AND FIX

MISTAKES.

"Holy crap. You knew that not doing the, uh... reaping thing, would sever your ties to The Penumbra, right?"

Folfrakka thinks on this for a moment, before shaking her large head once more.

SOMETIMES JUSTICE MORE IMPORTANT THAN DUTY. CHECCACHECCHUNDERAYONUS UNDERSTANDS. ICARUS NEEDS FOLFRAKKA. ICARUS STILL A CHILD.

"Still a child? He keeps telling me he died decades ago. But that's not true, is it?"

Folfrakka huffs, looking a little flustered.

OOPS. BOUNDARIES, BOUNDARIES! FOLFRAKKA NOT SUPPOSED TO SAY! ISABELLA NO MENTION ANY OF THIS TO ICARUS. GOODNIGHT!

And that's that. The monster turns on her heels and phases back through the door. Curiously, I look over my shoulder at Checcs. It seems like the little guy heard our conversation as well: he's somewhere else, his scaly brow furrowed ever-so slightly. When he notices me looking at him, he shrugs it off and changes his demeanor.

What? Izzie should go sleep. Busy days ahead.

"Yup," I agree, holding back a grin. "Bedtime."

***

Nightmares.

The kind filled with hellish screams of bloody murder. People running for their lives.

And that crunch of bone and spurt of blood. I've heard it before, and it has graced my nightmares ever since...

Only this time, I don't think it's another nightmare. This time...it sounds closer. It's like I can feel the vibrations of a hammer strike. Smell the black blood as it runs over the streets above.

Above...

Shit!

I'm out of bed so fast I nearly fall face-first on my way to the door. CheccChecc is alarmed, but I don't stop to hear his concerns. I'm charging down the corridor, through the cabin and up the stairs to surface level. I don't know what's happening - my feet are moving significantly faster than my brain is.

Out the doors and into the street. The storm has subsided, but those smoky gray clouds obscure the sun as it rises. The streets of Illaria are cast in an eerie glow, and it doesn't take long for me to realize that my nightmare wasn't a nightmare at all.

It's fucking reality. And I'm woefully unprepared for it.

My eyes hesitantly follow the trail of blood pouring down into a gutter. It leads me to the body of a poor woman, whose head is....is...

Fuck!

Go back! Too dangerous!

CheccChecc is trying to protect me. It's his job, I get it. But whatever happened here, it isn't over yet. I ignore my guardian-reaper and charge forward in the direction of more screams.

A few more dead bodies are scattered across the street. I don't want to look, but I have to. Most of them have head trauma of some sort, but unlike the woman back there, it isn't anything that should stop them from getting reanimated. At least I sure hope not. The scattering of personal effects, busted shoes, and broken glass tells me that nobody here went down without a fight.

Onward I go. An older couple runs past me, hand in hand. Like me, they're trying not to slip in the blood and leftover rainwater.

Foolish human! Turn back!

I feel claws tug at my arm and attempt to yank me backwards. It's Checcs again. I use everything I've got to yank myself free from his grasp and charge onward.

Past the theater, my heart is pounding. Past the town hall, my blood runs cold. And finally, not far from Dr. Farrow's practice, I see the culprit at last. Surrounded by a terrified audience. Hammer in one hand, gun in another, both covered in as much blood as he is.

Mikal.

He's smiling that awkward smile again, only this time his teeth are covered in blood, too. He's got someone tied up behind him, and he's using the gun to control his audience while he monologues. When my fellow warm-blood notices my arrival, he turns the firearm on me and speaks even louder.

"Ah, perfect timing!" he yells, his eyes lost in utter madness. "Behold, the girl responsible for setting Emery Farrow free from his first body! Because of her, Emery has been reborn! Like a phoenix from the ashes, so that he may continue God's work!"

Mikal bows towards me like a Broadway actor. One woman tries to use this opportunity to make a run for it.

Bad call. The psychopath before me shoots twice and hits her the second time, I think somewhere in the back. More screams from the crowd as her body hits the pavement. Before I can act, Mikal is already dragging her in.

"I warned you all," he starts hoarsely, "not to run away. Didn't I?"

The woman he shots flips over and tries to drag herself away. Mikal puts one combat boot on her leg and continues.

"All I asked for was your attention. Is that so much to ask?"

He puts his gun in his holster, just long enough to grip his large hammer with both hands.

"I ask myself what Emery would do. And I know...I know that he wouldn't let anybody escape."

"No!" It's my voice, but it sounds like it's coming from somewhere else. "Don't do it!"

Mikal freezes mid-swing and gives me another psycho stare.

Fuck! Do something!

"I'm the one who got your precious Emery killed! Let her go and you can take me instead!"

Did I just say that?

Stupid, stupid human!

I couldn't agree more. What the hell was I thinking?!

"Alright, kiddo," he says at last, lowering the hammer." Come and help her up. She'll go, and you'll take her place."

Slowly, I approach. A hundred ideas run through my head, all involving different means of tackling this murderer and beating him to death with his own hammer. But I gotta be careful. Everyone watches as I slowly approach the woman on the ground and extend a hand to her. My eyes connect with hers: scared and vulnerable, red with tears.

....
Oh, God...
....

   ...

      ...Please, this can't be real...

Unfortunately, it is. Mikal didn't keep his end of the deal. The woman before me is gone now, incapable of reanimation, and I'm wearing some of her blood on my face. I look up, trembling, to see that hammer dripping above me. Up that arm, to that face. That sociopath's eerie grin, quivering as much as my body is.

I have to go.
.... I have to get out of here...Oh, God...

"Oops," he says at last, "I changed my mind."

...No. Not again. Don't freeze, Izzie. And don't you dare run!

The gun is back in my face. I fight every irrational urge to escape. Instead, I raise my hands up and shoot him an unwavering death glare so unmistakable that it's enough to make Mikal lose a fraction of resolve as he continues.

"Back off," the monster says with a hint of nerves. "And nobody else has to die. I just want to be seen and heard, that's it. Okay?"

Without breaking eye contact, I fall back. I'm gonna stop this, somehow. I just need to be careful and decisive. Fight against my own worst tendencies...

So Mikal continues monologuing. It isn't worth my attention. On and on about how much he admires The Skin Craft Killer's work. God's work, greater purpose, pruning the weakest of humanity, blah blah blah. He's fucking crazy and that's all there is to it. I should have known from the moment I met this guy. I knew something was off about him. But The Skin Craft Killer's psychotic supporter? I didn't have a clue. Could this be the one who stole Emery's brain?!

Shit, I don't know...

If I had only figured it out sooner...Then maybe nobody would have died.

I could have stopped him before any of this even happened...

Fuck!

No. Looking back on it won't change the present.

But I can still change the future.

"And that's why I have to skin Emery Farrow's daughter, right here, with everybody around the world watching me. With Emery watching me."

What? Mikal yanks the hair of his hostage back, and finally I see who it is. Dr. Farrow. She's in bad shape, losing a lot of blood. Apparently, Icarus and I weren't the only ones to figure out who she was.

Fuck!!

Mikal replaces his hammer with a scalpel, and the crowd gasps in fear. It's obvious what he plans next. The gun is out again and pointed over his shoulder at his audience, as he slowly closes in on Dr. Farrow.

"The deli is closed, dead meat. Time to get packing."

Is that...a quote from Better Deader?

It's Icarus! The crowd parts and I can see him standing in the empty street behind us. He's got his hands in his pocket with Folfrakka standing tall beside him. Mikal snorts incredulously as Icarus continues.

"The Skin Craft Killer would never use a gun. If you're such a super fan, you'd know that. Stupid weirdo."

Gasps of disbelief fill the crowd.

"Icarus!" I hush him, but he keeps getting closer. Putting myself between him and Mikal, I stand my ground. "What the hell are you doing?!"

"What you're trying to do," he whispers back, sliding his glasses back up with a pointer. "The right thing."

BANG!

The gun went off again - thankfully, just a warning shot. Mikal is holding the smoking gun in the air, rage and embarrassment all over his bloodied face.

"Shut up, everybody! I-I'll kill every last one of you if you d-don't stop and listen to me!"

He's lost his mind, that's for sure. But he's also losing his resolve. I can see it in the way his wrist trembles ever so slightly. The darting of those eyes behind broken glasses. All we need is a moment.

Just one….

Little…

Moment….

Maybe he DOES read my mind.

Because just that one little moment was made when CheccChecc flew into Mikal, claws first.

Shit!

BANG! BANG!

Everybody's on the ground, covering their heads. Good call. Mikal is flipping out after being attacked by a monster he can't see. He's flailing, firing off the last of his bullets.

Click, click. Game over, asshole.

Onward. Icarus and I, we're charging Mikal together. CheccChecc got knocked off while in his material form, and that psychopath is freaking out after making contact with his unseen attacker.

"What the hell was th -"

Mikal's cries of confusion are quickly replaced with cries of pain as Icarus stomps on his foot. The kid is promptly lifted up under the armpits like a kitten, by none other than Folfrakka. As she carries him out of harm's way, I make my move.

And ask myself…what would Aunt Maggie do? If she were in a fight she had to win fast…

BAM.

It's a cheap shot, sure…
But it's effective.

Mikal is hunched over, clutching his crotch in agony. I was gonna try disarming the asshole next, only I didn't anticipate him making such a speedy recovery from my low blow. I'm stumbling backwards before I can even process the sharp pain in my thigh. This guy's flailing with the scalpel now. He's lost any control he thought he had of the situation. Adrenaline has me ignoring the pain, so I rush in once more with everything I've got. Only this time my target is one of those shaky wrists.

"Oh shit! Oh shit!" Our Skin Craft Killer fanboy can't take the pain. How ironic.

The scalpel shoots out of his hand and across the pavement. He's clutching his wrist and crying.

Icarus to the rescue once more. He trips Mikal, who promptly hits the pavement face first. Folfrakka sits her big bear butt right on top of him, pinning him to the ground.

BEST JOB BUSTING, TEAM ICARUS! ALL OVER NOW!

God, I hope so.

***

Dr. Farrow is freed and the crowd closes in on their new hostage. He's tied up and thrown into the side of a building.

"No!!" He yells pathetically. "It's too late! Everybody saw me! Emery Farrow saw me! The world is gonna know who Mikal Forrenson is!! They already know!"

It's like he hasn't caught up. He lost. His loud mouth is quickly taped up using the same roll of tape he had on him. The remainder of his delusional ramblings will go unheard. Good.

There is a lingering moment of silence as everyone catches their breath. The gravity of the situation lay all around us. Every one of us is shook. There is a lot of grieving that has to happen, as these people process the friends and family they just lost.

It's a lot.

But what has to happen immediately? Deciding what to do with the murderer.

The founder of Illaria bragged about how the city had no crime, and therefore needed no law enforcement: a revelation that Mikal used to his advantage. With no police presence and the founder of Illaria nowhere to be seen, the citizens themselves had to figure out what to do from here.

We talked about it altogether for several long and heated minutes.

What should we do?

Keep Mikal secured until Illaria's next landing, whereas we can turn him in to the authorities on the ground? Let justice run its course?

Or do we make our own justice here and now? Kill the killer where he sits. No reanimation and call it done?

The answer might seem like a no-brainer, but after what everyone just went through? Can you blame them for wanting their own justice?

And I'd be lying if I said I didn't want it, too. But I don't know. Aren't we supposed to be better than people like Mikal and The Skin Craft Killer? Do we have to answer death with death?

Sometimes, maybe. People who hurt other people SHOULD be punished appropriately for their crimes. Of course. But...damn it. Something about killing somebody who can no longer hurt anybody else feels wrong. Even if he really deserves it right now.

Death is the easy answer. It got easier when reanimation was invented.

"But life still has to mean something. Right?" I thought I was saying it in my head, but instead I find myself speaking loudly over the crowd. "Death can't always be the answer. This city is better than that. We're better than that. We can still do things the right way."

"You're just defending him because he's another warm-blood," spouts somebody from the crowd, and the frenzied voices resume.

That sure as hell isn't what I'm doing. Right?

"Warm-blood or reanimated, that doesn't matter! We need to hold ourselves to a higher standard as human beings! This psychopath will get the punishment he deserves. But we gotta be better than the people who wanna destroy us!"

"Says the warm-blood who BBQ'd The Skin Craft Killer!" Shouts another civilian. "Hypocrite!"

I'm not sure who heard me and who didn't. Hell, I could hardly hear myself over the arguing survivors. And honestly, what right do I have here to tell them what to do? This was an attack on their home. Maybe I'm just being too idealistic. Maybe I'm more like my mom than I want to admit.

Hmm? Something's up. I don't see Icarus and Folfrakka. I slide back through the crowd, and sure enough I spot them. They're standing by the mumbling Mikal. Upon closer inspection, I see what's going on. Folfrakka's looming over the killer with her head split open wide again, and once more she's releasing those weird spores. The foreign particles rain over the clueless Mikal, and slowly his muffled ramblings cease altogether. He sits upright and very still.

Mind control. What is Folfrakka doing?

The Skin Craft Killer fanboy struggles to stand up, his hands still tied behind his back. Folfrakka does nothing to stop him as he shuffles by, lost in thought. All of a sudden, his confused daze turns into something else altogether.

Terror. With a unique blend of shame, judging by the complete shift in Mikal's body language. He's freaking out again, but this time it's different.

The crowd stops arguing and watches as the killer screams bloody murder beneath his tape. He avoids eye contact with everyone and makes a run for it.

A run for the railing.

Shit!

It's too late. No matter what the people of Illaria had decided for Mikal's fate, Folfrakka decided it first. I watch with bated breath as the stranger who got us to Illaria plummets off its railing to his death. You know. The kind you can't get reanimated from.

I'm horrified and relieved at the same time. Does that...make me a bad person?

Everyone rushes to the edge and looks over the railing. Mikal has already disappeared into the clouds below.

It's over.

"You did that?" I ask Folfrakka as we stand behind the crowd. "You made him jump?"

I'm almost surprised when I get an answer.

NOT TRUE. FOLFRAKKA ONLY MAKE EVIL HUMAN FEEL ALL PAIN CAUSED TO VICTIMS. EVIL HUMAN CHOSE WHAT TO DO WITH THAT PAIN.

... Well done, guys.

There is some work that needs to be done here, no doubt about it. Icarus and I are eager to help these people however we can, even if we're still shook. Besides, we know all too well what it feels like to lose someone.

And some of us know what it feels like to do nothing about it, too.

Dr. Farrow didn't survive her blood loss, but she'll be okay. So will most of Mikal's victims, thanks to reanimation. Thank God. But two women died final deaths this morning. No do-overs for them. It's the end. And the finality of that...it's a scary thing. I'm not used to it, and these people are even less familiar. It's a terrible feeling.

Tiredly, I hobble over to Icarus and get his attention.

"Hey. Did you seriously quote Jason DeadHouse back there? From Better

Deader?"

The kid looks embarrassed.

"It was the first thing I could think of," he admits with a shrug.

I snicker and pat the kid on the shoulder. I'm honestly so proud of him. I want to tell him that. I have to.

"It's a terrible line."

He snorts, and I catch a glimpse of a rare smile.

"Yeah, yeah. I know."

Time to get to work. We'll get through this together. The morning is dark, but the day is far from over.

***

Cleaning the streets. Reanimations. Hellos and goodbyes. A somber mood has settled over Illaria, and the sudden departure of the person responsible has done little to lift any spirits. By the time Illaria's founder has the guts to show his face, most of the work has already been done. This community is going to have a lot to discuss moving forward. Some hard conversations are gonna have to be had, so nothing like this can ever happen again.

What to do about Mikal was unanimous this time. That psychopath desperately wanted attention for his actions, but he will be getting none of it. Any cellphone footage of his monologue was erased, and it was determined that there would be no mention of his name to the public in any of the upcoming reports. The Skin Craft Killer won't be watching him. Nobody will.

By the time the sun starts setting, Icarus and I are utterly exhausted. The next stop was postponed, understandably. We'll be leaving Illaria a day later. It's alright, though.

With the last of the glass picked up, Icarus and I plop down on a bench for a breather. All signs of the storm have passed. A beautiful purple and pink sunset greets us now, like a silent promise that things will get better. That there's hope here. And maybe, just maybe, the person responsible for reanimating Emery Farrow is finally out of the picture.

Damn, I am so hungry.

Folfrakka sits on the other side of Icarus, and they share a private discussion. Checcs is on my right, sitting on all fours beside the bench. We watch the sunset for a while, sharing the moment while keeping our thoughts to ourselves.

CheccCecc underestimated humans, Checcs says to me at last. **Capable of greater things. Kindness and courage. Stronger than Penumbrans thought.**

"Is that your version of an apology?" I ask him with a raised eyebrow. "Apology accepted."

CheccChecc grumbles under his tentacles and continues haltingly.

Penumbrans act like fear is human problem only. But...not so. CheccChecc was so afraid. Almost did nothing. Almost let Izzie die.

I'd be lying if I said I wasn't a little moved by this unexpected honesty.

"Welcome to being alive," I tell him quietly. "Fear is inevitable. It's how we react to it that counts. Right?"

Hmm. Right.

"Miss Cordona?"

I pop my head up and spot an undead nurse standing outside the double doors of the hospital across the street. She's looking right at me.

"Uh, yes, that's me."

"Dr. Farrow has asked to see you and your son."

Icarus and I look at each other in unison. We're both in shock. Are we in for another earful? The doctor was just reanimated. We follow after the nurse, confident that Dr. Farrow is in no condition to beat our asses...yet.

***

A few hallways later, the nurse stops at a random patient room labeled only with a number. She opens the door, and sure enough we see Dr. Farrow in a hospital bed, waiting for us.

"Thank you, Jessica," says the doctor tiredly, "you can leave us now."

The nurse nods and closes the door behind her.

It's painfully quiet.

In her hospital gown, Dr. Farrow somehow appears even more frail than she was before. She's also twice as pale. Her head wound is wrapped with bandages, and an IV drip is attached to her arm. There's something different in those pale eyes as they reflect on us. Indeed, the confident woman we first met is not the one sitting with us now. Before Icarus or I can break the long silence, the Skin Craft Killer's daughter beats us to the punch.

"I owe you two an apology. What happened today, it was my fault. I thought I could keep my family history a secret. Never did I imagine that anyone would discover my connection to this... Skin Craft Killer. Let alone another sociopath."

Dr. Farrow pauses to cough weakly. I'm so nervous that I'm sweating.

"My arrogance and my pride," she continues quietly, "cost some good people their lives. I never wanted to believe my father could be capable of such terrible things, but denial is no longer an option. The Skin Craft Killer must be stopped at any cost."

The petite woman struggles to sit up. With a deep sigh and a fold of her hands in her lap, she continues once more.

"You had questions about my father. I will tell you anything you wish to know."

CHAPTER TWELVE

Our departure from Illaria was full of gracious farewells and melancholy. Though I shook hands and offered condolences with smiles, on the inside I was fuming.

Why?

Because Dr. Farrow's intel revealed something terrible. First of all, that Mikal was NOT the person who reanimated The Skin Craft Killer.

Emery's got another fanboy. Someone closer to him, living in Dead Vegas.

Icarus could tell right away that I knew something. I was filling in the blanks with what Dr. Farrow was telling us. The kid kept prying, but I was still too busy processing it.

How should I feel about this?

Betrayed? Angry? Ashamed of myself for not realizing it sooner?

How could he do that?

How could he reanimate such an evil person who had hurt so many people?!

How could he lie to me? Right to my face, after everything I just went through?!

So we take another mach-speed elevator down to ground level, at some airport in Seattle. I could barely hear the annoyed vocalizations of my human companion as he tried to keep up with me, nor the attempts by CheccChecc to infiltrate my mind for answers of his own. I'm on a mission.

How could he have fooled all of us?!

"Hey!"

It's Icarus, and he stops me fast with a rough tug on my bomber jacket. I nearly fell backwards right there in the airport lobby.

"What the hell is going on? You gonna tell us what the plan is or what?"

Everyone is looking at me. I'm so caught up in my head right now, trying to figure out who to blame for what I'm feeling. But my present company deserves better. They need to know, even if I'm embarrassed about it. Even if I hate all of it.

"We're going back to Dead Vegas."

"Why? What does that have to do with anything?"

I sigh, defeated. "You know what Dr. Farrow said, right? About her brother's son out of wedlock?"

"Yeah. But we don't know where to start. She said the mother kept him a secret so she wouldn't be ostracized by their community for the affair. It's gonna take more work to find out where the kid's hiding, and we don't even know if he has a relationship with his killer grandfather in the first place."

I lean in closer, at a whisper. I'm so angry, I'm shaking.

"Not exactly. The kid developed a relationship with his grandfather alright, maybe in spite of the warnings about him. That I don't know. But they wrote each other often, and over time he began to idealize his grandpa as some kind of war hero."

"How do you know that?" Icarus furrows his brows at me, unconvinced. He will be soon. "Dr. Farrow didn't mention anything about any letters."

"Because someone who cares for Emery's illegitimate grandson told me. I've put it all together, Icarus. I figured it out. I know who he is now."

"How? All we got was his mother's maiden name."

A deep sigh escapes my lips. I clench my fists and fight against my own wildly beating heart.

"Exactly," I say at last. "Beckett. Eugene Beckett. I know him. And we are going to Dead Vegas so we can confront that lying asshole. If anybody's gonna know how to find The Skin Craft Killer, it'll be him."

***

I couldn't be any more pissed off.

First there was the new revelation about Beckett that threw everything I thought about him out the window.

And now, no available flights back to Dead Vegas for days. I'm stuck in Seattle while Eugene-fucking-Beckett is sculking around Dead Vegas and secretly cheering on his serial killer grandfather.

Did Olivia and Hideo know? Are they in on it? Was my friendship with them nothing more than some sick joke?

No, Izz. You can't think that. It's a bad road to go down.

But the alternative is even worse. What if Olivia and Hideo DON'T know? What if they're in danger?

...What if they're on Emery's radar? Should I call them up ASAP and warn them about Beckett? Or will that put them in more danger, especially without me there to stop him from retaliating?

I'm in a haze of anger and frustration. We walk down the streets of the city, end up on benches somewhere, and eventually I'm outside a dusty vending machine eating a bag of stale potato chips. I don't remember any conversation. Was there any? I'm just standing in the autumn chill air, eating chips like a zombie and looking off into the busy street outside some big old stupid building. Who even knows.

"Hey."

Crunch, crunch. I definitely feel crumbs falling down my tank top.

"Hey, Xanax."

This time I feel a light punch in my leg.

"What?" More crumbs escape my lips. Icarus dodges to avoid the spray.

"You need to snap the hell out of it."

The kid's not wrong, but it's easier said than done right now.

"You've been moping ever since we left the airport. I know waiting for another flight isn't ideal right now, but come on. Don't be a brat."

I pour the remainder of the chip fragments into my mouth and crumple the bag. It's tossed in the general direction of the nearest trash can, but it's a serious miss.

"I'm not being a brat. And yeah, the wait sucks, but that's not it."

Icarus crosses his arms and raises his chin. "Then what is it?"

"Dude, I just found out that someone I thought was my friend isn't who I thought he was. That he's related to the same psycho that started all this. That's a lot to fucking process, so please allow me to try. Okay?"

"You think I haven't been lied to before either?" The kid's getting annoyed. We have that in common. "Yes, it's awful. But you have to pick yourself up and keep going. If we freeze up every time somebody hurts us, we'd never go anywhere."

My next response wasn't my best. I offer an exaggerated apology soaked with sarcasm.

"Well, soooorry for not being able to brush off my feelings in under two seconds. I'll try harder next time I'm betrayed and my friends are in danger."

"What friends?"

I scoff and turn away from the kid. CheccChecc is looking at me from beside the dispensing machine, but I avoid eye contact. "Very funny."

"No, I mean it. I thought it was just you and your mom and your aunt back on the sanctuary island. I didn't know you had connections in Dead Vegas besides this Beckett kid."

I consider my response. Tell the kid to mind his own business? Offer a playful retort to lighten the mood and change the subject?

Or maybe...and just hear me out on this one...

I actually say what I'm really thinking?

"Yeah, I, uh...met some cool kids my age when I first visited Dead Vegas with my family. Besides Beckett, there was Olivia and Hideo. They're a little screwed up sometimes, but so am I. They made me feel normal. And there's also Frode, and Claudia - "

"So you DO know Frode Algar?"

I'm taken back by the interjection during my heartfelt share session. Icarus is staring up at me with big eyes.

"I didn't take you as another Frode fanboy."

Icarus is flustered, and it's enough to make me drop my guard a little more.

"Not a fanboy," he mumbles, pushing up his glasses even though they don't need the help. "I just watch the news, that's all."

ICARUS ADMIRES CONFIDENCE OF FRODE ALGAR. ICARUS OCCASIONALLY DRESS UPS LIKE FRODE ALGAR AND PRACTICES TALKING TO MIRROR.

Heh. I love Folfrakka.

"Anyway. My point is...There are good people in Dead Vegas I care about. If Beckett is secretly working with The Skin Craft Killer, then everyone close might be in danger."

I'm overwhelmed suddenly, unexpectedly. Are those...tears? I hate crying with a passion. But right now, I just can't seem to stop it. I squat down and wrap my arms around my raised knees like a little kid.

"I lost my mom because I didn't act fast enough. I was too afraid and I made the wrong decisions. I can't lose anybody else I care about for the same stupid reasons."

The words just spill out and I can't control them. I'm so frustrated. I ignore the concerned voice of Checcs in my head, and prepare myself for an onslaught of shit-giving from the kid standing in front of me.

"Cut it out," I hear him say. "It's not your fault. Not your mom, not The Skin Craft Killer, and not this Beckett guy either."

That...was not the response I was bracing for.

I low-key wipe my tears and raise my head. The diverse faces surrounding me share equal measures of concern and discomfort.

"You're not gonna lose anybody else, alright?" Icarus stands a few feet away from me, hands still in his pockets. "We are going to Dead Vegas and we are gonna stop Emery and his grandson from hurting anybody else. For good this time."

Folfrakka croaks and hops up and down, her heavy bulk bouncing with her. Checcs just nods at me.

TEAM ICARUS POISED FOR UNSTOPPABLE VICTORY!

CheccChecc believes in Team Icarus also. Even though Izzie crazy.

"But what if I try to run again? What if I can't face Beckett? Let alone THE Skin Craft Killer?"

Icarus scoffs. "Izz, I literally saw you stand up to Emery's copycat killer. Something that nobody in that entire floating city had the balls to do."

IZZIE BRAVER THAN IZZIE LOOKS, pipes Folfrakka inside my mind.

"And besides," the kid continues with a puff of his shoulders, "you've got us."

That's it.

All eyes are on me as I rise to my feet.

"The mental breakdown is officially over with," I say at last with a sigh. "Thank you for believing in me. And for carrying out this batshit crazy mission with me in the first place."

"Ah, don't make it weird. You're paying for the tickets to Dead Vegas, so I need you functional. That's all."

I laugh, picking up the crumpled bag and throwing it into the trash for real this time.

"Of course. Man, this whole thing is nuts." After dusting my hands clean, I look down the street and back to my companions. "So, what's next while we wait? More impressions of Frode Algar?"

The kid's face just got a few shades lighter.

"What did I tell you? Boundaries!" After angrily whispering to his monster pal, Icarus turns back to me with a mischievous smile plastered on his cherub face. "Well, whatever. I have an idea."

Oh, God. What am I in for now?

***

"Atteeeeeeen-TION!"

"What are you doing? This isn't boot camp, it's - "

"It's real life, soldier. And Sergeant Folfrakka and I are here to whip you and your guardian-reaper into tip top shape."

What is the whip into tiptop?

"He's saying we need improvement."

CheccChecc need no improvement. Perfect.

"Heh. Damn straight, Checcs. Icarus, we don't need to do this. You said it yourself. We handled Mikal just fine. We can protect ourselves."

"Enough insubordination, soldier!" Icarus takes his newly acquired stick and beats it on the floor in front of him. Folfrakka is once more in sync with her little companion, stomping a foot and crossing her little arms. Sergeant Folfrakka isn't messing around either.

I can't help but snicker just as Checcs lets out one of those warbly laughs beneath his tentacles.

"Silence!" the kid yells loud enough that his voice cracks. I stifle another laugh, and am quickly startled by the abrupt appearance of Folfrakka in my face. Both Checcs and I stop laughing and stand up straight, unwilling to push our luck with the hefty Penumbran before us.

ANGRY VOICES AND BIG HUMAN WORDS!

"Yes sir and madam!" I manage with the straightest face possible.

Icarus clears his throat and continues as he paces slowly around us. "Indeed, we managed to stop a first-time killer back on Illaria. However, The Skin Craft Killer is a totally different story. He has got far more experience and cunning. A well-timed kick in the crown jewels won't be enough to stop THIS psychopath."

The kid stops after making another full circle around Checcs and I. It's just us four standing in the middle of an empty park, mid-day. Monster vs. monster, asshole vs. asshole. Heh.

"Therefore, if we're gonna face off against The Skin Craft Killer and his grandkid," Icarus continues confidently, "you'll need to know how to defend yourselves by working together to your fullest potential."

Checcs and I look at each other. The little guy looks skeptical.

I, however, am game for whatever comes next. Admittedly, my guardian-reaper's lack of enthusiasm is adding to my abundance of it.

"Sir yes sir!" CheccChecc rolls his eyes at my salute.

Cue the training montage!

First, Icarus had Checcs and I do a variety of trust exercises with each other.

"Are you literally making us do trust falls?" I scoffed, preparing for a fall backwards into my guardian-reaper's arms. "I didn't know this was a couple's therapy session."

"Shut up, soldier," Icarus piped back, catching Folfrakka as she fell back ever so gently into his little arms. "I've seen the way you two interact. Your trust in one another needs work."

Checcs catches me whenever I fall, even though his use of claws could be mitigated. What proves more difficult is the winged monster's trust in ME. He maintains his incorporeal form three out of our four trust falls. By the time he finally let me catch him, I was so hyped. I was shouting like I just scored a shot in the basketball hoop behind us.

Careful. Don't make CheccChecc regret trust in Izzie.

"It's a start," Icarus shook his head, "but we've got way more work to do."

Next, we do blind runs through the playground. One of us would go through the course blindfolded, while the other relays instructions on how to get to the end safely.

It's a bit of a shit show.

Izzie go right of big half dome cage. Dodge springy fake animals. Other right. Big, big left. Climb dangly bars. North. Other north. West maybe.

I manage to reach the end eventually, but not without my fair share of shin bruises and dusty bars to the face. Icarus is having a good time watching, by the sound of it.

My turn.

"Monkey bars, go go! No, they aren't real monkeys! Duck under the swings and take five or so baby steps forward before standing back up! No, not real ducks! Oh shit, my bad! Watch it on the swing back! Ooh, shit! Okay, nevermind that, take a, uh...a wide left around the see-saw...No no no, it's not dangerous, it's not a real saw or anything. And, uh, let's see…"

I thought I couldn't possibly do worse than Checcs at dictating directions, but geez. It was SO much worse. By the time my guardian-reaper finally gets to the end, he rips off his blindfold in frustration and glares at me. I'm not the only one with bumps and bruises after this exercise. I'm sure he regrets observing our instructor's 'no phasing' rule.

"Sorry, little dude!"

Folfrakka is literally on her back holding her furry gut as she laughs it up with Icarus.

ICARUS SAY IZZIE SUCKS AND FOLFRAKKA AGREES.

Thanks, Fairy Frogmother.

The next exercise is all about cooperation. We're taking turns on an obstacle course Icarus built through the park. We have to work together in order to collect all the course's tokens (AKA quarters) and reach the end.

"Having an Eldritch companion is a rare blessing, soldier. An asset. Use your mental bond and unique abilities in tandem to achieve what normal people would consider impossible."

I'm sure as hell trying! Some elements of the obstacle course require Checc's flight and ability to phase through objects. Other parts include puzzle-solving and general human ingenuity. Gotta hand it to Sergeant Icarus. His time spent setting up the course this morning paid off. It's a clever exercise, and actually pretty fun.

This time we do a lot better. Checcs and I are helping each other through the course, offering solutions and powering through the various obstacles. Cheering and jeering each other on, and feeling unexpectedly competitive. It doesn't take long before we both have handfuls of quarters and palpable arrogance.

"Alright, alright," Icarus concedes, gathering in our hoard of tokens. "Not bad, I admit. But we're not done yet, soldiers."

Up next on the menu are mental gymnastics. Well, sort of. Icarus is trying to show me how to reach out to Checc's mind, and that's no easy task. The very thought sounds wild.

"Just as CheccChecc reaches out to you," the kid begins, "so can you reach out to him. Utilize your unique bond and learn how to communicate telepathically."

It's easier said than done. The kid tells me I need to hold on to Checc's words as he reaches out to me. Really feel them in my brain, whatever the hell that means. Find the connection, understand it, and turn it around to reach back into Checc's mind.

Again, easier said than done. I'm standing there with a slouch of my shoulders and a furrowing of my brow, no doubt looking like a constipated crazy woman. Checcs just sits there staring at me, unimpressed. The brain inside that bulbous cranium is a fortress, and there is no way I'm breaking in.

Folfrakka appears to be communicating with my guardian-reaper before promptly turning her attention back to Icarus. He hears something from her and pipes back up.

"Telepathic communication," he begins after a cleared throat, "requires the cooperation of both parties. CheccChecc, you're gonna need to let Izzie in, too. Remember, it's all about trust."

My guardian-reaper shrugs. He's stubborn, all right. Just like I am.

Still, I try again. Searching within my own mind, doing whatever I can possibly think of to try and reach out to the monster I'm bonded to.

"Ugly worm face, ugly worm face," I playfully repeat in my mind. If he hears it, I'm gonna know right away. *"You suck at directions and Folfrakka is way cuter than you."*

Still nothing. A few more attempts, and I'm ready to call it. My brain hurts and I'm getting a little embarrassed.

"It's okay, soldier," Icarus responds with a condescending pat on my leg. "It takes time to form the kind of bond Sergeant Folfrakka and I have. Keep trying and eventually it'll happen."

NOT TRUE. MAY NEVER HAPPEN.

The remainder of our training consists of physical exercises. Thank God. We're taking turns striking our pretend Skin Craft Killer, played by the good sport Folfrakka. She's walking around slowly with her arms in the air, wearing a paper plate mask. A crappy veil is drawn directly onto the plate with a black crayon. We practice predicting her next move and parrying her attacks.

"Remember, it's not just where The Skin Craft Killer's weapon is. It's where his eyes are, where his feet are pointed, and what his body language is saying."

"I can't see her eyes or her face, though," I say between breaths as I dodge another swing of Folfrakka's branch, "she's wearing a paper plate."

"Silence, soldier! Anticipate The Skin Craft Killer's next move and beat him to the punch!"

Bop! Cold bark snaps against my cheek. I definitely did not anticipate that move. I'm back on my ass, watching Checc flutter around madly like an oversized fly. He's dodging Folfrakka's swings better than I did, but it's far from graceful.

"Focus!" Icarus yells once more. "Don't get caught up on your failures. The Skin Craft Killer won't wait for you to get your shit together."

The fight continues, with Checcs and I exchanging light blows with Folfrakka. We're getting hit less, but we aren't gaining much ground otherwise.

"There's more than one way to win a fight, soldiers! Find a weakness and outsmart your enemy!"

Deep breath, take a step away. I try to put myself back in that moment with Mikal. When there was a gun pointed in my face, and there were various lives at stake. What did I do at that very moment?

I spotted a weakness. Just like Icarus said. The only way we can stop The Skin

Craft Killer is to find his weaknesses and exploit them too. Find our opening, and make a move.

So I watch Folfrakka for a bit. I see the way she swings wide. I see that her dominant hand is her right. She turns around slowly, and almost always left to right. Her big belly is currently under fire from CheccChecc's balled fists, but it is clearly not a weak spot.

Deep breath, take a step in. I dodge Checc's wings and move to Folfrakka's left just as she begins to turn right again. I yank her back by the left wrist and it's obvious that she didn't see it coming. She stumbles forward, and I use the opportunity to knock her weapon from her right hand. The stick goes sliding across the cement into the nearby grass.

"Haha! Good work!"

"Woohoo!" I'm so freaking proud of myself right now. "Move over, Jason Deadho-"

Thwack.

I'm back on my ass again, this time with the pain of a backhand burning my other cheek. Did Folfrakka seriously just....bitch slap me?

"Hey!" I'm still rubbing my cheek, but my pride hurts more.

Folfrakka stops and lifts her mask up. She looks at me and croaks, but I can hardly hear it behind the guffaws of CheccChecc. Some companion.

OOPS. FOLFRAKKA HIT TOO HARD?

"Never drop your guard, soldier! The fight isn't over until it's over!"

By the time the sun is setting, we are all utterly exhausted. Time to call it a day for Icarus's boot camp. We catch our breath on the astro turf before retiring to our cheap hotel room. Once there, we reflect on the day over glasses of water. I munched an apple I found from one of the park trees, but it's small and overripe. Heh. Better than nothing!

"Not bad today, Sergeant," I proclaim with a mouthful of mushy apple. "Not bad."

Icarus kicks back in his chair and crosses his arms.

"We're gonna find and confront The Skin Craft Killer, I know it. And when we do, we'll be ready. Right?"

"Sir, yes sir!"

Lights out, TV off. Just before I officially crash, I hear that all-too familiar voice passing through my mind.

CheccChecc not ugly worm face. Izzie the ugly worm face one.

Ha! Guess somebody heard my thoughts after all!

I sit up excitedly to rub it in to my guardian-reaper, but he's off in the corner pretending to be asleep. Maybe he just wanted to let me know that our secret communication was a success?

Or maybe he was just too much of a baby about it to let my telepathic insults slide. Heh.

Reaching out to CheccChecc once more, I do my best to convey one last message for the night.

"I didn't mean what I said back there, buddy. You did good today."

No answer. All I see is the glint of one glowing eye as it pops open long enough to sneak a peek at me.

Icarus is right. We'll be ready when the time comes. Emery and Beckett won't stand a chance against us.

***

Nobody ever warns you just how much waiting you have to do in life.

Because holy shitballs.

Waiting for the next flight to Dead Vegas feels like an eternity. I wish I could just flap my arms and fly there myself. Thankfully, we only have 18 hours left until we're in flight to confront the Red Bastard himself.

It's not all bad, though. We had woken up to some kind of parade happening down the main street. With a little luck, Folfrakka and I convinced Icarus to check it out. The four of us joined in a crowd of colorfully dressed undeads as they swung flags and marched to the energetic melodies played by their fellow drummers and trumpeteers. Though the sky above was dark and full of smog, the streets were full of life and laughter. CheccChecc and I enjoyed some shaved ice topped with thick strawberry syrup, while Folfrakka was mesmerized by the parade's more eclectic performers.

HUMANS CAN EAT SWORDS, FIT INTO TINY BOXES, AND SPIT FIRE?! The Fairy Frogmother shared with us, clapping her paws excitedly. FOLFRAKKA THOUGHT HUMANS SOFT AND FLIMSY, NOT SO. HUMANS CAPABLE OF MANY MAGICS!

"Must be nice," Icarus had whined, arms crossed tightly against his chest. "I can't see anything down here."

After slurping up the rest of my shaved ice, I stooped down in front of Icarus with my back facing him.

"What are you doing?"

"You wanna see above the crowd, right? Hop on my shoulders, twerp."

Icarus was quick to scoff. "Are you kidding? I don't need you to lift me up, not when I have Folfrakka."

But the kid's faithful companion was already following after another group of fire dancers, hoping to unlock the secrets of their sorcery.

I snorted. "What was that about Folfrakka being your loyal babysitter?"

"I don't need a babysitter. Now let's go."

And with that, the totally independent kid clambered onto my back and let me carry him on my shoulders the rest of the way. Together we marched on with the parade, cheering for the performers and giving each other shit for our shared status as fish out of water. Having others to be awkward with isn't so bad.

By late afternoon, I'm starving again and I regret not getting more shots of strawberry syrup. Good thing I stocked up on vendor chips. I never thought I would miss Mom's sweet potato pie so much.

Back at the park again, I read the news on my phone. Another double homicide, this time in Oregon. Same M.O. It's fucking awful, and sharing the article with my companions brought the mood down significantly. Indeed, the trip back to reality is always a harsh one. We've got to find and stop The Skin Craft Killer as soon as possible before anyone else dies.

As Icarus and I increase our resolve, Checcs and Folfrakka act more distant. I thought I was imagining it, until the kid beside me on the swings acknowledges it, too.

"Are you alright, Folly?"

Folfrakka croaks and steps behind Icarus. If she's talking to him, I'm not privy to it. She just starts pushing him on the swing. The creaking of the metal loops is deafening.

"How about you?" Checcs double-takes at me from atop his perch on the swing set. His eyes are downcast. "It's okay to be scared, you know."

No answer. I firmly plant my feet in the sawdust and steady myself in the swing.

"It's okay. I'm a little scared too. We all know how dangerous Emery is. But we'll stop him together. Right?"

Still dead silence. I wonder if he heard my thoughts that time.

"....Checcs?"

Icarus grinds his feet to a halt so fast that his glasses fall off. I can't help but wonder what Folfrakka must be telling him right now. My attention falls back on my own monster, whose gaze averts mine with shameful fervor as he continues.

The apocalypse is coming. Penumbrans stop it and save planet. Very soon.

"You keep saying that, but - "

Listen! CheccChecc no longer can hide. To Penumbrans, apocalypse... is humanity. Saving planet from humans.

***

Well. Shit.

How can I begin to process this information?

Saving the world and stopping an apocalypse sounds heroic. The sort of thing they'll tell stories about for centuries to come.

That is, if stopping the end of the world didn't mean having humanity kill itself off.

Let me rewind real quick.

CheccChecc powered through his apparent guilt as he revealed the true nature of this so-called apocalypse.

The planet is dying, and people are largely to blame for it. Can't say that isn't true.

To the Old Ones, that makes humanity the apocalypse.

How will they stop us from destroying the world with our greed and blatant disregard for Earth?

Simple.

Release toxins into our brains so that when the time is right, they can trigger our greatest fears and make us kill each other off.

288

I know. I thought the same.

Some extreme conspiracy theory of a rambling madman with a microphone. A Hollywood box office flop. Absolute, Grade-A, utter bullshit. Impossible. Ridiculous. The part of the story that goes completely off the rails.

But my guardian-reaper is convinced. Just telling me all this is difficult for him, I can see it all over his face.

Old Ones no longer want to invest in unreliable human souls for energy. Investing in life force of planet once human purge complete.

"'Human purge'? Shit, that's one way to put it. When and how are they planning to release these so-called toxins, then?" I asked him nervously.

Already have. Released into air months ago. Only waiting to activate when ready.

"Why use our own fear? Why not kill us off themselves?" I was furious.

Direct intervention not possible. Fear responsible for all humanity's destructive behavior. Humans already killing humans out of fear. Old Ones only accelerating process before planet suffers more.

I refused to believe it. I fought back all my anger and my hurt. My absolute fucking disbelief at this insane story. But as much as I want to disregard everything CheccChecc just told me, I can't shake this awful feeling.

The feeling that it just might be true.

Looking to Icarus for support, I find little. He's less shook, and I am reminded of when he casually brought this apocalypse thing up back in Grady's mansion.

"You knew?" I asked him, my knuckles white behind balled fists. "You knew this was happening all along?"

Icarus doesn't react to my raised voice, nor does he react when I shake him gently. He just stands there, head down.

"I didn't know it was real," he answers softly. "Folfrakka had warned me, but...I don't know. I thought it was a story. End time tales like the rapture, or something."

That's what I thought, too. I've seen enough apocalypse movies. This kinda stuff is too impossible to be real.

"IF what you're saying is true," I start quietly before my brain can catch up, "then millions, maybe billions, of people are gonna...they're gonna..."

Die, Checc finishes for me.

"What do you think of all this?! You can't think this is right! Please tell me you don't!"

Not anymore. Purge makes Old Ones bad as humans. Maybe worse.

"You fucking think?" It's all I can say, and it's worthless.

FOLFRAKKA NOT SUPPORT HUMAN PURGE EITHER. FOLFRAKKA ONLY TOO AFRAID TO DO ANYTHING. BUT NOT ANYMORE. FOLFRAKKA FIGHTS FOR TEAM ICARUS.

 "Thanks, Folly." I return my attention to Checcs. "Is there anything we can do to stop...this?"

The Eldritch creature visibly sighs. *No. But end of humanity not guaranteed. Effect only last for one human day. Fight off fear to survive.*

We only have to fight our fears for one day to survive the end of humanity?

Totally not absurd. Nope, no plot lost here.

Can I do that though? Fight my own fear?

Yeah. That's exactly what I did when I was buried alive. When I relived that fateful memory with Udolthra. When I confronted Mikal in Illaria.

I can do it again. Easy. Right?

It's my friends and family I'm worried about.

A pounding in my head like drums. Ignore it. Head for the park bathroom. Dry heave into a dirty toilet. Splash water on my face in a cloudy mirror. Pull out my phone. Aunt Maggie. Olivia, Hideo, and Beckett - fuck, not him. Fuck that guy. There's also Claudia. Hell, even Frode Algar. They need to know about this. I need to warn them. I need to warn everybody.

But how?

"Hey guys. Nice weather we're having. Oh, and by the way, the end of the world is coming."

"How? Magical fear toxins they released into the air months ago, absorbed into every human body living or undead. Toxins that will lie dormant in our brains until they're triggered on Apocalypse Day. So whenever that day comes, don't trust anything you see and try not to kill each other. Okay thanks, bye."

How can this happen? I feel like the clues were everywhere, and my persistent sense of dread wasn't as insignificant as I thought. Even if I want to refuse all of it, I can't. Too much is at stake, and I won't allow the only people close to me to face something so horrible unprepared.

Stare at the phone in my hand until I can no longer see it through the blur of tears in my eyes. Leave the bathroom in a hurry once some older lady waltzes in and gives me a weird look. Put on a confident face while regrouping with Icarus and our friendly Penumbrans.

"Are you...going to be alright?" It's Icarus.

"Yeah, I'm fine. I'll be fine. Will YOU?"

The kid grimaces and nods. Probably about as convincing as I am right now.

Fear not.

"Checcs. I said I'm fine. I'm not afraid. I already conquered my fear, remember?"

...Of course. CheccChecc protect Izzie from outside threats until contract expires. But Izzie must protect mind when fear manifests.

He's right. If this is happening... I have to pretend it's a zombie apocalypse and get my post-apoc mindset on. Craft a baseball bat with a barbed fence wrapped around it. Salvage a bunker. Hoard canned beans and trust no one.

However, before it comes to that...

I need to get my shit together fast and warn my loved ones, one way or another. They may believe me, they may not. But I've got to try. I've got to.

Because the clock

for humanity

just might be

ticking.

CHAPTER THIRTEEN

Calls made. Message received...to varying degrees.

"So it's true, then," said Frode solemnly. *"Guard your mind, girl. You must be strong. Get home fast. Warn your sanctuary. If you believe in any Gods, I suggest you start praying for some mercy."*

Aunt Maggie, on the other hand, was altogether unconvinced. I know how she is. I think the only thing that softened her was the obvious conviction in my tearful warning.

"Alright, Izz. I'll be on high notice, just for you. Don't worry about us. Love you, girl."

Good enough.

Olivia was excited to hear from me. Ready to tell me about her recent breakup. The dumb shit Beckett did the other day, the party Hideo was throwing this weekend. Her newest pet project: customizing a beater for street racing. Unfortunately, there was no time to catch up. Not yet.

Poor Olivia. No doubt about it, I've brought nothing but crazy to the girl and her friends since she met me. Though the gang had gotten proof that I wasn't ready to rock a straight-jacket after all, my latest revelation might be enough to make them reconsider.

"Manifestations of our own fears, huh? Hallucinations? I'll keep that in mind when I start seeing giant spiders and circus clowns everywhere."

"I know it sounds absolutely insane, but you gotta trust me," I pleaded. *"If, or when, it happens...you'll know."*

"Girl, you're seriously worrying me - "

"Please. Just promise me that you'll be careful and get ahold of me if shit goes south. The only way we can survive this is if we stick together."

"...Okay. I promise."

"And stay away from Beckett!"

"What are you - "

Click. Did I just...hang up on her?

Geez. Well. Good enough.

That's what I tell myself, at least. I don't know what else to do. The four of us wait at the Seattle airport for our late flight back to Dead Vegas, watching people come and go around us. All these undeads, going about their busy lives none the wiser. If only they knew what I knew. What Icarus knows. The grim truth I'm still arguing in my mind, even now.

I don't even.

Checcs has little else to say as we wait. Maybe it's guilt, or perhaps a shared sense of helplessness. He just sits there in the metal chair beside me, slumped over. Folfrakka is similarly uncomfortable, watching Icarus from a distance as he rests his head in his hands.

The supposed end of humanity. It isn't guaranteed, that much is for sure. But when everyone on the planet experiences their greatest fears all at once...what are the odds of our survival?

Can we survive ourselves?

Shit. I don't know.

It could be a week from now. A month. A year. I don't know what kind of timeline we're dealing with here. How soon is 'soon' for monsters too ancient to fathom? I hope we have time. I'm praying for the first time ever, asking for exactly that: time. It's like standing on the edge of a cliff, waiting for a strong gust to throw you off the ledge at any moment.

***

"Thank you."

A super pretty flight attendant nods at me and walks down the aisle. Like Olivia and Claudia, she's clearly rocking a synthetic body. You'd think I'd be more used to it by now, but it's just so uncanny. I wonder what body I'd choose, if I had the option.

Crumple. Pop. Smell the aroma of stale salted peanuts released from their decades-old plastic prison. It's enough to stir the stoic Icarus slouched beside me. Handfuls thrown down my gullet as I stare out the window. We're taking off now, at last.

That sense of dread persists, but nothing else has changed. The cabin is maybe half full, and everyone is at ease. That's good. CheccChecc sits silently at my feet. His pajamas are still comfortably stuffed away in my backpack for now, to his displeasure.

Gross smell. What is that?

"Peanuts," I whisper, waving the bag just out of reach of his tentacles. "You didn't notice 'em last time? They're good."

Checcs sniffs the bag again and coughs.

"Drama queen," I chuckle.

What is Drama Queen? Gross like peanuts?

"It means you're a big baby. But sure, you're a little gross, too."

He gives me this look. I stare right back, shoveling more peanuts into my mouth and flashing a cheesy grin. He's not amused, but I am.

"It's a joke. No need to be...salty."

Icarus lets out the biggest, most unnecessary sigh.

"Really? Jokes at a time like this?"

Izzie no comedian. Stick to causing trouble and eating gross nuts.

A little laughter is more than welcome right now. This might be the calm before the storm. I'm still holding out for the hope of no storm at all. For the hope that this apocalypse stuff is nothing more than monster gossip. Fake news. I might still be in denial, but it's a nice place to be thousands of feet in the air. The only thing I know for sure?

These peanuts are dope.

Someone coughs in the row across from us. I look up to see a middle-aged guy raising an eyebrow at me. Is it because I'm the only warm-blood on board, or because my pun game is on point? Who knows.

"Want some peanuts?"

I already know the answer, of course. But the guy sighs and returns his gaze to the crosswords in his lap.

The speaker system lights up with friendly updates from our pilot. He's got a voice meant for radio. My eyes scan the cabin for reassurance and I see smiling faces. Friendly neighbors offering up window seats and neck pillows. A woman dressed like a business exec snoring like a dinosaur. An undead hipster typing away on his laptop, ridiculously fast thanks to a pair of bionic hands.

Are they blissfully unaware of what trials supposedly await them?

You were overreacting, Izzie. You've already made a big enough scene over it to your friends and family. Don't freak out. Just think about these peanuts and getting back to Dead Vegas. Confront Beckett about his connection to the Skin Craft Killer and follow the clues before anybody else gets hurt. One step at a time. You got this.

Besides, what about MY greatest fear? I already faced it and survived. I'll survive again.

Damn. Nothing but dust left in the bag. Hold it up vertically to my lips, catching whatever salty bits are left on my tongue like snowflakes. Crumple it up and stuff it in the compartment ahead of me. Cross my arms and lean back, attempting as much comfort as humanly possible in these cramped seats.

"You're hopeless," Icarus sighs. Folfrakka raises her head to croak before resuming her position as the kid's furry footstool.

"Nah, asshole. Hope is all I got." I close my eyes. "Wake me when we land, Checcs. I'll get you another one of those overpriced milkshakes once we're done with Beckett. Sound good?"

Much yes. One thing. Sleep facing window, please. Nooo want smelly nut breath in face for hours.

Heh. Fair enough.

I'm going to be okay, though. Icarus, too. We've got an advantage - we already faced our worst fears. Hell, we're flying back to Dead Vegas to face more horrors. This can't be any worse than that.

1 AM

Woke up with a stifled scream. Some kind of nightmare roused me, ugly enough to make me legitimately uncomfortable and sweaty upon consciousness, but not clear enough for me to remember the gritty details. But when I did come to, I was unprepared for the reactions around me.

Everyone else seemed to wake from the same nightmare at the same time. I heard some sobbing behind me and some more up ahead. Fluttering before me is a very attentive CheccChecc, looking from one end of the plane to the other. To my right is Icarus, staring into the middle-ground with sunken eyes.

Something was happening. You could just feel it. At 1 AM in the morning, miles and miles above Nevada, the strangest, darkest feeling of dread washed over the entire plane.

Was it turbulence? I lean through CheccChecc and look out the window. Nope. It looks quiet out there. Nothing out of the ordinary.

Then why am I shaking? God, my heart is pounding. I feel sick.

Undead folks hyperventilating. Incoherent screams. I see some people fall out of their seats. The pretty flight attendant quickly shuffles by, trying to get control of the situation and calm people down, but to no avail. She gives up quickly and starts pulling those pretty blond locks of hers like she's going mad before my eyes.

Soon, it's total chaos. Some passengers who politely switched seats and shared neck pillows hours ago are now fighting each other like it's a battle to the death! Others start pounding on the windows, including one of the other flight attendants! There are no words from the charismatic pilot over the speakers either, and that worries me even more.

What the actual fuck is happening?

"Checcs," I whisper, my voice shaking, "This isn't...I mean, it can't be...what I think, is it?"

A briefcase goes flying towards me, and I quickly dip my head below the seat. The plane, it feels like it's shaking now. Shit, shit. Look to my guardian-reaper for answers, and his eyes seem to say it all.

Pity is what I see in those glowing orbs. The same pity I saw in the eyes of the doctors when they told me my mom was gone. Pity for a fate that was already sealed. Pity for pain that was inevitable.

It really is starting. The Penumbrans' psychological assault on humanity to end a supposed apocalypse.

Fear. Everywhere, all at once.

I wish it weren't true. I wish it was just a bad dream. But the strangest, darkest feeling of despair has washed over the entire plane, and the future of its passengers is undeniably bleak.

Turn to Icarus. He's holding himself now, a small fraction of the confident prick he once was. Folfrakka is trying desperately to console him, but he isn't reacting to any of it. It's like he doesn't even see her.

"Icarus!" I attempt weakly, shaking his shoulder. "It's happening! Whatever you're seeing, it isn't real!"

Plane heaves. More shrieks of terror. Someone is bleeding on the aisle floor, just a few rows down from us! Are they dead again? Fuck, I don't know. I gotta do something!

WHORE.

That familiar voice makes my skin crawl. Did I imagine it?

No.

Bury it. Bury it. It isn't real.

Fingertips start exploring my body. I panic. Look down to see hands coming out of my seat! Fucking shit! Masculine hands pulling out of the upholstery, utterly inhuman in appearance yet incredibly realistic to the touch.

Fuck!

Slap and pull and pry at the hands on me. I can feel them, and they're warm. They won't come off, no matter how hard I pry or what harm I try to cause them. More and more appear. Emerging from the back of my seat, grabbing me all over. Roving hands moving up and down my body, grabbing me in places...

IF YOU DON'T WANT IT, THEN WHY DON'T YOU STOP ME?

Tears. I'm in my own world, trying desperately to unbuckle myself and escape the clutches of these unwelcome hands. Catch a glimpse of myself in the window's reflection, only the girl looking back at me is 13 year-old Izzie.

Hopeless. Scared.

I don't want it

      I can't stop it

           Please stop

Please   stop

No voice

Can't scream

....

Izzie must resist!

What's that?

A new hand wraps itself around my throat. I'm coughing, gasping for air. I'm
alone in the plane, save for one spectator a few rows ahead. Standing there,
doing nothing. Pretending I'm not hurting. Too busy saving the world.

My mom.

"Help!!"

It's what I would say, if I had the words.

ALWAYS CAUSING HER TROUBLE. SHE WON'T BELIEVE YOU.

My mother, the powerful and brilliant woman she is. Her eyes turn away from
me, towards a host of disembodied voices surrounding us. Towards flashing
lights of curious cold-bloods and the adoration of humanity. Away from me.

Invisible.

I can't

      I can't

            I can't

Escape

"Izzie!"

Another familiar voice in my head. Am I imagining it?

Not real! Fight! Bigger danger surrounds Izzie! Real danger!

Heart pounding. Faster, faster. I know that voice. Why does it sound so distant? Why can't I remember?

LITTLE SLUT LITTLE SLUT LITTLE SLUT LITTLE SLUT

No! Not that voice! It's bullshit!

IF YOU DIDN'T WANT IT, WHY DIDN'T YOU STOP ME?

I don't want it

      I'm just so scared

          and alone

               and small

but I don't want it

      and I don't deserve it

I don't

I don't

OUR LITTLE SECRET

A few hands slink off of me, but those remaining tighten their grip. Skin goes clammy under their touch. Anger rising within me, boiling.

Something else touching me, too? It's different. Cold and slimy.

Is that...a tentacle?

Now I'm

       really losing it?

Fight! Stronger than Izzie thinks!

My mom's back is towards me, bowing before an invisible audience. Until The Skin Craft Killer appears with his sledgehammer, and...

It's fucking gruesome. Blood, bone, hair, and flesh...

...

Mama..

Then flames. She's burning...

A hell. Pits of despair, each deeper than the last. I have to end it.

It's the only way I can escape.

I have to escape

       I have to

Please

                                      Kill me.

Something sharp. Something, there has to be something in my backpack. More hands let up, allowing me to search my backpack for the instrument I need...

The touch of another hand, only this one is somehow different. Smaller, colder...

"Snap out of it, Izz!"

My backpack is yanked out of my hands, across the floor. Vision blips, and for a moment the gruesome murder is replaced with a cabin full of equally terrified passengers. And the strangely comforting gaze of an ancient monster inches away from my face.

...Checc? And...Icarus?

Hands tightening around my throat, groping at my body with blatant disregard for the person beneath the flesh they crave. Threats whispered in my ear, and I'm too young to comprehend how powerless and loathsome they really are.

YOU WON'T DO ANYTHING. GOOD GIRL.

No. I've had enough.

I don't deserve this.

I don't want this.

I won't be controlled.

I won't be quiet.

I won't be some plaything.

I'm not alone.

I'm not a victim.

Not anymore.

     Not anymore.

          Not anymore.

Somehow I manage to pry the fingers off of my throat and say what I've been wanting to say for so long.

"Fuck you, you piece of shit! I determine my worth, not you, or any other scum like you! I'll survive, while you fucking rot in prison!"

The anger in me swells, and the fear is replaced with something entirely unfamiliar.

Power.

Snap. I break the fingers around my throat.

Those inhuman hands become limp around me. I shake them off with ease, and they quickly melt away. Another blip, and I'm surrounded once more not by my own greatest fears, but by reality.

And it's not much better.

However, I'm done being scared. I catch my breath and give a tearful Icarus and watchful CheccChecc a nod of immeasurable gratitude.

CheccChecc proud. Move now.

The plane shakes again, and masks drop out from the ceiling. Alarms are blaring. Shit. Everyone is so caught up in their own horrors that they don't even seem to acknowledge this new and very real terror facing us.

We're gonna crash. We're gonna die, if we don't move fast.

But where?

I'm sweating more. Head is pounding. More turbulence rocks the cabin, and any passengers still standing heave with it. They're trampling each other, fighting and screaming and banging on the windows. The plane is going down, and if those passengers don't stop banging on the windows, we're gonna have a much bigger problem.

Checcs leaps off his seat, fluttering from row to row until he gets to the exit. He keeps looking back for me, waiting for me to follow. I drag myself out of my seat, grab my backpack and stumble down the lane. Dodging other passengers and flying luggage, stepping over battered bodies. The world around me seems to be pulsating, and I'm not sure if it is the turbulence or the fear tearing up everyone's minds. But I know I gotta keep going. If somebody breaks one of those windows, we're gonna get sucked out in mangled, broken pieces. But if we stay here, we die. Period. The emergency exit is our only chance, even if it's a long shot at this point.

I don't realize I'm prostrate on the ground until Icarus grabs my arm. With a little help from Folfrakka, he's dragging my ass over to the door. Unsurprisingly, I wasn't the first person to think of the emergency exit - a poor reanimated woman no older than 40 sits beside it, her eyes scratched out of her head.

All of it, it's a nightmare. Like a scene from a battlefield. Every fiber of my being wants to give in too, end this excruciating, engulfing terror. But I have to stay focused.

Think about my mom's strength and courage. I recall everything she had to endure to create a bright future for me and for warm-bloods everywhere. That stoic beauty, despite all the odds stacked against her.

I'm the daughter of Dayanna Morales Cordona. That same strength lies in me, too. I just need to find it, somewhere...

Slowly, I stand up. I push all the fear, doubt, and chaos around me out of my mind. Focus on my friends and the only chance of survival we have left.

CheccChecc gets his paws on the exit latch and looks at me. He's waiting, and time is running out. I give my companions a nod. Trembling hands are placed on the latch beside theirs.

Time to take our chances out there. Better than murdering each other thousands of feet in the air. Better than dying in a fiery crash.

I was not prepared. I'm suddenly whipping through the cold night air, violently. It's wholly disorienting, yet somehow less terrifying than being in the plane. As I spiral out, I see the other passengers fly out after me, whipping this way and that through the air as they all flail in torment. The plane is definitely going down, and I start to see flames now as it continues to take damage from the pressure change. I can't help but wonder what their fate will be, all these poor people in the wrong place at the wrong time. As long as their brains are intact after their landing, they can be reanimated again. At this point, that's all we can hope for.

Fuck, that's morbid, though.

As for me? I may not have packed a parachute, but I did have the next best thing: a winged Eldritch monster who is contractually obligated to save my ass.

Through the clouds we fall. It's freezing, and the air whips at me so hard that it feels like a bunch of tiny daggers all over my skin. CheccChecc has himself wrapped around my back and shoulders like a backpack as he tries his best to keep hold of me.

Icarus!

I frantically scan the sky for the little guy, but it doesn't take long to spot him. He's holding on to Folfrakka's furry belly for dear life as the monster falls through the air with mothy wings the size of parachutes.

Pieces of the plane are coming down. Shit! CheccChecc flaps those wings as fast as he can to flip us out of harm's way. I smell burning fumes, but also blood. Blood? I wanna choke. All around me, I see what looks like waterfalls of blood pouring down from the sky. I can hear the tormented wails of some invisible mass, as if I were getting a glimpse into hell itself. *It's not real, it's not real,* my mantra repeats itself. Gotta focus on what's very real, and that's what is fast approaching below.

Beneath a layer of smog, I can make out the multi-colored lights of Dead Vegas. It brings me some comfort in its familiarity, but not for long. More dread creeps in, as I begin to notice flames and smoke dotting the city from end to end. I'm not leaving the chaos above me. I'm just getting acquainted with an even greater chaos, and I am keenly aware of the fact that I may survive a fall from a plane but not a trip back to my hotel.

The drop feels like an eternity, lost in a strange void of time. At long last, ground is within reach. CheccChecc is working double-time, flapping and twisting like crazy to guide us towards the river waters. I feel like a useless sack of potatoes, but I understand that now is not the time to have a crisis of self-worth. I gotta survive this fall, and I gotta make sure my friends are okay. Shit. Please let them be okay.

2 AM

Soaking wet, freezing. Stench of garbage all over me, like perfume. The river certainly helped me survive the fall, but I still managed to dislocate my shoulder during my ungraceful descent. That shit HURTS. However, I'm in no place to complain. I'm alive, thanks yet again to my guardian-reaper. I get my feet on dry land and grit my teeth as CheccChecc forces my shoulder back into place.

I've never before experienced such a mixture of 'holy shit' pain and 'holy shit' relief in the same instant.

Icarus, on the other hand, had a much different experience. As I'm gagging on river water and nursing my shoulder, Icarus touches down gracefully on the dock. Folfrakka closes up those wings again and wipes debris out of her kiddo's tousled hair.

"You alright?!" he asks instead of giving me shit for the landing.

"...Peachy."

But the day is far from over. Together we stumble down the streets of Dead Vegas, feeling like we're in the middle of a war zone. Wreckage all over the place: cars crashed into poles, buildings, and other vehicles. Fires all over the city. Another plane is descending overhead, and I worry that it will suffer the same fate as the plane we were on.

Shit.

Somehow my cell phone survived the dip in the river, and thank God. I immediately try to call Aunt Maggie. No response, and my heart sinks. I wish she weren't so many miles away right now. Tears run down my face as I stumble along, trying to ignore the gruesome accidents and bodies all around me. Clearly, some people were jumping out of windows to escape their personal terrors. I worry so much that my aunt might have succumbed to her fears like all these people, and I worry that there is no way she could get reanimated again in a world completely gone mad.

I can't be without her, too.

I can't be all alone, please don't let me be alone.

My own terrors aren't gone either. My mom's ex-boyfriend continues to belittle me in my mind, and I see visions of him and the asshole at the fundraiser all around me. CheccChecc stays by my side, keeping an eye on me as I hobble along, trying my hardest not to vomit.

Boom. A loud crash, followed by a car alarm. Look to my right and just a few feet away, I see the body of another jumper on top of a van.

Please, God, let this nightmare end.

We press on, somehow. At this point I've texted Olivia and Hideo. Aunt Maggie and even Frode Algar. But not one of them responds to me.

Until now.

My cell phone buzzes at last. Shakily, I swipe the cracked screen and take a look. It's Olivia! She's alive! Her message is straight and to the point:

"Izzie thank God, I'm ok but need help ASAP!! Beckett snapped, having PTSD. Police can't help. Where r u???"

Fuck. Beckett.

I have no clue where I am exactly, but I find the nearest street signs and text Olivia what I see. Hopefully she can find me, and get here safely. Somehow.

Blinding lights ahead bring my attention up from the glow of my phone. It's a taxi cab, barreling straight towards me! Without another thought, I lunge out of the way and farther up the sidewalk, landing very poorly on my side and shoulder. I manage to sit up, and to my surprise I see no sign of the taxi cab at all. Another hallucination?

Gotta keep it together, Izzie. Keep reminding yourself what's real and what isn't.

But honestly, right now, it's just so hard to tell.

A shrill scream beside me. I turn and find Icarus curled up on the pavement, eyes so wide they could bulge out of his face. Apparently, I'm not the only one fighting more episodes.

"Icarus!"

I get down on the ground in front of him and attempt to get his attention. His eyes are everywhere, looking right through me at some unimaginable terror.

"...M-mommy?"

He sounds so frail. Like a totally different person.

"Hey, no, it's me, Izzie."

More car horns go off in the distance, followed by some kind of explosion. The noise shakes both of us and prompts the poor boy to start crying harder.

No time! Hurry!

"I know, give me a second!"

My attention is turned back to Icarus. Though he still isn't acknowledging my presence, I continue regardless.

"You gotta fight it, kid! You're supposed to be the tough one, remember?!"

Still nothing. He's mumbling incoherently, heaving for breath between his tears. Folfrakka is trying her mind control thing, but apparently that isn't working either.

New tactic. Quickly, I embrace Icarus right there on the ground and offer a tearful note of my own.

"Fight, Icarus. For me. For Folfrakka. For Michael."

We're rocking there for what feels like an eternity contained within minutes. At last I feel the kid's body loosen in my arms.

"...You smell awful."

Heh. That's more like it.

I grab Icarus's hand and together we regroup with our monsters. We should stay off the road, avoid any and all other people. Try not to look at the carnage. Blank out the screams, the smoke, the stench of fear hanging everywhere. What's real, what's not.

Just gotta survive and do what I can to protect the only people I have left.

4 AM

When Olivia finally found us, I had already vomited twice and was curled up in a fetal position outside a corner boutique beside an equally disheveled Icarus. Her red truck was pretty busted up, like it had been struck multiple times. Windshield busted out. I wondered if she was real or just another illusion, but her tearful embrace gave me my answer.

However, there was no time to reminisce. Beckett was in trouble, and by the sound of it a danger to himself and others. I'm not interested in helping that lying asshole, but I'm gonna have to if I want my chance to confront him about The Skin Craft Killer.

"I tried talking him down over the phone," Olivia sobbed as she drove, "but it was like he was somewhere else. Back in the war. He didn't even recognize my voice."

I ask about Hideo, but the Aussie hasn't heard from him either.

"Hopefully he's at home, in his penthouse. Fuck, I don't know. Izzie, I'm so scared, I don't know what to do."

But we did know where Beckett was: in his fourth story apartment, or at least that's where Olivia tried her best to keep him while talking him down on the phone. That's where we gotta start.

"Who's the kid?" Olivia asked, only after he jumped into the truck with me. She'd be more alarmed if she could see the two monsters piled into the bed behind us.

"Icarus," he says, extending his little hand for a handshake. "Thanks for the lift."

Roadblocks are everywhere. More accidents, more bodies, more wreckage. There's no police presence at all. Hell, there are busted up and empty cop cars along the streets, too. Thankfully, Olivia knows these streets like the back of her dainty hand. She weaves this way and that, getting us closer and closer to Beckett. I can't help but notice that all of the mirrors on Olivia's truck are busted out, including the rearview mirror. A discreet glance at Olivia's hands on the steering wheel reveals damage to her knuckles. I want to ask questions, but now sure as hell isn't the time.

"Holy shit!"

We seem to say it in unison. Falling down ahead of us is a giant neon sign from one of the casinos. Olivia yanks the steering wheel hard, throwing all us passengers to the left of the truck.

"Hold on tight, Checcs!"

A brilliant, ear-piercing crash. An explosion of glass, lead, and twisted metal fills the road behind us. Now THAT...was real.

Holy shit!

A few harrowing turns later and we're there at last. Flames are licking out the windows of the topmost floors of Beckett's building. Time is ticking. Olivia, Icarus, and I try to open the door, but it feels like something is blocking it on the inside.

"Checcs," I reach out to the Penumbran telepathically, *"you gotta get us inside this building. You gotta find a way in and open the door for us, please. Please."*

There is no argument from my little monster. He phases through the wall and we wait for what feels like an eternity. Olivia stares at me, and I know she still has some doubt about my invisible partner. But she says nothing, and soon enough the wait pays off. There is a loud clang behind the door, and moments later it cracks open. Olivia sees a doorway dotted with broken glass and busted furniture, but I see a very earnest little creature sitting on all fours, ready to lead the way. Time to go.

5:45 AM

Shrapnel and wood fragments erupt from the wall as another shotgun blast sounds. The old apartments had seen very few repairs over the years by the look of things, but the damage was rapidly getting worse. Olivia and I are hunkered down, crawling across the ugly hallway right outside Beckett's unit. We're trying to get inside, but the serial killer's grandson isn't having it. He's hysterical, and what's worse? He's armed.

"Leave me the fuck alone, Gibbons!" he screams through the door. His fear is palpable, overwhelming. "I'm not gonna do it, I'm not going anywhere!"

"THAT'S Beckett?" Icarus raises one brow incredulously.

Another blast, this time through the door. I look from Olivia to CheccChecc, and neither one seems to have a plan of action either.

Think, Izzie! Think!

Suddenly, an older woman in a nightgown and some slippers busts out of her unit a few doors down. She's wailing bloody murder, and I feel my heart up in my throat. Beckett definitely heard that.

Beckett's door cracks open, and sure enough he's standing there in a bloodied wife beater and camo pants with gun in hand, ammo over his shoulder. The look in his eyes is pure madness, like he's seeing through reality into a nightmare all his own. He's barely recognizable. He cocks his shotgun and prepares to shoot at the woman running down the hall.

"Beck, don't!" Olivia screams.

I don't know what I was thinking. But I'm abruptly aware of the fact that I'm charging at an armed man twice my size.

Boom. The shotgun fires, but its target is the ceiling. Thank God. The woman finishes running down the hall and out of harm's way. She may be safe, but the rest of us sure as hell aren't.

Beckett grabs me by the throat with his robotic hand, and I immediately start to panic. He's spouting some nonsense as tears and snot run down his face, talking about people and places I am utterly unfamiliar with. CheccChecc rushes my attacker and grabs the arm holding me. With both claws securely wrapped around Beckett's fake arm, my guardian-reaper pulls and pulls until the fucking thing literally snaps apart. Olivia gasps in dismay as she sees the arm choking me get snapped apart seemingly out of nowhere. I'm on the ground now, and Beckett is somehow even angrier than he was before.

Gasping for air, I scramble across the floor back to Olivia. She's starting to have an episode too, I can tell. Her eyes look right through me as I try to comfort her. We have to move, and fast. But she's just sitting there, holding herself.

"Olivia, we gotta go, now!"

"My name...is not Oliver!" she screams at the top of her lungs, shoving me away.

Shit, what do I do?

There's no time to think. Beckett might be down an arm, but he's still got more weapons on him. He exchanges his shotgun for a handgun, and he's aiming it now. CheccChecc takes a page out of my book and charges into the veteran, tackling him to the ground. Beckett clearly thinks he is still fighting his own nightmares. He hollers at Gibbons, his father, and a slew of other personal demons as a very real monster fights to keep him on the ground.

I have limited time, and I gotta use it wisely. Noticing my dilemma, Icarus grabs my arm and yells,

"Help your friend! Folfrakka and I will help keep that psycho down!"

I nod and turn my attention back to Olivia, who is still rocking herself and yanking at her own hair. "I'm not Oliver, I'm not Oliver," she keeps repeating. Her eyes hesitantly move to the corner of the hallway, near the ceiling. I can tell she wants to avert her gaze, but her hallucination refuses denial. "Mum, why...why did you do it? It was my fault. It was my fault..."

I've never seen her like this. So vulnerable, so fragile. It's like looking into a mirror at my own lowest lows, alone at the sanctuary. Alone with...him. Feeling responsible for my mother's death, even if I know deep down it wasn't my fault either. I get down in front of her and force her to look me in the eyes.

"No, it wasn't your fault!" I yell at her, holding back my own tears. Her suffering, I am familiar with it, even if I don't understand its specific nature. "You can't keep blaming yourself for the horrible things that happened to you, or your mom!"

I wonder if she can hear me. Her eyes are fully dilated, quivering as she looks from her ghosts to me and back. She tries to yank out more hair, but I grab her hand tight to stop her.

"Dad says it's my fault. She couldn't live with what her son was. It's my fault, it's my fault..."

"Well, your dad's full of shit!"

Those eyes flutter and come back to me. Big, pretty wells of despair. But I've got Olivia's attention, and Beckett's continued barrage of obscenities reminds me that I need to get her back ASAP. "You're right, you're not Oliver! You're Olivia, the most gorgeous, talented, and badass chick I've ever met! You're my friend, and right now your friends need you! Beckett needs you! Please, snap out of it!"

The look in her pale eyes changes. I can almost see the fear wash over, perhaps not permanently, but at least for a moment. A very, very important moment.

"Beckett," she stammers, and I help her to her feet.

CheccChecc, Folfrakka, and Icarus all continue to struggle with Beckett, who is clinging to his handgun despite the clawed toes holding his arm down. He's got some kind of otherworldly strength. A gunshot at floor level, but thank God it hits nobody. Olivia steps past me and kicks the gun out of Beckett's hand.

"Fuck you, Gibbons!" he yowls with spitting rage. "I won't kill her, I won't!"

314

My friends are clearly tiring from the struggle, and I see Beckett starting to make headway. He's reaching for his hip, for a knife I think.

"I'm sorry, Beck," Olivia apologizes. She gets down and, with one solid right hook to the jaw, knocks Beckett the fuck out.

7 AM

"Where...am I?"

He pulls at his restraints. One arm tied to the leg of a heavy table, both legs bound together in an impossibly tight knot, courtesy of boy scout Icarus. The veteran looks around frantically, and it doesn't take long before he realizes all weapons and ammo were stripped from him. Understatement: he isn't happy about it.

"You're in your apartment," Olivia offers carefully, standing at a safe distance. "In Dead Vegas. It's me, Olivia. You're safe, with friends."

"Fuck you," Beckett spits, thrashing around. "I'm not your fucking prisoner. Torture me all you want, I ain't saying shit!"

It's my turn. This one is hard to approach. I can't imagine what horrors he must be reliving right now. Swallowing my anger for the moment, I do my best to help. "The Undead Wars are over, Beckett. What you're experiencing right now, it's not real. They're just nightmares."

But he isn't having it. Beckett throws his body around so hard that the table slides across the floor and Olivia and I both take another step back in unison.

"I didn't mean to, I didn't want to," he cries, lowering his head to the floor. "He made me do it. I didn't wanna kill anybody."

I see the alarm in Olivia's face, but she maintains her cautious poise. "I know, Beck, I know. You're a good person. You need to snap out of it, before somebody gets hurt. I know you don't want to hurt anyone."

Icarus scoffs and crosses his arms. Can't say I disagree with him.

Beckett starts crying more, and it is so devastatingly sad that I can't help but feel something as I watch. He's tortured by his own memories of war. Maybe guilt, too. Fears I can't begin to fathom.

"I didn't mean to," he repeats, utterly broken. "What was I supposed to do? And that fire...it burned so hot. Hotter than anything. I can still feel the heat. I can still feel it...Oh, God..."

I'm pleading with him alongside Olivia. "Beckett, I know you carry a lot of pain with you. But you gotta fight this."

"I can't," he whimpers, sinking lower to the ground. "Those people were innocent. I don't deserve to live. You gotta kill me, for good. Please."

Olivia hurries over to Beckett and gets within reach. I want to protect her, pull her away from this dangerously unpredictable and tormented soul. But she's dead set on it. Carefully, she helps Beckett sit upright. He just looks through her with those vacant pools of despair, on the verge of complete surrender. Olivia grabs his hand and forces him to look at her.

"Whatever happened during the war," she starts softly, "you can't take it back. But take it from me. You can't let your past define you. Who you are now, and how you treat others today...that's what matters."

"I have nothin' to offer anybody. My dad was right. I'm a fuck-up and a mistake, that's all I'll ever be."

"That's a bunch of bullshit and you know it. Screw your dad, he was an asshole. The people you have in your life now, they care about you and see your worth. Please, Beck."

"...Livi?"

A breakthrough! He recognizes her!

Olivia embraces Beckett as CheccChecc and I stand by.

"That's right, it's me. Hideo still needs our help. If we want to survive today, we have got to stick together. Okay?"

"I don't...know if I can."

"Yes you fucking can. We need you. And who else is gonna be the comic relief if you stay back here moping around?"

That actually gets a little chuckle out of the reanimated veteran. "Yeah, I am...pretty hilarious. But I'm gonna need a hand, though."

He coughs and chuckles a little more, shaking his busted stump of an arm. Olivia is so ecstatic, she goes in and plants a big kiss right on Beckett's lips. His eyes widen, and I can tell we share the same disbelief before he gives in and kisses the girl right back. As much as I hate to admit it, it's actually pretty adorable.

When Olivia finally pulls back, the veteran gets this tired but giddy smirk on his face. He looks like his old self again.

"You DO like me... I knew it."

Olivia just slaps his chest playfully. "Oh, shut up, dummy. Now let's get the hell out of here."

9 AM

Slowly, Olivia's red truck weaves us through the burning city. Hideo's loft feels so very far away. When her truck stops working, the girl hot-wires an old hatchback without a second thought. Icarus and I exchange looks before hopping in our borrowed ride. Thank God Olivia is a good driver, because we've had so many close calls with delirious pedestrians and escaping vehicles that it's a wonder we're all one piece. Well, except for Beckett. He's sitting shotgun, with his busted up prosthetic in his lap. I've avoided eye contact with him ever since he rejoined our merry band.

Pull out my phone, see no new messages. Shit, that's not good. I call up my aunt again, this time leaving a voicemail. It's a bit of a scattered mess, but I at least got the important stuff; let her know I'm alive and with friends, that whatever terrors she's facing exist only in her mind. All she has to do is survive until tomorrow, when this whole madness is supposed to end.

"Love you, Aunt Maggie," and I hang up. She better make it.

"Shit," I hear Olivia call out from the seat ahead of me. "Shit, shit."

The rest of us look up in unison. We're at the foot of the right skyscraper, but there's no way we can get up to Hideo's penthouse. A helicopter crashed into the side of the building! The doors are blocked with wreckage and half the building is in flames! It's gonna collapse!

"Fuck, fuck," Olivia is freaking out. I get it.

"Maybe he isn't up there," Beckett offers weakly. I'm not sure if he believes it, he's just trying to make us feel better. Unfortunately, it only makes things worse.

As the two of them discuss their options, a better idea occurs to me. Something equal parts insane and dangerous.

"I can do it. I'll find him, if he's there."

Both Olivia and Beckett whip around to give me this look of disbelief. I look at the kid beside me, and his expression suggests he already knows what I'm planning.

"But you guys gotta trust me, okay?"

After a moment, Olivia and Beckett concede. I hop out of the hatchback with CheccChecc close behind me.

Looking up at the skyscraper from here, I get this horrid sense of vertigo. More screams in my head, a rattling reminder that my own sanity is still in question. But the fires above me are real. The smoke and the wreckage and the horrified screams from the building, they're real. I wish I could save everyone, but I gotta start small. Right?

"CheccChecc, will you help me save Hideo? Please, I can't do this alone."

The Eldritch monster shares my sense of urgency. He becomes tangible and grabs hold of me, flapping those wings as hard as he can to get my fat ass up to the fire escape a few stories up.

"Holy shit, use your leg! Switch on your ankle! "

Is that Olivia yelling at me?

I can feel the heat dumping off those flames, and I have to fight another panic attack as I hustle up the stairs. CheccChecc helps me bust open the door at the top, and together we enter the stairwell.

Floor 10... Floor 11...Floor 12...

The smell of smoke and rotted blood is getting thicker. Bodies, I'm finding some here and there on the stairwell and it's heart-wrenching. People plummeting to their end, intentionally or otherwise, trying desperately to escape their own demons. I can see The Skin Craft Killer staring at me from the top of each floor, full of hatred and disgust. I gotta stay focused. I wrap my jacket around my nose and mouth, wearing it like a bandit.

He's not real. Keep going. Don't give up.

Floor 14...Floor 15...Floor 16...

Everything hurts. I'm literally crawling up the stairs. I'm learning I shouldn't have skipped cardio so much. Still so many floors to go...I feel CheccChecc's trunk-like paws grab hold of me.

Go outside. CheccChecc fly Izzie rest of way.

"But you're hurt," I manage between heaving breaths. "You can't carry me all that way. And there's all that smoke."

No time. Must fly. Now.

"Checcs," I mumble weakly. Then I hear my mom's ex-boyfriend's voice again. His deep voice saying things I've told myself for years.

"See, you're weak. You can never handle your own problems. You always need to be rescued."

"Fuck you," I whisper under my breath, hoisting myself up.

Wait a second. Olivia was telling me to use my leg? Something about a switch on the ankle...

On my butt to Checc's dismay, and off with my shoe. For some reason, I never paid much attention to my prosthetic leg since Olivia messed with it. She even gave me a handwritten 'manual', but I forgot all about it after I got on that plane to Wyoming. Sure enough, though, I see a switch on the ankle.

Dare I flip it?

Um. Better take a look at that manual first.

Crazy human! No time for reading break!

The 'manual' I pull out of my backpack is borderline pulp after hitting the river, but I can still make out the crude drawings.

Holy crap. Olivia is nuts. And she just might have saved more asses than mine with her ridiculous modifications.

It's time to go.

Back onto the fire escape, and once again we're hit with blankets of dark smoke. CheccChecc lifts us off once more, and I can feel his little body heave with every ounce of strength he has left. Every flap of those powerful little wings is as much of a struggle as it is for me to breathe.

"Hang on tight, buddy," I reach out to him, pressing my good foot against the switch on my fake one. *"I might be able to help after all."*

A little struggle. A little pressure. Little more. And then...

Click.

I watch the robotic foot beneath me pull back at the ankle, converting my prosthetic leg into what can best be described as a cannon. Whir of metal, toes flipping up and over to reveal some kind of opening. I can't see what's in their place from this angle, but I can only imagine once I see and feel what comes out of the robotic stump.

A burst of smoke and sparks. CheccChecc audibly gasps in surprise when my prosthetic leg aids our lift-off with...

Rocket fuel?

Olivia is absolutely nuts and I fucking love it.

Our slow and steady flight up becomes twice as fast. My rocket leg shoots Checc's trajectory diagonally towards the neighboring skyscraper, and the both of us scramble to redirect our course. Fighting the force from my leg, I struggle to get the rocket directly beneath my center of gravity. With my monster's help, we regain control and continue our flight up the side of the skyscraper at almost three times the speed we were going before.

Way cool.

A gorgeous balcony with a large in-ground pool. Various flags posted up on the banisters outside the screen glass doors. I've been there before.

"That's it!" I cry out. "Hideo's penthouse, land here!"

Turn off boom leg first!

Boom leg, right. But how?

Hideo's balcony gets smaller and smaller as my leg keeps propelling us upward. Shit, shit! Using my other foot once more, I manage to kick the switch back. Smoke and flame dissipate rapidly as my robotic foot slides back down into its normal, unsuspecting position. I wanna hoot excitedly, but I'm too busy falling down at 'shit-yourself' speeds. Even Checcs is freaking out, clutching at my body even tighter to regain control as we fast approach the balcony once more. Second time's a charm.

Bam, sweet, sweet ground. The little guy and I tumble across the floor, exhausted beyond belief. I've never seen the Eldritch monster look so weak.

"You did a great job," I tell him telepathically, *"Now rest, and I'll find our friend."*

I don't have to look far. A shirtless body is floating in the pool.

It's Hideo. And he isn't moving.

"Hideo!!" Coughing and choking, I make a run for the pool. Jump in, splash my way over to his body, fearing the worst. He's so heavy. These synthetic bodies are no joke.

My head is spinning. There's a strong taste of iron in my mouth. I think my nose is bleeding.

Come on, brain. Keep it together. Now is so not the time to slip back into your own nightmares...

More sirens. More smoke, more noises. Hideo's body is dropped outside the pool, and my body drops right beside his, exhausted. But there's no time to rest.

Flip Hideo over. He's not breathing, but by the look of it he's not gone yet. I've never done mouth to mouth before, but no time like the present. Right?

A few pumps on his chest. Some small breaths into his mouth. No reaction.

Frequent pumps on his chest. Larger, more panicked breaths into his mouth. Nothing. *Come on, come on...*

A burst of water erupts from Hideo's mouth, and he's coughing and gagging. I'm so relieved I could cry, but we're not in the clear yet. His eyes roll back, and he's looking right at me. Sort of.

"...Izzie?" He is completely confused.

"Yes, it's me! Look, there's no time. The building's gonna collapse! We gotta get the hell out of here, fast!"

"I can't. You wasted your time."

That doesn't sound like the Hideo I know. "Yes you can! Come on!"

I grab his arm, try to lift him up. But he's completely limp.

"I can't move," he cries softly. "I'm paralyzed again. I'm fucking useless."

"No, you're not!"

He scoffs. "Sure. I have an athletic career built on illegal modifications and bribes funded with inheritance money. And no real friends, just people who wanna gain something from knowing me. And I don't care if they're using me either, because I'm scared to death of being alone again."

The athlete is just lying there, holding back tears. I don't see the ultra charismatic, life of the party flirt I had become so accustomed to. I see something else in that synthetic husk, something so utterly familiar in its vulnerability.

"See?" he says at last between weak coughs. "I don't deserve any help. I don't deserve anything I've got. I was a better person when I was alive and disabled, and everybody knows it."

"That's not true! I don't care who you were, or what you think you deserve. Your real friends are here for you but we're running out of time! What you think you're experiencing right now, it isn't real! You need to realize that, and real fucking quick!"

"You gotta leave without me. I'm not holding anybody else down, never again. I can't fucking take it. Go."

The building seems to buckle. I thought I imagined it, until I see Hideo's eyes widen too. We're in real danger.

Ignoring Hideo's defeated assertions, I sit him up and slap him across that pretty face. He's gotta come out of this. He's got to.

"Olivia and Beckett are waiting for you below. We came all this way to save you.

You're not useless. Living or undead, synthetic body or not. You're you, and enough to make a car full of crazy people race across a burning city to save your ass."

He's focusing on me now, and I think I see the breakthrough I was searching for in those misty eyes. I continue with levity. "And if I show my face down there without you, Olivia is gonna kick my ass to next Tuesday."

Hideo manages a chuckle, but he's still not budging.

"You need to be brave, Hideo. Like you showed me. Believe in yourself. You can move. I know you can."

Another buckle. Hideo sighs deeply and focuses on his legs. His inner struggle is all too apparent, and I have to keep talking him down every time he discusses giving up. It just isn't an option.

I've never been so thrilled...to see a big toe wiggle. And apparently, neither has my waterlogged friend.

"See?" I give him a playful slap on the shoulder. "I know this isn't easy. Come on. You got this."

Little by little, Hideo is coming to life. A toe wiggle followed by an ankle shake. A raised knee followed by a propped shoulder. It's sluggish and shaky, but he's returning. He's got it in himself, he has all along. And slowly but surely, he's believing it again, too.

I've got him standing now, and his face reflects an expression of triumph. It's the kind of change that would look miraculous. I see the old Hideo returning, the one brimming with confidence. We might survive this yet.

"Remember the night we first met? When you egged me on to jump buildings with you guys?"

"A mile ahead of you, new girl."

He gives me this tired wink before starting some stretches. As he prepares, I get CheccChecc's attention. He's curled up on the ground breathing heavily, but he drags himself up as soon as we make eye contact. Shaky wings pry off his back, and he's ready for action.

"Ikuzo!"

And with that, Hideo does a parkour jump across the side of the wall. I know where he's headed, and I do my best to follow. CheccChecc claws up the wall behind me.

A few more hops and stairs, and we're at the vantage point we need to make the leap. Hideo does a running jump off the ledge, somehow getting more air than he did the first time I saw him jump. A graceful tumble down on the other rooftop, and now it's my turn to try and follow that up. Spoiler alert: I'm not quite as graceful.

However, the jump was a success and I land in one piece. One very, very sore piece. I almost stumble backwards, but Hideo grabs my hands and pulls me back. Almost shit myself there.

Gotta keep moving. We move across the rooftop of a lower-rise skyscraper, hopping and maneuvering across until we reach a spot to jump with the highest chance of success. And shit, that timing is so cinematic. Behind us the skyscraper begins to collapse, and I'm floored by just how close we cut it. A giant cloud of smoke pillows out, threatening to obscure our view and fast.

"Jump!!" Hideo and I seem to shout it in unison.

We make a leap of faith as the smoke bellows all around us. The hard contact of cement on my rear end tells me we made it...But now we can't see anything. At all.

My mouth is covered, and I'm doing my best to hold my breath. I hope Hideo is okay too, I can't see him at all. I don't know what to do. Wait it out? We sure as hell can't jump blind.

The loud rumble of a chopper, somewhere beyond the smoke. I don't know what this means, but I'm praying for good news.

What I got was something I could not have anticipated. There's a chopper alright, but it's being led by a terrifying and giant beast, with long arms and bug-like features. I've seen it before. A monster that is consuming the smoke like it's brunch, clearing the way for a silver chopper bearing a brilliant, bright logo on its side.

"ESTRID Industries".

Frode?!

It is! As the chopper lowers and the doors open, I see a figure of familiar stature and poise. I don't know how he found me, but I'm so incredibly grateful he did.

I look at Hideo, whose jaw-dropped expression begins to appear beside me as the smoke clears. I know what he's thinking. Maybe this sheltered islander wasn't lying about knowing his idol after all. I feel a little smug, but I keep it in. Head up high, poised for one last jump.

"Get in!" Frode calls out, extending his hand.

This time, I'm first to jump. I fall into Algar's arms and stumble into the chopper, where I'm greeted once more by his ever-radiant assistant. Hideo comes next, followed by my bushed guardian-reaper. Frode gives him this little nod, and CheccChecc seems to understand it. A job well done, even if it isn't over yet.

"Our friends! They're on the ground, we gotta make sure they're okay!"

Right on cue, I turn around to see Olivia and Beckett seated by each other in the back of the chopper. They're smiling from ear to ear at me.

Beckett reaches into his pants pocket and pulls out a phone. My phone.

"You left this behind," he simpers, "and a certain somebody was blowing it up. Texted him for ya. Hope you don't mind."

A very uncomfortable Beckett grins tiredly, pleased with himself.

Icarus and Folfrakka are there, too. Thank God. The kid is laying back in his monster's furry belly, locking tired eyes with me behind his cracked glasses.

"That was nuts, Izz."

I can't help but laugh. A sort of cry-laugh. We're reunited at last, the whole gang. Somehow, we got this far. It's a joyous regrouping, but Frode is quick to bring us back to reality.

"The day is far from over," he reminds us as he pulls the doors closed, "and the devastation is just beginning. Time to go."

1 PM

As the chopper continues on its path, things seem to be calming down a bit. Well, sort of.

As Hideo and Olivia fangirl out over meeting THE Frode Algar, I'm sitting in the corner attempting to watch live news on my phone.

It's worse than I thought.

Most of the stations are out, nothing but static or emergency broadcasts. Whatever channel does come in has erratic coverage pieced together by newscasters and spokespersons on the verge of losing their own shit on camera. But the message is clear: everyone around the entire planet is suffering from this.

The pope, missing.

The United States nuking China.

Peace treaties broken.

Countless suicides, everywhere.

Shootings.

Plane crashes.

So much destruction and despair.

And it's only 1 PM.

I curl up and cry into my knees softly.

"I'm sorry."

Beckett's voice surprises me, even though he's been sitting across from me this whole time. This asshole has the gull to apologize?! He continues, avoiding eye contact with me.

"For earlier. I wasn't in my right mind, ya know? But that's no excuse. I'm sorry, Izz."

What do I say to the grandson of The Skin Craft Killer? Is this my moment to confront him?

"Water under the bridge. Just glad you're okay now."

Wait. Seriously, Izz? THAT'S all you have to say?

"It ain't alright, though." The veteran sniffs and twitches his shoulder. "It ain't alright."

I'm furious. And terrified. But I have to confront The Skin Craft Killer's grandson now. Because here, amidst all this chaos, as the world wants to crumble all around us...I don't know if there will even be a tomorrow. As Icarus power naps in Folfrakka's lap, I take a deep breath and seize the moment.

"Beckett. You're Eugene Farrow, The Skin Craft Killer's grandson. The one who stole his brain from the coroner's office. Aren't you?"

The Red Bastard didn't have to say anything when his face said it for him. Another worst fear awaits the vet.

"Is this...real?"

I can't help but scoff and lean forward, holding the full extent of my venom behind a hushed voice for civility's sake.

"Unfortunately for you, yes. This is fucking real."

The asshole's eyes immediately swell with tears. Fucking tears! After ensuring that nobody else is listening in, he continues more quietly.

"I- I can explain…"

"I don't care why you did it. All I need to know is how to find him."

"Nobody gave a shit about my grandpappy after he got out of the army. Not his country, not his family, not nobody. Do you have any idea what that feels like? I - "

"I said I don't care, Eugene. Just tell me how to find your serial killer grandpappy before he kills anymore people."

Beckett jerks up with eyes even wider.

"W-what? No, it's not him. I…t-tried, but… his brain…it couldn't be - "

The chopper rocks abruptly. The monster flying above us screams - it's awful. We all lunge across the interior, until suddenly half of us are tumbling out into the forested area surrounding Algar's hidden estate. I swear I hit every branch on the way down. That'll leave a mark or twenty.

Look up through the brush and busted branches. The chopper is crashing down, and the monster that was protecting it is already tumbling across the ground ahead of us. By the look of his flaming wings and smoking shell, he got hit by something alright. A missile, maybe? A bomb? Fuck! Was the monster the target, or was it Algar's chopper?

"Thylohtanncasenka!" At least that's what I think Frode said. I can't see him, but he's somewhere in the forest near me.

"Checcs!" I yell at the top of my lungs. "Icarus! Olivia! Hideo!!"

My friends call back to me, and I can see CheccChecc and Hideo from here. I follow a small groan to my right and spot the wiggling legs of Icarus emerging from a bush. Thank God, everybody survived the crash. All thanks to Algar's

Eldritch monster.

Wait. What about Claudia?!

I get my answer moments later, and it isn't a good one. Algar's standing over his assistant's body, which now has a thick, broken branch penetrating her chest all the way through. It doesn't look good. The Viking is distraught as he holds her, watching her final moments of pain and confusion as her synthetic organs fail her.

"Claudia!" I yell, hoarse.

"Mr. Algar," she mumbles weakly, "I'm...s-so sorry..."

She coughs up blood, and there's no other word from her. It's heavy.

"We're under attack," Algar shouts with a trembling voice as he pulls his assistant down. "We need to get to my estate! Everyone, follow me!"

The Viking hoists Claudia over his shoulder and takes the lead.

So we're running. Darting through narrow trees, leaves and bugs everywhere. I try to maintain my breathing and favor my bionic leg. Ignore the explosions around us. And soon...gunfire.

We are so screwed.

It looks like police officers maybe. No...are those army fatigues? What's happening?

Duh. The apocalypse isn't over yet. These guys could be seeing eight-legged aliens for all we know.

It's pure pandemonium. We're all booking it, diving between trees and brushes and confused deer in varying zig zags. One time I bump into Beckett as the asshole is running with his detached arm still in hand. And then, right there in the forest, I see her...my mom...

Focus, Izzie. It's not real, it's not real...

But the army guys, they're closing in. I can hear their voices everywhere, and they're clearly holding on to control by a single thread.

Beckett freezes, and I can see in his eyes that he is somewhere else again. It's the soldiers, I'm sure of it.

"Eugene!!" Olivia beats me to it. She ignores the warnings of the soldiers and continues. "You're not in South Africa! You're not at war anymore!"

Olivia continues to ignore any warnings, calling out to Beckett until that crazy look leaves his countenance. The soldiers are now pointing their guns at our frozen pack with a primal sort of paranoia. A few of them scream and throw their walkie talkies away out of nowhere. I don't know if I should laugh or be more afraid. Probably the latter, considering they're still armed to the teeth.

"This is all just a misunderstanding, gentlemen." Algar gently lowers Claudia and raises his hands, but his hesitance appears to be less out of fear and more out of procrastination. "I'm sure the president wouldn't want to know that the maker of his prosthetics was being harassed by a few scared and lost soldiers."

It seems to work. Somewhat.

A couple of soldiers put down their weapons. One starts crying. Several more keep their guns out, but their aim is significantly shakier. And another one just pivots and shoots the soldier beside him instead. More scared gunfire ensues.

I guess there's no talking our way out of this.

Algar acts first. He rushes forward and grabs the soldier in front of him by the arm. With some quick and precise positioning, he straight up chops at the guy's arm and makes it break. Poor dude is crying. More indiscriminate gunfire follows. Beckett has to forgo the arm for a second so he can disarm the soldier behind him. He's got that trained precision regardless of being down one limb. He's got the gun now, and he's using it to dispatch one attacking soldier, then another. I can't help but notice that he's careful to avoid headshots. It's difficult to admit, but the Red Bastard's company is definitely a life-saver...for now.

More rounds are shot, but this time most of them come from Algar and Beckett's new firearms. The soldiers are going down one by one, but it's not over yet. They have backup running our way.

One soldier fires at me, only to be utterly confused when the bullet bounces off of seemingly thin air. It's CheccChecc to the rescue again, with that thick skin of his! I use the moment to charge at the soldier before he can come back to his senses.

Charging people. Is that my primary attack strategy? Maybe I should play football.

BAM. I don't know why I didn't expect that to hurt.

But it worked. We're both on the ground now, his weapon just out of reach. I wanna grab the gun, but this guy's still putting up a fight! I have to roll and pull him back to avoid getting hit or stabbed. It's an awkward struggle, and I'm losing.

"Checcs!" I yell, putting my hand out. "The gun!"

My little reaper looks around until he spots the gun in some leaves. His tentacles grab it, then his front claws. But instead of bringing the gun to me, smart guy decides to try it out himself. Poorly.

Pop pop. Directly into the tree next to us.

"The hell, dude?!"

The soldier seems to notice that a gun is hovering in mid air, firing at him from waist height. He loses it a little more, taking off his helmet and screaming bloody murder. I don't know how to handle that, so I just ball up my right fist and clock the soldier in the jaw. Turns out that was a pretty good idea, and it's lights out for one more tough guy.

I return my attention to Checcs, who is still holding his new toy excitedly.

"I think I better take the gun from here, trigger finger."

He complies with the same enthusiasm as a child told no.

Another enormous thump. Trees crackle and fall. Dust and leaves and dirt, everywhere. Knocked back to the ground. What is it this time?

Algar's monster. It's back, but no longer airborne. Seems like it belly flopped right on top of the backup. Squash.

The soldiers lose their remaining control precisely at that moment. A few of them run the opposite direction. Wise. But I happen to notice one soldier near Olivia reaching for a grenade and my heart stops right there.

"Olivia! Behind you, he's got a grenade!"

The green-haired girl finishes head-butting a soldier then whips around for the bigger threat. She spots it quickly and punches the guy square in the throat. Grenade's out of his hand now, but so is the pin.

"Everybody, clear!" she yells.

We all spread out, and Olivia chucks the grenade as far out as she can. It explodes in the clearing behind us, and nobody is harmed. Shit. I frantically scan the area for Icarus, and I'm relieved to see him taking cover behind a nearby tree. But where's Folfrakka?

Frode runs out of bullets, so he pistol whips the guy in charge before he can radio for more backup. Beckett takes out a sniper before the rest of us even know he's there. Hideo eggs on the last soldier a bit, dodging his sloppy strikes with ease before knocking the guy down to his knees and putting him in a sleeper hold.

"Sniper posted at your estate, playboy." Beckett straps his robotic arm onto his belt buckle. It's a little unsettling visually, but it works. "Either you ain't telling us somethin' or your bachelor pad was compromised."

Frode mumbles something angrily in his native tongue.

"New plan. We head to my - "

Something switches in Algar. He falls to his knees, dropping beside Claudia's body. He starts sobbing so abruptly, it's almost like he's possessed. I've never seen him emote like that. He's full-on shaking on the ground in front of us. We're looking for leadership, but the man that was standing there a second ago checked out.

"Estrid!!" He cries out at the top of his lungs. He repeats his daughter's name over and over again, accompanied by something else in Old Norse most likely. I don't need to know the words to understand the meaning. His voice is so sincere in its torment that it's painful to hear. And it goes on for a moment, until...

...

It's the worst thing I've ever seen in person. One second I'm looking at Frode, vulnerable for what must be the first time ever. Next moment my head is ringing and his is just...gone. And I can feel that I'm wearing some of it on my face.

God...

I'm blacking out. Am I deaf? But everyone is screaming. How do I know? It sounds like it's on a different plane. But...

It's on my face. It's fucking real.

....

Flashbacks to that morning in Illaria, with Mikal...

Fucking awful. I ...

....

My eyes are closed tight. I hear the screams of my friends around me more clearly now. Another gunshot, this time from Beckett's firearm. I'm shaking. It's happening again. I can feel it. The fear, creeping back in. I'm shrinking again, and by the sound of it I'm not the only one.

"Stay with me, guys!" It's Beckett this time. He fires a few more times. More snipers, we should have known. But not anymore. Beckett makes sure of it this time. Afterwards, he takes his gun and checks the perimeter.

"Clear! We gotta move!"

"Oh my God..." Olivia is losing it. I force myself to open my eyes and face reality. The Aussie is just standing there, staring at Algar's headless body on the grassy floor. "Mum...why did you do it? Why?"

Shit, it's awful and I can do nothing about it. Ignore the fear, the returning visions of my mom's ex-boyfriend and Mikal and The Skin Craft Killer, the trauma splattered across my face.

"Olivia, we gotta go! I've been here before, I know there's a cellar we can try!"

She's sobbing. "It wasn't my fault, dad...It wasn't my fault...It wasn't my fault..."

Beckett talks her down as Hideo does a quick search of the soldiers lying around us. Next I locate Icarus, who is still cowering behind the same tree crying. As I feared, no Folfrakka in sight.

"Where's Folfrakka?"

The kid doesn't look up at me.

"We got separated when the chopper crashed," he sobs. "I tried to find her, but I don't know where she is. I'm scared, Izzie."

"Izz, let's go!" Hideo is in a hurry to leave, and I don't blame him.

"Don't worry, you're not alone. I'm here. Come on, we gotta go."

"What do you care? I'm not your brother."

Ouch. That sounds vaguely familiar.

"You're right, you're not. But Folfrakka isn't here, so that makes me your next best shot at survival. We gotta move, now!"

"But, Folfrakka - "

"She'll catch up if she's still out here! You know she will! Now, hop on!"

Icarus wipes his eyes and climbs up on my back.

"Checc, cover us!"

On it.

I'm trying hard to not be afraid. Trying hard to be decisive. The situation demands it.

Olivia is doing better now, but she's still frozen in place, speechless. Beckett hollers for her to come back to us as he struggles to lift up Claudia's body. Hideo jumps in to carry Claudia for him.

"Cover Izz and the kid, got it?" Hideo instructs, and Beckett answers by readying his gun and signaling for me to step forward.

"Lead the way."

"Um, guys..." It's Olivia, gaining her composure long enough to lose it all over again. She's pointing at Algar's corpse.

Today is going from batshit to holy fucking batshit.

The Viking's body is now floating in the air, erect as if he were standing. That insect-like monster towers over the levitating corpse, and a bunch of tiny long arms pull out from his torso, dripping with snot-like strands. All these arms start working together, forming tiny symbols with fingers the length and width of pencils at each joint. It's some kind of magic, no doubt about it. I see curls of red smoke conjure up and start swirling around Frode's upper body. It gets weirder, though. Pieces of flesh, bone, and brain rise up from the ground. The splatters on my face wiggle and fly off towards a ball of red smoke swirling over Frode's shoulders. The unholy process doesn't end until every piece of his head has floated up to take its original place. Blood comes back in straw-less streams. We all look on in terror as Algar's head rebuilds bit by bit, bone by bone, ligament by ligament. Not a drop of his blood is left on any of us. A perfection reconstruction of the brilliant mind that had just been annihilated. Frode told me he was immortal, but this isn't exactly what I expected immortality to look like.

The playboy drops back to his feet, and the monster who rebuilt him just chitters and scuttles forward without looking back.

The playboy fixes his hair and adjusts his coat. That fragile man seconds before his gruesome death has checked out. He seems confused by the blatant stares and mouths agape.

"Where was I? Hmm...Yes. Change of plans. Follow me!"

I don't know if I can look him in the eyes. I'm still shaking. But not a single one of us is prepared to call this the final destination in our descent into madness. We press on, and judging by the direction, I'd say that Frode is taking us to the same place I was going to take our crew: the cellar, not far from where I was buried alive.

We're running as more helicopters and explosions can be heard off in the distance. Ash is falling in the forest, from who knows where or what. Birds fly overhead, headed the opposite direction with urgency. Icarus wraps his arms around my neck tighter. I'm paranoid as hell. Even though Beckett is armed and ready for more soldiers, I'm horrified at the thought of another sniper somewhere. Frode might be able to regrow that thick head of his, but the rest of us aren't as lucky.

A deep rumble approaches from a distance. We almost stop in our tracks, and I'm prepared to see more soldiers.

No. We see something else.

It's a fucking bus! Barreling through the woods, battered to shit, coming straight for us!

Fuck!

Horrified screams from the group. We try to run, get out of the way in time. But it's coming down the hill at us fast, length-wise. It's gonna fall over!

The world goes black and white. The bus is tipping three times as slowly, and it looks to be miles ahead. Immediately in front of me is something else.

My mom again.

Only this time she isn't smiling that smile. She's looking at me with disgust, as if I'm nothing more than a smear in the grass.

"...Mama?"

"You're a coward," she tells me through gritted teeth, fighting back tears of rage. The bus continues to tumble towards her in slow motion, spewing shards of glass around us like confetti. It feels like my body is rushing forward even though both feet are planted.

"No...You're not real..."

Despite my desperate pleas, that vision of my mother continues with the same earnestness I've always known her for.

"You disgrace me and my name. I wish it were Dante who survived instead of you."

Falling to my knees, I sob gracelessly at the words I've always feared the most.

"Mama," I cry, "I'm so sorry. I think about him all the time, and you're right. It should have been Dante. It should have been Dante..."

"Snap out of it, Izz!"

A firm shake of my shoulders sends the vision of my mom into a pixelated spasm. In its place are fragments of reality: the chaos surrounding us in technicolor, desperately trying to return.

"If my dumbass could break free, then you sure as shit can! Now, do it!"

"It should have been Dante..." my mom echoes, just before she catches ablaze before my eyes. Her gorgeous hair burns up first, and then...

Oh, God...

Another shake, and the vision of my mother is twisted and dissipated like smoke. I rub my blurred eyes and see the distraught face of the person responsible for bringing me back.

Him? Of all people?!

"There ya, are," Beckett sighs, and I realize that he's carrying me. How long was I...elsewhere? "You were like a deer in the headlights back there. That reminds me, wanna hear a joke?"

"God, no." I hop out of the vet's arms as quickly as possible, turning my head to hide my surprise. "But...thank you. Really."

The veteran just nods before sniffing and twitching his shoulder nervously.

Suddenly I'm aware of my surroundings. That toppled bus is far behind us now. It WAS real! It looks like The Hulk punched it. How did we survive?

Nevermind that, we're there! The cellar, I can see the doors now. Olivia's also got control of her fear again, and she takes an extra gun off Hideo.

"All yours, Livi," he tells her, taking up the rear of our group when we come to a stop. "I'm a lover, not a fighter."

"Yes, I'm sure you love yourself frequently." Olivia reloads the gun with ease.

"Not a fighter my ass," Beckett chuckles, still eyeing the perimeter with gun in hand. "I saw your skills back there. Not bad for a pretty boy."

"Everyone, quiet!" Frode has our attention once more, just in time to watch him unlock those cellar doors. "You gentlemen can kiss later. For now, we need to get the hell underground."

One after another, we jog down those stairs and into a very small room full of gardening tools. It's cramped and dirty, but knowing Algar I'm sure that there is some kind of hidden doorway behind that unusually bare wall ahead of us. The playboy files in at the end, closing the cellar doors above us. I watch as the last remaining light is closed out, leaving us nothing but darkness and the mutterings of our own private insanities.

5 PM

Waiting. It's all there is. Listening to what sounds like war over our heads. Feeling every time the furniture shakes. Checking our phones every couple minutes, hoping and praying for enough reception to check on our loved ones. Disappointment, paranoia, and waves of fear. Relief, disbelief, and utter exhaustion. But we're safe, at least for now.

Frode's panic room is more like an underground guest house. It's spacious and well lit, sleek and modern.

I start snooping. Cans of food in the kitchen, believe it or not. The cans are like five years old judging by what I can make out on the label, but it's good enough for me! I struggle to open a can of beans until CheccChecc gets tired of watching me suck and just pops it open with one claw. He looks like shit. I can't begin to imagine the train wreck I must resemble after today.

"You saved my ass back there," I tell my Eldritch familiar, "Hell, we couldn't have made it without your help. You're a badass, Checcs. So you know. Thank you."

Little guy sighs under those tentacles and looks me in the eyes.

Izzie very brave. Maybe Old Ones wrong about humans. Some at least.

A weak smile spreads over my lips. "Is that...an actual compliment? Are you being nice to me?"

Checcs looks away and flicks his wings.

Human look awful. Eat gross goopy can food and catch breath.

Next I check in on Icarus. He's just sitting in the corner, fidgeting his broken glasses in his lap.

"Hey," I start with a nudge to his shoulder, "how was the piggy back ride?"

"Very funny."

"I totally carried you like a widdle baby boy."

340

"Cut it out."

"Your little legs all danglin' and - "

"I said stop it, alright?"

The raise in his voice stops me short. He isn't in the mood for jokes, and I guess I can't blame him.

"Hey, my bad," I respond softly, "are you alright?"

Icarus sniffs, but doesn't raise his head from his lap.

"Folfrakka...I haven't been without her in ages."

I lean down so that I'm eye level with the kid, should he choose to look back at me. "Hey, it's okay. I'm sure she's alright out there. She's a badass like you, right?"

Finally the kid looks up at me. His eyes are red and puffy.

"I know she survived the crash. I can feel her presence. But...I don't know how hurt she is. And without her, I just...feel so small and helpless again. I hate it."

It's almost like..I'm looking at myself when I was a kid. So I embrace Icarus then and there, and I'm pleasantly surprised when he doesn't resist.

"What if I'm nothing without her?" he cries into my shoulder, defeated.

"None of that bullshit, kiddo. I couldn't have made it this far without all the lessons you taught me. You're a hell of a lot stronger than you think."

Icarus forces a weak smile before wiping his face with his torn sleeve.

"I'll stay up and wait for Folfrakka. You go catch up with your friends."

"I thought that was what I was doing. Heh. But...yeah, I gotcha."

I overhear Olivia interrogating Frode in the living room area, not far from where

Claudia's body was placed. She isn't about to let his resurrection slide. I'm cramming spoonful after eager spoonful of beans into my mouth as I discreetly watch the interaction unfold in the connecting room.

"I saw you die!" Olivia's shouting now. "You were dead, as in DEAD dead!"

"The day has been full of terror," Algar begins carefully, "and we have seen all manner of nightmares and hallucinations."

"But I watched you get your head blasted off! Hell, we were wearing pieces of your brain, for fuck's sake! We all saw the same thing, didn't we, guys?!"

Beckett stops tinkering with his arm long enough to raise his hand hesitantly. Hideo's got his arms crossed as he leans against a pool table, looking uncharacteristically unsure of himself.

"I don't know what I saw," he says at last, "but Mr. Algar is right. I've seen all kinds of shit today. We all have. So I dunno."

Olivia is frustrated. She looks to me for confirmation, but I just want to eat my beans in peace. Not sure if I should give Frode away or not. Though certainly, I considered it.

In the end, though, I just shrug.

"I saw giant monsters and blood dripping out of the sky, to name a few things. It's been a long fucking day."

It wasn't the answer Olivia was hoping for, so she gives up. Her focus is quickly redirected to Beckett, who continues to struggle with his busted arm.

"Let me take a look at that, Beck. I'm, um...good at fixing things."

Beckett grins weakly. "So I've heard."

"Have fun, lovebirds." Hideo stretches. He's acting nonchalant, but it's clear as day that the guy is still very shaken. "I'm gonna take the longest nap of my fucking afterlife. Wake me when Apocalypse Day is officially over."

Frode stands up, groaning like the old man he is. His attention returns to his assistant, who is laying on a table near the wall. "Good plan. Our own fears will continue to threaten us until the day ends. Safest bet is to sleep it off, as it were. Deal with the aftermath tomorrow."

There is little opposition to that. Olivia heads off with Beckett to continue working on his arm, while Hideo falls back to have a moment apart from his friends. He looks over his shoulder before leaning in closer to me, hands in his pockets.

"I almost died twice over back there," he says quietly, "the kind you can't come back from. You saved my life, Izz. Thank you."

It's not something I'm used to hearing, and there's so much weight to it. So I say nothing, just smile awkwardly and nod. I suck at this. Hideo returns the gesture and heads off to one of the rooms.

I'm left alone with Frode and CheccChecc. It's uncomfortable.

"Is Claudia gonna be...alright?" I ask. She looks so peaceful now, despite her blood-soaked torso. Poor lady didn't deserve to die like that.

"There's a reanimation chamber in the basement below my estate. If I can get her there safely within 24 hours, she will be fine."

"That's good."

Before my guardian-reaper and I can leave, however, Frode stops me.

"Thank you for covering for me," he says quietly, avoiding eye contact. I'm assuming he means the magic head-regrowing trick. My skin curdles at the memory, and I wish that I too could believe it was only a hallucination.

"Yeah," I say at last, also avoiding eye contact. "You're lucky. And I'd be lying if I said I didn't enjoy watching an ancient asshole get what he deserved, if only for a moment."

I AM lying. There was nothing enjoyable about it at all. But not because I like Frode or anything. Just because that kind of violence...there's just nothing fun or cool about it at all. It's not like the movies. It's awful. And I'm afraid that it's all I'll see from now on when I look at this Viking dickbag so insistent on being in my life.

But there's more than that. Something I didn't wanna face, but there's no escaping it now.

"I don't think I truly understood what you meant. You know, when you first told me about the deal you made for immortality. Not sure what I was expecting. But after seeing...that. Remembering your partial confession, plus what Udolthra showed me..."

The former Viking avoids eye contact with me at all costs, only serving to reaffirm my suspicions.

"You had to sacrifice someone else's soul for that immortality. You sacrificed your own daughter, didn't you?"

Frode is getting unhinged. Pupils dilated, hands trembling, on the verge of tears almost! As much as I wanted to be wrong about this, his reaction only confirms the accuracy of my accusation. My heart sinks and an ugly rage begins to bubble up within me.

"You have to understand," he starts at last, "what I thought I wanted back then...It was all wrong. I was scared, weak, and prideful. Every day I wished would be my last, but my contract could not be undone!"

I've never seen him this upset before. The guy barely emoted before today. Now he looks on the verge of a psychotic break, mumbling between breaths in his old tongue. Soon he's actually crying - sobbing like a baby! It makes me angrier. He doesn't have the right to a pity party. Not then, not now, not ever. Some shit you can never come back from.

"So what am I, then?" Frode quiets down a bit, but he still can't look me in the eyes. With balled fists, I continue. "Your second chance to prove to yourself you can be a good dad or something? Is that it?"

"I understand if you never want to see me again after tonight."

I wanna slap him. I feel betrayed. Pissed. Disgusted. Utterly exhausted.

"Did my mom know?"

"Yes...Despite my past, she believed in me. She gave me hope in humanity and made me believe I could be a better version of myself. But one thing long life has taught me is that I am exceptionally good at ruining every meaningful relationship I'm lucky enough to forge. You have every right to hate me."

"Good, because I do. After this shit day is officially over with, I want you to stay the fuck out of my life."

Resisting the urge to scream, to throw something, to say something else hurtful...I grab my shit and head for my room. I'm not about to let one more revelation tear me apart. Yeah I'm hurt, but it's a drop in a very big bucket. The whole world is hurting right now.

The engineer's shameful cries fall behind me when I close the door. I ignore the concerned looks of my guardian-reaper and just bury my head in the pillow beside him.

Seven hours to go. Is it too much to hope I spend them passed the fuck out?

9:30 PM

Yep. Too much to ask.

Wake up from more nightmares to the sound of loud banging on metal. Checcs is fast asleep, no doubt more exhausted than I am. Stumble out of the guest bed, put my ear against the door. I hear agitated voices outside...and they aren't familiar.

Fuck.

Am I imagining it? Normally I'd be more scared. But after everything else today...

Open the door, slowly. Peek outside...

Just what I thought. We're no longer alone down here.

Small group of armed undeads, eight that I can see from here. Not soldiers - these are regular people dressed in homemade riot gear like they're ready for a zombie apocalypse. Six men, two women. Aged early twenties to mid forties, maybe. They have a woman with them: a maid, by the looks of it. She's tied up, with a gun to her head. Shit! If I had to guess, these invaders came through Algar's mansion and forced the maid to grant them access to the panic room.

They're making demands, but they're incoherent. They're trying to intimidate, prove to themselves and their other captives who's in charge. But it's obvious that these guys are still dealing with their own demons. Unfocused, scared shitless. A combo as dangerous as it is advantageous to the only person left unaccounted for down here.

Me.

One last glance at the Eldritch monster sleeping beside the bed. I almost rouse him from his sleep, but decide against it. I think this is literally the first time I've seen him sleep. He must really need it. I can take it from here.

Am I crazy?

Maybe.

But a little crazy is the only way my friends and I will survive one more threat to our safety on this painfully long night.

A quick look for the gun I acquired proves fruitless. I must have left it out there. Firm grip on my pocket knife. Head out the door slowly, quietly...

The invaders' attention is solely on that asshole Frode the Chode, who is currently tied to a chair having demands yelled in his face. Two people are sitting on the floor unconscious, tied back to back with bags over their heads. The exposed green curls and reattached steampunk arm leave no doubt over their identities. Claudia's body is notably gone from the table behind Frode. But, Icarus...where's Icarus? Or Hideo?

Survey the immediate threats: a pistol pointed at my unconscious friends, a knife at the maid's throat, and two other dickwads with rifles in hand.

Suddenly I feel a little under-armed with my pocket knife.

Wait. That's not all I have...

Knocked out of my own thoughts the moment one guy back-hands Algar across the face. I can't make out what they're saying that well from back here, but it's safe to assume that the playboy isn't cooperating how they'd like. Some of the other invaders start bickering amongst themselves. Hard to have an organized coup when every member is being tormented by private fears and hallucinations.

Movement in the kitchen, behind the island. It's Hideo! That's a 6/10 in clearing the premises and taking hostages, assholes. The reanimated athlete and I make eye contact before turning our attention back to the problem at hand.

We have to act, fast. But what do we do?

Clang! A pan drops in the kitchen. Hideo's lack of surprise tells me it was intentional. The group of invaders are immediately on edge, sending one of their own to check the kitchen. Dude with a beer belly armed like Rambo swaggers towards the source of noise, rifle still in hand. The closer he gets, the more I see his hands shaking. He's mumbling to himself, too. He's almost in the kitchen now, peeking around the island...

A howl of pain, courtesy of a kitchen knife to the foot. Rifle fires off into the cabinets once before Hideo sends an aluminum elbow into the shooter's groin. Ouch. Guy drops fast, cursing and calling for help. A punch to the jaw and it's light's out. Hideo grabs the rifle and stands up fast, pointing the weapon squarely at the group of attackers ahead. Only problem is, they've already reacted.

"One more dumb fuckin' move and we'll paint the walls with your friends' brains!"

Lots of bustle and panic, but their apparent leader isn't lying. The gun that was once lowered behind Olivia and Beckett is now placed directly against the back of the veteran's head. One shot for both of them. Three more guns are pointed back at Hideo now, all quivering to different degrees. It's their fear and lack of resolve that just might get us out of here alive...if we choose our next actions wisely.

Hideo isn't taking their threat lightly. There's a standstill for a moment before the athlete concedes.

"Alright. Nobody else has to get hurt. I'm gonna put the weapon down, okay?"

He lowers the weapon slowly, slowly.

"Hurry the fuck up!"

The rifle is on the ground now. As an apparent display of further cooperation, Hideo gently kicks the firearm across the floor, further out of his own reach. The onlooking assailants appear satisfied with this gesture, unaware that the weapon he kicked away is now within arm's reach of somebody else.

Me.

Never shot a gun before. But judging by Hideo's sideways glance, there's no time like the present to learn.

As another armed guy closes in to take the athlete captive, I make my move. Down on the ground, sliding the rifle into my hands. My only saving grace is that they weren't aware of my presence. Before the guy can react, my finger's on the trigger. *One shot, Izz. Don't fuck it up...*

Bang. My eyes close for a second as I recoil, but a scream of pain tells me I hit my target. Look again and see the asshole is on the floor, clutching at his gut as black blood oozes out.

Pandemonium ensues. Hideo uses the chaos to pull out another kitchen knife and expertly throw it into the chest of a fast-approaching guard. Before the poor guy even hits the floor, his other friends are shooting through him indiscriminately. Bullets spray the walls, forcing Hideo to take cover behind the kitchen sink. I wanna take another shot at the assailants, but I'm too afraid of hitting one of my friends in the process. I drop the gun nervously.

"Wait!" yells their leader, bald guy in his forties with the build of an ex-marine.

"Stop shootin'! It's a warm-blood!"

The four remaining invaders eventually stop firing and turn their attention to me.

Shit.

"Kill the Jap. Take the girl."

Fuck you, assholes. But if being a warm-blood makes me valuable...

I quickly take out my pocket knife and hold the blade up to my own throat. I watch the approaching woman's eyes widen in dismay. Good.

"Kill him and I'll kill myself."

It works. Thank God. Another dickwad is waved over to take care of Hideo. The girl stands there, glaring at me but not touching her rifle. I keep the knife to my throat as I watch the other guy head for Hideo with plastic ties in hand. Thankfully, my friend complies. Keeps his hands up as the rail thin youth grabs them and ties them behind his back. Hideo is then led back to the others, propelled forward with a salty shove.

"Happy? Put the fuckin' knife down now."

This blonde chick isn't messing around. She's got her gun aimed at my face again, though I can't help but feel like it's an empty threat. Still, I comply. Drop the knife and let her bind my hands the same as Hideo's. It's alright. I still have another trick up my sleeve...

BAM. That hurt.

Lights...

out...

???

Blur of faces. Jumble of voices ranging from pissed-off to scared shitless. Shake my head, clear my vision. Shit, my head hurts. Nothing compared to the aftermath of getting brain-raided by Eldritch monsters, but it still sucks hard.

I'm tied to another chair, hands bound behind the back, tight. I taste blood.

Maid is on the floor, crying under a piece of duct tape. Olivia and Beckett, I hear their scared voices muffled beneath their bags. Hideo's been beat up, unconscious on the floor. Fuck. Frode is still conscious in his chair, though he's looking particularly awful. I see an otherworldly rage on his face as the invaders' leader moves in on me.

"I'll give you anything you want," he says behind gritted teeth, pulling at his restraints. "Money. Prosthetics. Hell, even priceless prototypes. Just don't hurt the girl. Please."

The assholes merely laugh. The tall guy hits the Viking with the butt of his gun, knocking a couple teeth out.

"You know how hard it is to come by one of these nowadays?" chuckles the leader, petting my hair. I spit at him venomously, but he only seems to relish my anger. "Warm-bloods are more valuable than any of that bullshit technology you got. Better than any cash you think you can offer. This right here, is a gift that keeps on givin'."

He leans in even closer. I can see every wrinkle. I can see the fog in his eyes - he's been dead for a while. Scratches and gun wounds and stitches all over. Not a single prosthetic - he's oldschool undead for sure, and so are the rest of his friends.

Fingertips run across my cheek, and I feel an all-too familiar clamminess return to my skin. Not again.

"Young, warm flesh like this," he continues, eyes up and down my body, "will fetch a pretty penny indeed."

The other guys laugh and look me up and down, too. Stupid, horny, undead dickbags. It pisses me off, and the lack of care from the only two females in their group infuriates me further.

Algar spits out black blood. "You want warm-bloods? Let this one go and I'll introduce you to ten more."

"Empty promises." Asshole's hand travels down my throat. "The world's goin' to shit. You can't guarantee any of your 'warm-bloods' are gonna be around. All that's for sure is what we've got right here. And she's plenty to go around."

More laughter from our captors. There's talk about 'trying me out'.

Fuck that.

Fuck all of these pieces of shit.

More enraged and empty threats from my friends. Nobody to save me. Not Frode. Not CheccChecc. All I have...is me.

In my peripheral vision, I see more hands sprout from my chair and start grabbing me.

OUR LITTLE SECRET. NOBODY HAS TO KNOW.

Not again, brain. I know what's real and what's not. And I know what's NOT gonna happen this time.

Because I'm not the prey.

Not anymore.

Not ever again.

Quietly, I move one foot to the ankle of my prosthetic one.

"Getting that burning feeling in your loins, pervert?" I scoff. "I might be able to help with that."

Click.

Their confusion once again works to my advantage. My robotic foot moves up and converts into a rocket. I raise it up so that it's square in the leader's crotch.

I've never felt as titillated as I am at this moment. Watching rocket fuel blast into the junk of the last pervert to try hurting me. He's screaming at the top of his lungs. The other captors are flipping out. If ever there was a time to act...it's now.

Boom. Rocket fuel sends me falling backwards in my chair to the ground, hard on my bound wrists. I'm propelled into the wall, where the head of my chair protects my cranium from being smashed by the force. Quickly I turn off my 'boom leg'. The room is shrouded in smoke, and more gunfire sounds off. Thankfully, the high-pressure fall wrecked the chair I was strapped in. My wrists are still bound, but I'm able to get up and stand now.

The fight I return to is a mess. It is quickly evident that my unexpected attack triggered the fear again in our captors. Thank God. The woman who bound me hits the ground with a gunshot in her chest, courtesy of her own terrorized companion. The tall guy is on his knees, crying and staring at some invisible horror on the wall. I take my robotic leg and give him a good, hard kick to the back of the head. No doubt that hurt him waaaay more than it hurt me.

A splatter of dark blood and more screams. Turn around and see a familiar set of bat wings flickering in the smoky haze. It's CheccChecc! He's late to the party, but I'm so grateful he's here. He's tearing the back off another guy, claws going this way and that under the narrowed glare of those glowing eyes.

More gunfire, but none of it hits their targets. I shoulder the other woman hard, forcing her gun flying out of her hands. She takes a swing at me, and misses badly. Crying and mumbling to herself, she's fighting her own fears and losing. I take a page from Aunt Maggie's book and headbutt the girl, hard. Now THAT hurt. But she's on the floor now. One less asshole to worry about.

"Miss Cordona, please duck."

That voice. Is that...Claudia? Had Frode snuck off to reanimate his faithful assistant while we slept?

It's still a little hard to see in here, but there's no doubt about it. That petite girl standing in the doorway, holding what looks like a prototype of sorts over her shoulder. Future tech. It isn't readily recognizable, but the closest thing I could compare it to is...

A rocket launcher.

You better fucking believe I'll duck.

"Checcs, get down, now!"

BOOM.

The remaining captors left standing are blown away with a crackling thunder. The room lights up, and I feel a whoosh of air pulling at my hair and clothes as the blast dissipates. When the air clears, I see only friendly faces remaining. Well, except for the single asshole left, making a run for it. Well, less of a run and more of a limp.

It's the leader. Claudia is ready to fire again, but I stop her.

"I've got this."

I barely think as I make a run for the cowardly piece of shit. I overtake him in no time, tackling him to the ground with all of my body weight. He hits the floor hard but struggles to right himself. With my arms still tied behind my back, I wrap my legs around his neck and get him in a choke hold. Tighter and tighter I hold him, hearing him choke and curse and cry all at the same time.

"Fuck you, you piece of shit," I spit, hearing him struggle for his final breaths. "My name is Isabella Cordona, and I'm nobody's prey."

We struggle a little longer, me fighting against his flails and him prying at my powerful grip. After a few more pathetic cries and gargles, the fight leaves him. His body sinks. My heart pounds out of my chest. After a few long moments, I finally release him and stand up.

We did it. We won.

Fuck.

11:50 PM

The air in the room is thick. Everyone is quiet for a while, catching their breath and resisting the cruel grip of fear just a little longer.

The Eldritch monster claws off everyone's zip tie restraints, save for Frode's. His assistant is quick to put down her weapon and take care of his. Together, with bloodied wrists and tired bodies, we go around the room helping one another up. The maid is okay, thank God. She apologizes profusely for giving in to the invaders' demands for access to the panic room, but her employer makes it clear that he places no blame on her.

"You did what you had to do," he says tiredly, wiping the blood from his beard, "and I'm not worth dying for."

As I stand here, surrounded in equal parts by conscious friends and defeated enemies, I feel no fear. I'm shaking, and my heart's still pounding. But I'm not afraid. Not anymore. It doesn't take long before I notice the curious looks of my battered companions. I detect a mixture of fear and awe, concern and respect. It's a different blend than I'm used to.

"Nice use of that leg of yours," Frode breaks the silence hesitantly, "though I don't recall including an incredibly dangerous rocket-fueled modification in that build."

At that point, Olivia raises her hand with a sheepish grin.

"That...might have been me."

The Viking raises a single brow at the pretty girl he apparently had very different opinions of prior.

11:58 PM. If what I learned about this whole fear apocalypse thing is true, then that means we only have two minutes left to survive.

We hug each other. We cry. We laugh, or at least try to. We complain about our aches and pains. But more than anything, we share a critical moment with one another that may never be accurately measured. I look around the room and I see familiar faces in an entirely new light. Together we shared our darkest moments and deepest fears. It's as uncomfortable as it is a relief. Perhaps this group of very different people has much more in common than I initially thought. And reanimated or not...we're all so painfully human.

Shortly after midnight passes, there is a palpable shift in the air. The unnatural constriction of my mind that had been bending my thoughts and fears for the last twenty-four hours loosens itself, replaced with a raging migraine. Still, it's a tremendous relief, one that echoes itself in the faces of my companions.

We're free.

We survived.

It took everything out of us. Almost drove us off the edge into complete insanity.

But we made it.

The only question that remains is...what about the rest of humanity?

What will the next twenty-four hours look like?

It's an answer I don't think any of us are prepared to face yet.

For now, there's only one thing we need for certain.

Sleep.

However, I have one last obstacle between me and a pillow: a certain Eldritch babysitter who is less than enthusiastic with his human's actions.

"You alright?" I ask him cautiously.

Foolish human. Could have died. Stupid human. Stupid.

He's mad, alright. But the concern in his warbled voice is not something I'm imagining. It feels like I'm getting scolded by my mom all over again.

It's a little frustrating for that reason. But mostly? It's comforting. In its own weird way...it's nice.

"I get it, Checcs. But there was no time and I had to act fast. I know you can understand that."

Saving other humans not Izzie's job.

"You're right, it's not. But I care about these humans, and it was the right thing to do."

Hmm. CheccChecc understands. Still very stupid.

A sigh escapes my lips. Out of the corner of my eye, I see Checcs flick his wings about nervously.

But, Izzie very brave also. Selfless. Such behavior from humans unexpected.

Compliments make me uncomfortable. But more than anything right now, I'm just tired. So I laugh it off, and for the first time I notice the new wounds on CheccChecc's little body. The worst of them is a tear in his right wing that goes clear through.

"Looks like somebody clipped you along the way, Checcs. I can help with that. If you'll let me."

My guardian-reaper looks from his wing to me, then back again. Maybe he didn't even notice it until now? He looks utterly confused for some reason.

Why? Izzie in worse shape. Look terrible.

I laugh. "Have you looked in a mirror? Or are you a bad liar, too? Come on. Let me help."

Hmm. Fine.

I wasn't expecting him to actually accept! Admittedly, I'm a little touched. He hobbles tiredly on all fours back to our room. The bodies of our captors are relocated for our safety and peace of mind. They'll be dealt with later. Final goodnights and wordless 'thank you's are exchanged, and I leave my friends to spend the morning after the apocalypse stitching up an ancient monster and sleeping off what feels like an eternity of torment.

Just as I finish playing doctor with Checcs, my door cracks open. It's Icarus! Thank God, he's okay.

"Where were you? Are you okay? Did you go looking for Folfrakka or something?"

He avoids eye contact with me.

"Can I...sleep in here? With you?"

Hmm. Guess he isn't in the mood for questions. I'm too tired to push. Just glad he's okay.

"Of course." I pat the opposite end of the bed. "Up you go."

He says nothing. Just crawls into bed and slumps into the pillow. He'll be hearing no more jokes from me.

Indeed, like everyone else in this bunker, I have nothing left. Utterly spent.

Goodnight, world. If you and I are still here in the morning...we'll have to find the courage to move on and rebuild. Somehow.

CHAPTER FOURTEEN

A cold wind. A silence as peaceful as it is deafening. A bouquet of roses cradled in my arms. A prayer on my tongue.

It's only been a few weeks since the world almost ended.

The devastation was unimaginable. Not just in Dead Vegas, or here on the sanctuary island. All over the entire world.

Millions dead, hundreds of thousands incapable of being reanimated. Millions more still fighting to restore their sanity.

Cities in ruin. Political and social upheaval. Alliances between nations torn apart.

They didn't know what hit them. They called it an act of terrorism. Chemical warfare, it had to be. Nation against nation, person against person. The news was full of speculation and finger-pointing. Nobody would ever believe the truth. Humanity's only hope for moving on was to come together, but we all know that's easier said than done.

I place the roses at the foot of a gravestone I've been too afraid to visit. *Dayanna Morales Cordona, Beloved Mother and Friend.* It's heart-wrenching. Beside her is a more familiar gravestone: *Dante Aiden Cordona, Beloved Son and Brother Returned to God Too Soon.*

So much loss. So much grief. As I stand here now, honoring my mother's memory, I'm reminded of every other person who has lost someone permanently during the apocalypse. Candlelit vigils all across the U.S. Mournful songs in Israel. Mass gatherings and prayer in India. The names of lost loved ones scribed onto millions of paper lanterns in Japan. Families and strangers alike crying and holding each other, asking God how he could possibly let this happen.

If only they knew God had nothing to do with it.

"Mrrreow!"

The brush of a synthetic fur tail across my skin alerts me to Eckerd's presence. He's purring as he zig-zags between my legs. The affection of my favorite reanimated feline is always welcome, especially now.

Next I feel a cold hand press gently against my back. It's Aunt Maggie. I had gotten back home to the sanctuary island as soon as I possibly could after the apocalypse. Everything here was fucked, still kinda is. People died, structures were damaged, and crops were burnt to ash. Aunt Maggie was one of the casualties of that fateful day, and I blamed myself for not being there for her when she needed me. Thank God her long-time friend Roger was able to get her reanimated in time. No slump trucks on an island full of warm-bloods.

"I miss her more every day," I utter softly, "but I'm so glad she didn't have to go through that hell."

"Couldn't agree more." Aunt Maggie sighs. "It's gonna take a long time before we can recover from all this. Hell, before the whole fucking world can recover."

"Meeeeerow." Eckerd agrees, too.

We stand in silence for a moment. CheccChecc perches on a distant tree branch, well out of reach as he keeps his eyes on me. There's been a lot of silence between the two of us as well. It's like none of us know what to say to make things better.

Aunt Maggie breaks the silence with a topic I'd rather not discuss. "Have you heard much from Frode Algar lately?"

"Nope, and I'd rather keep it that way."

The reanimated woman beside me steps forward long enough to place a single lily on my mother's grave. I told her all about Frode the Chode. There was no love lost from her for the rich playboy, but I could tell she had some sort of reserve.

"He told me that my mom knew about his sacrifice, but I still don't believe it. There's no way my mom would let somebody like that around her only daughter."

Another long pause. Aunt Maggie to the rescue once more.

"Have I ever told you much about my life before I met your mom?"

"I know you used to be a pop star called Rita Venus and you had a chimpanzee sidekick."

She chuckles weakly. "Ding ding ding. But I was also a grade A asshole. You think I'm bad now, but I was so much worse back then. Spoiled rotten, selfish, angry, and ignorant. Pretty much a shit person. Everybody hated me, but not as much as I hated myself."

"Geez, uplifting story there." I sound dismissive, but she has my attention.

"What I'm trying to say is...Meeting your mom and caring for her made me a better person. It offered my miserable life meaning and hope. I mean, she believed in me when nobody else did. And look what we went on to accomplish together."

"Are you trying to tell me that I should make up with Frode?"

"I'm not gonna tell you what you should or shouldn't do. You're not a kid anymore. But it's good to remember that people CAN change. Your mom had a way of bringing out the best in those around her, and so do you. So just...don't give up, alright?"

"...Not bad."

Aunt Maggie cocks her head. "What's not bad?"

"Your motivational speech."

She grins that cheshire cat grin and gives me a wink. "Yeah, huh? Probably my best yet."

"I wouldn't say your best," I tease, "but it's definitely up there."

Before Aunt Maggie can get sassy back, I give her a surprise hug.

"I'll think about what you said. Thank you."

She hugs me back. "Anytime, kiddo."

It's heavy. All of it. There's a lot of work to be done on the island. I've already heard murmurs of distrust and paranoia among the other warm-bloods. If I don't step in, knowing what I know, then the members of this fragile community will continue to turn against one other. The future of humanity can't afford that, especially not now.

"We're gonna make this right," I say out loud, an attempt to convince both Aunt Maggie and myself. "The sanctuary is gonna survive this and come out stronger. It has to. For Mom."

Aunt Maggie lets me go and kisses me on the forehead.

"For Dayanna," she agrees. "I'm headed back in. Town hall in thirty. You coming?"

"I'll be there," I offer with a tired smile. "Just need a few more minutes."

Aunt Maggie nods and heads back to the mansion. Eckerd follows after her, tail perked up. With a sigh, I sit down on folded knees before my mother's grave and offer one last prayer.

CheccChecc is quick to fly back over and sit next to me. I wonder how the apocalypse affected him, and what he thinks about the future.

"Checcs," I ask at last, eyes still on my mother's grave. "If you weren't stuck babysitting me...what would you do?"

CheccChecc not understand question.

"Your job. That contract that keeps you stuck with me. If there was no job, and you were free, what would you choose to do?"

CheccChecc seems utterly puzzled. It's like after Grady's Mansion, trying to get him to think about 'fun'. I can almost see the wheels turning.

His next response rings a little more clearly in my head. It's like he's whispering in my ear as opposed to mumbling in the distance of my consciousness like usual.

Remember when CheccChecc say protecting Izzie only job?

"Hmmm? Back in that cheap hotel, forever ago?"

The little guy nods.

CheccChecc lied. Izzie was supposed to die, same night Izzie jumped off building. CheccChecc saved Izzie instead of reaping soul.

My jaw just drops.

"What? Are you for real?! All this time, I thought –"

Point is. CheccChecc already doing what CheccChecc wants.

I'm utterly flabbergasted. So many questions. I don't know where to start, so I just...do.

"But if I was supposed to die back then, and you disobeyed Penumbran orders by saving me...what does that mean for you?"

CheccChecc shrugs and looks off into the distance.

CheccChecc no return to The Penumbra. Stuck in human dimension.

My Eldritch companion finally turns his attention back to me, and I swear that I detect a hint of...embarrassment?

"Why?" I ask him, blinking away tears. "Why did you do it? Why did you save me, if you knew the cost?"

CheccChecc knows what loss feel like. Izzie had much loss, not fair. Death of Izzie too soon, not right. CheccChecc chose own path. No regrets.

"But your home! You can never - "

No worry for CheccChecc. Human dimension not the punishment Penumbrans made to believe. CheccChecc happy here.

...

"Checcs, I - "

Stop. Silly human. More work to do. Yes?

Deep breath.

"...Right. Thank you."

Not another word is uttered between us. I sit at my mother's grave, hands folded in my lap. CheccChecc sits beside me in the grass, and I swear I can hear a sigh under all those tentacles.

He's right, though. Despite the solace I so desperately seek, it's time to get up and head back. However, I'm stopped the second I feel something leathery touch my side. It's CheccChecc, tangible once more as he leans against me.

Ever so carefully, I raise one hand up to see if I can touch the monster where he sits. Sure enough, my hand doesn't pass through this time. I make contact with that dinosaur-like skin, and I'm warmed by his little body. This is new and unexpected. But...it's nice.

My cautious touch becomes a careful stroke down and back again like I'm petting Eckerd. CheccChecc closes his eyes and says nothing more. We sit at my mother's grave in peace - something all too rare in this new and broken world.

***

This job isn't easy. I can't imagine it was before, but especially not now.

Forty-eight warm-bloods died during the apocalypse, most of them from accidents or self-inflicted wounds. This pushed forward an ongoing debate on the island: what should our official stance be on reanimation?

Everyone had a lot to say about it. Should the warm-blood sanctuary retain our initial anti-reanimation beliefs to ensure a moral standard for the future we're building? Or should every individual maintain their freedom of choice? It was contentious, so we put it to a vote. Freedom of choice won out, but barely. I believe that was the right call. Certain stipulations will have to be made for it in the upcoming bill to discourage reckless or intentional death for the purpose of reanimation. We wanna keep the majority of our population living. But we're gonna have to figure out where and how we're gonna build a reanimation chamber on the island.

Then there's trade. The apocalypse led to a lot of renewed distrust between nations and foreign entities. Unfortunate, but not surprising. The sanctuary had just signed a trade agreement with the UK, but the union was cut short by apocalypse-induced xenophobia and anti-life-ism. We must increase U.S. imports, sell fish and crops to passing traders, and pursue new trading alliances with neighboring islands. We reject all offers to sell warm-bloods for goods and services - which, by the way, are as frequent as they are unnerving.

Understandably, our sanctuary island had lost momentum after the apocalypse hit. Most nations' efforts would be redirected towards rebuilding, securing borders, and signing peace treaties. Xenophobia may be at an all time high, but the universal desire to prevent further terror and loss of life is still winning out. Thank God. There's hope yet.

Then there's the day to day stuff. The fishermen need more supplies. Farmers need new equipment. The people need additional medicine. The school needs more materials and teachers. More children are being born, and we lost one of our best doctors during the apocalypse. The demand for everyday commodities and important services is staggering, and we're barely meeting those demands as it is. We gotta outsource, and fast.

I didn't realize how much work went into running the island, and my naivety makes me feel guilty for leaving so much of the responsibility with Aunt Maggie. It's a lot. And I hear the way folks here talk to her. Though she was my mom's partner, a lot of the warm-bloods are still unhappy being led by a cold-blood. It's not fair, not after everything she does for them. But it's reality. I'm hoping that by standing with her, the people will show her more respect. I think it's helping, but the unrest is still ever present.

However, I get it. After the apocalypse of course, but also before. People risked everything and traveled far and wide to start a new life on this island. They escaped prejudice, violence, and great hardship, just like my mom did. They too came here for a better future. We owe them that.

That's why taking care of the sanctuary my mom built is not a privilege. It's a promise. It's a responsibility to every human who had to fight for survival and learn to put their trust in strangers not so unlike themselves. To people like my mom, who believed that humanity was capable of greater things when they worked together. It's a sentiment I share now more than ever.

That being said, it's tough. All the time.

We make a choice to fund one group, then another group suffers. Make one person happy, anger two more as a result. Every action intended to better the sanctuary has its consequences. There's no easy answer. It's stressful as hell. I have no clue how my mom kept her positive attitude all the time. But I do understand that ever-present burden on her. It's the weight of the world.

The island and its needs are evolving. As our population continues to grow, electing officials is the obvious next step. We'll vote on everything. After all, the future we're making here belongs to all of us.

After spending hours debating with fellow islanders and taking shit tons of notes, I spend the remainder of my night upstairs in my old bedroom, brainstorming more solutions. For now, I'm thinking of ways to raise money. Public awareness and foreign aid are necessities. I can't pretend I'm an expert, but I CAN put that proverbial 'A' in Social Studies to the test.

"This shit is hard, Checcs. Taking care of all of these people. Trying to do the right thing. I thought it would be easier."

My Eldritch familiar continues to pet a very sleepy Eckerd by the window. He's rocking his old pair of bunny pajamas again, and enjoying the attention it garners him from unsuspecting humans.

Taking care of one human hard enough.

"Heh. I believe that." I raise my pen for a moment, observing the prehistoric entity sitting so casually across the room. There's something wrong with him, I can tell. Maybe he's bored? Life on the island is a lot different from life in Dead Vegas. I couldn't blame him.

"Hey," I start softly, watching those bunny ears bounce up. "I was gonna surprise you with this, but I think you should know now. I talked to Aunt Maggie and her manager about getting a fast food place built here. Milkshakes all day, any day you want! Sounds pretty rad, huh?"

No excitement on the creature's face. If anything, he looks more disappointed. Those tentacles lower, and his eyes turn farther from mine.

Kind. But not necessary.

"What's wrong with you? Human girls know when something is wrong, you know. It's like a sixth sense. You can tell me."

Nothing wrong. Izzie should focus on humans who need Izzie.

I'm not buying it. It's obvious that my companion is as stubborn as I am.

"I'm here for you too, Checcs." I pause for a moment, almost too afraid to ask the question waiting on my tongue. "Are you...unhappy on the island? Do you...want me to bring you back to Udolthra's sanctuary? So you can be with your own kind?"

No. CheccChecc not forsake friends.

I don't admit it, but I'm relieved.

"Then what's wrong? What's on your mind?"

...Folfrakka. Icarus. The mission. Did Izzie forget?

My hand stops writing and I slide the paper aside. The Penumbran deserves my full attention.

"No way. Of course not. Icarus texted and told me he's fine. He found Folfrakka and they both needed time to heal. As for the mission...I assume you mean finding The Skin Craft Killer?"

Checcs nods, flopping those bunny ears once more.

"I didn't forget. But there's just so much to do. You know? The people here, they need me."

CheccChecc knows. Understand.

"Besides, if we're lucky, that asshole died during the apocalypse, too. No reported killings since."

...Yes. But everything Team Icarus endured. Together. Many adventures. Everything, just to find killer. So close to answers. Izzie can't give up so easily.

"I'm not giving up. I just...have to shift priorities a little, you know? I have a lot on my shoulders, so just...cut me some slack, alright?"

Yes. CheccChecc understand. Many responsibilities here. No time for more adventures.

I still don't feel good about it. But I don't know what else to say, so I back off.

CheccChecc says nothing else. Only continues to pet my aunt's reanimated cat as he purs like a little engine and I go back to my notes.

***

A new day full of work, planning, promises, and compromise. But also, something else.

Visitors! Very special ones at that, hailing all the way from Dead Vegas. It's Hideo and Olivia!

They arrived by private jet, courtesy of ESTRID Industries judging by the giant logo sprawled along its length. I didn't ask questions. Only greeted my friends with exclamations high enough in pitch to break windows. It was the first time I've seen them since the apocalypse. I ask the obvious and inevitable question, though: where's Beckett?

"He's visiting some people from his past," Olivia answers softly. "First time since he left the service. I offered to join him, but he said it was something he had to do on his own. He didn't elaborate, but it seemed pretty important to him. I hope it helps."

I hope so, too. But I also can't help but wonder if any of these 'people from his past' include The Skin Craft Killer.

No way.

We exchange pleasantries. I reintroduce them to CheccChecc, who is now much more visible thanks to his fluffy attire of choice. I introduce them to Aunt Maggie, who charms them immediately with her brazen personality.

I show them around the island, and the pair look about as out of place as I must have back in Dead Vegas. It's comical and oddly gratifying to be on the other end this time around. Hideo takes an immediate interest in the docks, so we head that way next as the athlete fills me in on what's new.

Apparently, the social media star is no more. I'm shocked by how casual he is as he tells me. Hideo confessed to using illegal body modifications and was banned from playing at least two sports professionally: soccer and kickboxing. His sponsors dropped out. His social media following plummeted. The money stopped rolling in, and the fame was replaced with notoriety. It's the kind of thing that would humiliate most folks or send them into spiraling depression. But Hideo? He seems...happy.

"Everything I had," he tells us, "was what I thought I always wanted. But none of it felt real, you know?"

We greet the fishermen with smiles and waves. My undead companions are met with a few double-takes and cautious stares, but nobody stops us from passing through.

"Do you miss it?" I ask him quietly as he absorbs his surroundings like a curious child. "The lifestyle and the fame, I mean. It's a lot to leave behind."

He shrugs. "If it is, it doesn't feel like it. I'd rather be someone I like again. Do more good with the inheritance I have left. Start fresh."

Olivia appears as proud of our mutual friend as I am as she gives him a hefty slap on the shoulder. His bashful reaction is uncharacteristic for the ever-assured bachelor I first met almost a year ago. Like his wardrobe, Hideo has changed. And as I watch him observe an unfamiliar world with endearing enthusiasm, I'm happy to know that I'm not the only one changed by the revelations of apocalypse day.

Apparently, this trip was more than just a visit. Hideo makes it clear that he wants to help.

"I'll do anything," pleads the undead pretty boy, "I mean, I don't know much about any of this stuff to be honest. But I want to learn. I'll donate money. I'll get my hands dirty, too. Just let me help. Please."

A smile spreads over my lips. How could I possibly say no?

"There's always work to be done around here. If you're interested in the fishery, I can introduce you to Cho-Hee. She runs the docks down here and she's one of the nicest islanders. As long as you don't mind smelling like tuna all the time. Oh, and not having any mirrors to check your hair in."

"Lucky for me, natural beauty doesn't need much maintenance." He winks. "Plus I like the smell of fish. So count me in."

"The stench of fresh tuna is still an improvement over his cologne, anyway."

Hideo rolls his eyes and simpers. "Livi's not wrong, though. Girls always hated it."

We laugh like old times. Like before the whole world changed. Before WE changed. It's comforting, during all the chaos and uncertainty the apocalypse left us with.

Cho-Hee is introduced to an eager cold-blood as comfortable around the water as she is. The dutiful woman is skeptical, but not about to turn down such a capable volunteer. After a brief evaluation of the pretty boy's demeanor, her expression softens. She hands Hideo a pair of smelly overalls and even smellier boots.

"Get changed," she tells him, hiding a smile. "And I'll put you to work."

Hideo and I exchange looks that say far more than any words could suffice. A sort of mutual admiration and gratitude after our shared terror, still too fresh to discuss. Olivia and I watch as the former athlete grabs his new wardrobe and follows briskly after Cho-Hee.

***

Olivia and I catch up. A lot has happened since I last saw her. Helping rebuild the auto shop. Volunteering at Dead Vegas relief programs with Hideo. A particularly exciting development is Olivia's new job. Apparently, Frode Algar was more impressed with the undead girl's modifications to my leg than he let on.

"No more pill-peddling for pocket change, because you're looking at the newest paid intern at ESTRID Industries, girl!" she shares, positively giddy. We cheer and hug. Even my bunny-hooded monster gets involved in the excitement, accepting an enthusiastic high-five from the both of us.

Olivia sighs and takes a seat beside me on a nearby bench. There's a different air about her. She's more vulnerable, that's for certain. But at the same time, I detect a confidence unlike any I've seen from her before. It's something that goes deeper, beneath her perpetually cool surface.

"You know, for the longest time...I hated Oliver. I thought he caused all my problems and represented all my weaknesses. Everything I didn't want to be. I wanted to bury him forever."

Olivia pauses for a moment. I turn my body so that I'm facing her more. She has all of my attention.

"My dad spent my natural life convincing me that Oliver was something to be ashamed of. But I realized something, you know? I may not identify as Oliver anymore, but he's still an important part of who I am today. That's why I'll be happier if I can learn to love the past, present, and future tense of myself. Besides, self-loathing is tiring as fuck."

"Amen to that. I am SO proud of you, Olivia. Seriously."

The Aussie smiles at me, her platinum curls gently blowing across her face with the low wind.

"Thanks, babe."

I give Olivia a hug so sudden that it elicits a startled giggle from her. She returns it, and we share a few peaceful moments in silence watching the waves hit the rocks below.

"So how is Beckett holding up exactly?" I ask at last, carefully. "I haven't heard from him since that night."

Olivia lowers her head and sighs deeply.

"He's having a tough time. PTSD worse than before. He never really had a proper outlet for dealing with what happened in the war. The apocalypse forced everything back to the surface. We're working through it. Trying to, anyways."

"Poor guy. We gotta stick by him. His country may not give a shit about him, but his friends do."

What am I saying? Beckett is Emery Farrow's grandson. The asshole responsible for reanimating that serial killer. So why do I...feel sorry for him?

Olivia curls her legs up and wraps her arms around them. "I just hope he can forgive himself, too. It's hard for somebody to accept any kindness when they're sure they don't deserve it. Trust I understand that."

"He's got the support of people that have seen him at his highest highs and lowest lows. Plus the genuine affection of the coolest chick I know. He'll be okay, in time. I'm sure of it. Don't give up on him, Olivia."

A raspberry leaves the girl's lips, visibly startling CheccChecc. "Not a chance, Izz. I'm in it for the long haul. He's not the only stubborn arsehole in this relationship." The girl pauses to really look me in the eyes. "Thanks, Izz. For everything."

I don't know what else to say. This is all so new to me. For the longest time I thought I would only ever feel this close to my mom and Aunt Maggie. But after sharing in each other's lowest moments and overcoming them together...I feel a bond with Olivia and the others that I never anticipated. It feels unbreakable.

"How about you?" she asks hesitantly. "I mean. After whatever fears fucked with you that day. How are YOU holding up?"

Silence all over again. I'm still uncomfortable thinking about the long-suppressed fear I was forced to process on that plane. I would be lying if I said I didn't cry over it in fleeting moments of privacy between sanctuary obligations.

"It's okay. You don't have to talk about it. Just wanna make sure you're okay, girl."

"No. I appreciate it. I really do."

But am I ready to talk about it? Share the trauma I've kept buried for over six long years? It still feels so daunting. Hell, I could barely even acknowledge what happened to myself, let alone to somebody else. The whole thing is an ongoing process. But the good news? I'm done pretending what happened didn't happen. Done accepting blame for shit that wasn't my fault. And ready to understand the mental roadblocks I set up to keep my inner demons at bay.

What happened to me. The self-doubt and the unmerited outbursts I directed at my mom time and time again.

Bury it. Bury it...

No. Not anymore.

...

The fact is, I was a victim of sexual assault when I was only 13 years old. I blamed myself when I shouldn't have. And I blamed my mom for letting it happen to me. That woman was poised to save humanity, but she couldn't even protect her own daughter at home. And when I was nearly assaulted again at the fundraiser, it brought all of that resentment and self-loathing right back. I was positive that my greatest fear would be The Skin Craft Killer, but I couldn't be more wrong.

This revelation is oddly freeing. It's the first time I've said it in my head. The first time I've made it feel...real.

I realize now that the blame I placed on my mom wasn't fair. She didn't know what was happening at first, but she acted decisively as soon as she got her proof. She wrote guys off after that, and became the over-protective helicopter mom I would grow so accustomed to. She loved me with every fiber of her being, even when I insisted on being a total dick. I don't doubt her love one bit. I regret suppressing the trauma and misdirecting my anger for as long as I did. My relationship with my mom and all relationships to follow suffered because of it.

But like Olivia, I'm done running. I can't change what happened to me, or to my mom. I can, however, change what happens next. I've got no time or patience left for the fears that already dictated enough of my life.

"I'm gonna be fine," I tell her at last, and I mean it. "All we can do is move forward, right?"

Olivia concedes with a smile. "Right."

CheccChecc lightens the mood with an involuntary jump. Apparently he didn't notice Eckerd sneak up behind him until those little murder mitts were around his ankle. Olivia and I laugh as the pajama-wearing monster almost falls over trying to escape the feline half his size. He runs off on all fours, Eckerd close behind.

"You're invisible friend is pretty cute," admits the Dead Vegas native. "Weird as hell. But cute."

"If only you could hear some of the shit he says. He's worse than I am."

"So what's next for Miss Isabella Cordona? More monster hunting?"

"One ancient creature is enough for me." I pause, gazing off at the docks below. Hideo is still out there, his professionally-styled hair a comedic contrast to his filthy overalls as he gets his hands dirty with unruly fish. The people he's helping are just laughing at him and going about their business as usual. But I know better - the uneasiness is palpable across the entire island.
"The folks here need peace and guidance more than ever. The only way this place is gonna survive is if we can better unify ourselves from within and garner allies outside the island. I'll help my aunt right here and carry on my mom's legacy."

"To prove to yourself that you can? Or because you feel like it's your job as her daughter?"

I smile. "Neither. Because it's the right thing to do. A lot of people are suffering, now more than ever. And I am so done fussing over my own problems. Booooring."

Olivia snorts. "Amen, girlfriend."

We chat about lighter shit until the sun starts to set. Olivia is still a little jet-lagged, so Checcs and I walk her back to the mansion where she can rest up in one of the guest rooms. Watching my bunny-eared companion return her wave goodbye is too cute for words. Don't tell him I said so.

Shortly after, I meet back up with Aunt Maggie. We discuss new concerns among the islanders, needed supplies, and potential traders. The former pop star is considering a fundraising concert in the States, getting the other half of Lass Galaxy and her guitar-playing chimpanzee to join her. Now THAT...I gotta see.

When I return to my room for the night, I find my mind and my body at odds with one another. Exhausted, yet incapable of sleep. I lay in bed, thinking about everything that needs to get done as CheccChecc slurps a milkshake in the moonlight by the window. I look at my phone for the time, but end up thinking of something else instead. Something I haven't really wanted to face.

Unlock the screen. Flip through an admittedly short list of contacts. It's the only person under the letter 'I' besides Icarus.

"Immortal Douchebag".

Sigh.

Aunt Maggie's right. I know it, deep down. Hell, she's living proof. Or should I say undead proof?

Anyways. People can change. A lot can happen over a millennium or so. I mean. I guess.

Right?

And even though he's an asshole, he was there for me and my friends when all hell broke loose. There's what you see on the news, and what you hear in the tabloids. And then there's what the people I trust think, and what my actual experiences indicate.

When there are no cameras rolling. No front to put up. No scripted words or pleasant disguises, only deeds and intent. What do those say?

Tick tick tick. Backspace. Rewrite. Backspace. Auto-correct. Tick tick tick. Rinse and repeat until something that resembles an actual sentence appears on my glowing little screen. A few revisions and poop emojis later, I finally hit 'send'.

It's not much. But it's a start.

And that's what everything is about right now: fresh starts and second chances. Rebuilding the world, one relationship at a time.

I trust my mom's judgement. But above all, I trust my own.

CHAPTER FIFTEEN

"Nice entrance, Mary Poppins."

It's what I said to a certain little dark-haired boy that had traveled via Folfrakka Airways to visit me on the island.

"What?"

I was unsure if I would ever see him again. That maybe the apocalypse was just too much to come back from.

"Oh sorry, she's way before your time. To everybody else you must have looked like a cute little dandelion spiraling through the air…"

But seeing Icarus now, sporting new glasses and his matronly monster once more, Checcs and I couldn't be happier.

"Very funny."

"…carrying the wish of a small cherub…"

"I'm adorable, I get it."

MUCH TRUE. ICARUS CUTE CUTE CUTESY. MUCH UNLIKE IZZIE, LOOKING MORE HAGGARD THAN NORMAL.

I missed the pig-headed kid and his painfully honest pal more than I'd care to admit.

The best part was how I knew he was arriving. Farmers yelling outside about the boy floating down from the heavens? Priceless. If they could see the battle-scarred toad-bear with wings, they'd feel even more crazy.

We catch up. Well, kind of. I ask a lot of questions, but as usual, I don't get a lot of answers. Turns out the kid is less interested in getting sentimental and more focused on the matter at hand.

"He's still alive. And he killed two more victims."

I sigh, clenching my teeth.

"Yeah. I saw it on the news. A father and his son. Both are incapable of being reanimated. The psycho's a fucking cockroach. He just won't die."

"Are you ready to change that?" Icarus is smiling that smug smile, arms crossed alongside his Fairy Frogmother.

"I wish. But Beckett didn't get us any closer to finding him."

"Guess again, lady."

Pulled from out of the kid's coat pocket is something old, bound in leather.

"Folfrakka and I found this at that Beckett kid's apartment," he tells me, presenting the object with his head held high. "It's a diary."

I take the small book and flip it around in my hands. There are no markings on either side, but it's covered in blood stains and bookmarked in several places with dirty envelopes.

"I didn't take Beckett as the 'dear diary' type."

"That's because it's not his, dumbass. The diary belongs to Emery Farrow."

What the hell?

"What the hell?" I repeat out loud, throwing the pages open deliriously. "You two are fucking legends for finding this! Seriously!"

Page after page. Fast, then slow, before accepting defeat and closing it right back up.

Unfortunately, the book is filled with the sort of scribbled, violent nonsense you would imagine for the diary of a serial killer that escaped an insane asylum.

Some pen marks are so deep that they nearly cut clear through the pages.

"It's an awesome find, but...there's nothing useful in here, unless The Skin Craft Killer's current address and phone number are on one of those letters."

Icarus swipes the diary back from me and huffs. Folfrakka quickly does the same.

"Lucky you, I already read it inside and out. You're right, most of it is incoherent babble. However, there's one consistency amidst all the crazy. One big clue that puts the whoooole picture together."

Checcs and I lean in real close. Icarus waits until a curious spectator passes by before continuing more quietly.

DRUM ROLLING!!

"The reason Emery could see your guardian-reaper? The 'voices in his head' that made him kill? The reason why his brain rejected reanimation? His whole reason for going crazy in the first place?"

We lean in so close that we're practically face-first in Folfrakka fur.

READY THE GASPS OF SURPRISE!!

"It's got a name. 'Akatantis' is what he calls it, every time."

My jaw just drops. "Holy shit. You're saying that he's got his own Eldritch familiar and IT'S the crazy one?"

BINGO BONGO!!

Icarus nods proudly. "Exactly. Somebody made a deal with the Old Ones to bring Emery back from the dead during the war. He didn't know about it - had no clue. The guardian-reaper whose job it was to protect Emery is a sociopath who corrupted Emery's mind up until his soul was ready to be taken. Emery was meant to die for good the night he encountered Dayanna Cordona and her daughter. And he did."

Incredible! Icarus and Folfrakka much smart!

CheccChecc is positively giddy, wings fluttering about faster than a hummingbird. It's his mission. The excitement and adventure he's been longing for. The resolution to our long journey before the world stood still.

AKATANTIS REAPED HUMAN'S SOUL ON TIME, BUT NO RETURN IT TO THE PENUMBRA. BROKE CONTRACT WHEN AKATANTIS ABSORBED HUMAN'S SOUL INTO SELF INSTEAD.

"The killer knows how to perfectly replicate Emery's murders. And that's because - "

Another hearty smile behind shimmering glasses as Icarus finishes my sentence for me.

"The new killer is Akatantis, Emery's guardian-reaper. He absorbed Emery's soul and stayed behind to continue their work."

FOLFRAKKA's TURN AGAIN!! ICARUS AND FOLFRAKKA LEARNED HOW TO SUMMON TOPSIDE PENUMBRANS USING NAME AND OLD MAGICS. CAN SUMMON AKATANTIS DIRECTLY TO TEAM ICARUS. THE END!

"What do you say?" Icarus is grinning as he sticks his hand out towards me. "Ready to finish this once and for all?"

I am. Absolutely, I am.

It's just that...things are a little more complicated now.

"Icarus...The people here need me. There's still so much work to be done. I can't just..."

The kid furrows his brows. "What? Too busy now to stop the monster behind the murderer? The one who destroyed our families?"

"No, that's not it. I mean, not exactly."

"Then what is it? The great Isabella Cordona assumes power over her mother's kingdom, and loses interest in saving anybody else's lives?"

"You're being unfair. I don't have power nor do I crave it, asshole. We're about to have our first official election, and it'll be one of the elders. Not me. I'm doing my best to protect my community and save lives from here."

"Sure. This island is your ivory tower, keeping you safe from The Skin Craft Killer. You sound like Dr. Farrow."

I've had it. "You think I'm scared of Emery Farrow? He's fucking dead! And this Akatantis? Nothing can beat the fears I endured during the apocalypse. The world is a fucking disaster right now and I'm trying my best to put the pieces back together. So excuse me for having other adult responsibilities."

A silence - an uncomfortable one. I shouldn't have raised my voice. Icarus drops his hand to his side and looks at his feet. Folfrakka avoids eye contact with me as well, and I officially feel like an asshole for losing my temper.

"I'm sorry. It's just...this sanctuary, the entire world...they need all the help they can get. Sometimes it just feels a little overwhelming, that's all."

"No. I'm sorry, Izz. I should know you better than that. You're trying to do the right thing for your people here, and for your mom. It's just..."

As quickly as the tears begin to form, they're wiped away beneath those red-rimmed glasses. Icarus has a weird knack for annoying me and melting my heart simultaneously. He continues a little more quietly.

"I need this, Izzie. I'm not like you. During the apocalypse, after Folfrakka and I were separated, I was terrified and useless. I need to prove to myself that I'm stronger than that. Confronting Akatantis and ending the legacy of The Skin Craft Killer will save lives and offer me a chance to move on. Please."

He's so earnest, it's heartbreaking. Multiple voices compete for attention in my brain, equally matched in their sincerity.

MUCH TRUE. ICARUS NEED IZZIE. CAN'T FACE AKATANTIS WITHOUT IZZIE AND CHECCACHECCHUNDERAYONUS. TEAM ICARUS GO!!

Must finish mission together. Izzie return to saving sanctuary after. Please?

I sigh. The answer was never 'no'. My desire to put an end to The Skin Craft Killer's reign of terror has never wavered. My plate just got more full, that's all.

But I'm settled. The world can wait. I owe it to Icarus, for everything we've endured together. And to CheccChecc. And to my mom.

Thrusting my hand out towards Icarus, I say with a smile,

"Count me in, sergeant."

Icarus shakes my hand vigorously. "Now, let's catch ourselves a killer."

***

How do you kill a monster older than humanity?

The space shifts and illuminates around me and Icarus, and we're bathed in an eerie red glow.

It's a question we debated heavily. And according to the friendly pair of Penumbrans in our company, there is no easy answer.

Icarus and I, we stand our ground as the air thickens. In the caves beneath the cliff, facing the southern coast of the sanctuary island, it's only the four of us. But not for long.

Every Eldritch entity is different. Some are fireproof, like CheccChecc. Some hate water or loud noises, like Folfrakka. And as Udolthra could attest, guns are generally ineffective.

The tall silhouette of some strange entity appears before us, seemingly out of thin air. I grab Icarus's hand in mine and stand tall, ready to face whatever horror awaits. The end of The Skin Craft Killer's legacy may indeed be upon us, as long as we can figure out that one tiny detail.

How do you stop a serial killer monster? We'll have limited time to figure out what his unique weakness is, but we're prepared to troubleshoot. Icarus seems pretty confident in his planning, and I trust him on this one.

And for once, I'm not afraid.

His presence is otherworldly yet familiar at the same time. Broad shoulders, four arms, and a bug-like face full of humanoid eyes that bore into your soul from behind a thin black veil. It's clear that Emery Farrow's body modifications were intended to make him resemble the beast that tormented him.

Icarus and I don't budge. Neither do the Penumbrans at our sides. We watch as Akatantis drops his bloodied sledgehammer at his wolfish feet with a resonating clang. Those bloodshot globes scan us for a moment, followed by the slimy appearance of human-like teeth as the monster grins knowingly.

FLIESSSSS.

That voice. It's like daggers into my brain. Shivers run down my spine. A gasp from the little boy beside me says that he heard it, too. Awful, dripping with hate as it rings through every crevice of your mind. Icarus grabs my hand tighter. I don't know who's comforting who more. CheccChecc and Folfrakka are frozen beside us. I guess even Penumbrans aren't immune to fear.

"Akatantis," I utter with a trembling voice that betrays my inner resolve. "We have unfinished business."

UNFINISSSHED?

Icarus's hand clenches mine harder still.

"Don't play dumb," the boy spits, "you know why we're here."

Akatantis tilts his enormous head. Drool drips down those gums as he grins wider.

NOISSSSY. ALWAYS SO NOISSSSY, LITTLE THINGS. AREN'T THEY?

That's it. I take a step closer to the behemoth, ignoring the warnings of my guardian reaper.

"You and Emery killed my mom, asshole."

"And my b-brother, dickweed."

A big gross tongue licks black lips beneath the veil.

DID WE? PROBABLY. OH YESSSSS.

He's so nonchalant. I can feel my rage building. My heart pounds louder.

"You're not hurting anybody else."

LAMENTING PAIN? NO. TINY THINGS REVEL IN IT. WE REVEL IN IT, TOO. DON'T WE?

Despite the horror in front of me, I can't help but notice the little boy beside me trembling. I assumed it must be fear, but on closer inspection I think it's something else. Nerves, maybe? He's got a hand under his little petticoat and his eyes dart from his person to the beast ahead. What's going on?

Akatantis laughs.

SSSOOO MUCH. FFFFFEAR. SUMMON USSS FOR THIS? WE ACCEPT YOUR OFFER. TOGETHER WE SQUASHHH THE FLIESSSS.

All my attention is back on the behemoth that taunts us. I'm trying to figure him out. Trying to find a way we can end this without getting ourselves killed. Or worse.

So for now, I gotta buy some time for my own plan.

"Alright, so you like to talk, huh? Who is 'we'?"

EMERYYYY AND AKATANTIS.

"Emery's dead, no thanks to you and your psycho grooming."

NO. AKATANTIS LIVED IN EMERY. NOW EMERY LIVE IN AKATANTIS. ONE IN SAME. AREN'T WE?

The monster pauses only to laugh. Icarus tries to retort, but I can't hear it over the next penetrating vocals in my mind.

FLIESSSS. SQUASH THE FLIES. EXPOSE THEIR WEAKNESSES. DRINKK THEIR FEAR.

CheccChecc ready. Give signal.

My hand nervously inches down my thigh, towards the switch I intend on flicking momentarily. Our plan should work. It has to. We just need to get a little closer...

Akatantis doesn't back down. He grins down at us, a towering bulk with quivering limbs. I can see the eerie luminescence of those diseased-looking eyes beneath his veil, each blinking separately.

"Why? " I ask, taking yet another step closer. "Why torture and kill random people? I know how you Penumbrans feel about humanity. You think we're nothing but violent, selfish monsters. But how does what you do make you any better than us?!"

Akatantis tweaks his head from side to side like a glitched toy, taking a few wobbly steps closer.

SO NOISSSY, AREN'T THEY? ALWAYSSSS BUZZING. SQUASH THEM ALL. THEIR FEAR. SO DELICIOUSSSSS. DRINK DRINK DRINK.

Did I truly expect any real answers? He's not even original. There's no reasoning with a psychotic murderer. It's no wonder his thoughts perverted Emery. Akatantis has no villainous exposition to offer in his shining moment.

Only his hunger and his madness.

I look to Icarus and nod.

It's showtime.

But before I can give Checcs the signal, Akatantis grabs one of his own eyeballs and yanks it out. What the hell? My mind seems to fall out for a second as I watch the behemoth before us grab Icarus and press that rogue eyeball against the kid's forehead.

And the kid is spiraling. I can see his face from here: eyes rolled back, body twitching violently in our enemy's grasp. I know what's happening. Icarus is getting brain-raided by Akatantis, and I gotta stop it, ASAP!

"Let him go, asshole!" I scream. The plan starts to allude me as my panic grows. "Checcs, do it! Do it now!"

My guardian-reaper leaps forward with a swoop of his wings. From under his tentacles he spits alcohol all over Akatantis, careful to avoid Icarus. The psycho is confused, but at least understands that he's under attack.

"Checcs, move! Move!" I'm taking my shoe off as Folfrakka holds me up. A blast of leg ignition will light this asshole up like the White House Christmas tree.

A warbled yelp destroys my focus momentarily. It's CheccChecc! Akatantis took one of his four arms and just backhanded my little guy into the cavern wall, hard enough to crumble rock.

"Checcs!!"

He's lying there on the ground in tattered pajamas, motionless. Fuck!

I desperately try to put my foot down, to run to my guardian-reaper's aid. But Folfrakka holds me back and shakes her head. She reminds me what I have to do, that I can't let Checc's actions be in vain.

"Trektikzt!! Die, you ugly motherfucker!!"

Click.

Mechanical foot turns and transforms into that familiar cannon. Folfrakka holds me up as I dip back and aim my weapon straight at the monster's face. Fumes and smoke and flame pour out, and in that split second the darkness is lit with a furious red glow.

Akatantis is screaming. Fire runs up his arm, across his torso, along his neck, and to his head. His veil ignites and turns to ash, just in time to reveal the putrid popping of eyeballs from the heat and flame now raging across his face.

Icarus is released at last, and his captor's creepy arms are flying everywhere inches above. Claws slice through stalactites. Icarus narrowly avoids a claw to the shoulder as he rushes to knock that sledgehammer out of reach. Folfrakka spots the eyeball Akatantis dropped, and promptly crushes it beneath the weight of her furry foot. Gross. Meanwhile, our enemy rages on. As two hands fondle his poor face, the other two are reaching out blindly. They don't connect with anything, until suddenly they do.

Me.

My mechanical leg is hit so hard by his wrist that it bends. The heat builds up inside the cannon, unable to escape.

Panic sets in. I scramble desperately to turn off the ignition before something explodes. Smoke begins to cover us.

WE SSSSTILL SMELL YOUR FEAR! WE WILL TEAR THE FLESH FROM YOUR BONE!

He's got me by the leg now, dangling me like a fish. Smoke continues to emit from the corners of my mechanical leg. More heat and pressure are building. There's no way I can reach the switch from here!

Shit!

"Izzie!" It's Icarus, crying out from below. It sounds like he thinks I'm gonna die.

And maybe I am.

What...was the next step of the plan again?

The moment lingers on forever, in slow-motion. Checcs still on the floor, silent. Icarus rushing towards me, Folfrakka towards the sledgehammer. A large mouth opening up beneath a melted face. Two monstrous arms closing in: one holding me steady while the other begins to dig its claws into the top layers of skin on my thigh. The pain is tremendous, but somehow my adrenaline is winning out. I should be terrified. Done for.

I'm sorry, Mama.

I'm sorry, Aunt Maggie.

And I'm so sorry, Checcs.

It's likely I won't survive this.

But I still have one last chance to end this killer's reign of terror.

The pressure in my leg is mounting. All I can do is hope...

Hope that it will be enough...

BOOM.

Slipping in...

...and out...

...

Ringing in my ear turns to pure silence.

I see nothing.

Then suddenly I see snippets.

Flame engulfing the behemoth's head and torso once more.

I feel.

The rush as I drop hard onto the rock below.

Someone is yelling.

Is it...me?

Or maybe Icarus?

Fade in….

Fade out…

Try to breathe. Remember how to breathe, right? In, and out….

I smell.

Blood. My own.

And smoke. Black smoke, and burning flesh. Not my own.

Fade...out…

Don't you dare, Izzie! Not now! Hold on!!

Struggle to push my torso off the ground and get a better look. My limbs are wobbly, and I can't see straight for shit.

I…

…

Hold on, damn it!!

Akatantis is somehow still standing! He's whirling in pain, fending off a sledgehammer-wielding Folfrakka and gripping the bloody stump that only moments earlier was the hand holding my leg. He's hurting, but he's not done for. We've successfully pissed him off. He'll squash us all.

I just...gotta...do something...

Fuck! My own bleeding stump looks like something out of a horror movie. It's nothing but shredded meat and shrapnel down there, up to the knee.

...

Come on! Stay awake!!

But as Akatantis rages with himself, I manage to make out a familiar tiny voice beside me.

Icarus...

"Don't you die!" I think he yells. "Get out of this cave, NOW! I'm gonna end this once and for all! People need you, so you have to survive!! You better, okay?!"

What?

What is he...talking about?

The kid grins at me and wipes his tears away one last time. I watch as he takes his petticoat off, revealing something large strapped to his little chest.

Holy shit! Is that a...bomb?!

Is he crazy?!!

"Icarus!" I try, a gargled, drooling mess. I'm utterly devastated. I can't watch someone else I care about sacrifice themselves for me. "No!!"

"Thank you for everything," he says to me confidently before turning his attention back to Akatantis. "This is for Michael!!"

I reach out to him, but I'm helpless. The boy makes a run for the monster. Folfrakka's big eyes are easy to read, even from here. It is obvious that she too was unaware of her companion's backup plan. The distress on her countenance is heart-breaking. Her croak of despair echoes through the cavern as she drops the sledgehammer and runs on all fours to stop her only friend from suicide.

"No!!! Stop!!"

But something happens.

Folfrakka reaches Icarus before the boy can reach his target.

Between black outs, I see Folfrakka's head open up.

The subtle glow of those spores…

And Icarus drops to his knees, just long enough for Folfrakka to pull the bomb off him.

Stopping wasn't the only thing she made him do, though.

Icarus seems to be fighting within himself, crying out against his body as it acts out of his control. His legs carry him swiftly out of range - farther and farther, until he's right outside the cavern. He's crying and yelling in dismay. Whatever he wants to do, Folfrakka won't let him do it.

Suddenly my body is sliding across the wet stone floor, farther from Akatantis and closer to Icarus. I struggle to see who's pulling me by the arm.

It's CheccChecc!

I attempt words, but nothing comes out. I'm still fading in and out. My bloodied and battered guardian-reaper is trying to save my ass one…last…time…

My head lays flat on the sand, and I peer at the action ahead from outside the cavern. Akatantis is regaining his composure, at least enough to turn his attention back on us. That asshole is resilient. Folfrakka is the only one close to him now. The bomb she pried off her companion is now draped around her neck, and the trigger is in her paw.

ICARUS THINK NO LIFE FOR HIM AFTER AKATANTIS. NOT TRUE. PLEASE TAKE CARE OF ICARUS. TAKE CARE OF EACH OTHER.

It's her. Folfrakka peers over her shoulder at Icarus. I can only imagine what she's communicating to her little boy in this final moment.

And then...

BOOM.

The ground quakes beneath us. The rock walls tremble. Flames and smoke fill the large cavern until I can see nothing else.

...

I'm...gonna...

...

"Checcs," I reach out, suspended somewhere uncertain in space and time, *"show me something beautiful from your world. I want to see...something beautiful..."*

Something cold on my skin. My mind begins to slip away slowly...gently...

Suddenly, I see something...An alien landscape beneath a maroon sky, darkened by the shadow of another planet's surface. Broken chains miles ahead, piled so high that they looked like a wall. A blanket of golden stars weaving between wispy orange clouds. It's so quiet...and peaceful. So vast and fantastic, unlike anything I could have dreamed of. And I see them there. My mom. My dad. And Dante, if he were my age. He's got my mom's eyes, and my dad's smile. And he smirks at me, like he knows exactly what dumb thing I'm gonna say next...

And suddenly...there is nothing…...at all...

CHAPTER SIXTEEN

It's...strange.

Cold and numb. I'm standing in some space where I can't feel my own feet, like they fell asleep on me. When I look down, I can see that both legs are fully intact. However, the darkness surrounding me now is heavier than anything I've ever felt. The darkest dark, an endless void of confusion and despair.

But there are also these lamp posts. Pale, glimmering beacons of hope lighting the way through this lonely void. The whole change of scenery begs the question...

Am I dead?

Though I'm a little uneasy, the lamp posts seem to beckon me towards them. They lead somewhere. Hopefully some place far from the emptiness that threatens to swallow me whole.

Long moments later, a strange shadow appears underneath a lamp post a few feet away. I walk numbly onward, only to be greeted by a very unexpected individual.

It's an undead kid my age sporting glasses and a little goatee, as tall as he is wide. He's covered in scars and the stitchery of a quilt, yet he's got such a peaceful presence. It's the weirdest thing. Somehow I just know I can trust him.

"Where...am I?" I ask the question, but I can barely hear or feel myself say it. Still, the mysterious kid doesn't skip a beat in answering me.

"Welcome to limbo, little homie."

Limbo?

"It's true then. I'm...I'm dead? For real?"

The mysterious youth sighs and puts his hands in his pockets.

"You, uh...better come take a seat with me."

I'm led a little off the lit path. It doesn't take long until an enormous fountain appears from the shroud. The water spewing forth from the ornate gargoyle centerpiece seems to be frozen in motion. It's as if time has stopped on this single, solitary moment within a moment. It's here that my new friend of sorts takes a seat, right on the cobblestone ledge of the rounded fountain. He groans visibly when he sits, like he's older than he looks. Then he gives me this little grin and pats the ledge beside him.

" Siéntate conmigo. I'll catch you up to speed, alright?"

So I listen and sit my ass down.

"As you might have guessed, you're...ya know. Dead, little homie. Game over."

He gives me a moment of silence to process that. I stare at him, unblinking. It's still a bitter pill to swallow, but he goes on.

"This is a crossroads. A destination for souls trapped in the transition between life and the afterlife, you feel me?"

"Does everybody go here before they're reanimated?"

"Not everybody. Some folks croak and see nothin' at all. Others see visions of their future, or the afterlife they believe in."

I'm nervous. "And...what about hell? Is it real? Do bad people go there?"

The big guy sighs deeply, slinking further into himself as if it's a question he doesn't like to answer.

"It's real, but...none of it is what folks think, you know?"

"So what is it? And, um, no offense, but...who are you and why do you know all this?"

He puffs out his chest proudly. "Name's Gabriel, but you can call me Roca. And I guess you could say I know about Hell 'cuz I've been elected to watch over it for the past 50 years or so."

My eyes widen at that, and it must look comical because the big dude snickers at me.

"Yeah I know," he shrugs, "I don't look the part. I get that a lot."

"So does that mean you're here to drag me to hell or something?" I'm getting a little worried.

"Nooo way!" He lets out this hearty chortle and pats me heavy on the back. "Unless, of course, that's where you think you belong."

"What do you mean? I don't think I belong in Hell. I mean, I'm an asshole sometimes to the people I care about. I haven't always made the right choice. I've been selfish, lots of times. And I have DEFINITELY said some...um...bad words."

"Ay, you're a hardened criminal, time to lock your scrawny ass up for eternity!"

Something tells me that if Gabriel wasn't dead, he'd be laughing himself until he was red in the face. Once he eases up, he catches me staring at him looking a little less amused. He continues with a straight face.

"Heaven, hell, purgatory. Even The Penumbra. They're just celestial planes competing for souls. But reanimation kinda screwed the pooch for all the celestials, ya' know? Nobody stays dead long enough to be collected. But limitation inspires innovation sometimes, like mi mamá used to tell me. I think we're gonna come to a peaceful agreement soon about a universal change in currency, feel me? I can be very persuasive. Especially with the ladies."

Gabriel dusts off his shoulder and laughs some more. He's like a big teddy bear. Not exactly what I expected from the self-proclaimed Watchman of Hell, but clearly I don't know shit about the afterlife. This whole dying thing...it's a little new to me.

I gasp, fearing the worst.

"Icarus! Is he alright? And CheccChecc? Did they survive the blast?"

Gabriel - er, I mean Roca - smiles and gives this cheesy thumbs up.

"The kid survived - he's a tough one. As for your prehistoric little buddy, I don't know. I can only see humans who pass through."

"Shit, Checcs better be okay too. He has to be." My heart skips a beat. "My mom! Can I see her? Please??"

"I'm sorry," he begins softly, "but she isn't here, and it don't work that way. Not exactly."

Crestfallen. Old me would have raged out. Refused everything. But right now, sitting here in limbo, after everything I've gone through? Somehow, I get it. It's not the answer I wanted, but I understand that all this...Well, it's a lot bigger than me and what I want.

There's an uncomfortably long silence between us. He's literally twiddling his thumbs beside me.

"My mom died when I was real little," he says at last, still looking at his thumbs. "Almost 60 years ago now, and it still hurts. I felt lost. And angry. I'd do anything to bring her back. But not everybody comes back...ya' know? It ain't fair. I know that. But reanimation can't solve all our problems. Sometimes it just makes things worse."

"Says the reanimated kid," I snigger, despite being moved. "Tell me something. How did you end up here, greeting the newly deceased? You're just a kid. No offense."

"None taken," he grins, wiping his eyes. "Getting reanimated, landing this job after it 'opened up', so to speak...Sometimes we don't get the luxury of choice. I know enough about you to get that's somethin' you understand well."

I lower my head. I'm twiddling my own thumbs now. "Yeah. I get it."

A silence thick enough to cut with a butter knife ensues.

"What should I do now?" I ask at last. "Is this...really it for me? Where is my soul supposed to go?"

"Heh, you sound like an old friend of mine. Where do you think it should go?"

I wasn't prepared for that question.

"I dunno, Watchman of Hell. I thought you were supposed to have the answer to that."

Roca laughs this wheezy laugh.

"The system only works when people believe it does."

"Easy, anarchist."

He chuckles and pats my back again, this time even harder.

"For real though, you would've ended up as 'soul bucks' in The Penumbra if it weren't for your little buddy breakin' script back there. Guess your fate's your own now. Yup."

Holy shit. That's right. That night I jumped off the building in Dead Vegas, CheccChecc saved my life instead of reaping my soul. That means the contract is null and void, then? I'm really....free? Just like that?

I gotta make it count. All the sacrifices. All the loss, pain, and growth.

"I made up my mind. I wanna go back. CheccChecc, my friends, the sanctuary - they all need me! And I made a promise to look after Icarus!"

"Heheh. You chose wisely, hermana. But I don't think you have much say in it this time around. Your crew is electrifying your ass as we speak."

Roca snaps his fingers, and a puff of dark smoke appears out of nowhere, swirling over his head for a moment before descending to the ground at his sneakers. It twirls and shifts until it suddenly takes form! Some weird little monster. Nothing like CheccChecc and the other Penumbrans. This thing looks like a hideous mutation between human and bulldog, although its features always seem to be changing. I'm freaking out, and I nearly fall into the water behind me.

"Chill pill," the big guy laughs. "He's cool. Aren't ya?"

Roca is treating the demon like a cute little pet. I would have thought this sight was absolutely bonkers before, but after witnessing Eldritch monsters and magic, I guess I shouldn't be that surprised.

"Hey, show her what I taught you," he whispers loudly to his cuddly mutant. I watch as the two attempt a secret handshake. The pair make up for their lack of coordination with a shared enthusiasm that is oddly adorable.

"You saw that?!" Roca hoots, his demon hopping up and down excitedly behind him. I can't help but clap. "Way cool, man."

The big guy leans in closer to me and farther away from his partner in crime.

"We're still workin' on it," he whispers to me. "He says I go too fast, but he always gets the last couple steps backwards."

My brain feels like it's pulsating. I feel like my consciousness is slipping in and out in rhythm with my heartbeat.

"Wait. I still have so many questions!" I know I'm about to make my return to the land of the living. Back to my body, but never the same. No longer warm-blooded, special. Just reanimated. Another member of the undead majority.

It's like Roca can read my mind. As he pulls out a lighter and chills with his demonic familiar, he offers one last bit of advice:

"Being reanimated is what you make it. Folks will try to tell you what you are, what to do, and what you're capable of. But all that's for YOU to decide, Izz. Make that momma of yours proud and live your next chance at life without holdin' back."

"For a plus-sized gatekeeper of Hell, you're not so bad. Thank you." That's what I try to say, but I don't think it actually came out, I'm slipping again, and faster.

Looking at myself sitting by the fountain now. Out of my own consciousness. It's like I have the front row seat for watching my soul get ripped backwards at mach speed, across foreign planes of existence, across a world as old as time...

Through that light everyone talks about...

Through shades of gray and an unfathomable silence...

Until I feel the low buzz of electricity pulsing through my body...

It's...

***

"....ALIVE!"

My eyes flutter open. It's all a blur, but that smug voice is all too clear. So is the smell of tuna.

Hideo. He continues enthusiastically.

"Welcome to the unofficial afterlife, girl! Sorry, we're fresh out of buttons. How're you feeling?"

No response leaves my lips. Only the driest coughs I've ever had. Like I've been lost in the desert for weeks.

"She can't speak yet, dummy," a little voice sighs. It's Icarus! He DID survive!

Next I hear Olivia, with that all-too familiar accent. "And it's her first time. The first one's always a doozy."

Olivia's gotta be right, because I feel like I was hit by a semi-truck multiple times while hungover. I just lay there, still on the table as the shock doc removes my restraints. The lights are waaaay too bright. I keep my eyes closed tight.

"I know you are all very excited," the doctor speaks plainly, "but this patient needs more injections and rest. You can visit her again after 6 PM."

"Bullshit, Fabio. I'm not leaving my niece's side unless you're prepared to take a Gucci purse to the dick."

Aunt Maggie! She's here, too?

I struggle to open my eyes. It's still painful to focus, but I can make out everybody here, I think. My friends, and the only family I have left. They're all here for me, huddled together by the door of the reanimation chamber. Plus two unexpected visitors in the very back: Frode Algar and his assistant, Claudia!

I wanna celebrate with my friends and thank them for being here. For wanting me back. For making me feel worthwhile for a change. But did I mention that I feel like a bag of dog poo? Words are a little too hard right now. Thoughts are hard too, even for me. Heh.

A little retching. Dry heaves. The mumbled complaints of my well-groomed shock doc as he argues with an overprotective Aunt Maggie.

I fade in and out. Still numb all over. Will it always feel this way?

....

When I come back to, I see that I'm in a hospital bed. Scan the room. Dark, but only because the curtains are closed. The clock says it's after 11 PM. My friends and family are gone. A nurse says a few things to me that sound underwater before smiling and leaving me to myself. I struggle to sit up, and for the first time I see my leg post-explosion. Poor thing. You'd think I have a vendetta against this appendage, getting it wrecked twice now. An ESTRID Industries prosthetic is in its place, even nicer than the last. And by the look of it, it's been signed by my friends.

Is it possible to feel so unlucky and lucky at the same time?

My heart skips a beat. I struggle to sit up just a little longer, hoping to spot one last familiar face excited to see me.

"...Checcs?"

No answer. No glowing set of eyes staring at me curiously. No sarcastic words echoing through my mind. No bunny pajamas, or slurps of milkshake.

My guardian-reaper simply isn't there.

'Not friend', he had told me once before. *'Just doing job.'*

A lot of things changed between us. I could tell he cared in his own way. And to me, he WAS a friend. There for me when I had nobody else, and he risked everything for me time and time again. And right now, I miss him more than anything.

Did he die in the blast with Folfrakka and Akatantis? No, he had to survive it! Please, I can't lose him, too!

Fall back heavily against the bed. My tank is still on 'E'. The shock doc is right - I need to rest and regain my strength as soon as possible. I might have kicked the bucket, but life most certainly goes on. There is way too much to do. So much to rebuild, and too many people who are counting on me.

But for now...

Night night.

EPILOGUE

ONE MONTH LATER

"The warm-blood sanctuary concluded its first democratic election last Tuesday, making history as - "
Click.

"-your skin will glow like you're alive again. 2nd Chances: You got a second chance at life - shouldn't your skin get the same?"

Click.

"Following a month of no attacks, The Skin Craft Killer was finally identified as Emery Farrow. His grandson, Eugene Farrow, confessed to stealing the serial killer's brain after his death last year and has been cooperating with authorities in the brain's return and destruction under court law. This new development brings much-needed resolution to the victims' families and puts an end to one horrifying saga."

Click.

" - and the party responsible for that global act of terrorism is obvious: it's those damn lizard people, polutin' our water and turning our - "

Click.

" - attack changed everything, Katie. It changed the world and it changed us. Chock it up as an act of God."

"Oh, my. I didn't think you were the God-fearing type."

"That's exactly it, Katie. I've never been religious, but there is absolutely no evidence anywhere to indicate that this was a terrorist attack committed by one nation or another. It's as if God himself was trying to teach humanity a lesson."

"Goodness. And what might that be?"

"Simple, Katie. That we need to get off our asses, stop blaming one another for our problems, and start working together to make the planet a better place before it's too late."

"Well. Don't you think that's a little idealistic?"

"Maybe so, Katie. But if any of us are still standing here today, living or undead, then we've already survived our worst fears. Working together despite our differences can't be any worse than that."

Click.

"Show's over, cocksucker. You're cockle-doodle-dead."

"Wait, don't change the channel! I love this movie!"

Icarus freezes with the remote still in hand.

"It's almost over, though."

"Who cares?" I grin, watching Eckerd stretch and jump off the cat tower. "It's Jason Deadhouse."

"Yeah, in the worst movie of Felix's career."

"Debatable. And besides, you chose the last movie. It's my turn."

Icarus sighs dramatically. "Fine."

The kid puts the remote down and sinks back into the couch. Eckerd is making a b-line straight for his lap. Together, the three of us watch as Jason Deadhouse kills the evil owner of an underground cockfighting ring.

It gets better every time I watch it.

Poorly choreographed fights accompanied by a symphony of gunfire and an energetic brass section. The lights of the flat screen TV illuminate the darkened living room in shades of red, white, and blue. But mostly red.

"This movie is so stupid," says Icarus as he leans forward, eyes glued to the screen. Eckerd paws at his hand for pets, but the kid is clearly...occupied.

Heh.

Credits roll. I clap exuberantly to the embarrassment of my pint-sized roommate before standing up to stretch.

"We have a few hours before the next sanctuary meeting. What do ya' wanna do, kiddo?"

Icarus sighs, his eyes glued to the undead feline purring on his pajamas.

"Hmm. You ever play soccer?"

"Nope. But it's just kicking a ball around, right? That's easy enough."

The kid raises an eyebrow. "I'm glad you feel that way. It'll make it easier for me to beat you."

"With those tiny, little legs of yours? I'd love to see you try."

"You're old. So your heart will probably give out early on. Wouldn't want you to kick the bucket again."

"Ha ha, very funny. Come on, put some real pants on and meet me outside, Icky Sticky."

Eckerd meows and bails from Icarus' lap as if on cue. The kid gets up and shuffles over in his slippers. I'm about to give him more shit, until I notice his face.

"You alright?"

"...Folfrakka used to play soccer with me, too. I just...miss her, that's all."

My heart aches for the little guy. I get down so that I'm eye level with him and put a gentle hand on his shoulder.

"Hey, hey, it's alright. I get it. Not a day goes by where I don't think about CheccChecc either. Nobody can replace them."

Checcs. The cave was sealed after the explosion. Still, I check the beach every day for signs of my friend, hoping that my worst fears are wrong.

"Does it bother you?" he finally asks. "That nobody else could see them? That nobody around here understands what we lost?"

I sigh deeply. "Sometimes, yeah. But WE understand. Whatever it's worth, you've got me, kiddo."

Icarus raises his head to look at me, and this time he's smiling.

"You'll need me if you want to survive your next trip to Dead Vegas."

"It's a date, then." I give Icarus a motherly kiss on the forehead and stand up. My attempt to annoy him was successful as usual.

"Gross, you weirdo," he says, wiping off his forehead with the cuff of his shirt. "I don't need your granny kisses."

"Get dressed and meet me downstairs, you big baby."

Is this what it's like...to have a brother?

Out the door and down the stairs I go. Once I'm in the lobby, I pause to look out the large window overlooking the beach. My hand presses against the glass. A cold, pale hand that I'm just starting to get used to.

Being dead...it isn't so bad. I don't know what I was expecting.

But is it weird that I never felt this alive and in control when...well, I was actually alive?

I had always thought I was alone in my fears, and that my trauma made me weak. But I was wrong about everything. Everyone has their own fears to overcome, and when we confront our trauma and release its power over us, we're stronger than we ever thought possible.

Life is weird.

And unpredictable.

Full of suffering.

But also, full of something else. Something wholly unexpected in the aftermath of the apocalypse, especially for The Old Ones responsible.

Hope. The whole world is still hurting, only now it's spending more time seeking peace than shifting blame. Indeed, our values are changing. I wonder what CheccChecc would've thought if he could see the palpable change in the humans he left behind. Maybe he'd have hope, too.

Who knows what the future holds for my mother's sanctuary. For warm-bloods and cold-bloods alike. For the planet itself.

All I know is that I'm so incredibly grateful for the opportunity to spread a little more hope, one day at a time, alongside all the wonderful humans and monsters alike who helped me become the person I am now.

I hope I make you proud, Mama. And you too, Dante.

"Excuse me, Miss Cordona?"

It's Cho-Hee. She's disheveled and out of breath, accompanied by a few other fishermen who look equally startled.

"Hmm? What's up?"

"You're not going to believe this, but we caught something very peculiar in our nets. It seemed to know you, Miss Cordona. It reacted when it heard your name. It's a funny little faceless thing wearing a burnt rabbit costume."

THE END

PLANET ROT